Praise for Tales of the Astonishing ~~Black~~ Spark:

"You'd need lightning to combine the satire of Paul Beatty, the rueful humor of Lorrie Moore, the deranged superheroes of Charles Yu, and the twenty-first-century inheritance of *Invisible Man*—and then you'd have Charlie J. Eskew's *Tales of the Astonishing ~~Black~~ Spark*, a funny, nerdy, and biting look at race and contemporary life, celebrity, and power. Buy it for the superheroes; read on for the humor and the wisdom. This is a rich and furious debut novel."

—Daniel A. Hoyt, author of *This Book Is Not for You* and *Then We Saw the Flames*

"*Tales of the Astonishing ~~Black~~ Spark* is a scintillating journey into the distance between villains, heroes, and superheroes. In swift, edgy prose, Charlie J. Eskew gives the reader a beautifully created world where 'superhero' is a business and ethics grow murky. You'll be thinking about the smart yet earnest Black Spark and his 'T Believers' long after you've turned the last

—Soniah Kamal, award-wi

Unmarriageable: Jane Aust

Pakistan ⸱ ₋ent

TALES OF THE ASTONISHING ~~BLACK~~ SPARK

CHARLIE J. ESKEW

LANTERNFISH PRESS

WWW.LANTERNFISHPRESS.COM

LANTERNFISH PRESS
399 Market Street, Suite 360
Philadelphia, PA 19106
lanternfishpress.com

COVER ART
Design by Michael Norcross.
Illustration by Ronald Ackins.

Printed in the United States of America.
Library of Congress Control Number: 2018933663
ISBN: 978-1-941360-16-3

TALES OF THE ASTONISHING ~~BLACK~~ SPARK

CHAPTER 1
DISASSEMBLED

SUPERHEROES ARE BULLSHIT. I've been sitting here for half an hour, waiting for the rude awakening of my redeye to set in, wondering where to start, and, well, that's what I got. That's the thesis statement. That's what my Black ass should have known from years of stroking one out to the fantasy of capes, cowls, colors bright, and spandex tight. I should have just jumped the line to become your cautionary tale sooner.

I'm skipping ahead.

I was never supposed to be someone, you see. Most people, the *untalented* people, go off and get a career that doesn't involve chafing and electromagnetism. They might have an origin story. They might get a character arc and a few crossovers, but ultimately, they're supporting characters in someone else's tale. Thanks to—well, we'll get to it—I have to tell you a different story, the one I wasn't supposed to have. This is the story of a man of substance, who had something fantastic, something *astonishing* happen to him—but who wasn't built to accept it.

This is a story of heroes and villains.

The kind you got to read about in the comics, but not so much. Yeah, before the Almighty Asper, before the White Flame, before me, all we had were the books. Years of reading Marvel and DC led us to believe that those guys weren't even human beneath the knockoff luchador masks.

When I was eight, my dad gave me my first comic book: *Wolverine vs. Spider-Man.* So badass. You couldn't separate me from that trade. I carried it to every NA meeting he dragged me to, and my pseudo-sister Kat made sure to bring it to me in the hospital after mishaps with rocket skateboards and later, of course, sparks. I ran that fucker through my danger room of a backpack; it was with me from bus stop to bus stop, on dark nights and through dead daddies. I knew every page and every detail, every *snikt*, *thwip*, and *bub*.

The world that existed within those thirty pages always seemed *fair.* The good guys beat the bad guys or the bad guys beat the good guys, but you never felt that it didn't make sense. You always knew that somehow, in the end, things happened just the way they were supposed to.

This isn't the story of things ending just the way they're supposed to.

These are the Tales of the Astonishing Blunders

These are the Tales of the Astonishing Age of Heroes

These are the Tales of the Astonishing
World We Always Wanted

These are the Tales of the Astonishing
World We Can't Give Back

I remember where I was when the Almighty Asper first appeared, as I'm sure most of you reading do, too.

I was fifteen then, and I was playing a game. By that time, I had my feet firmly sunk in the muck-filled basement that is geek culture, which, I would note, is a distinct thing from nerd culture. The difference being that, while nerds are harassed for unlocking the secrets of the universe, geeks are harassed for rallying to bring back *Firefly*.

So I was sitting there in the (literal) basement of the comic-book shop, playing this geeky game, wowing my buddies with my meticulously crafted Versus deck, when there was a shrill sound like stones shredding against plywood. Tremors through the shop shook dust speckles free from the ceiling. Entranced, in a miasma of stupidity and curiosity, we—those to whom the earth had been promised—bolted upstairs, leaving our bubble of fantasy to find the store above in shambles.

Aedan, the pale, freckled shop owner, had often regaled us with tales of the glory days, the Golden Age of comics, when heroes were heroes—not like the rubbish they put out now.

"Silver Age?" he would scoff. "More like Shitty Age."

After the boom, though? There were no scoffs. There were no debates. There was only a Moffat-inspired silence. There was only me and the other gamers, and Aedan—lying there, but not. His neck twisted around from where it should have been. I waited for a reboot, a retcon, goddamned Dragon Balls, anything that would make sense of it. There were only the pages of ruined stories spilled over him.

I screamed.

I guess what I'm getting at is that seeing the bludgeoned, ripped-ragged remains of Aedan, his ginger hair twisted darkly by blood, was the beginning of the end for the Golden Age, that place where you find out just how fragile your heroes are. I couldn't look away from Aedan's body. I didn't see what everyone else was seeing, that of course being the first-ever recorded battle of two Talented individuals: Almighty Asper and White Flame.

Not that any of those guys knew at the time what the hell was going on. They only knew that He was the answer. He was that fleeting dream that had tucked itself into the corners of their eyes as they spent hours scanning page after page of adventure. He was everything the world needed.

He wasn't Aedan.

They watched as the seven-foot mass of spandex and caviar dreams brushed glass from his blond crop of grade-A American hair. They were hypnotized by the sight of his scarlet cape, billowing in wind that streamed through the new opening his super-brawl with White Flame had torn into Aedan's shop.

I can only give you a sketch of what happened after that, mostly stuff the guys told me later. In that moment I forfeited my opportunity to witness the first appearance of the Almighty Asper.

"Who are you?" one of them asked as the Almighty Asper patted dirt from his blue leggings and cream-colored tunic.

"Me? I, citizen, am the Almighty—" Before he could finish, an elongated tendril sped through the gaping hole and wrapped around the Almighty Asper's head. It dragged him back over gravel and back-stocked Milestone comics that had been sitting in the same box for years. The others rushed outside, while I tried to take my eyes off of Aedan. I wouldn't find out until later that night, after the coroner had taken Aedan away, when I finally had it in me to go home and watch the news, that the tendril was from the White Flame.

I guess the reason it's easy to remember the day the first superhero arrived was because it would also prove to be the last day I ever went without seeing *that* as my image of Aedan.

It was the last day I argued with Aedan over who was the best Green Lantern (Rayner, of course) and the last time I walked into a comic-book shop in my life.

After Almighty Asper and White Flame, spandex would catch on just like any good American fad, and we'd see an overabundance of Wild Wombats and Bold Revengers, of Ultra-Insertnames and Great Whatshisfaces. For the most part, none of them really had what Almighty Asper had—what my agent, Christopher Row, would fool me into thinking I had, which he aptly named *it*.

It, for those who don't know, is what makes the difference between having the movie about you made by Scorcese or motherfucking Uwe Boll. But I digress.

As I sit here in this coffee shop, I can't turn away from watching you people, you Talentless mob. I suppose that I'm one of *you* now, but I feel like something else entirely. I watch with tear-drunk eyes as you work on your nifty little novel or memoir or poem on your nifty little laptop, and I can't help but wonder *why*. I can't see it. Nikolas says the meaning is there if you look hard enough, past all the bullshit. That between iPhones and WIC cards there's a silver lining—that something, somehow connects us all and intertwines everything that we are or will be. But the harder I look, the more convinced I get that it's not there.

These are the Tales of Someone Who Thought
They Could See That Silver Lining

These are the Tales of Astonishing Saturday
Mornings and Taffy-Tickled Thumbs

These are the Tales of Rocket Skateboards
and Gravity's Lack of Mercy

These are the Tales of the Astonishing Applied
Uses of Misogyny in Refrigeration Systems

These are—

I should really stop beating around the bush, because my coffee's getting cold and the barista—Tad, I think his nametag said—is starting to give me funky looks and whisper to his coworkers while pointing at me. I'm pretty sure I know what they're saying.

"Nah, can't be."

"But dude, look at his *hair*, how many *Black* people have *white* dreadlocks?"

"He could just be a fanboy, some creepy, cosplaying fanboy."

"No, I think that's him, man. I think that's the *real* Black Spark."

CHAPTER 2
ORIGINS

WELL, WE SHOULD JUST get into it. You're probably tapping your finger right now, pissed that I haven't gotten to the whole mass-murder thing yet. Don't worry, True Believers, we'll get there. You know what, though? Go on ahead, if you want. I'll even give you the title of the chapter: "The Night Everything Changed." There. If you're so invested in the moment I became The Deviously Dark Spark, skim on over! But I'd like to begin with a time not so beaten and bronze.

We'll begin with the boom.

I'm Donald, by the way, though you've probably gathered that already. I looked for myself online the other day as The Black Spark. With this cluster of collectible catastrophes being my life and all, I get curious to see what you all are saying about me.

When the screen returned *Did you mean Donald McDougal?* I deduced just how utterly screwed I am. Anyway, where was I?

Oh yeah. *Boom.*

The A&E biopic—*A Spark of Courage: The Inspirational Tale of the World's First African-American Negro Black Superhero*—wasn't exactly spot-on. The story doesn't start with me doing work with the Peace Corps in Africa.

It starts with me and a toilet. Fighting a losing war in my throat, crouched over a bowl at Paul Hughes's New Year's Eve party. The sounds of everyone outside the bathroom mixed into an amalgam of empty promises and drunken vows for the upcoming year. Thunder rattled the window. It was a weirdly warm December night; I guess the weather gods were displeased.

I was busy vomiting what looked like trail mix when I heard a pounding at the bathroom door. This was followed by a jiggle of the handle. I bumped away from the toilet to the flat of my ass.

"Gimme me a minute." I gathered they couldn't hear me, as the jiggling and pounding continued. After the tenth attempt, I lunged for the door handle and unlocked it. Paul, my brother from another, burst in. I gave my best *I'm okay* smile, but it didn't really work, since the trail mix had spilled down my tie. Paul quickly made sure that no one else was around, shut the door, and crouched down in front of me.

"You're a mess."

"You're a dick," I said, with a laugh that nearly lurched what remained in my throat up the pipe. Paul scratched at his clumped beard. I felt his hand reach the underside of my arm, coiling tight against the tweed blazer, and I jerked away.

"I want to sit here for a while." I wiped his toilet seat clean with my forearm, ever the courteous lush. The outsiders persisted with their knocking until Paul kicked against the door.

"One minute, fucking hell!" The voices stopped and feet trailed away. He turned back to me, shifting some dreadlocks away from my face and tucking them behind my ear. My reluctant hero surveyed the area, paying a sigh to every spot of chaos I'd caused, though I knew he could afford it. There was a shattered frame covering an artsy photo of an opium den. Sigh. Potpourri spilled from a wicker basket, trailing towards me. Sigh. One best friend with a blazer between barfs. Sigh. "The ball's about to drop. New Year, new possibilities, all that."

I almost projectile-vomited again when Paul grabbed me beneath my arms, but I fought it. After sloshing to my feet, I snapped away from him, the shift so sudden his Ankh necklace swayed. "I got it," I said, straightening my jacket.

"Yeah, you got it." While I, as you read, *had it*, he still waited a few moments before opening the door.

The party was too busy to notice anything beyond the sounds of slushed say-say, magical incantations like *conscious rap* and *Well, NPR said—* I leaned against the kitchen sink. Paul grabbed a beer from the fridge.

"So, is um, is Thandie coming?" I asked.

Paul draped his arm over my shoulder in his best attempt at a bro hug. It had been about a week or so at that point since she'd left me nearly naked in her living room, with *Ten Things I Hate about You* playing on her flat-screen TV. Joseph Gordon Levitt's proclamations about *being back in the game* will forever remind me of getting dumped.

"What do you do when you lose the woman of your dreams?" I turned to look Paul in the eye, but the furthest I got was the top of his tie.

"You wake up, I guess."

"Yeah. I guess." I whipped my head up and stared at the ceiling to avoid drowning in all the feels. Eventually, after a chuckle from Paul,

I splashed a bit of cold water over my face. Paul handed me the dish towel and patted my back.

He walked me back into the living room with everyone else. His iPod seemed to have forgotten there was anyone in hip-hop beyond Badu or Common. No one seemed to mind, though. Hakeem, one of Paul's coworkers, was the first to notice me and waved, making everyone else turn too. I froze. They froze.

I tried to save the day.

"Zapidy-do!" I crowed, making a show of *accidentally* straightening my vomit tie with my bare hand. There were chuckles, a few *Oh, Donald*s. I tipped my invisible hat and stumbled toward the couch, making certain to trip over my own foot. It's the details, True Believer. They laughed. I shuffled over the speckles of pride I'd left lying on the ground, heroically pulling myself up to the couch and flopping down on it. Paul didn't laugh; he summoned his best Laurence Fishburne face and sat down on the other side of the room.

These are the Astonishing Tales of
John Singleton Sorrows

"I think GRAVI-Tina is doing the ball drop this year," someone said.

"No, I think it's DEATHRAGE this year."

"Wasn't he banned after the whole accidentally-shooting-into-the-crowd thing?"

"There was no indictment; I saw it the other week."

"No, no, it *has* to be Almighty Asper, he does that thing with his freaking laser eyes, and smaboosh! The ball turns into a million pieces and, like, snows down over the crowd."

"A million pieces of glass sounds . . . kind of *not* like a good idea," I say, but they don't hear me—to them I'm just Paul's drunk friend, the relic of his yesteryears in cultural irresponsibility, who probably has an entry-level job and works next to Latisha in the Sky with Cubic Zirconium.

As the countdown continued, thunder boomed outside. There was a flash of light—and then everything went black. The forty-five-inch plasma screen shut down along with the rest of the power in the house. A chorus of *aw* and *no!* and *what the actual fuck, man?* filled the air.

Now's my chance, I thought. While everyone griped and Paul yelled back, letting them know he was going to fix everything like only he could, I seized the moment and escaped into the black.

So, yeah, it was a stormy night—you know, the kind where lightning strikes? If I'd only remembered my wallet and cell phone, I'd probably have called a cab, or Kat, and I might not be here in this café, chugging down this overpriced Verona blend and telling you this story. I would have gone back to Paul's house the next night for his New Year's Day party, and he would still be trying to save me.

I cursed at the unseasonable rain, sniffling as I shuffled. I needed to breathe. I needed to feel the cold and the fury and the bite.

What I really needed was another fucking drink.

Without my wallet I had to walk from Bexley, a neighborhood of Blocks Bagels and brick buildings, through downtown Columbus, Ohio—filled with A&B Coin 'N' Liquors and a legion of hair salons—to my one-bedroom apartment on 21st Street.

Drivers passed me and honked, but I wasn't stupid enough to flip them the bird. My black and dreadful locks were soaking up water and weighing my head down. I was wobbly and cold. I was thirsty but not for water. I was thirsty for Thandie. I was thirsty for my rocket skateboard and the push, even the fall.

There was another boom of thunder. It wouldn't be long, but I couldn't know that. I was thirsty to be naked with clothes. Another boom. I was thirsty to know what you probably already do. Another boom. I was thirsty for nothing. Another boom. A flash. A spark.

CHAPTER 3
THE LIGHTNING SAGA

MAY 18, **"THE SUPERPOWER** *Hour with Keith Kelly Kurskovitch,"* *Hound News Station:*

"It was a close one, that's for sure. Thankfully, I'd soon get a *spark* to my system." When I said it, I turned to the camera and let some sizzling electricity bounce around the copper emblem of my costume.

"That's amazing—no, *astonishing.*"

Laughter.

"So, after you saved the chief's daughter, what happened next?" Keith was sitting on the edge of his seat. I waited a moment, just like Chris had told me.

Good, that was good—be approachable, be funny, be everything they need you to be, he'd tell me after the interview.

"Well, they just sort of stared at me."

Keith, still on the edge of his seat, gave a knowing shake of the head.

"So, I'm losing a lot of blood—I won't go into the details, but it wasn't a pretty sight. And they bring me to their shaman, this hulking, beastly figure of a man. I was afraid at first, like *anyone* would be. He was like a hybrid of nightmare and beauty, his body riddled in tribal markings I couldn't understand and didn't try to, since the pain from the attack was radiating through me. He put a hand on me and another to the sky above. The rest was a kind of a blur. He started to convulse, which really freaked me the hell out, to be honest, man, but then in a sudden burst this light beamed over me. A gentle stream of pure, powerful lightning, coiling around my body. It was then that I was reborn as The Spark."

"That is truly a harrowing story. So—so dignified. And if I may say, you are just so well spoken."

"Oh, well, thank you, Keith, thank you very much."

I must have told that story a thousand times by then. Each time I did, I believed it all the more.

* * *

January 1, 1:53 a.m., Spirit Hospital

"Crash cart, goddammit!"

I wish I could give you a clear recollection of what happened in the hospital that night, or even those first few weeks. But I'm surprised I remember anything at all, aside from the smell of burning cotton and the stinging of bright florescent lights.

"Ugh, soiled himself, that fucking smell. . . . Insurance? ID?"

I'd be told later about the thrashing, about the sedation that didn't sedate, about the absolute resistance of my body.

"Only on News Channel 8. . . . Coffee later? . . . Patient's name is Donald McDougal. . . . Nurse!"

I'd be told later that America averages 120–125 lightning-related accidents each year.

"Emergency contact Paul Hughes."

I'd be told later that of these lightning attacks, about 90 percent involve serious injury. Decreased quality of life. Paralysis. Nerve damage. Scarring, but not the cool kind.

"Twenty bucks says . . . eight weeks already . . . wasting good taxpayer . . . like Obamacare . . ."

I'd be told later that the other 10 percent are fatal.

"Can you hear me, Donald? *Christ*, Donald, just wake up!"

I'd be told that, after racking up eight hundred thousand dollars in medical bills, I beat the odds. I was a miracle. God had a plan for me.

"Perfect, he'll do perfect."

I'd be told that the local news station had screwed up and displayed my picture at about three-fifths the size it was supposed to during the report of the accident, so no one saw me—no one except Paul.

"Integration complete."

I was told someone was looking out for me. I was told I had a hero.

* * *

When I finally came back, it wasn't in the middle of the road like I expected. It was in the peaceful dark of my hospital room. I knew it was a hospital because you *always* know it's a hospital when you've watched someone close to you die in one. What I didn't know was how I'd gotten there. I remembered the power going out, and staggering out of Paul's, but not much else. The only thing that came through clearer than Paul's party was the pain. I remembered the sensation of skin tearing. A steel porcupine tumbling down my spine, settling atop my heart, tiny pins poking over and over, never stopping.

I began screaming. I twisted. I coiled.

I sparked.

The hairs on my chest, pallid white, trembled against the ECG electrodes with the low, humming whisper I'd soon come to know so well. The lights on the attached monitor began flickering.

I remembered lying in bed with Thandie on a Thursday morning, teasing the curtains open to wake her with spurts of sunlight.

I remembered falling from a skateboard and being rushed into a hospital that blinked incessantly with fluorescent bulbs, a mess of ten-year-old blood beneath white sheets.

I remembered licking batteries through the small gaps of freshly fallen baby teeth and fiddling at electrical outlets with forks.

I'd surged. That's what Nikolas would call it, later on. Everything was burning but nothing was on fire. I felt my muscles contract and release. I was the boy who'd been struck by lightning. I'd come back, but I'd come back wrong.

Contract and release.

The ECG machine smoked and popped. Contract and release. A nurse rushed in, but I couldn't hear what she said over the buzzing and throbbing in my ears from that first surge. She touched me and got catapulted back, slammed into the wall. I squeezed my eyes shut. Contract and release. I slipped into unconsciousness.

* * *

"Ugh." When I awoke, it was to the familiar smell of Cherry Coke and clove cigarettes. Turning my head, I blinked the fuzziness away and saw Kat, her short blob of straight, black hair hanging eerily over one of her eyes, emo-style, though the blonde roots kind of ruined the effect. I thought of high school days, hanging out in the bathroom, sitting on a closed toilet lid while Kat cursed and hair dye drizzled down over her eye.

Kat was my oldest friend. I guess I'd grown closer to Paul over time, but she and I had always been there for each other when it counted. She slept soundly, curled up in a thin ball on a chair with hands cradling her knees. My throat was painfully dry but it had nothing on my lips, so I decided not to talk. I just let her sit there sleeping.

When I felt a bit calmer, I shuffled myself to the bathroom. I cupped water in my hands, splashing it against my face. I guess by this time I'd developed some pain tolerance, because even though it bit my skin, I didn't freak out like I had earlier. I just reached for a towel blindly, like it was shampoo in my eye. I threw the towel to the side and opened my eyes to see a stranger in the mirror. Well, okay, maybe stranger is a *bit* dramatic, but that's how I felt when I saw my dreadlocks transformed into a bounty of snowy tendrils.

"What the hell?" I said aloud.

If there's a checklist of superhero habits, talking to yourself has to be on there somewhere. I once attributed it to lazy writing in the comics when you saw Super-whoever speeding across the sky with speech bubbles instead of thought bubbles, conversing with themself about whatever catastrophic event they were on their way to stop. The bad comic writers had it right, though. I stared for what felt like forever into my own eyes in the mirror. They'd shifted to a silvery hue from the brown I'd always known.

"Is this supposed to happen?"

I ran my fingers through my hair. At first, I tried to deduce who around my comatose body would go through the trouble of dyeing my hair white. Would Kat or Paul—

But it was the same on my arms, my body, my legs. For good measure I locked the door and took off the hospital gown, only to see more snow in the south of the garden. A long scar wrapped around my left shoulder, traveling diagonally across my body like an off-kilter ring of Saturn. Even weirder: this body *had* to belong to someone who hadn't smoked a pack of cigarettes a day or spent their Sunday afternoons watching reruns of ~~Gilmore Girls~~ a show about cars while inhaling microwavable burritos smothered in lard.

I touched the pack of muscles that had somehow snuck their way into my abdomen in place of the charming beer belly. My arms, my legs, everything—I belonged on one of those workout videos that told you over and over how much better you could be if you just fought the urge to do nothing.

"Donald, are you in there?"

I scrambled to put the hospital gown back on. "One sec!" I said, trying to be loud enough for her to hear me but only managing a raspy whisper.

Before I was even one step out of the bathroom, Kat pounced on me, laughing.

"How are you feeling?" she said.

"I don't know? I guess pretty good, all things considered."

It wasn't the first time Kat had seen me in a hospital bed, but at least this time it was the universe and not some childish flight of fancy that had put me there.

"Dude, you were struck by lightning," she finally said over a huff of laughter. A few dewy drops welled up in the corners of her eyes, but she was too stubborn to let them fall. One wrong word and I knew she would make this one of the awkward moments we always tried to retcon in the history of us.

"I know, right?" I said.

I guess I'll spare you the next fifteen minutes of us going back and forth, the *oh my god*s and *you're so lucky*s. It's enough that you know they were there, I guess.

"How long have I been here? The last thing I remember is Paul's party. It was weird, Kat. I remember voices. I remember waking up for a minute hooked up to machines. Hearing Paul, and a few other things."

"It's been a while. About two months. The doctors say it was touch and go for a long time. Paul's been coming in almost every other day to hang out with you, and I try to make it up here when I can. He'll be pretty pissed I was here for the big wake-up scene and he wasn't."

I almost made the mistake of placing my hand over hers, breaking her cardinal no-touchy-less-you-want-destroyee rule, but a familiar flame in her eyes stopped me.

"Don't get weird about it," she said.

"It's really awesome that you're here, Kat. Thanks."

"Well, I'm really, really glad you're not dead."

* * *

They released me about a week later with a clean bill of health, or at least as clean as I was going to get without insurance. Paul drove me home, not wanting me to hoof it for fear of another lightning attack—in the middle of a sunny March afternoon.

"So, how does it feel to get back to the world?" he asked.

"Surreal." I'd been staring out the window at everything scattering like fading lines on an Etch-a-Sketch.

"Guess that's to be expected. You were struck by lightning. You survived, your *Black ass survived*. Hell, I have half a mind to write a piece about you."

"I *didn't die*; the whole *survive* thing is still up in the air." A group of kids threw a ball back and forth from opposite curbs while we sat at a red light.

"It's nice to know this hasn't messed up your ability to rain on a parade," Paul said, rolling his eyes so hard I that I didn't have to look over—I just felt it.

"I have two months of rent to catch up on, a migraine, and a pound of hospital meatloaf in my stomach that isn't going to come out without a fight, not to mention the bills that are gonna start floating to my mailbox any day now. You decided to bring your parade through my shitty little village."

The light turned green, and everything moved without moving again.

I didn't know why Paul would want my story for his online "magazine" (blog), *The Kuumba Kollective*. They mostly published political stuff—antiestablishment rhetoric—and he received enough side-eye as a young editor who was relatively successful, so it didn't seem like veering off into a fluffy piece about an uppity retail worker (who happened to be his best friend) should appeal. I eventually settled on telling him that I'd consider it, just to prevent him from giving his usual speech about how everyone has a story that needs to be told.

I also kept the bit about the ECG machine and the whole nurse-electrocution thing to myself.

(Thankfully, she was fine, save for a bitch of a headache and some admittedly convenient short-term memory loss. I *wanted* to tell him. If you decide to pick this up, Paul: I *really* wanted to tell you. It wasn't a lack of trust, man. I just had enough to deal with. When the hospital chalked up the ECG busting to faulty mechanics I figured it best to let you keep thinking that. Looking back? It'd probably have been nice if you were there at my side for this next bit.)

* * *

At my Shoebox of Solitude there weren't any streamers or noisemakers. No Thandie D. Nettle lingered, and my beautiful Believers didn't exist yet. What I did find were empty cupboards and a cloud of buzzing black gnats swarming over the now-fungus-encrusted bowl of microwavable pad thai that sat on my Craigslist coffee table. The electricity had been shut off. I'd expected as much, though.

Paul made it his mission per usual to save me, trying to drag me from the beautiful dark of my apartment to his townhouse with the always-open doors. It's one thing to deal with a little darkness; it's a whole other to deal with a constant stream of guests discussing the Black plight of the new millennium. *No thanks, I'm good*, I told him. Kat made a similar offer, but she basically lived in a shoebox also, and squeezing anyone else into it would be an exercise in defying physics.

When I returned to the Stereo Hutt the next day, it was as much a graveyard of capacitators and crooked adverts as I'd left it. There were a few bearable things about the place, though, one of which was Allen, my manager. When I walked in he gave me the best nigga nod a Caucasian man has ever mustered.

"You're a little late for your shift."

"Got struck by lightning, boss."

"That old excuse." He extended a hand. I took it and was pulled into a quick pat-hug.

I'd been promoted to keyholder a few weeks before the lightning strike, which meant the same pay with a few extra bits of metal on my belt. When it was decided that I would be Lord of the Keys, Allen made a big show of pulling out the spares from his desk, calling in my coworker Natalie to act as a witness. I'd like to think I received this honor due to my exceptional ability at selling over-priced batteries to an older crowd who gasped and fawned at my vernacular. Or possibly it was Allen's innate talent for sensing ini-tiative, drive, and get-the-job-done-ness.

I stocked product for most of the day and more than once nearly busted my ass pulling boxes from the ground. I remembered them being at least twice as heavy, but I disregarded it—we'd had our share of messed-up orders. What was odd, even then, was how much I loved working that day. Each box of batteries I unpacked made my skin crawl and muscles flutter. Throughout the work day I became harder, better, etc. I'd never known the clock to speed by so fast—in a blip it was done.

After work I climbed into my Corsica to enjoy what little night I had before starting over from the top. No matter their creed, color, or comic-book origin, anyone can feel power behind a wheel. Bonus points for stick shift, of course. I loved clouding my mind with gears and glinting moonlight.

These moments had been hijacked as of late by Thandie D. Nettle. I found that all she had to do was infect a moment in time and that was that: she was wedged there like a granule of sea salt that wouldn't melt.

(If you decided to pick this book up, Paul, I know you're probably saying, "Bro, get over it," and don't worry—only 9, at most 10 percent of this book is about her. I promise.)

I slowed down at the red light and fumbled through a tangle of headphones and power cords wedged in my coin tray to find the half-full box of menthol mayhems. My smoking habit could play as metaphor for any Black Power movement after the 80s: not fully committed, reluctantly active.

Less than a mile from my shoebox I considered driving all night, blowing puffs of deathstream into the familiar night. But the oasis of chill I'd found myself in thinned as quickly as the dissipating smoke when flashes of red and blue summoned a stop from behind.

These are the Astonishing Tales of First Times

Every nigga has a cop story. This will, unfortunately, always be our great unifier. It's one of those things we promised to teach you later. It's become so redundant that a guy, no matter how kinda sorta brown he is, getting pulled over is equivalent to a fart joke in your favorite Adam Sandler movie.

I digress, and apologize, as I'm aware that two more racially aimed comments will officially land this little memoir in the dusty African-American section of your local bookstore.

These are the Astonishing Revolutions
That Cannot Be Categorized

The sirens are the worst part, always; they rattle my skin like it's covered by a Marvel symbiote. At the sound I dropped my cigarette and then cursed while swatting at my fiery crotch and simultaneously pulling over.

Amid this reckless flailing, I tapped the gas pedal over and over and heard the stutters of the police officer's car *woop wooooping*. When we finally parked he waddled up to my window and acknowledged with a grunt what a burden I'd been. *I'm tired too*, I wanted to tell him. *I'm so, so tired.*

I'm not a moron, though, so I bit the words back.

"Do you know why I pulled you over?"

These are the Astonishing Tales of Cause I'm
Young and I'm Black and My Hat's Real Low?

I didn't let my Jay-Z-inspired insolence escape. I avoided eye contact.

"No, sir."

"You don't? I know that your registration stickers are on the wrong sides of your plate. I know that you should take that bass out of your voice when you're speaking to a police officer."

There was no bass, no treble, just a scared soon-to-be superhero staring at his own waist, wondering if he'd be the next name on a picket sign under things that mattered.

He rolled his eyes and I ducked mine low, the inevitable dip in our dance. I almost went for my ID but thought better of it. I sat. I waited.

"Your ID, sir."

I complied. When I reached into my side pocket and there was a reassuring lack of *pows* I was free to start feeling the fire.

Don't you hear my voice? Don't you know that I'm one of the goddamned smart ones?

He didn't.

The sound of breaking behind my ears began then, and I don't know if it's ever stopped.

"Please step out of the vehicle, sir."

I climbed out. I didn't ask why, because, well, not a moron.

"Where are you coming from?"

"Work."

His eyebrows rose at that. "Where's that, exactly?"

"The Stereo Hutt."

"Mind if I search your car, sir?"

It's no secret, or at least it shouldn't be, that you have every right to say *no* to a question like this. You can also raise a middle finger. You can laugh in their faces. You can beg them not to make you part of the hashtag hailstorm. There's a lot of things you *can* do.

"Sure," I answered.

The officer tore through my vehicle like a beast from the east or some other juvenile thing. He found nothing but seemed so pleasantly exhausted afterward that I considered bumming him a cigarette. I stared around my car at the accumulating mess, the cost of a disorganized life. Amongst the amalgam I saw old printouts of weekly work schedules and comic books I hadn't gotten around to reading yet, still bound in the plastic they were shipped in.

Passersby, few that they were, stared for a moment before blazing off. Shitty as it was, this was the good part. For a moment I became the badass, the one I ran from through the halls in my high school. The onlookers gave me that gift: turned me, with one magical glance, into that darkness.

I was brought back to life, back to reality, by the sound of a clinking coin. During the ransack it had glanced off the accumulating pile of crap at an odd angle. It wasn't a coin for spending, just keeping. It signified five years of my father's sobriety from narcotics. When I was fourteen I'd found it on top of his dresser while pilfering change to avoid the embarrassment of having to use a free lunch ticket. I'd found it at a time when I thought any Roman numeral was fancy and to be admired. I wasn't much for photos or movie stubs, but that coin, that *goddamn* origin-story-starting coin.

It dropped out the open door and started to roll away into the darkness. I wanted to ask permission to run after it. I couldn't, though. I was powerless.

These are the Astonishing Tales of Fuck That

I reached out a hand like the five-year-old you once were. The one who saw *The Empire Strikes Back* one too many times and tried to use a Force you didn't have. I don't know the why of this next bit, just the how. Twinkles of blue sparks danced from my fingertips to the coin as it shot up to my hand. Before the officer had time to turn I was already holding it.

"Ho—fuck!" I yelped.

The officer turned with a hand over his firearm. I was too connected to care.

* * *

Yeah, that was how it started.

* * *

I didn't go to work the next day, or the one after that. I'm not really sure if I ate even. Sitting there in the beautiful dark, afraid of the world and the wonderful ways I could tear it apart, I found the courage to open my eyes and hold my palm in front of my face. Sparks fluttered about, staying mostly between my fingers. The charge circulating through me quickened and I welcomed it like a cigarette after a toss, a smooth bite that picks everything up, though I pretend it slows it down.

Contract and release.

The spark wanted me to be more. I could feel it. The first skill I'd been learning, without even knowing it, was using a low amount of electricity to work my muscles. Throughout the day I'd feel the spark clutch and let go, until it decided on a good point to stop for recovery. It gave me that body you wanted for your high-school reunion or that civil dinner with the ex. Contract and release.

"Okay," I said. "So, I've got superpowers. I was struck by lightning, and now I have superpowers." I repeated it over and over, each time sparking and flashing.

I must admit that, yes, it is pretty fucking cool to shoot lightning out of your fingers. I mean, it's fucking lightning, out of your *fingers*. It takes some getting used to, though, True Believer.

Like most who find themselves in uncharted territory, I decided against baby steps. I ran, unrestrained and full of something like daring, but honestly? It was mostly about survival. I had to be smart about this and learn everything I could about a subject that I couldn't exactly buy a book on from Amazon. The comics don't tell you about that part. Research. Fucking research. The countless hours that turn into days until soon enough, it's been two weeks, twenty-six broken toasters, and twelve fried surge protectors. Five hundred dollars that I'd borrowed from Visa, spent on that junk, earned me a modicum of control. What I didn't think of until it was already at my front door was the bill for recently reactivated AEP service. I was learning all too fast that *with great power comes a great need for more income.*

Before I was Astonishing, I'd guiltily waste away in front of episodes of *The Superpower Hour.* The host would ask the inevitable question: *What has your life been like since freak accident X occurred?* Following that would be a moment of silence and then an admission of how much they wanted to be *normal.* I would listen and think, *Yeah, jackass, because flying or walking through walls is such a burden, boo-friggin-hoo.* That was, of course, until the five-hundred-dollar electricity bill, not to mention the six-figure medical bills sitting in a corner. Then there was the two months of rent, which landed somewhere a bit over a grand, and still sitting at the bottom of the well was the twelve thousand dollars I owed for a degree program I'd never finished.

What I wasn't going to do, or even consider, was the whole super-*villain* route. I would never hurt anyone, not really. But I mean, as long as no one got hurt, there wasn't such a problem, right? It would be more like liberating money than stealing it.

These are the Astonishing Tales of He
Who Doth Protest Too Much

It was supposed to be the perfect crime. Actually, the word *crime* is giving it too much credit. I'd been a hermit after my first spark, avoiding, as much I could, going out during the daytime for fear of hurting someone by accident. There had been too many supervillain sob stories of losing control, someone getting hurt or dying, and the hero having no choice but to take them down. The biggest problem with the villains, the mainstreamers who seem to get in and out of prison like there's a revolving door, is that they go too big. They want to make some kind of statement—it's what leads to them getting caught every time. Me? I was just a guy who needed a little help. I wasn't searching for a new deal, a handshake, or a handout. I just wanted to keep doing the whole eating thing.

The option I'd settled on was to try hitting an ATM with a power surge. Just like the movies promised, an unlimited amount of bills would then spill out at me, begging to be taken. It was a victimless crime as far as I was concerned. While the bank was most likely insured, my renter's agreement wasn't, so if there was anyone who didn't have a choice—if there was anyone *entitled* to this—it was me.

I didn't really have to go all out with the black hoodie and sweatpants, but the cosplaying geek in me needed to play dress-up. The plan was to hit the shoddy ATM at the twenty-four-hour gas station where I used to resupply on snacks during late-night gaming sessions. Andrew was working that night, per usual. He was a good kid, eighteen years old, and he enjoyed sparking conversations about comics whenever I walked in, especially after eying my Ben Reilly T-shirt. He wasn't a big fan of the heroes, and I respected him for that—still do, because if Aedan were still around I'm sure he'd share the sentiment.

"I like the classic stuff, you know, like Ditko and Lee, or—or Kirby, Kirby had some amazing stuff. These *real* superheroes, it's like, I don't know, like a bad deconstruction we can't turn away from," he'd said once. He was a student, so politics, philosophy, and anything concerning the internal plight of the Silver Surfer validated his fandom as an *art*, all while giving him a half-chub.

"Isn't everything a deconstruction we can't turn away from?" I'd asked.

"God, I hope not."

Tonight Andrew was skimming through an old issue of *Hardware* when I accidently stumbled into a magazine rack.

"Smooth," he said with a chuckle.

I forced a laugh and picked up the sprawled-out issues of *People* and *Super People*. I made a show of flipping through them during the slow trip to the back corner where the ATM was. *This is it*, I thought, standing in front of the shoddy tank of a cash machine. *This is my perfect infallible foray into crime.* I placed one hand over the metallic keypad and the other over the display screen. Then I started trying, well, anything.

This was not one of my proudest moments as a superpowered

individual. In case you didn't know, True Believer, you can't just overload a machine with electricity and expect it to do what you want. Shocking, right?

I watched with sizzling hands and a sinking heart as the display blinked crazily before stagnating on a blue screen. Then a puff of smoke burst from the keypad. I waved my hands and coughed, swallowing the fuck-you fruits of my spastic ambition.

"Shit," I whimpered between coughs.

"Everything okay?" Andrew called from the front of the store.

"Yeah, just, um, I think this thing is busted," I responded.

In modest defeat I decided to peruse the aisles for my poison of choice, salt-and-vinegar potato chips, in preparation for another night of gaming followed by a wrestling match with Leftonya Handson. While I stood there facing the eternal dilemma between name-brand or Quik-E-Mart potato chips, the store bell chimed. Another late-nighter, who stumbled into the magazine rack just as I had and tipped it over, though he didn't take the time to pick everything up. I watched from the back of an aisle as Andrew slapped his magazine down on the counter and stared at the newcomer, who, like me, was clad in black from head to toe. That went on for a while, until Andrew succumbed with a groan, taking a knee to pick up the mess of papers.

Then I saw the newcomer circle around behind Andrew. Tucked in the back of his sweatpants? A gun.

I couldn't make a sound. I just watched as he put the gun to the back of Andrew's head. There were beads of sweat running down the robber's face, sticking thin strips of blond hair to his forehead.

"Oh god. Oh god. Please don't kill me. Please, *please* just don't kill me." Andrew's hands were in the air and he was shaking. The man with the gun, who couldn't be any older than me, was shaking too.

"Shut the fuck up! You're gonna—go to the drawer and give me all the money. Now!"

"Please, please, please, just—god, just please—" Andrew started sobbing. He'd seen the man's face. He would talk to a sketch artist; he would tell anyone he could about the most interesting thing that had ever happened in his life. The news would loop the picture. The gunman seemed insane, but not stupid. He knew what had to be done. He'd known it before he even walked in. What other options did he have?

Life is easier when you *can't* do anything about these things, because it makes self-preservation more of a priority than moronic hero-itis, which I'd steadily been developing a case of. The robber cocked the gun and pushed it a bit harder into the back of Andrew's skull. *This is it*, I thought. I edged forward a bit, filling my hand with tingling needles as I stretched it towards him. But I wasn't stealthy enough. Potato-chip bags rustled as my arm brushed them.

"The fuck?" the robber said, turning his attention and weapon in my direction.

There was just enough time for me to shoot a bolt of electricity from my fingers. The spark connected with his gun and traveled through him, not giving him the chance to make a sound. Instant unconsciousness, a pain I knew all too well. I closed my hand and the stream stopped. He toppled over, convulsing, mouth foaming.

"What just happened?" Andrew shouted when he turned around to see smoke rising over the gunman's soon-to-be corpse.

I ran over and slid to the ground.

"Come on, come on, wake up!" I barked, slapping the gunman's face lightly.

"What's wrong with him?"

Andrew was still panicking. I ignored his questions and focused on the unconscious—kid, he was a kid. A teenager. *He's dying*, I thought. *It'll be on my hands. I'm responsible. I have to save him.*

These are the Astonishing Tales of the
Man Who Disobeys Traffic Laws

When we arrived at the emergency room he was still twitching.

"Help!" I screamed. "Someone, I need some fucking help!"

Calm down. You fucked up, but calm down, I thought. I calmed down. I settled. I got my shit together and carried him through the sliding doors.

Someone from the front desk spotted me and rushed out. After a back and forth of *what the hell are you doing*s I finally got my mystery gunman into a wheelchair and we pushed him in.

He'll be okay, I thought. *You saved him.*

I think I've mentioned this before, but I hate hospitals, like Batman hates boom-tubes and Superman hates magic, like Indy hates snakes and Kirk hates Khan. I really, really hate hospitals.

In a list of things to hate, it's probably one of the most unfortunate if you stumble into this line of business, because odds are you'll end up in one at least once a week. You'll be on a first-name basis with the MDs, the nurses, the friggin' vending-machine operators.

"Are you the one who brought in Mr. Splam?"

Dumbass kid had had ID in his pocket. I was standing in the waiting room with a cup of coffee. I'd taken off the black hoodie, hoping I'd look a little less burglarish. I turned to see the lab coat and the glare of methodical indifference that usually accompanied one.

Did I mention I really don't like hospitals?

"Yes, I am."

"How do you know the patient?" the doctor asked.

Well, funny story, we just happened to be trying to pull a quick heist at the same time. Small world, right, doc?

"I don't really *know* him per se, I just, I mean, he was robbing this store I go to, and he had some kind of seizure or something. And Andrew, that's the cashier, he was *really* scared, so I drove him here. I mean, I drove the robber here. After the stroke, or seizure, or whatever."

"Shit," said the doctor. "Did you call the police?"

"Uh, no. Andrew was on the phone with them when I left, though." That wasn't true, but I was pretty sure it was the next thing he'd do.

"Ugh. There's gonna be a ton of paperwork. Don't go anywhere, okay?" He turned back to the automatic doors.

Shit. "So he—is he going to be okay? The robber, I mean."

The doctor gave me a weird look. "I think he'll pull through," he said. "Just have a seat, okay? The police are going to want to talk to you."

So I sat there, drinking coffee that wasn't nearly as *premium* as the vending machine claimed, waiting for my next reckoning. Telling myself over and over again there was no way I could get blamed for this one. I was the hero, goddammit. I'd *saved* this lowlife piece of shit. *And* Andrew.

I thought of the heroes. I thought of their mighty deeds and their mightier paychecks: the Almighty Asper doing ads for that shoe company; the Neutrogena commercials with Sergeant Snakeskin.

There was an easier way to take care of my problems than busting up ATMs. As such a rabid fanboy, it's sad that it took nearly frying someone to realize just how to do that.

I'd be a hero. I'd be a Superhero.

CHAPTER 4
TALES OF THE MIDWEST MARVEL

OHIO'S FIRST SUPERHERO?
THE MIDWEST HAS A DARING NEW TALENT!

Violent crime is a growing epidemic. With a surplus of superpowered threats to the United States, sanctioned heroes have been placed throughout the country, most prominently in New York, Miami, and Los Angeles. Yet some states, such as Ohio, have yet to receive protection from the North American biological-defense unit, PantheUS.

"We haven't had contact with the so-called 'Midwest Marvel.' As of now, he is an unsanctioned vigilante under the Supreme Powers Act of 2003. We strongly urge him to register within the allotted period," said General Gunther Grey of PantheUS.

Analysts say there is a strong possibility that official registration of the Midwest Marvel would result in his relocation, however.

Continued on B4

IT WASN'T THAT I hadn't thought about it before, but after the thing with Aedan, I just, I don't know.

What were those guys really protecting? They sure as shit weren't protecting Aedan. There was no letter of apology sent from the Almighty Asper to Aedan's wife and daughter after he became a casualty or collateral damage or whatever you want to call it. What would Aedan think of me now, becoming one of *them*?

I tried to put it out of my mind, but after a while—*I'm so sorry, Aedan, God rest your soul and all that jazz, but I need funds, dolla dolla bills y'all.* (Yeah, I don't feel right even typing that.)

What was I talking about?

Oh yeah, Midwest Marvel. So, it started like this.

TERROR IN THE HEARTLAND
THE MAVERICK MORALIST'S REIGN OF FEAR

Not even the heartland is safe anymore. A costumed individual using the alias "Maverick Moralist," who claims to be trying to purge the world of "abominations," has been linked to a string of kidnappings throughout the city. As seen in recent video footage, the terrorist wears a gray robe and has a facial tattoo in the form of a crucifix. Anyone with information relating to his whereabouts is asked to contact local authorities immediately.

"Can you believe this shit?" said Paul, slamming his tablet down.

We were finishing up our regularly scheduled pretentious coffee outing. I slid the tablet over to where I could see it. The news page displayed a picture of the Maverick Moralist, or—as we now know him, my True Believers—Levert Duterman, the first true Super Predator to grace the heartland after White Flame.

Lucky us.

"A Super Predator, in Columbus?" I said, catching myself smiling like an opportunistic douchebag. I frowned as best I could, mustering all the skills a two-thousand-dollar Acting 101 class had given me.

"A Super Predator! And the damn *Central Dispatch* scooped the story!"

"Wait, you're pissed about the story? Not really *Kuumba Kollective*'s type of headline, though, right?"

"We could have used the story. Our sales are, per usual, shit." Paul rubbed his temples.

Watching him have yet another existential crisis over cover stories, I did feel bad for him. But my heart couldn't stop racing at the best news I'd gotten in the last few months.

"Sorry, man."

"Whatever. Anyway, I gotta go," said Paul. "I'll catch you later, Donald."

"Yeah, sure. Later, man," I said, not paying much attention to his departure. All I could think of was the Maverick Moralist, aka Levert Duterman: my first big, fat paycheck.

After the robbery at the gas station, I'd become a bit obsessed. I brushed up on current events, putting in a subscription to *Hero Quarterly* and another to *Super Style Weekly*, the latter because everyone knows that the first appearance is what people remember. If you're the schlub who's seen in *last year's costume* you can kiss whatever opportunity you think you had goodbye.

Back when I read comics I'd have been bored with the business of becoming. What do I mean when I say the "business of becoming"? I mean the trials and tribulations of costume development, name recognition—branding and advertising. They're like the awkward parts of sex that get skimmed over in movies. Everyone would rather slide past them.

After going through it, though? I have a newfound respect for it. And if I had to deal with it, so do you.

The dilemma, of course, was that I still wasn't making enough to keep up with the bills. It didn't leave much budget for tailoring. What I *could* afford was the ever-stylish array of options at the Salvation Army.

"Excuse me?" I asked, tapping the shoulder of someone folding clothes.

She turned around and chilled me with a look only the deadest of eyes could offer. I tried smiling back to fix everything that had gone wrong in her life, but it only served as a reminder that I, like so many others, would probably only make it worse.

"Yeah?"

"Um, where is the men's section?"

Translation: *Where is the section where I can find clothes to cut and paste into a superhero uniform?*

"Right there?" She pointed to the alarmingly oversized sign which read *Men*. I gave a nod and took my ineffectual smile with me to the *Men* section. I was glad to see that not many people were out and about at two o'clock on a Wednesday afternoon, because you see, True Believers, I worried that somehow *someone* would notice that Donald McDougal was there to buy his superhero costume.

After unsurprisingly failing to locate the perfect crime-fighting costume among the donations, I settled on a black T-shirt, a thermal long-sleeve to keep warm beneath, and a pair of black slacks. With a little snip here and an iron-on transfer there, I'd be golden-age glossy. I snuck through the ladies' section and nabbed a pair of black stockings: I needed a mask, or at least I thought I did at the time, but more on that later.

"How much is it?" I asked the cashier after she'd rung everything up.

"$10.50?" she said, or asked—I couldn't tell.

"Okay? Thank you?"

"You're welcome? Have a nice day?"

After the uplifting experience of visiting the Salvation Army, I felt so warm and cuddly inside I'm surprised I didn't crap bunnies and unicorns on the spot, but somehow I fought the urge, heading home instead to play a bit of dress-up.

I was still behind on my electric bill, but I'd learned enough about the manipulation of electricity to keep things running instead of draining the meter. The electric bill's henchman, however—the internet bill—had sneak-attacked me from behind. Thankfully, I could always count on that one neighbor with the password of *password*, and the world was mine.

These are the Astonishing Tales of Just a Little Snack, Guys

I typed in *fantasy lightning bolts* on Google Images. It returned pictures from *Harry Potter* and *Shazam!*—neither of which would look good on a T-shirt—and then of actual lightning bolts, which, while oddly soothing, were too authentic. I wasn't going for authentic; I was going for astonishing. Finally I settled on a yellow clip-art-type lightning bolt that had about two more edges on it than that of a certain speedster from DC Comics (Detective Comics *Comics*? Does that bother anyone else?), so that way I'd avoid any wrongful implications of running really, really fast. I'd have to figure out how to get it from the screen onto my classy black T-shirt, but I could do that later.

Because really, the costume was the least of my problems. Becoming a legitimate hero was going to be more of a challenge.

General registration in PantheUS cost four hundred dollars. While I'm sure the fee helped weed out the uncommitted, I couldn't quite make that kind of investment. However, the website said I could get special registration for free if I "assisted law enforcement with the capture of a superpowered individual engaged in criminal activity."

The Maverick Moralist was an obvious choice. He was local. The footage of him from News Channel 7 had been uploaded to YouTube, and already there were over three million views. Below them, comments that only internet anonymity could enable:

> REIBAUGH1439: First comment, woot!!!!!

> THE WOND3RFULOZ: So horrible, why can't we all just get along??????!!11

> HELLERKELLER: His costume is lame.

> ASPER-FAN34: I do't know, look at his robes, look at his conviction, whatever he's doing its obv gods work.

> TAKA101: BIG GREEEEEEEEENNNNNNN!!!!!

> M_D_BAHAHAHATTI: He is setting an example, round em up, cut em down, make em bleed...

After picking through thirty-seven cult webpages, a few fake blogs claiming to be his, and one very disturbing music video that spliced the original news report with *Creed* songs, I still had bupkis.

I was no detective. The choose-your-own-adventure mystery books I grew up on had obviously misled me into believing this was much easier than it really was. I watched the video the Moralist had sent in repeatedly, hoping for one of those "there it is!" moments

39

where I'd recognize some seemingly arbitrary detail that made me snap my fingers before exclaiming loudly in front of no one: *Holy handkerchiefs, they only sell that brand of napkins at x location on x day!*

I would then proceed to find x location, where (1) I would pummel a lackey nearly to death, heroically of course, and frighten them with the prospect of being electrocuted. (2) Said scoundrel would direct me to the appropriate hidden bastion, where I would shock (heh, shock) my would-be nemesis with my astounding skills in detection. Then I would (3) brawl with him, and (4) leave the murdering bastard tied up with rope, ready for police officers to come and claim him.

It never works that way, though, True Believers. Not while you're still in the minors, at least.

* * *

A call from Kat gave me a great excuse to take my mind off of all this detecting. We decided to meet at Margarine's Pub, in the brilliant suburban ignorbliss of Gahanna, Ohio. When I got there, I saw that she hadn't arrived yet, so I grabbed a beer while I waited.

Margarine's Pub wasn't anything special to people who weren't on a first-name basis with the bartenders. I'd been a regular patron for about four years at that point, which may or may not have had anything to do with the fact that in Gahanna it wasn't hard to pick up women favorably disposed toward my parental-rage-inducing complexion. (Keeping them was an entirely different story.)

I had wounds there, markings on the walls of the men's bathroom where I'd drawn, among other anatomically incorrect creations, women's breasts, or turned to other urinaters and laughed while I wrote the word *niggers* on the wall in the delusion I was being ironic.

There were scuffs in the dance floor from when I'd enacted a rendition of Michael Jackson's "Thriller" to please the masses.

They loved it; they fed on the spirit I gave so freely, just for the chance to call this *our* house and not *their* house. I'd earned my keep; I was one of them. Even if separated by epidermis, I was the epitome of what they needed, that face in the crowd who could tell them everything was okay if the hard *r* was left off.

"Hey, D," said Kat.

"Yo, Kat."

She shuffled into a seat next to mine, raising a hand, and the tender brought her a beer. We were quiet, as usual when drinking on slow nights and watching sports games we couldn't hope to understand. Since we were both cut from the same nerdy cloth, we didn't waste our time with awkward comments about ball when there were more important things we could talk about, like whether Joss Whedon was overrated and what made Patton Oswalt bae.

When we were bored enough and drunk enough to start smoking we headed out to the front of the bar for a cig. The cancer collective was out and about. I took the pack from my back pocket, fingered two from it, flicked one over to her, and we enjoyed the drag. I leaned against the window. My dreadlocks shook a bit, and there was a tug.

"Oh my god, I *loooove* your hair! I didn't know you could color it like ours!"

She was drunk—whoever she is, she's always drunk. Her fingers picked through the pallid mess of locks that I hadn't touched with a latch hook in weeks. Kat rolled her eyes, because she knew what was coming.

"Thanks! I'm Donald. What's your name?" I said to, um . . . Becky. Let's call her Becky.

"I'm Becky!"

"Awesome! Hi, Becky. Are you here on your own?"

"No, that's—that's my boyfriend, right—there." She pointed her cigarette like a wand toward the proud Adonis behind her. I gave a nod and the boyfriend nudged in behind her, wrapping his hands around her waist. Her hand in my hair, his hands round her waist. I don't have to wonder who's the tool in this tripod.

"Hey. I'm Rad," he said, giving me of all things an upward nod. He'd obviously watched his fair share of music videos.

"Yeah, you sure are."

Kat huffed. I nudged her stomach with my elbow, or at least I tried to, but I ended up grazing her breast by accident instead and we placed it in our jar of awkward moments. Rad was probably the worst name I'd ever heard—until Tad the barista, at least—but unlike my current barista, Rad was probably one of the worst people as well. You've seen him before:

1. A shirt that gleams with a slogan along the lines of *Affliction* or *Hey Notice Me Please.*

2. A rubber bracelet that asks or commands you to *Live Strong* whilst having two testicles. (I know this last part because of number three.)

3. A pair of jeans that are strategically ripped and tight enough to stylishly outline a package you don't have to sign for.

He was the kind of guy who made Kat proud she had no interest in male types at all, but his Barbie—sorry, Becky—didn't quite support the notion that women were any better.

Okay, sorry. I guess I'm being judgmental here. For all I know, Rad was a weekend warrior at a soup kitchen and Becky read Plato's

Republic to starving children in South Africa. But first impressions are a hell of a thing, and I generally don't give much benefit of the doubt to those who are able to do something about them.

"So where are you guys coming from, that club up the street?" said Becky.

"No, we just came here to grab a drink or two."

Kat finished her last drag and without so much as a sarcastic grunt went back inside.

"Yeah? That's cool. We were gonna go but there's like—like a line out the front door. It's dollar drink night over there so it's like wall-to-wall urban types. I mean, no offense or anything. It's just urban types don't come out to this side of town much. And there was a fight. I saw it. I'm like, keep that shit downtown! We don't want anyone getting shot down here or anything, you know what I'm saying?" She laughed.

I don't know why I put up with that shit. No, I do. I just really, *really* liked being in our house. It was more comfortable than sweating in front of a club, that's for damn sure. I could have argued with her. I could have pointed out that there are more brawls at Margarine's Pub than there are mythical, nonexistent club shootings in Gahanna, or even disputed the economic differences in our drinking rituals. That was Paul's bag, though. That *Superman IV: Quest for Peace* shit.

Instead I just detached Becky's fingers from my hair, waved bye, and exaggerated a drunken wobble on my way back into the bar. Kat was staring at the TV screen. At first I thought she'd discovered a new love for sports.

I was wrong.

"I, the Maverick Moralist, am doing the will of my father, blessed be! I, the Maverick Moralist, am the avenging angel—AH! That the world has been waiting for—AH! Do you hear me out there, you abominations? Do you hear me out there, all you sinners?"

A newscaster appeared. "The disturbing message received today from the local costumed kidnapper and cult leader known as the 'Maverick Moralist.' Reports say Maverick is currently holding an unknown number of hostages at an undisclosed location in the city. Maverick himself has released several blurred photos of the scene on social media. Caution, these images may be disturbing for some viewers."

The photos showed hostages blindfolded, hands tied behind their backs. One caught my eye—a little girl whose face was scrunched up like she was crying under the blindfold. Kat noticed her too, and it sobered the both of us. Where were the heroes? Sure, none of them were stationed in our little Midwestern lair of lost lambs, but hell, hadn't they ever heard of the airport? And that's not even considering that PantheUS included fliers—and teleporters.

Wherever he was, it wasn't a church; he'd just had enough self-righteousness to bring his own altar. People were sitting in booths. Okay, that was a start, I thought, but it was Kat who got me to the finish.

"This guy is ridiculous," she said, ignoring the bartender, who was trying to ask if she wanted another round.

"I can't believe no one's found him yet," I said.

As we watched the report, I think it was the first time I had a moment—some sudden spark (yeah, I know)—of wanting something more than to line my pockets. These people needed someone, anyone, to save them. Kat squinted at the screen.

"Oh, oh my god."

"What?"

"I think I know that place. Look at that trash can with the weird broken flap."

I saw what she was pointing at a second before the photo disappeared. "It's the Crimson Lobster that closed down. I used to eat there all the time."

These are the Astonishing Tales of Finding X
Brand of Napkins at X Location on X Day

It was time for Donald McDougal to make his heroic debut.

"You, uh, better maybe call the tip line or something? Is there a tip line?"

"Yeah, I should," said Kat.

"I, uh, gotta go, anyway. Getting up early tomorrow."

"Wait, Donald?"

I was already rushing out. The bartender gave a shout, thinking I was trying to skid out unpaid, but I tossed a twenty on the counter for her. I then realized that I was far from being in a place to just throw away twenty dollars yet and ran back inside to get change. Kat looked bewildered. I winked at her as the bartender handed me $13.45.

"Zapidy-do," I said, feeling sparks of excitement start to dance through my body.

* * *

It wasn't until I stood in front of the old Crimson Lobster in the pouring rain—yep, it had started raining—that I started to tremble out of something other than excitement. I was about to fight someone, *with my hands*. Sure, my hands had lightning now, but still. I hadn't been in a fight since grade school, and it wasn't like Maverick had just stolen my chocolate milk or called my kufi a *goofy*. He was a full-grown, crime-committing, kidnapping asshole.

The door was unlocked behind the sign that said *No Trespassing*. I slid in. The front lobby was empty, so the beautiful dark gave me invisibility. I could hear him, doing his psycho preaching thing like that embarrassing uncle no one wants to invite to Thanksgiving. He was going on and on. I started pacing back and forth, throwing punches at imaginary monsters to warm up. It was silly, but hey—anything that helped get me amped up couldn't hurt, right? I also wrung some rain out of my costume and did a few pushups, which was a complete waste of time since the electricity I store does all the working out I could ever need. I was stalling, and I knew it.

"The people need a wake-up! Do you hear me! Say that you hear me people—AH!"

"We hear you!" the hostages said in dispirited unison.

I slunk to the edge of the dining area. The Maverick was evidently too preoccupied with the business of himself to notice the five-foot-nine cosplay reject who'd started crawling on all fours behind the masses of people to find a seat for the weekly word.

In the center of the room there was a spiral pattern of shattered floorboards. Beneath it, a pit that looked like it would have taken some serious heavy machinery to dig out. A smooth, flat grunk of stone rose from one side of the pit, and there was a camera propped on it—he was *recording* this. The camera turned to sweep across the crowd. No—the stone pedestal itself was rotating.

Slowly I put it together. *He can control the earth around him*, I realized, feeling that my plans for an endorsement campaign might be prematurely cut short. That was how more than seventy people had disappeared so easily: he was hiding his captive congregation underground.

"We should all make a run for it; he can't stop us all," whispered an older man nearby.

"Yeah, maybe that's a good idea," a woman next to him responded.

"I think you should sit tight," I said, laying hands on their shoulders. I expected the gesture to have a calming effect, but I didn't realize how off-putting it was to have a hand on your shoulder in a room filled with people tied at the wrists. They squirmed. I begged them to hush with a *shhh!*

"Who are you?"

"I—I'm a hero. I'm here to stop this guy."

"So . . . isn't there something else you should be doing?"

"Right." I gave a quick double pat to the back of the man's shoulder. This was it; this was the moment. I stood up.

"Hey! Hey you!" I shouted. I put my hands on my hips and puffed out my chest as heroically as I could. He hopped down from the pulpit. I could hear people crying; I could smell their sweat. It was too much. It was just enough.

"Who are YOU to interrupt the word—AH!"

"I've come to bring you to justice, you *fiend*!" I actually said that, aloud. The hostage I'd spoken with snickered. I nudged him with the heel of my boot, then stretched a hand toward the fiend.

My moment of truth: the first time I'd do something for everyone to see. I tried to expel the surging electricity from my hand. Instead, my damp skin sizzled and I screamed. It felt like glass shards were piercing me, over and over. I convulsed and fell flat.

It wasn't the worst pain I'd known, but it was a close second. I tried to shake it off, but my muscles stayed rigid. And the Maverick Moralist was slinking through the crowd towards me. You know what I should have done during all that toaster-busting "training," True Believer? I should have tried using my powers while saturated in water. Much as it would have sucked, I'd rather have convulsed like a fevered slug in the privacy of my own shower than learn it there. Eh, I digress.

"You see? Can you see this?" Maverick shouted for the camera. "This is divinity in motion; this is the proof!" A kick. "This is the proof that I have GAWD on my side!"

I can't let this be it, I thought. *I can't let this be the end of the unnamed superhero formerly known as Donald.*

The Maverick Moralist finished sermonizing and tossed me over the serving counter, where, True Believer, I played dead very, very well.

I thought of my father.

I thought of how they'd never see me coming.

My body was stiffer than I'd gotten in the sixth grade when Paul snuck "a video" from beneath his brother's bed, but the pain was fading. I was still ready to be more.

"The greatest thing—AH! Is the Lord—AH! And I see you here! You abominations—AH! Your gallivanting in the streets! Isn't it time—that you paid—for your sins!"

The evangelists of the world, for all their moneygrubbing, do have a certain flair for the theatrical that can't be denied. Even the villainous ones.

While on the ground, I crawled. I lived those days, I think, in a constant state of crawl. I pushed myself up with a grunt. When he saw me, Maverick attacked again. This time, it was a stoning.

Ducking while running, I found my way back to what I think used to be a stockroom, while rocks that seemed to fly out of nowhere shattered a glass mirror overhead, raining royal hell for me to pick out of my dreadlocks later.

I crashed into the doors and they swung open. I tripped, smacked the ground with one hand, pushed up and kept running. Slid behind a stack of old boxes before Maverick could slam shoulder-first through the doors, his camera floating on the ragged stone not far behind him.

"I can smell you, sinner, mmhmmm; the *word* tells me that you're close by, you and your sinful ways—AH!"

Oh, how he could go on.

As I crouched behind the stacks of boxes, watching him thrash about with small stones like bullets hovering around him, I considered my options.

"Okay, okay!" I shouted. "I give up! I'm coming out. Don't hurt me, okay?"

I shuffled out from my hiding place looking as bewildered and harmless as I could, hands up in surrender. The stocking cap was mushing my face and one or two of my dreadlocks poked out from the bottom.

I could tell that Maverick hadn't expected it to be so easy. He kept a hand raised, a flat stone floating about his index finger, ready to sledge it at me.

I peeled the mask off.

"Sorry, I'm just, you know, I'm kind of confused. I came here to—hah—I came here to, I don't know, fight you or something, but come on, it's not like I can win here," I said.

He lowered his hand with a kind of grace, and the stone fell to the ground beside him. Then he said something in a language I couldn't understand—but when it's one o'clock in the morning and you find yourself in the midst of your first superpowered fight, you should just roll with it.

After he was done with his chant he breathed in deeply, evidently thinking he'd worked some kind of spiritual mojo on me. "So, then, *my brother*, do you repent—AH! I see you stay in your ways of abomination, but as you repent you start toward the path of the righteous—AH!" He embraced me then, so sudden it snatched my breath.

Remember, True Believer, just roll with it.

* * *

When I was a kid I was obsessed with collecting action figures, mostly Marvel stuff, saving up my three-dollar-a-week allowance until I had $105 and then splurging to my heart's content. When my grandmother, God rest her soul, caught wind of my obsession and wanted to do something nice for her grandbaby for Christmas, she decided to one-up my beloved little plastic golden calves and buy me one of the year's most popular dolls (note to any grandmothers out there reading this: *action figures and dolls, two entirely different things*). It was called "My Buddy," and she wholeheartedly believed this would make my six-year-old heart burst with joy. She planned it so I'd wake up with the doll tucked gently in my arms.

What Grandma didn't know about was something a bit more popular at the time: a horror film called *Child's Play*, which featured a sadistic murdering doll named Chucky who ran around with a kitchen knife asking if you wanted to play while he butchered.

True Believer, you don't know true terror until you wake up cuddling an abomination that's staring you in the face with deadly eyes.

After screaming for fifty-eight seconds with no break for air, and two slices of chocolate cake later, I was diagnosed as fine, but the worst part would be the nightmares. They weren't anything to write home about. Chucky would terrorize me until, as expected, I'd awaken just before the kickable mass of plastic killed me. One night, however, I was smart enough, or cowardly enough, to stop, turn to Chucky, and really have a heart-to-heart, you know, just a standard dialogue between a six-year-old and a murdering plaything that haunted him.

"Can we talk, Chucky?"

"*Wanna play?*"

"No, no, but can we talk for a minute?"

"That's not really my thing."

"Talking?"

"*Not murdering*, to be specific."

"Well, did you want any, um, help?"

"What?"

"With the murdering, did you want any help? I could cut my birf-day cake the other day, so I think I know how to use knifes."

"Wow, you know what? Yeah, why not, kiddo—I could use the company."

What followed was me shaking my marvelously malicious doll friend's hand and then waking up happy, safe in the knowledge that I'd outsmarted my doom. When I got to the bus stop the next day and regaled Kat with tales of my newfound ingenuity, she had a different view, delivering the understanding that I could be a bit of a chicken shit.

* * *

"Well, one down—AH! Just one nation of abominations left—AH!"

Standing there in the stockroom with Maverick hugging me—realizing that I wasn't going to wake up, no matter how much I wanted to—being a chicken shit felt like the way to go. Sure, I'd dried off a bit, maybe from all the sizzling and steaming I'd just done. I was probably dry enough to use my electricity again—but I didn't want to yet. I wanted him to keep talking.

"Um, Mr. Maverick? I don't mean to pry, but—why are you trying to kill these people?"

I didn't really have to ask; I'd seen it on the news. The cult Levert grew up in had given him a whole instruction book, more than eight hundred thousand words of authorization for visiting the wrath of God upon unbelievers. But, as Nikolas would eventually let me know, it's all about connecting; that's just what we try to do. So I tried to connect, no matter how pointless it felt.

"Kill?" he exclaimed. "Good Loooord in heaven hallelujah, I don't want to *kill* anyone! Exodus as my shield and sword, I tell you that we shall not kill anyone, my nameless brotha! We shall obey every word! My work is to bring them the truth—AH! The light—AH!"

At that moment I started to feel a bit useless, True Believer. Maverick was never in this to *kill* anyone; he was just trying to get someone to listen to his side of the story.

"*Unless* of course the heathens reject the truth! Then I have no choice but to have them—AH! Burrrn in the core of the earth! Because—AH! It is the Will to have them follow or die! Cursed be he who holds his sword back from blood!"

Or, you know, not.

He wrapped his arm around my shoulder and led me back out to the masses of people in the main hall, with the camera perched on a rock following us. I noticed one of the victims trying to break free. Without words I begged for him to stop, to wait for me to save him. But when I reached the pulpit with Maverick, I saw what everyone there could see: I was doing nothing.

"So, abomination, are you ready to help me spread your own repentance to your kinsmen?"

"Abomination?" Just when I'd thought we were past that.

"You stand there in robes of cotton and polymer blend, and you deny your abomination!? Do not back-step when you've come so far, my brother!"

"What."

"Thou shalt not wear a garment of diverse sorts, as of woolen and linen together. Deuteronomy 22:11, my brother! See these, these abominations!" He went right up to the crowd, leaning into the face of a little girl. She whimpered. "And that's only the beginning of their sinful ways! Aw *Lawd*, we're gonna have church today—hallelujah!"

"*What?*" I couldn't form words. Feeling purged of my rainy-day baptism, I remembered that I wasn't there to talk after all.

I brought my palm up and tried to spark with my fingers. I felt it—the tremble across my skin—and it shot off, connected, but not with him.

It streamed into the sweaty headphones wrapped around the little girl's neck, trickling down the cord into the MP3 player at her waist. I was thankful that I'd decided to use a minimal charge, hoping to just stun the Maverick and not obliterate him like I had the gas-station robber. The girl yelped, but only a static sting's worth of electricity seemed to have dispersed beyond her player. She was okay.

The Maverick seemed pleased—stunned, to be sure, but pleased nonetheless. He wrapped an arm around my shoulder and playfully shook me.

"I know how hard it is to contain yourself—AH! But you must be patient! Give them time! To repent their abominable ways!"

I wish I'd taken the time to learn how to break boy-sized boards in karate class when I was younger, because I reached back, fist rolled, feeling the sickening stretch of rubber over my fingers, and punched into Maverick Moralist's face.

I cried out and cradled my hand. He toppled back. Snapping up, he sent jagged stones bolting through the air, and so the dance went on. There were people, too many people in the room. I rushed toward the front of the building. Stones shattered glass at the front of the restaurant and skimmed my arm, leaving gashes, but I couldn't stop, not until he cleared the building.

You might guess my oversight there, True Believer, but thankfully the rain had let up. Maverick Moralist hadn't. He ran out to meet me in the derelict dark, still flinging stones. They bruised my back, my legs, whatever I couldn't cover. I knew it couldn't last for long; my health bar in the versus game we'd found ourselves in was hastily diminishing, so I just tried to evade what I could. An extra-chunky block of stone hurtled past me. I dropped to the ground to avoid it, and it went on into the street. Smashed into a passing car. But—*blessed be*, I thought—the car was a police cruiser.

"See what you've made me do!" His teeth ground the words into a slurry, but I ignored them and leapt at him. If I couldn't aim the electricity, I'd have to close the gap between us.

I pounded flesh against flesh, stuffing my hand into his face, jabbing at his eyes. It was enough to stun him, at least. I didn't let the sounds of incoming police cars deter me as I forced my way around the mounds of stone he was raising to protect himself from my embarrassingly telegraphed blows. I didn't listen to their screaming, their cheers, their feast of eyes and idle hands. I focused, and I finally connected. My hand around his throat, I sent a spark shuddering throughout him.

It wasn't enough. He clenched all over but didn't fall. If I were to give Maverick Moralist anything, it's that at the time I thought the guy would never fall, ever.

"You don't understand, do you? None of you do—AH!"

The noise was drawing people to the parking lot. In Columbus, a city without spectacle, it wasn't surprising that one of the only superbrawls ever to go down would cause a bit of a ruckus.

They were just more liabilities, more problems, more things that made the day more of an abomination than it already was. His hands raked across my face, lances of a spurious salvation, in the name of a God we both served. My God, though, he told me something different. He told me that those caught in the storm? Their blood and bone wasn't mine or Maverick's to broker. He told me to fight.

"You—AH! Try to stop me, but you can't! It has been foretold. Corinthians 2:15, the spiritual man makes judgments about all things, but he himself is not subject to any man's judgment. I am the spiritual man! And I have been appointed to righteously judge you all—AH!"

"Wait!" I spat. "It says that?"

"You ignorant! You do not seek knowledge, so you do not know—AH!"

"No, no, it's just—well, I could have sworn it went, 'Therefore judge nothing before the appointed time; wait till the Lord comes. He will bring to light what is hidden in darkness and will expose the motives of men's hearts.'"

The stone he'd been twirling dropped to the ground. "You're thinking of Corinthians 4:5. You abomination!"

"Huh. Well, isn't that kind of confusing, then? Which one do you go with?" I said.

The Maverick Moralist tried to start a sentence, but from the sweat starting to build on his forehead all the moisture must have left his mouth. He started to fidget, to falter.

I threw my best-aimed punch of the night. When it connected, lightning jolted through him. The blacktop parking lot began to crack beneath us and beneath the officers behind me.

"Run!" I yelled.

Maverick wouldn't stop yelling. He was still preaching, but really he was crying out for some semblance of control, and for the first time that night I think he and I wanted the same thing.

I clamped both hands on the sides of his face and sent more electricity than I had ever used before coursing through him. He winced and wailed, and the earth yawned. I didn't stop. I couldn't stop. The crack widened. We started to slide toward it, both of our bodies nearly dropping deep into the nothing. As we hung on, he tried to send one last evangelical message to my head in the form of a slab of torn concrete. Before it reached me, I saw one of the onlookers pointing. I had time, just barely, to lean to the side. There was a loud *crunch* as it smacked Maverick in the face instead; his body went limp. I reached for him as he fell toward a hole of his own making. I must have read too many comics, of course, thinking the weight of an unconscious man could be offset by one hand. He fell, twenty feet, and landed unmoving at the bottom.

The fight was over. I'd won.

I'd finally be a hero.

"Who are you?" I started to hear from the surrounding crowd.

I wanted nothing more than to tell them *I'm Donald McDougal,* but self-promotion lost out to self-preservation. I tried to think fast, but—

"The Midwest Marvel," I said through a few exhausted gasps for breath, still fixated on the body—lifeless?—at the bottom of the pit. Don't worry, True Believer, that name won't stick around for long.

They kept pitching questions at me, looking for answers they thought they were owed, but I was tired, I was hungry, and I was wondering if I'd just killed a dude.

A ragged moan from him gave me as much of an answer as I cared for. I reached out a hand out to the electrical billboard above the restaurant, deciding to give the overexcited crowd something to see. Sending out most of what I had left in me, I made the screen burst in a brilliant rain of tiny lights.

That created just enough darkness and confusion for me to dart around the other side of the building and get in my car.

I couldn't stop laughing as I drove. I should've been freaked out—I'd just fought a thirty-seven-year-old man with, like, legit rock powers. There was nothing like fear for a jolt, though, and I was on cloud seven hundred and thirty-two.

I was the Midwest Marvel, Donald McDougal.

For a while, I was honestly going to feel Astonishing.

CHAPTER 5
MASKS

"OUCH," I WHIMPERED. BECAUSE at moments like that—lying face down, nestled in ash and blood, unsure if the blood was mine or theirs—I needed to be reminded that something was alive. I needed to hurt.

Only New York ever knew how to kiss me like this. Pushing up, my arms like Styrofoam sheets ready to break, I tried not to look at the charred body beneath me. I'd done this—we'd done this—and everyone would pay. The shackle on my right wrist jingled as I shifted a hand to my side. It was warm, and there was no mistaking the sting I felt at the touch: this was me, pouring out of myself like sand. This was the end. It was really the first time that day that I'd realized it, this was—

* * *

Oh, wait, apologies, getting ahead of myself. Tend to do that sometimes. Let's take a few steps back.

* * *

"Ouch!" I said, but the phlebotomist busy violating my arm with a needle didn't seem to hear; she never really did.

After the fight with Maverick Moralist, I don't know what I was expecting. It's not like I knew how any of this worked. I found myself still entirely broke, with a tattered costume I hated but had no other choice than to repair, and so I did what I usually did in a tight spot: whored out my plasma.

The plasma center smelled like mothballs, like things that wanted to die, like people who didn't know what else to do. The black-and-white tile floor squeaked as the vampires shuffled around, strapping us in for two hours of arm squeezing and watching whatever daytime show helped remind us there were worse people out there than us.

For me, this place was a lifeline—a glass I'd break in case of emergency, which basically meant every week. Granted, emergency is a relative concept:

'Sup Donald, it's Kat. Want to throw a few back?

Poke

Donny, Paul here. Some people I want you to meet, man— look nice.

Poke

Baby, these people matter, you can't actually show up looking like that. You should really buy a suit. Do it for your Thandie candy?

PokePokePokePokePokePokePokePokePokePoke

You meet the most interesting people in the blood-whoring business, and build the most suspicious scars. My costume would hopefully hide my veins; if not, an armband would be worth the investment. *It's all about getting there. Eyes on the prize, Sparky, eyes on the prize.*

What I really needed to spend money on was something a little more durable, a little more refined. For that, of course, I'd have to know that whoever built my superhero uniform was someone I could trust with the burden of my new late-night antics.

Oh, and I'd also need, like, *all* the fucking padding. Pain sucks.

* * *

Later that morning I stood outside of Kat's door with my stomach not so much in knots as in heavy blocks that wouldn't shift.

Is this a good idea? The remaining spark I had from the other night contracted the muscles in my abdomen furiously. *Calm down,* I thought. *Don't panic.*

I banged on the door.

At this point, True Believer, I hadn't slept in twenty-seven hours.

"Who is it?" Kat sounded half-asleep.

"It's, uh, it's Donny."

She grunted before cracking the door open. Her hair was a thin black mess on her forehead and her glasses hung diagonally off her face. "D? Everything okay?"

I nodded, regretting that I hadn't thought to at least give her a call and say I was on the way. She left me in the living room and went to her bedroom. When she came back she'd changed into a pair of black sweats and a white T-shirt that read *Xenogears,* featuring an ensemble with at least three characters she'd made costumes of in the past.

"Sorry, I figured you'd be up."

"No, it's fine, so what's up? You were acting real weird last night."

"I, well, I um—do you have anything to drink?"

"It's ten thirty in the morning, Don."

"Yeah, yeah. Um, never mind."

"Dude, you're jumpy as fuck. What's wrong?"

"I, well, it's just that I *kinda* have these . . . powers."

"Powers."

"Yeah." I took a deep breath. "You hear about that guy they're calling the Midwest Marvel? That's, uh . . . that's me. I can, like, do stuff with electricity? Since the accident." I let a few sparks of electricity bounce around my hand. "Anyway, I wanted to tell you that I can do, like, *stuff*, and you're cool, and seven ate nine!"

"Huh," Kat said after a while, which probably was less time than it felt like. "So, you, Donny McDougal, are this new Midwest Marvel?"

"Yes, Kathryn. I am." I opened my palm and let a flash of light erupt.

"The Midwest Marvel."

Still no real reaction. Weeks, True Believers. Weeks that I'd walked around, wanting to tell someone, anyone, that yes, *I was special*.

"So, you are a super*hero*, right? It'd be a bit much, you as a super-villain, I mean."

Oh sweet foreshadowing god, you have *no* idea, Kat.

"Of course! Well, I did try to crack an ATM. Rent was late, and—"

"Oh my god, that's crazy! How much did you get?"

"Well . . . nothing. All it did was shut down on me."

"Yup, sounds about right."

In hindsight, I realize there could have been worse reactions. As stupid as it was to tell anyone, I don't regret Kat being the first one, not for a moment.

She took a second to walk around me, inspecting me up and down before taking a seat near her computer.

"You're a goddamned superhero!" she said.

There it is, I thought, unable to hold back a grin. "Yeah. Nifty, right?"

* * *

When Kat and I were eight years old and had our first sleepover, I'd felt a bit awkward, since I'd never had anyone else sleep over, let alone in the same bed. So, fast-forward to us waking up in the middle of the night, the bed saturated in remnants of Yoo-Hoo and one too many Capri Suns. Me screaming and crying, unlike her, who sat with this haunting expression devoid of anything.

I began to point at her and yell, "Bed-wetter!" (I was quite the little politician.) She only sighed, shoved me off the bed, and called me a goober-head before proceeding to say,

"There's only two of us. I know I didn't pee-pee the bed, *you* know I didn't pee-pee the bed. So let's just wash these before your daddy wakes up." She showed me how to wash clothes for the first time in my life, and we cleaned up the crime scene.

The next Monday, at the bus stop, with the all-important eyes of other third-graders upon us, she kept her mouth shut. And that, True Believer, is real friendship.

* * *

"What else?" she asked, catching on. Her superpowered ability to call me out on my shit had only advanced in the last eighteen years.

"Okay, well, I need your help," I said, plopping down on her couch.

"How can a mild-mannered woman possibly be of use to the *Midwest Marvel*?"

"Mild-mannered? Where's she?" I said.

She tossed a pillow at my face. "You should be less of a douche to people you're asking favors from."

"Right, right. So, I need you to help me with my, uh, look."

"Your what?"

I peeled off my hoodie. Every inch of my scathed skin awoke as I did. Finally I revealed what was underneath: the black T-shirt with the iron-on lightning bolt and the yellow spandex long-sleeved shirt beneath it. By the time I slipped on the winter gloves I'd dunked in yellow paint she'd already started to crack up. When I added the black mesh stocking cap she let loose. I gave her a minute to get it out of her system.

"So, yeah, this is what I'm working with right now."

She finished her cackling before wiping her tears away. "Oh, god. You should have called sooner."

Her truth wasn't always welcome, but I could never say it wasn't necessary. I guess if it weren't for her skill with a needle I might have told Paul first, but I didn't need a reassuring pat on the back. I needed to make a statement, and if anyone knew how to help me with that (not to mention for a relatively low price), it would be Kat.

When we were younger and had more time on our hands, most of our weekends had been spent parading around in costumes at Japanese animation conventions. I guess I got into it after everything went down at Aedan's shop. I'd been disillusioned, for a while at least, about what Western comics had to offer. And if you're a bona fide geek, self-exiled from regular society, that doesn't leave you many other options. Unless you're willing to get into LARPing. But even I have standards.

Anyway, Kat had always been gifted with a sewing needle, but it was at the conventions that she really hit her stride. You know the crazy costumes you see people wear? Yeah, those don't just make themselves, and more often than not the good ones—hell, even some of the mediocre ones—take weeks or even months of work. When it came to the particular realm of geekdom called cosplay, Kat had an unparalleled talent, and once she realized that, she capitalized on it.

You'd be amazed at the profit you can make selling people the chance to dress up as their favorite fictional character for all of seventy-two hours. When it came to me, she'd usually give me a decent discount, partly out of friendship and partly out of knowing that any time our convention friends wanted to do a theme or a set of costumes from a show, I'd end up taking one for the team.

"Awesome idea, everyone! We're doing a group costume from *Shaman King*—it's going to be *amaaaayyyzing*."

"Oh, really? That's cool, I started watching that a few weeks ago. I really like Yoh, he's badass."

"Not a bad idea, Donald, but you're like one of the funniest guys we know, why not dress up as, ugh, the one guy, I'm forgetting his name—the comic-relief guy, you know?"

"You mean Chocolove McDonnell . . . the Black dude?"

"Oh, I guess he is Black, hadn't noticed."

Or:

"Okay, guys, *Dragon Ball Z*! It's old, but vintage cosplay always wins best costume."

"*Dragon Ball Z*! Dude, Gohan is like my favorite character of all time. Well, aside from Piccolo."

"Actually, we have both those guys covered. We don't have Mr. Popo yet, though."

"Um, you mean the indentured servant in blackface?"

"Whoa! Why does it always have to be about race with you, Donald?"

You get the idea.

Anyway, I had thought it would be cool to give Kat a change of pace, let her use some of those creative muscles she seldom got the chance to flex, or at least that was what I told myself to justify making her a part of all of this. Really I was more concerned with not having to run around town looking like a luchador's fever dream anymore.

Kat picked up a sketchpad from her coffee table, kicked her feet up, and flipped the book open.

"All right, so, what's your name?" she asked.

"Donald," I answered.

She rolled her eyes.

"Oh, you mean, like, my hero name?"

"Yeah, Donald, like, your hero name. 'Cause obviously it's not going to be 'Midwest Marvel.'"

"Well, I've been leaning toward, um, Electric Boy?"

"Donald, you're a twenty-six-year-old adult male."

"Electric Man?"

"Didn't realize you were a Mega-Man villain."

"Okay, Ultimate Man!" I raised a sizzling finger, as if it could make the name any less horrid.

"That is just lazy. I swear, this is why I don't read Western comics. Donald, you have this astonishing chance to reimagine yourself here. You can have a name that makes a statement. I'm sure it doesn't need to just announce your gender, although if you're really that insecure I can sew on a couple of arrows to highlight your junk."

"Okay, okay, I get your point. Oh! How about Eye of the Storm?"

"Better. A little wordy, but better." She scribbled the name down in her pad.

I smiled, realizing that it was the first time I'd had fun since this whole thing started. But this went on for a while. Two people, even as nerdy as us, were apparently not enough to screw in the lightbulb. I wondered: how many more nerds would it take? If only I'd kept in contact with some of the others from our cosplay days, or even the comic-book store, maybe it would have gone faster. But then I would have been the Ethnic Electrician. The Melanin Mayhem. The Brown and Beastly Bolt. I would, unfortunately, have been just fine with this, because *they* would have been fine with it. It's easy if you do it long enough, True Believer. The mask, the real one.

I always figured that on some level they needed me to wear that mask. It fit a little snug and was musty as hell with that pungent breath of mine I had to smell, trapped within it from all the times I said stuff like, *Nah, you're right, stereotypes do exist for a reason* or *Yeah, we don't really talk about blackwashing much, do we?* But there was always the hope of something at the end of the lie, when maybe, just maybe, they'd reach a state of comfort and you could pull off the mask. When they were ready to see you.

"How about I just go nameless?" I said, one order of Chinese food and three Red Bulls later. "Keep the mystery. It'll be really deep."

I was sprawled out on the floor, throwing a rubber-band ball up at the ceiling and catching it as it came down. Kat was back at the computer, checking the availability of whatever we came up with on Wikipedia.

"Because, Donald, I need a name. It helps me with a costume. I can't just come up with some random design, that'd be the worst idea ever. Hell, you'd probably end up in some haggard green-and-yellow blob of fabric. You're my friend. I won't do that to you. Come on, just think of something that works around an idea, something that defines you."

Something that defined me? It sounded impossible, not to mention insulting, the idea that one word could encapsulate everything that made me feel, that made me unique. That in this world of words the only one people would have time for would be this singular one.

"The Spark," I said. It just came out, like I'd been fighting it for years—mangled and frayed.

"The Spark," she echoed. "It's clean, and . . . kind of catchy."

She never got around to asking me how I came up with it, but if she did I'd have just bullshitted something about it sounding neat, or electricity relating to sparks. It felt like more than that, though.

It was a beginning.

"Well, *Spark*, I think I can get started," she said after sketching for a bit and taking some measurements.

I opened my wallet and shuffled past the few fives to find lonely Ben. I'd nearly fainted that morning when I drafted it, but it was required. I'd never have asked Kat to work for free.

"It shouldn't take me all that long. I'll call you when everything is ready."

* * *

I left, head held high. I had a name, my *own* name. I'd have a costume soon enough, and whether I liked it or not, I was about to start one of the shortest careers as a superhero the world had ever known.

CHAPTER 6
THE AMERICAN COLLECTIVE FOR RESOLVING OVERTLY NEGATIVE YOWLED MISCONDUCTS

SORRY, HAD TO TAKE a pee break, True Believers. You didn't know that, did you? You couldn't have, unless I told you. Writing is nifty. Anyway, before Tad, my barista boy wonder, comes back, I guess I should finally get to these assholes.

The next morning, I called in sick to work. As much as I needed the money, I was essentially a giant bruise and needed the rest more. As my apartment afforded zero luxury, I decided to use Paul's pad to recuperate. Thanks to the key he'd given me once when I watched his now-deceased cat while he was on vacation, I could waste away in front of a TV that afternoon.

> These are the Astonishing Tales of Just So You Know,
> I Didn't Kill the Cat; It Died of Kitty Cancer

Paul was at work, as it seemed he always was. I hobbled to his cabinets first, rustling through them to find the hidden box of sugary cereal. There was a Post-It Note slapped on it that read, *C'mon, man, don't be that guy*. Since I of course was that guy, I tore it off and crumpled it before pouring a bowl with some of the almond milk from his fridge.

I watched a few episodes of *The Sidekick* to start. I was something like a season behind and didn't have much idea of what was going on. The only realism to be found in the show, amongst the well-rehearsed outbursts and obviously scripted twists, were the occasional moments when someone tripped on their cape or misused their powers when they sneezed. This season, it seemed Sapling was everyone's favorite. She hoped to impress Almighty Asper for the chance at winning her own fully funded hideout, or maybe even placement into a high-traffic city by PantheUS.

Flip.

I slurped my milk down and landed on a superhero procedural, *Super Investigation Unit: Terse Looks*. I let it suck me in for a while. There'd been so many episodes that you could always find a new one to watch amid the torrent of reruns. The Introspecter, a real-life but non-Talented registered hero with PantheUS, starred in it, and each episode began with the discovery of a new violent supercrime. I liked the episodes when they didn't try to force in a special guest star, some B-list hero whose agent was still working overtime. This one looked promising.

"So, our vic was a Jamaican immigrant. From the markings it seems someone was performing a voodoo ritual, which caused the vic to have an aneurysm."

"Bumbaclot," I said at the TV through a mouth full of cereal.

"We better find this guy before he makes another bumbaclot," said Introspecter gravely, before staring directly into the camera with a terse look.

Flip.

"We don't know that much about him yet, but he doesn't seem to be affiliated with PantheUS. The video footage, as you can see, displays a strange, violent power set. The vigilante, seen here subduing a white male known simply as the Maverick Moralist—if he's unregistered, then he's just as lawless as the man he's subduing."

I'd ended up on Hound News, and my narcissism kept me there. Playing the station within the walls of Paul's condo was one of the few atrocities I'd fear him banning me for, but I was on the *news*, man. I'd expected local stations to pick up the story, maybe, but national? I didn't consider myself that astonishing just yet.

These are the Astonishing Tales of I'm Sorry Because
That Use of Astonishing Was Pretty Cheap

"I mean, look, the liberals are going to say, like they always do, that this is a race thing, but don't listen to them. Don't let yourself feel guilty over their conspiracy-mongering hootenanny."

"Heh, *hootenanny*." I giggled.

"We have with us Dr. Logan Jean, professor of sociology at Some Institution Donald Can't Remember."

"Thanks for having me, John."

"So what is going *awwwwnnnn* here? This new hero—they're calling him the Midwest Marvel—he clearly has no idea what he's doing. Look at this clip, see—this is why superhero registration is important. This guy, this Midwest Marvel, took the law into his own hands and could have really hurt someone. He did hurt this—this Maverick Moralist, and the jury is still out on whether Maverick was actually a villain at all, as opposed to an emotionally disturbed individual."

"Well, I really concur, John, I mean this kind of thing just can't be tolerated in a civilized society. There's freedom and then there's anarchy."

"Because wouldn't you say that there are reasons we have PantheUS validation? Without it we get thugs like this, who can't be trusted to make sound decisions regarding who is and is not a true villain."

"Absolutely."

"In your opinion, is this Midwest Marvel acting on the kind of anti-white rhetoric we've been hearing day after day?"

"Well, I absolutely think it's important to underline the fact that *all* lives matter, especially when there's violence involved. Because all lives *do* matter."

"Right, well, thanks, Dr. Jean, I don't want to take up any more of your time, but your wisdom on this topic has been really appreciated. When we come back: Is national policy on superheroes restricting their ability to enforce the law? We'll take an in-depth look at DEATHRAGE's recent hearing."

Well, shit. I'd fallen a few more times than I remembered. It was like the time Paul had recorded my drunken rendition of the "Thriller" dance to teach me that I had not, in fact, killed it.

Mostly, despite the expected focus on what of course they would never focus on, I was bummed to see just how sloppy I looked on camera. Maverick took the lead on everything, including his own downfall. I needed to be better. The next reality that smashed inward, like a deeply Southern wave, was that my Blackness was blatant. I'd hopefully find some escape from that with Kat's costume, as well as a fuckton of padding.

To feel better, I indulged in another bowl of sugary splendor.

Flip.

". . . seem as if the American Collective for Resolving Overtly Negative Yowled Misconducts has met their match. We have live footage of an attempted bank robbery by a masked figure. Reports say the masked suspect has paralyzed Patches, the Boy Band-Aid."

Hero News Distributor, the only twenty-four-hour news outlet that exclusively followed the antics of us, the costumed and catastrophic, was reporting live in New York as the American Collective for Resolving Overtly Negative Yowled Misconducts attempted to subdue a villain. It was a rare sight: all of them, *the* premiere superhero association within PantheUS, during an actual encounter, not some pre-edited sludge reminding us that once again our tax dollars were hard at work.

They were all there, and yes, when I say "they" I am most definitely talking about *them*. The original, unequivocal superhero association. The one every hero hoped to join, at least every hero who didn't realize what a hero actually was, like, you know, me.

The main roster, all five of them. GRAVI-Tina stood out front, her eyes a spectacular, shimmering violet beneath the half-mask. Behind her was DEATHRAGE, maybe the most impressive member of the Collective since he had no powers to speak of. He only had what seemed a limitless supply of firearms slung over his shoulders, strapped in holsters, or tucked, pinned, and shoved anywhere he could fit them.

Then there was Patches, the Human Band-Aid, a sixteen-year-old kid from North Carolina who'd skidded past age restrictions due to the rarity of his ability, which was to heal anyone of *anything*—even, within some limits, death. Floating in the sky, as expected, was the Almighty Asper, cape rippling, hands covered in dust from the hole he'd punched into the building to get at the robbers inside. And lastly, there was Afrolicious Samson.

A quick note on Afrolicious Samson: I hated Afrolicious Samson. More on that later, though, True Believer.

Their challenger was clad in black from head to toe. It didn't seem nearly as thrift-store-inspired as my first costume had been, however; there was a high-tech plastic sheen to it. The only visible part of his body was the pasty fingers; his gloves were cut out to leave them exposed.

Asper seemed to have run out of what little patience he had, and his eyes began to shimmer with a bright blue glow, ready to send an incendiary eyebeam at the black-clad man despite the fact that Patches, who seemed to be paralyzed, was in the line of fire. DEATHRAGE smiled through clenched teeth and aimed a shotgun to back up his teammate. GRAVI-Tina gaped. You couldn't hear what she was saying, but I imagine it was something like this:

"Asper, what the fuck?"

"We do not negotiate, GRAVI-Tina! We do not turn a blind eye to terrorism. We are the American Collective for Resolving Overtly Negative Yowled Misconducts!"

"Aw, hell," the villain said with a sigh as Asper shot off a patriotic eye blast.

I'd never seen someone move so swiftly. Nothing the black-clad man did seemed wasted. Every motion was calculated. He dove at Patches's legs, rolling over the blacktop to save them both from the beam. Patches seemed to regain a bit of movement then, as he grunted and shuddered after the two of them stopped tumbling. Asper zoomed over to hover above them, his eyes flaring again. The villain, like most who followed the antics of America's great alien hope, must have known it was a bluff—Asper never fired one of those incendiary beams within a few minutes of another—so he turned his attention instead to DEATHRAGE, who had decided against the shotgun and was whipping twin pistols from his belt while Afrolicious readied a super-punch. At the last minute the villain jumped high into the air between DEATHRAGE's pistols and Afrolicious's fist, letting the two clash with each other in a superheroic meet-cute. DEATHRAGE took the worst of the clash, falling unconscious to the ground.

"Bitter Hanukkah," Afrolicious said with a wince.

Before the villain could find a new footing, Asper had gripped him in a super-bear hug and was ripping him upward into the sky.

They soared so high that the cameras couldn't show much detail, but I thought I saw the villain tap the sides of Asper's temples. They plummeted—but he probably didn't plan how he landed first, so that he came to rest trapped beneath Asper's paralyzed body. There he shimmered violet as GRAVI-Tina augmented gravity just enough to make it impossible for him to move without letting Asper crush him.

"So, we can try this again. Who are you? What dastardly deeds are you doing here?" GRAVI-Tina said. "Who do you work for? Or are you a freelancer?"

So, side note? *Dastardly* is a hard word to shove into any sentence, but per regulation, negative modifiers must be employed during moments of "banter," to help draw the dichotomy between them and us (and, most importantly, you).

(Or you could always do what I did and take the fifty-buck hit to your compensation. Convenience and not sounding like a moron are sometimes worth the pay cut.)

"I suppose you can call me the Emancipator. Freeing you of . . . movement! Yeah. That. And, doing? Well, it's more like what I aim to end."

By that point all the superheroes left standing had formed a circle around the Bent-Kneed Emancipator.

"The superheroic structure, thanks for asking," the villain continued. "The everything that you, all of you, do nothing with."

"Says the guy who's robbing a bank. Kind of shits on that moral high ground of yours," Patches said, crossing his arms.

GRAVI-Tina chuckled at that. So did DEATHRAGE.

So did The Emancipator.

I would eventually learn what happened afterward, but in that moment the screen flashed a few times before going to static. The spoon fell from my mouth as I yelled something like *What the hell!* or *Come on!* When the video returned, GRAVI-Tina lay flat on the ground beneath Asper and Patches. The Emancipator was picking up his sacks of money, the only remaining comical thing in the image, as Afrolicious Samson, barely standing, looked on.

"Muh fuckin . . . bitch ass . . . cowardly fuckin muh fucka," Afrolicious said, losing himself to an anachronistic 70s spiel. The Emancipator, I imagined, grinned beneath the now-cracked mask.

"Yeah, I am. I'm fixing that, though," the Emancipator said, turning to go.

Afrolicious took that moment to rush at the Emancipator. To his credit, he didn't yell his catchphrase. Either his two doctorates, his pain, or something else that he hid behind the bell bottoms and yellow vest made him smart enough to attempt stealth. It was a bad move, maybe the worst he could have made, but—we'll get there. The Emancipator waited for him to get close enough and then somehow summoned a steel pipe from the beneath the slabs of rubble. He swung like a baseball analogy I don't deserve to make against Afrolicious's kneecap, caving it in. As Afrolicious fell, the Emancipator sledged the pipe against his shoulder, not stopping until there was a loud *crack*.

These are the Astonishing Tales of Yahtzee

The Emancipator dropped the steel pipe, breathing deeply, nearly falling over. It was about as difficult as you'd think to render a Talented individual with enhanced durability broken using nothing but a steel pipe, regardless of how exhausted they were, but the Emancipator had managed it.

He didn't pay any more attention to the cries of Afrolicious Samson, or at least it didn't look like he did. He just picked up his cartoon sacks of cash and looked into one of the cameras before *flash*, *boom*, white noise.

CHAPTER 7
MISHAPS AND MONTAGES

THE NEXT DAY BROUGHT a shift I desperately needed at Stereo Hutt, even if my body wasn't all that ready to take it. It passed the time, at least, while I waited for Kat to get back to me about the costume.

"Hey Donald, could you grab the shipment from the back and then help Natalie stock batteries?" my manager asked, popping up behind me as I leaned on the counter.

Usually, I could hear the *shlick shlock* of his $12.99 soles skidding wherever he went; they gave us all a spider-sense we never asked for. But between the Emancipator, Hound News's brief coverage of the Midwest Marvel, and the broken parts of me that hadn't quite come back together yet, I was a bit preoccupied.

I obeyed, following the boom tube of a hallway back to the mostly empty storeroom. Natalie Normsley was the kind of girl I imagined high-school jocks fell in love with. Her sandy blond hair, thick and lustrous, was a perfect frame for her blissful suburban face. Beneath violet-framed glasses, jade eyes hinted at introspection.

"Donald McDougal! It looks like we're working together tonight!" she burst when I met her at the battery display case.

I painted on my face, the smiles my father taught me to share. The news in the background caught our attention; it was only noon, but the Midwest Marvel was already on their radar. I was apparently *hot shit*, as Natalie called it, because every other story seemed to concern either me, my shitty costume, or what this meant for the Midwest.

Ex-fucking-celsior, I thought.

"Have you heard about the Midwest Marvel? He's getting a lot of coverage. He's pretty hot shit right now, huh?"

See. I told you.

"Yeah, spicy," I groaned.

A box of batteries primed for stocking waited on the browned carpet. My skin started crawling when my hands got close to them.

Surging on empty is, well, a lot like a sweet nicotine drag on a bender. Even if you just had one, you can easily find yourself in front of a bar on a Saturday night in frost-forged February smoking another if you catch even the whiff of someone else's. I lifted the box from the ground and walked behind the counter where Natalie was leaning, watching the hanging TVs instead of our nonexistent customers.

"Did you hear the thing about him being, you know, a Black guy?" she said, *so* sweetly.

"Um, yeah, what do you think about that?" I asked, rolling back my white sleeves to the elbow and revealing the prickly, pallid hair on my arms. I reached into the box for a battery package, pulled the plastic frame away from the paper backing, and let the metal tickle against my skin. I'd never get enough.

"What do I think about that? I think it's great, Donald. I think it's so diverse and unconventional."

"Really?" I said, enjoying my last fifteen seconds of being able to give her the benefit of the doubt.

"Yeah, really! I mean, it's about time. I mean, like, you know, my friend, she tried to say that maybe he's not all that, because of how he was stumbling around when he was trying to beat that Maverick Moralist guy, and I was like, *Don't be such a racist, um, Amy!* God, you'd think we're past that kind of thing, right? You'd think that nowadays white people wouldn't be so moronic."

Aaaand fifteen seconds over. Usually I'm not so slow to pick up on it, True Believers, but in that moment I realized that my newest soul sistah's enlightened opinion, poorly expressed as it was, had become null and void. Natalie brimmed with fervor to be seen as both nonchalant and passionate on the subjects of race, economic inequality, and other Tumblr causes of the week. Quick to let me know just how normal I was and that my hair was, like, *so* cool. But there was no friend Amy. I knew it as soon as she said it.

I could spot girls like Natalie fifteen miles away, on the other side of that neighborhood-defining stop sign in Bexley. She never crossed the street, much as she'd protest that things on this side were ever so much more soulful.

"Don't get me wrong, Donald, I know that I'm just, like, some privileged white girl from the suburbs, but it was so upsetting! I'm just so sorry about that—the only thing Amy should have complained about is how he really does deserve a better costume. I was thinking about starting a collection for him at my school. It's the *least* we can do."

Oh, Natalie; sweet, sweet Natalie. I've never hated the Natalies of the world, for all their ignorance. At least it's cute and sort of progressive? I'm aware that it was in part thanks to the Natalies that I was eventually elected into the American Collective for Resolving

Overtly Negative Yowled Misconducts, so maybe I was judging too harshly. Maybe this Natalie was an actual ally, a true sidekick. So I kept stacking and threw out a simple test.

"Well, I don't know, maybe your friend Amy was right. That nigger *was* stumbling a lot."

Natalie's face contorted, her knuckles paled, and her legs quaked for a soapbox. She looked like she might faint.

"I don't appreciate the use of that word, Donald! It's such an ugly word. I'm going to—I mean why would you say that word? I have friends, Donald, who are not defined by that word. You should be ashamed of yourself!" Afterward, carrying a burden over four hundred years in the making on her shoulders, Natalie marched to the front of the store and took a moment to calm herself. For the rest of the shift she avoided me and also any topics that were marvelous or Midwestern.

I stocked batteries by myself for a while, watching her center her chi, until Paul texted me: *Coffee?* It seemed more of a command than a question. I'd been a lump of wreckage all day anyway, so I dragged my ass to the back and told my boss that I'd need to leave early and use a little sick time. He reminded me for the nine hundred and fucktonth time that sick leave didn't exist at Stereo Hutt, but I counted the thirty or so bucks I was out as an acceptable loss to get the hell out of there.

* * *

Paul and I met up at the coffee shop near his office, Hotep House. It was filled with rustic tables that tried too hard to look like they weren't from Ikea. Thrift-store-style art and famous faces in Black history were strategically disorganized over all the walls, with Malcolm and Martin above the bar. Every waitress was, I assumed, contractually obligated to have a perfectly picked Afro and Black Power fist comb. I once asked the owner, Shakur Shakur, if he'd ever considered using the transcript of King's "I'm Black and Beautiful" speech on the placemats—in jest, but he hit up Wikipedia and then got fired up about implementing my stellar business idea.

Real talk, though? I am kind of proud of it.

Paul and I sat at "our" table in the center of the room without saying much of anything at first, not breaking our silence even when his Java Baldwin with two sugars and my Fannie Lou hibiscus tea came out.

"Peace be unto your refreshments, my brothers," the waitress said before leaving the table. Paul took a gulp of his coffee while I looked around at all the faces. No one seemed to notice me. Eventually, I decided my identity was safe: between the Salvation Army mask and the spotty camera footage, I'd stayed anonymous.

"So what's up, man?" I said.

"Ah, nothing, just wanted to kick it, man. What's up with *you*, Don?" Seeing Paul Hughes with a full-toothed, childlike smile was one of the greatest terrors I'd ever known.

"Nothing really. Went out with Kat the other night, had a few drinks, that was cool. Oh! I finally caught up on *One Piece*."

"That. Now *that* is real interesting. So, my turn? Well, okay, what have I been up to. Oh, shit, yeah, I did have a weird morning. Did you know that a superhero with electric powers took down the Maverick Moralist? Someone hit me up with a link to this video. This dude is silly, but he's a brotha. A *brotha*. With *lightning* powers."

"Oh. Oh, wow, so we have a superhero in Columbus? How *crazy* is that? Wait-wait-wait, I *did* hear something about that. That Midwest Marvel dude, right? I wonder if he—"

Paul interrupted me with a sigh as long as winter. He took his glasses off and pinched the bridge of his nose. "Man, don't be . . . I *know*, D."

"You—" I lost my voice for a minute. "Shit."

At one of the other tables, a waitress was dropping off a platter of George Schuylones; the customer was laughing and throwing up a Black Power fist.

"So Kat told you, then?" I said.

"What? No, you have white dreadlocks, my nigga!"

"Right. Well, um. I was going to tell you, I just—"

"Donald. What exactly do you think you're doing, man? I saw how bad you got your ass whipped. Is this gonna be a thing with you now?"

"I'm thinking," I started, but I realized the other patrons could hear too much as Paul's volume had twisted up my own, so I leaned in. "I'm thinking I have to make a difference. I'm thinking that maybe I'm meant to do something, I don't know, something fantastic. Something astonishing."

He just stared at me.

"I'm thinking you're just pissed I didn't come running for help from big brother Paul before I did anything," I said.

"Bullshit," said Paul. "What Donald is thinking is 'Hey, how can I make a quick buck? How can I avoid having to do any real work and throw my dumb ass in front of a camera without giving two shits about the people who care if my ass lives or dies?' For the record, that's why I'm pissed. And it kind of hurt that you didn't bother telling me, but at least now I know where I stand."

You're probably getting the feeling that something's missing here.

When we were young, dumb, and full of shared experiences that gave us a Lego-style interlocking awareness of each other, Paul and

I had started the *Kuumba Kollective*. We believed. Our belief was tethered to the moment and the caustic nature of ever-changing circumstance. Nonetheless, we believed we were changing the world, bringing its absurdities to light.

It was idealistic and inane, thinking we could form a news source that dealt in the "real" stories no one else was putting out there. Stories about disparities, racial and economic, in the health-care system. Stories about the adverse effects of superhero interference in political campaigns. Stories that sounded off the cries beneath black and blue sticks. Stories that in the end only mattered to the ones you have listening to you.

Paul was never coy about finding my writing to be shit. It was shit, mind you, but only in the sense of not being twice as good as that of our competitors, which meant it wasn't good enough by half. Before he went the way of the winding tubes of the internet, back when we used to print *Kuumba*, I'd become a man on the street instead, with no name but plenty of mislaid hopes.

Even so, we never sold that many copies. What good was it to burn your lungs for empty ad spaces and lackluster interest, I asked? When I presented the idea of lowering our standards, cutting back on the sad, sappy shit we'd been shoving, Paul flatly said no.

It wasn't *all* he said; there's never an *all he said* when it comes to Paul. I threw back that I needed a real job to afford inclusion in our passion project, and that maybe if he couldn't afford to compromise a little, then he couldn't afford my involvement in something that wasn't going anywhere. In response, he asked me to help him. To stay the course, all that.

These are the Astonishing Tales of Heroes

I left, and, well—welcome to Stereo Hutt, how may I help you?

Afterward, one of Paul's fill-in writers gained some notoriety thanks to a piece she wrote criticizing PantheUS's publicity-minded placement of heroes. This led to someone backing a paper I'd pissed my time away on, and then partnership with a New York–based news outlet with similar aims, and a hell of a lot more readership. I briefly considered going back to peddling papers and links with Paul, since he'd told me there was a place for me there forever and always. It'd be a poor investment, though—he just hadn't realized it yet. Eventually, people would stop wanting to hear *those* voices. There'd be a regression, and for a long, dark December we'd tell ourselves, *maybe things aren't so bad.*

Superheroes, though? Who gets tired of that?

These are the Astonishing Tales of Your
Previously Scheduled Pissing Contest

"You know what? I bet it's *real* easy to sit up there and say that shit when you ain't making $8.50 an hour, but I don't get to live on the other side of the bridge. I don't get to afford whatever the fuck you're drinking. I get to buy mine black."

"Nigga please, don't even try that with me. You, D. You in yo own way, and this is jus you tryn to skip the line, yet a-fuckin-gain."

We switch codes like skipping stones across a lake.

"You wanna bring up that old shit?" I said. "What, Paul, do you want me to keep shelving batteries and—and fuckin depending on *your* ass? You get off on that? Knowing you have poor old Donald to follow yo ass around and look down on? Maybe that's what's really biting your ass, that your favorite little failure is finally coming up in the world."

He didn't say anything for a moment, and I thought I'd won the game he wasn't playing.

"Donald, you're something, man, but you're no hero." He shuffled a hand in his pocket, pulled out a ten, and plopped it on the table. "Don't worry, brotha, I got this one," he said, barely audible, and left me.

These are the Tales of the Astonishing
Things We Wish We Could Change

It wasn't the worst fight we'd had, but it was up there. The Spark inside would flutter through the rest of the day when I thought about it, forks and faceplates in my apartment shuddering whenever I let the frustration take hold.

I went to see Kat at work. When I showed up, she thought it was about the costume, which, she informed me, was completed. She told me to stop by her place after she was off work. But she wasn't too surprised when I didn't leave and instead leaned against the back of her register, spilling my tragedy-stricken soul. It was a Saturday, so the store was in disarray, fabric strewn everywhere and middle-aged women out for blood, thunder, and bias tape.

"And then—that ankh-wearing asshat—he says I'm doing this all for me. Like, for real, man?"

"Uh-huh. Ma'am, would you be interested in one of our rewards cards today?"

The everyone's-grandma kind of customer that stood in front of her rummaged around in her purse and flicked a rewards card onto the checkout counter.

"I'm already a member. You know, it's pretty unprofessional to talk to friends while you're working. If I was your manager—"

Kat put a finger over her name badge: the words in sparkly Times New Roman font read "Kathryn Oldgoer, Manager." Grandma scowled, snatched the bag of yarn that would probably end up being the sweater her grandson never asked for, and huffed out the door.

For your information, True Believers, Kathryn wasn't a manager, but her immense experience with costumes had also given her an aptitude for working with props. She carried an extra name badge in the pocket of her smock, reserved for those times when I forced myself upon her work day.

"Don, listen. I get that you're going through some stuff, but I'm busy. Can't you, like, go kiss and make up? It sounds like you're both being children."

"You know who else is busy? Paul 'I'm-better-than-everyone-in-the-world' Hughes. I probably saved the lives of half the people in the city—you know, the city he lives in? You'd think I could get a thank you or something. What an asshole."

Kat groaned; I wasn't sure why. Was it the sudden decrease in customers? The fact that her supervisor was glaring at her from the customer-service desk? She put a hand to each of my shoulders and pulled me out from behind her register.

So I left, and tried to get excited that I'd have an actual superhero costume that evening.

* * *

I knocked on her door at seven o'clock.

Would there be a cape? I didn't need one. I hated them anyway: they billowed; they lied and told you that you could fly when you couldn't. But there had to be a mask, right?

"Hey, Don, come in."

I wandered down the hall past the figurines on her radiator, most of them different poses of KOS-MOS, Yoko Littner from *Gurren Lagan*, and—with a bullet—Asuka from *Neon Genesis*

Evangelion. She had a very melon-focused vision as far as fictional crushes went.

"So I decided to go with more of a simple feel. Since your powers are based in conducting electricity I didn't want to overstate the point by stitching lightning bolts all over the place."

"Can I see it?"

"In a sec. So, the hardest part wasn't the emblem. I thought it would be, but dear god, have you ever worked with stretchy fabric? It's such a pain in the ass."

"Can I see it?"

"In a sec. So then, blah blah blaaaah blah blah, bias tape, blah blah blah blah, inseams, blah blah blah, blah blah, and that was thirty-five dollars, blah."

* * *

Blah Blah Blah Blah Blah of the Blah Blah Blah.

* * *

I grabbed her shoulders. "Can. I. See. The. Costume."

Kat finally gave in and snatched my forearm, dragging me to her bedroom, where a black futon amid clear tubs of fabric was the only relic of our time as roommates.

The tubs formed a fort-like construction around it, and a medley of other artifacts confused me more than a giant penny in a dark cave ever could. A sculptured dress form looked, to my untrained eyes, like a sadistically decapitated mannequin. There was an array of sewing machines that hadn't been touched in years but stuck around for nostalgia's sake. I'd heard all of their tales from Kat at one point or another.

Her closet was so wide she'd been able to squeeze a little table in it with her working sewing machine. She walked into the closet with nothing and came out with The Spark. She threw it across the futon and smoothed it out.

These are the Tales of the Astonishing Spark

"I wanted to go for a clean look."

She started to deconstruct its simplicity, but I barely heard, my eyes affixed to the stretchy fabric. It was a full bodysuit, a pure white that I hadn't an inkling of an idea how I'd keep clean, but throughout Kat had used a blue lining that bled into the white like the lightning that had started it all. The suit puffed out with some sort of insulation, which—she explained—incorporated a padded compression shirt and leggings. Her ceiling light reflected off the copper emblem stitched onto the center. I'd thought she would give me a letter, but I should have known Kat better than that: it was a symbol I didn't recognize.

"It's an *adinkra* symbol, West African in origin. Totally free of trademark, and only connected to what matters."

The same symbol was printed at the top of the oversized hood, which I could take off if I wanted to. It would help a ton on rainy nights.

From the waistline, royal-blue stripes ran down to the ankles; the same stripes started at the shoulders and ran down both arms. I knelt to feel the booties sewn into the stretchy fabric. The soles were thin and hard: copper, Kat said. There were copper tabs at the fingertips, too.

"I figured, with the whole electricity thing, conductors couldn't hurt."

"Hah! Yeah, of course." I had to admit, my aim hadn't been great so far. I remembered connecting to the robber's gun, the little girl's headphones. Maybe the conductors would help.

"This is—wow, Kat. You're amazing."

She shrugged. "And you're astonishing. So, you like it, then?"

"Yeah—I mean, you thought of everything. You've got, like, friggin electric-conductor thingies! And the chest piece looks so badass! And—wait."

"What?"

"Where's the mask?"

"Oh, yeah, about that. I didn't make one."

"You didn't make one . . . yet?"

"No, Don, I didn't make one."

"Kat."

"Don, it's okay."

"Kat, I need a freakin' mask!"

"Why? Why do you need a mask?"

"You know, because of this thing?" I did my best John Cena impression and waved a hand in front of my face.

She lit a clove cigarette and took a drag. "Donald, let's be real for a second. You're clumsy enough as it is. I saw the video of you fighting the Maverick Moralist. Maybe a mask isn't the best idea in your case. You could look at the whole protecting-your-friends-and-family thing, but your parents and your grandma passed away a while ago. You're an only child. Really there's just me and Paul, who already know about the whole superhero thing you're trying to do. It's not like villains will take the time to track you down, wait for you to, like, call up one of your two friends, and ambush us in a vulnerable moment." She poured the words like they'd been sitting in a pitcher, chilled to serve when I arrived.

I groaned but didn't argue. The lonely Ben I'd given her couldn't possibly have covered the cost of this suit. I flopped down on the futon.

"So, what now?" Kat asked.

"Well, if I'm going to do this, I can't get around registering. I guess I'll have to take a hit to my savings. Since I'm actually, you know, *Talented* I can probably get onto a superteam somewhere."

She raised an eyebrow.

"What?" I asked.

"Well, I mean, haven't you heard? I thought you'd be all on top of this." She picked up the remote, flipped on her gaming system, loaded up YouTube, and typed "Afro Samson retired."

A few vids popped up. She scrolled down to one of the Hero News Network ones. You probably remember this next bit—in fact, you probably saw it before I did. Without access to Paul's house, and with a limited data plan on my phone, I hadn't kept up on what had happened in the world after the Emancipator reared his diabolical head. I'd just assumed that Patches healed Afrolicious Samson.

What I learned, sitting there with Kat, was that Patches had been ordered to use his powers on the Almighty Asper, in case he had internal injuries from the fall. Thankfully for us, True Believers, Asper was fine. Afrolicious, however, was not, and since he then had to wait twenty-four hours for Patches to be able to use his powers again, the damage had been done.

He would, per his contract with the American Collective for Resolving Overtly Negative Yowled Misconducts, be given a sizable retirement package. What this meant for schlubs like me? Opportunity.

I didn't cry over the end of Afrolicious's career. Not only was he now set for life, but, as mentioned earlier, I fuckin hated him. Why?

Because I know every insignificantly significant detail there is to know about Afrolicious Samson, as anyone of color does regarding the only Black hero in the American Collective for Resolving Overtly Negative Yowled Misconducts. I'd heard his platinum album *Samson Stunner* and I'd watched his critically acclaimed movie, *Diary of a Mad Black Superhero*, in which he played both Tyrone, a mean kid from the streets with a desire to escape, and Grannie Nay Nay, a sassy black woman with a heart of gold and no-nonsense attitude. But for some reason I just couldn't get behind his fan club.

This is another canonical error, by the way, which needs to be cleared up: I was not the first African-American superhero. Never mind what they've said whenever I've appeared on the Black station. Afrolicious Samson was the first.

Afrolicious Samson was born Bartholomew "Jamal" Jenkins IV, son of Bartholomew "Arthur" Jenkins III and Cynthia Lois Vanderhoot-Jenkins. Growing up was a bit of an ordeal for young Jamal. There was no silver spoon, which the news coverage was sure to point out to you over and over again. He was born and raised in Flint, Michigan, and while his family had little in the way of economic riches, there was a Black gold about the place, a reassurance that what he had wasn't less, just less considered.

It was expressed to Jamal—by his parents and by his teachers, who marveled at his exceptional scores in math and science—that he'd have a wonderful future if he figured out how to get away. So he did. He worked his ass off until the black went blue, until the scholarships rolled in. He bit, tore, and anything else you can imagine possible by dint of teeth and tenacity to become Dr. Bartholomew Jamal Jenkins, Ph.D. After that, he thought it prudent to invest his time in bettering the place that built him. That much, I can't help but admire him for. What he didn't have, though, was funding.

So, we all know what's coming, right? Science plus good intentions plus no opportunity? Jamal's freelance experiments for improving the water supply eventually imbued him with the powers of—as he'd soon be called—Afrolicious Samson.

His super-strength was immense but directly tied to the length of his now-enormous Afro. He celebrated beloved heroes from the seventies with his special brand of dynamite justice. From his bell bottoms, tight vest, and yellow-tinted, full-circle sunglasses to his inane catch phrase of "Bitter Hanukkah," he was everything we'd had shoved in our faces about the golden age of Blackness: the hip, the inherently masculine, and the mad cool. What I also knew about Dr. Jamal was how little the "Dr." part mattered after he came to the American Collective for Resolving Overtly Negative Yowled Misconducts, and it didn't seem to matter all that much to anyone else, either.

These are the Astonishing Tales of So Yeah, Fuck Him

You should go throw on some music right about now, True Believer, maybe "Eye of the Tiger" or "The Spirit Never Dies," because after taking the time I needed to feel sorry for myself, I was about to take part in the most sacred ritual of any up-and-coming hero: the holy training montage.

Through karate classes populated mostly by twelve-year olds, I would become a hero.

Through nights at the library spent studying in silent corners and poring over science texts, I'd be a hero.

Through deciding to set aside the hunt for another Super-Predator in favor of starting from the bottom up, taking down devious purse snatchers, I'd be a hero.

TALES OF THE ASTONISHING ~~BLACK~~ SPARK

Through renting a storage unit to bask in heroic solitude, hanging my then-small collection of news clippings on the walls, I'd be a hero.

In the metal shop, crafting aluminum and copper rods to conduct copious amounts of electricity, I'd become a hero.

These are the Tales of the Astonishing Similarities
between Hero and Superhero, and the Astonishing
Ease with Which They Can Be Confused

When you turn the music off, you'll find me: The Astonishing Registered Spark.

CHAPTER 8
DO YOU EVEN LIFT LOCOMOTIVES, BRO?
(OR: THE LIGHTNING THIEF)

"SO, WHAT IS THE Caped and Captained package?"

I was sitting across from the polo-and-khaki-clad Wonderful Wanda. Her blond-and-pink hair had caught my attention as much as my fresh and frill-light costume had caught hers. She'd winked at me, a joke I didn't realize we were both in on, before digging into her drawer and yanking out a pamphlet, carefully handing it to me as if it'd burst into flames otherwise. She gleefully clasped her hands as I read through it, then chimed in as if I didn't know how to words.

"This package is only $224.76 quarterly. With it you get two free sessions a year with a sanctioned PantheUS member. Also, by agreement with PantheUS, we own the rights to any new superhero names that start with Captain. This package guarantees you first dibs on such names if that's on your superhero vision board. Also, thanks to our partnership with Wuwu Capes, you receive one discounted cape or cowl—marked down by 35%!"

"Ah, gotcha." I scanned the next page. "How about the Heroic Heart package?"

"Oh, this one is wonderful. It's $74.92 a month and an additional $3 each quarter. We give you full gym and locker services, as well as access to our video library of archived PantheUS brawl footage, which could give you a leg up—maybe even into the newly opened position in the American Collective for Resolving Overtly Negative Yowled Misconducts, if you play your cards right. Also, access to the Hero salad bar, a monthly supply of fish-oil pills, and we donate one dollar a month to a charity of your choosing!"

"Cool, cool, and the . . . White Flame plan?"

That one turned her smile up to eleven (and ninety-two cents). "Can I ask you a question, Black Spark?"

"It's *Spark*, but yeah, sure."

"Well, who is the most notorious villain in the US?"

"White Flame?"

"Oh-ho, looks like we have a student of superhero history. That's impressive! As you make your way into superheroics, we at Planet Asper want to make sure you're ready for any encounter. So, for a one-time fee of $499, a $200 activation fee, and a $200 nonrefundable service charge, you get—okay, are you ready? I don't think you're ready. Yeah? Okay, you get a one. On. One. Virtual. Call. With. THE Almighty Asper. Not to mention we give you access to the full gym, snack bar, and costume mockups if you're looking to shake things up." She shimmied at the phrase *shake things up* and then leaned back in her swivel chair.

"That sounds, um, logical. Listen, I'm just trying to get a little exposure, get some direction, get a little more in . . . fighting form, you know? Do you have something simple for that?"

"Ah." The Wonderful Wanda rifled through a few more leaflets before finding an old, crumpled mess of one and sliding it across the desk.

"Decent Samaritan package, for the heroic hobbyist. $37.45 a month, common gym area only. You'll have one free slice of pizza per month and one picture with a visiting PantheUS member per year."

I flashed a quick smile when passing my prepaid credit card to her, and she returned the same: an all-too-familiar exchange of a mutual *fuck you* behind feigned familiarity.

A step back? Yeah, let's do that.

While I was slowly working to better myself as a superhero, I wasn't necessarily gaining any traction in what was *important*: brand recognition. It was, as expected, announced that the American Collective for Resolving Overtly Negative Yowled Misconducts would be searching the nation for a new hero to join them. There were rules, always are. The applicant had to either be Talented or have a record of three years' active hero status; they had to be a citizen of the United States; most importantly, they had to be registered. So I drafted from my savings, built from my daddy's bones, or more accurately from the meager life savings he'd had that was given to me when I turned eighteen. It was scrimped and saved for, that $20,000, and each time I spent part of it I felt I had a little less of him. By the time I had to pay $2,000 to register with PantheUS, it was already down to $6,000. That slash cut deep, but I'd plant the beanstalk if it meant gaining the privilege of stillness instead of running from one dollar to the next.

The registration, coupled with my dwindling hours at Stereo Hutt, had made me more reliant on my savings than I would have liked. But the forced budgeting helped my life as Spark more than I realized. The spark inside always worked to train my muscles, but it worked even better when I couldn't afford to order piles of greasy takeout. I pretty much gave up on my power bill, which forced me to learn more about controlling the levels of electricity I distributed, if only to run the lights in my apartment without shattering lightbulbs or draining myself before skipping around the city in the nighttime. There were fewer nights out at Margarine's with Kat and more street patrols.

About street patrols: apparently, your average criminal can't be found on the nightly news like Maverick Moralist. Hell, finding *any* crimes to stop was hard. After perusing all the hero blogs I could find using the free internet at the library, I discovered felonyspotlight.com. You could select a city and find different crimes plotted on a map with goofy emoticons. I tried using it to predict whether it would be more worthwhile to spend the gas money driving to Hilltop or downtown, off-campus Columbus, but I still stumbled across disappointingly few red-handed evildoers. At best I'd draw a few admiring glances as I stalked up and down the sidewalks (rehearsing my self-made theme song, because priorities). At worst, if I patrolled too close to the wrong neighborhoods, I would have to flash my laminated registration card with my hero ID to a curious police officer who would ask a codex of questions before letting me go my way.

Then one day the news was everywhere: Almighty Asper, on behalf of PantheUS's Gunther Grey, would be searching his trade-marked Planet Asper gyms for heroes who might fill the open spot in the American Collective for Resolving Overtly Negative Yowled Misconducts. As any good nerd does, I became obsessed and scoured every news source I could find.

Asper was a vocal fan of Hound News and let a few more things slip when they were the ones interviewing him than he did otherwise. What he let slip—what eventually got me sitting across the desk from Wonderful Wanda—was in response to prodding from his golfing buddy Keith Kurskovitch.

"You gotta give us something, Assy. Are you seriously going to sit there and tell me that General Gunther Grey doesn't have someone in mind already—that you all aren't just trying to milk the hell out of this thing? I hear membership at Planet Asper gyms is up 137 percent since your tour was announced."

Asper, who floated in a seated position above his chair, chuckled. "All right, there may be a few Talented individuals that we've been keeping an eye on, but who knows, right? This isn't just to get our membership up. We are seriously considering *anyone*—but if you're not serious enough to be training in the only PantheUS-backed gym in the country, how serious of a candidate can you be? We *hope* to find some fresh blood. We're hoping to keep things, uh, open, and show that *anyone*, from *any* background, can be a hero."

What I heard was: "Donald, this is your chance. Donald? Donald McDougal, please save us—you're our only hope."

These are the Astonishing Tales of the Any Background Spark

During my initial walkthrough with Wonderful Wanda, she explained to me that everyone who came through the doors deserved to feel like a hero. They should feel immersed in the *altruistic zone.* To highlight this, they affixed an astonishing adjective to each employee's name, while also covering the cost for each employee to be registered, talented or not.

If I'd known that bit up front, I probably would have saved some money and just applied for a job. Hindsight, though, and all that.

I was part of a massive wave of hopefuls who'd heard Asper's call to arms, but like Charlie dreaming of the Chocolate Factory, I only had the one ticket—a $37.45 one at that. There wasn't a set date for Asper's arrival, either, so every day I shuffled into the gym, hoping to catch the eye of someone who would make me matter. My first few days I did catch some looks, but that was more about Kat's adept hand with a sewing needle than anything else. The occasional askance eye scanned me up and down. Once in a while, when I went to nab a slice of pizza before starting my workout, I would catch a remark:

"—doing here? Shouldn't he be in the VIP area?"

"Is he a scout? Maybe a cheap-ass—"

"—awesome costume—"

"—saw him downtown, mumbling to himself. It was weird."

It became easy enough to ignore after a few weeks. I spent time on more important things, like GETTING JACKED, BRO.

The problem was that I didn't know the first thing about doing so. I couldn't afford the classes led every other hour by registered PantheUS instructors, so I settled on working with the machines those first few weeks. Since I was still pissed at Paul, at least I had something to push toward: becoming exactly what he told me I was never going to be. Imagine my surprise, then, about my third week into my Planet Asper aspirations, when I lifted the thousand-pound weights, slid them onto the surprisingly durable bar, and completed three back-to-back sets of bench presses.

I looked around for a moment, removed one hand from the bar, and lifted it again with one hand. *LIGHTNING GAVE ME SUPER STRENGTH, OHSHITYES!* But why had this power arrived so late? I hadn't felt anything super about the punches I'd thrown at Maverick Moralist—I mean, sure, I was stronger than before, but I was no Afrolicious Samson.

These are the Astonishing Tales of Wait for It

As I left the weight rack, sweat still unbroken, I went to award myself yet another slice of recovery pizza. Before I could enjoy it, however, I stood with mouth agape as one of the gym janitors whistled while picking up and putting away one of the weights I'd left lying on the ground. He did it with one hand. I marveled at what had to be the single most intimidating cleaning man I'd ever seen. Until, of course, I heard laughter behind me.

It was a Great Saiyaman wannabe of a man in a black compression T-shirt and swishy basketball shorts. He'd been sliding a hand into one of the cheese pizza boxes. His skin was a pale, nearly translucent white, like the hairs on his eyebrows and across his arms and legs. "Oh, sorry," he said. "You just looked *really* into yourself over there for a while. I was wondering if you realized." He shoveled a piece of the pie into his mouth, speckles of grease clinging to his moustache.

"What?"

"The weights. They're fake. It's a way of *making everyone feel talented*," he said, drawing air quotes with his fingers.

"Oh. Well, I . . . dammit."

"Sorry, I didn't mean to be an ass or anything. I thought you people could take it." He grinned, and I thought I sensed an eye roll beneath the 80s-style sunglasses this douchebro was wearing indoors. At a gym.

"You people?" I knew what he was referring to, of course, but since he'd humiliated me I hoped to gain the high ground.

"You know. Black people." His face went hard, cut by the shadows in the room.

"The fu—"

The man laughed again. "You, my friend, are too easy. *Talented* people, dumbass. Anyway, have a good workout."

I made a point of trying to avoid him during the following weeks, but I'd show up, and there he'd be. He must have caught me glancing over at him every now and again, because whenever I did he'd grab one of the half-ton weights and grunt loudly while lifting it. It was annoying. But whatever his deal was, I had to keep my head in the game. Asper, or some undercover scout, could pop their head in at any moment.

* * *

I kept away from the weights and pretty much everything else except the floor mats for a while, until the day I apparently forgot that I was a walking lightning bolt and tried out one of the elliptical machines. Cardio, when you cough up a lung at the mention of running, isn't likely to be a favorite activity, but I'd already started cutting back on the smokes at that point, because if Maverick Moralist had taught me anything it's how winded the whole heroic hustle can make you. As I ran, though, it was as if I were wasting away on the floor at one of Paul's parties: something climbing up my chest, wanting to get out. I was so, so far behind where I needed to be, though, that I kept pushing, pushing . . .

These are the Astonishing Tales of Boom

The machine, bursting out in smoke and sound, shuddered before croaking over to the ground. A spark I didn't mean to share had erupted from me and trashed this very expensive piece of equipment.

I looked around, hoping no one had seen, but I guess it was hard to miss. Everyone in the room was watching me with crimped, scissor-slit eyes as I tried to wave smoke away. I could feel my credit card folding into itself inside my pocket to die. I tried to laugh it off, but they, and more importantly my douchebro friend from the pizza counter, had plainly seen that fiery, toothy thing my pops had always ordered me to keep clandestine until it mattered.

These are the Astonishing Tales of
Who's Got the Power Now, Bro

"He's Talented," I heard someone say.

I moved as fast as I could to the locker room, but that guy, that pizza-eating, shades-wearing sack of cynicism, was still staring harder than the rest. Was he some kind of gym security?

Nothing happened, though, until a few days later, when Wonderful Wanda got on the intercom to demand that I report to her office.

"I wish I'd known you were Talented when we first met," she said. "And you're also *registered*? You're full of surprises, aren't you?"

I didn't know what she was playing at yet, so I remained silent, feeling like I had when the school principal stared Kat and me down after an unfortunate series of events involving mIRC, the entire series of *The Secret World of Alex Mack*, and a network-wide adware epidemic.

Wanda just looked at me, waiting.

"Um, I'm sorry?" I said. "I suppose I should have . . . am I in trouble? Like, the machine, it's . . ." I wasn't sure how to finish the thought. *Dead and costs more than a year's rent?*

"Oh! No, not at all," Wanda said. "We encourage the membership of Talented individuals, and we're fully insured. The reason I asked you in here was that someone is very interested to meet you."

"Oh, yeah, someone sure as shit is," said a voice on speakerphone from her desk.

These are the Astonishing Tales of Gunther Grey

I didn't know who it was at first; the voice of one old Southern white dude sounds mostly indistinguishable from the rest.

What I did recognize, however, was that sword-to-stone, gritty twang that existed only in those who'd known authority and power. It was when Wanda introduced him that my stammering began. I saluted the answering machine, bowed, and eventually remembered how technology worked before stilling myself.

"So, I'm speaking with the Midwest Marvel—no, sorry, you go by Black Spark now, right? Unless you prefer Donald? Well, son, it's good as goat milk to finally have a chance to speak with you."

"Spark is fine, unless—how did you—?"

"My boy, it's my job to know everything about anyone who's worth anything."

I looked to Wanda, who only shrugged.

"I've been *watching* you, my boy. I've gotta say I'm impressed with what I've seen. It's time you step your game up though. I'm not a man for tiptoeing around the bushes. You got *moxie*, boy. You have a lot of power, a lot to give back. To be honest, this whole eager-to-serve thing isn't very common anymore. Too many kids lining up to get an iSomeshit instead of an iCanhelpmycountry! Hah, that was pretty good." His laugh rattled the static on the line. I laughed back at the speaker phone, and so did Wanda.

"Sir, your honor, sir, I'm—I don't know what to say."

"Listen. Your story, and more importantly your talent, well, it's something. I can't say I've seen anything like it, or you. You successfully corralled an elemental talent on your first go, no training, no nothing, just you and that little stun-gun thing you do. You were obviously trying to get someone's attention, and I figured you'd rear your head out the right gopher hole one of these days," Gunther said. "And with everything that's happened—"

"You mean Afrolicious Samson, sir?"

"Yeah, sad thing. Sad, sad shame of a thing. But new blood is always a good thing, I think. Gets the old folks riled up, puts a fire under my team. America's team."

His team, I thought. It was a hell of a thing to feel right for once—that I'd been working toward something more than just how to waste all my money and time as fast as I could. "So, you're saying that—that I have a position on—"

"Whoa, Nelly." He chuckled. "You don't just get to skip the hairy tit for the milk right this minute. You are, however, on my radar, and that's a good place to be. I'm sure you're aware we have an emergency election coming up. Lots of talent, but let's just say I already have a shortlist in mind."

"And I'm . . . on that list?"

"Yes, Donald McDougal, you are on that shortlist. Keep your nose clean, keep up the good work, and I might be seeing you in a few months out here in the hero capital of the world."

* * *

That night, hitting the streets, I broke out in laughter more than once. Not the greatest move when trying to cultivate that crucial brooding, devil-may-care hero vibe. Then again, neither was a suit with a bright-white base and royal-blue accents, so I mostly just accepted that I'd never be your grim and terse dude with a cape who jumps around a lot. I ended, as usual, by shocking and silencing a few minor miscreants you probably don't care to hear about.

A boom of thunder shook the night as I headed for my storage unit. I used to get nervous about storms, but now I was excited. If I could catch the lightning ahead of the rain, I'd have a free full charge.

The powers that be were kind. I heard the *croom*, that connection. There was a tingle, a fire-forged net that caught over me, letting me know the lightning was charging up and I was in queue for the next jolt. But before that could happen, for the first time, the net snapped. I smelled singed flesh, but it wasn't my own. When I turned around, there he was.

"I really couldn't have timed that better! I mean, it kind of says everything, doesn't it?"

Thin vapors of smoke rose from his body. He wore a getup like the one that I'd seen him in at the gym, all black from head to toe, contrasted by his pallid head of scraggly white hair and silver-tinted eyes.

"Sorry, my name is Nikolas. Nikolas Tess."

Really, douchebro?

"I'd like a moment of your time, Mr. McDougal," he said.

These are the Astonishing Tales of That Asshole

CHAPTER 9
HEROES AND VILLAINS

THE RAIN PICKED UP to a full pour as we watched each other through the heavy, beading drops. Nikolas Tess, my very own lightning thief, sloshed towards me.

"So, can we get inside? Rain isn't very kind to me, though I'm sure I don't have to tell you that."

"I've been learning karate!" I said, putting my fists up defiantly.

His face contorted. "That's adorable. Listen—I didn't come here to fight or anything, if that's what you think."

"So you just creep up on superheroes in the middle of the night and flash your powers, dressed in all black, to . . . what?"

"To talk, Spunk."

"It's Spark."

"I know."

The geek in me wanted to smile back because it's what the cool guy was doing, but I tried to sizzle a spark inside just in case, keeping it dim enough not to throw my body into convulsions under the rain.

Slowly I turned to the gate of the storage unit and pulled it open.

Why? Well, how many talented individuals can you name who can absorb, contain, and manipulate electricity? Sitting here in this coffee shop, I can still name only two.

I motioned for him to go in before me. He jogged in out of the rain, shaking himself dramatically and sifting a hand through his pale hair. I followed and let the gate fall shut. We stood in the darkness for a moment and I heard him rustling around, drying off his hand on something, before a flash of light erupted from his palm. From each of his fingers, lightning fed into the center of his hand in a perfect marble of energy.

It was fucking cool.

I dried my hands on a dingy towel before igniting a small spark between the conducting tabs over my pinky and index fingers. It took me a moment to find my external battery, but when I did I recharged it with my other hand before attaching a USB desk lamp to it.

Nikolas shut off his orb of light and looked around my fifty-dollar-a-month storage unit of solitude. The biggest newspaper clipping on the wall was the picture of me and Maverick, my personal favorite.

He raised an eyebrow. "So how long have you been able to do what we do?" No more smiles, no more gleams or glitzing, just us and what we do.

"Not very long. Since a little after New Year's."

"And how did it happen?"

He asked, so I told him. I told him about hospitals, about sparks and booms and all the parts of me that I'd been waiting for someone to understand.

"So," he said. "After all this, after you realized what we could do, it took you all of a week to decide to go electrocute someone?"

Ah, the Evil and Mischievous George Splam, my first villain—who probably wouldn't have a multi-issue arc.

"That was before I'd even gone out as the Midwest Marvel," I said. "How did you know?"

"Because—obvious as I thought this would be—I didn't just pop up at Planet Asper. I didn't coincidentally end up in Columbus a few weeks after the Midwest Marvel, flashing his very unique power set, hit the national news. I came here for you, to see what you were about."

It was hard not to feel a bit flattered, if I'm being honest. I wondered if this made Nikolas my first superfan, but his tone dismissed that theory relatively fast. He'd been scoping me out, like Gunther Grey—like everyone at that gym after I may have not-so-intentionally destroyed some equipment.

Nikolas dusted off a beanbag chair I'd stuffed in the corner before flopping onto it.

"So what *am* I about?" I asked.

These are the Astonishing Tales of Acknowledge Me, Senpai

Nikolas sighed. "You're dangerous. Electricity can mess you up, bad. You really, *really* don't know karate, or much of anything, do you?"

"What do you mean?" I was indignant. I'd been *studying*.

"You've electrocuted two men. One, Mr. Splam, suffers from heart palpitations and will need help going to the bathroom for the foreseeable future. Yes, you've got power; yes, you're at least *trying* to protect people with it, but in a messy-ass way. I thought maybe you were, well, something more intentional, but you're not. You're working with something you have no idea about. You're ignorant, and you think you're not, and, well, yeah. That pretty much sums it up."

My mind had stopped absorbing his words at *need help going to the bathroom*. That phrase turned my stomach into a stone. It must have showed on my face, because he softened, in his way.

"I'm sorry if I've upset you," he said. "But you have to understand that, well, you *don't* understand. I came because I realized that you were different."

Needs help going to the bathroom.

"I think that, if you let me, I can teach you how to control this," said Nikolas.

I'd hurt people—not goons, not comic-book cannon fodder, but people. The fear of that had never left me, not with my new copper rods or minimal progress at controlling the flowing spark or karate lessons. I'd always known what it was to live painfully conscious and subtly enraged at all times, but the added weight of this on my body was too much. I needed him, and he knew it.

Rumor had it that roughly a tenth of a percent of the country's population was talented. There weren't schools for the gifted—at least not for what I had in my bank account—but right there, in front of me, was Nikolas.

"So what is it you think I need to learn?" Of course, I knew the answer was *loads*, but I wanted specifics. I wanted to see if he wanted to teach as much as I needed to learn.

"For starters?" He opened his hand. When sparks leapt from his fingertips, one of my copper rods flew from its shelf directly into his grip.

"It's not just the science of electromagnetism and conductivity. It's about *connecting*. It's about realizing that this thing we do is bigger than us and bigger than anyone or anything. It's about realizing what it means to be a moth circling the flame."

Riddles. Awesome.

He tossed up the rod and it stopped in midair; then, with a flick of the finger, he whisked it back to its rightful place but knocked the rest of the rods down onto the ground. They made a violent melody smacking the concrete floor. I bit back a laugh.

"See, certain skills should be exercised in moderation. The first thing is to learn how to turn the switch off. Avoid collateral damage."

Just like that I was no longer an equal but a student, which hurt my pride but soothed everything else. He closed his eyes and breathed. There was an uncomfortable pull between us, much like when he'd stolen the lightning, but it didn't last this time. Instead it rattled for a moment before snapping like a broken rubber band and falling flat.

Nikolas grunted and staggered back; beads of sweat seeped from his forehead. When he opened his eyes again they weren't like mine anymore—the silver in them had turned a brilliant blue.

"Come here," he said. I cautiously obeyed. He took my hand and placed it on his arm. "I take it you've siphoned off electricity before, from your surroundings?"

I nodded.

"Do it now. Take mine."

It should have been one of the easiest voluntary acts I could perform, but when I tried it nothing happened. He smiled again, taking my hand away and putting it back at my side.

"What did you do with it? Your power?"

"It's still here," he said, putting a hand over his heart. "Do you know how a light switch works?"

"Yeah, you flick it. Up or down."

"No. Well, yes. But do you know what happens when you turn that light switch on and off?"

I shrugged my shoulders.

"The electricity doesn't stop flowing through the walls. The switch just opens or closes a certain connection."

More riddles.

"What I'm saying is that there is no separating you from the power. You *are* the power. But I felt it, each way it snapped throughout my body, and learned each way it could go. I learned to cut it off from this path, or that. I *controlled* it. You can't get rid of it, trust me—but you can install some switches. Direct the energy."

"The spark," I corrected.

He closed his eyes for a few seconds, then opened them to reveal that the silver tint had returned. "Of the energy. Sorry, don't mean to go all hippie on you or anything, but it'll be easier if you think of it as energy. A flow, not a zap."

These are the Astonishing Tales of "The
Energy" Is a Terrible Superhero Name

Yeah, I was sold.

He would tell me later how he'd practiced that little moment of ours a few times on the way over, and I'd give him the appropriate level of shit over it, but at the moment none of that mattered. I'd finally be saved.

He scribbled a time, a phone number, and an address on a little piece of paper.

"If you want to learn, be there on Friday at 7:30 a.m."

Nikolas lifted up the gate of the storage unit. The storm had passed quickly and the rain was already subsiding.

"Oh, and no costumes, Spark," he said before leaving.

"It's Donald," I said, hoping he'd heard before the gate slammed shut with him on the other side of it.

111

* * *

It had been a Sunday when he showed up, so I had to make my way through four days of living without my walking Wikipedia. I suddenly had this promise of a thing I never knew I could have—*actual* control—and then just *hey, see you next week*. I didn't know at that point how he'd even found me, so when I was at work during those long, long days, I would look up as the door chimed, in the vain hope it was him. When Kat called I rushed to my phone like a lost puppy. Basically, every day was Christmas Eve and I was reduced to living like the eight-year-old Donald, aching for Milestone action figures that never materialized.

I persevered, though, True Believer, and eventually the day of answers arrived. The address was an abandoned building on South High, a dead area of town that I'd never spent much time in. Water and neglect had made the walls weep over the long years, leaving me surrounded by streaky gray. *There's metal everywhere. An abandoned steel mill?* I thought, surveying the bits, bolts, and girders protruding like broken bones.

For a guy who didn't like costumes, Nikolas definitely had a flair for the theatrical.

"Nikolas?" I called, squinting as the sun danced through haggard holes and shotgun illumination blasted me. I looked down and pushed at the litter of nails on the ground with my toes.

A few of the nails started to rattle, though nothing else shook. They burst upward and danced in the dust-ridden air surrounding me. At first I was foolhardy enough to think that I was doing it, but of course it was Nikolas, off in a dark corner of the building. I finally saw him when he made the nails all point needle-end towards that corner.

"Hey, Donald. Glad you could make it," he said.

"Yeah, me too. Let's get started, Sensei."

He ignored my exaggerated bow.

I knew that the first lesson Nikolas wanted me to learn was how to control myself. It had long been the most important item on my to-do list, and was coincidentally the most boring item on the to-do list.

"There are two things you should know, Donald," Nikolas said, letting the flow connect us. "First, all materials, conductors or otherwise, have a certain level of resistance to electricity." He let the flow pulse into me at a higher level, before dimming it down until it stopped. "That includes your body. When you switch a light off, a separator blocks the connection between two wires. Your power, your *spark*, streams throughout your muscular system from your nervous system, which is finally controlled from your noggin. You don't need hardware to stop the flow, just will. It's movement. Subtle movement. Like flexing a muscle."

"Okay, so what you're saying is, I just scream, like, *Shazam!* and lights out?"

"No, you don't say anything, you just do it. You feel it and you do it."

"I'd really like to say *shazam*."

"Please don't."

So I didn't. No costumes. No codenames. No understanding of relatively mainstream comics references. Even the abandoned warehouse turned out to be a practical choice. Training with Nikolas should have been as fun as living out an early 2000s superhero movie, but it felt more like . . . work. I closed my eyes instinctively, thrusting myself into lessons learned from old kung fu flicks my father had forced me to watch. I thought of stopping. I thought of waiting. I thought of being silent to let the rest of myself be heard.

A flash. A boom. A Spark.

I felt a sharp sting across my chest and abdomen, and I realized: It's resisting my resistance. It's saying *no*.

I fell to my knees. My eyes swam in their sockets; Nikolas, approaching, was a blur. I stuck out a hand to stop him.

"No, I got it." I really needed a win for once. Heroes were supposed to have those, after all.

I touched the jagged teeth gnawing inside my body, popping the seams of my bones and breaking the brackets of my muscles. Nothing worth having is easy to obtain, I guess, except obvious aphorisms. Nikolas crouched down next to me, telling me that I was capable, that I shouldn't give up. I doubted how natural this off switch really was, since it felt so unwelcome. I remembered Paul's words—*you're not a hero*—but I had to try. *They'll never see you coming*, I heard in my father's voice. But what if I never got there at all?

I thought of the things that could change. I thought of keeping everything the same, and how easy it was, how natural *that* felt. But to avoid hurting others, to dance in the rain, I would have to accept change.

"Well, look at the fast learner," Nikolas said.

He didn't have to tell me tales of my brown eyes; I could feel it, or rather, couldn't. I stood up and I was normal. I was Donald, and someone had a plan for me.

"I call this the state of Absolute Resistance," said Nikolas.

"Catchy."

Nikolas shrugged.

"Is it supposed to hurt like that?" I asked after catching my breath.

"No, not if you keep practicing."

So I did.

As expected, Nikolas gave me homework, but in that first session alone I cut the amount of time it took me to shift into and out of Absolute Resistance by half.

I wanted more. I wanted everything he had, or at least the SparkNotes. But, again, I'd have to wait a week.

* * *

After that first meeting I considered calling Paul, but then I remembered how well our last conversation had gone. I thought of calling Kat, but how could I expect her to understand?

The only person I really had now wouldn't be speaking to me again for another week.

Every week I found myself going through the motions just to get to the next lesson. It took me about three weeks to learn how to properly switch off and on in under five seconds, and as we progressed I learned exactly why we'd focused so hard on it to begin with. It was, if there is such a thing, a gateway skill. As versed as I was in wax on and wax off from the pre-Spark days of watching Mr. Miyagi movies, it hadn't prepared me for the actual application of such methods.

After that door was opened, everything else began to flood in. There were some Fridays where we would just maintain Absolute Resistance, leaving our warehouse and wandering around German Village or Sharon Woods without so much as a sizzle. From the pieces I shuffled together during Nikolas's anecdotes about his own trials and errors, I knew he had at least eleven years of experience over me. I knew that he loved to tinker, deconstructing stun guns and coils to get accustomed to the amount of electricity he could exert.

Only once did the role of teacher not seem to come easily to him. We were muddling about on a stormy afternoon, coming back along

115

a trail to the warehouse after grabbing coffee, sloshing across puddles of water. He started to talk but never lifted his eyes from the ground.

"So, about . . . having the sex," he said.

These are the Tales of the Astonishing Ways I Really Need to Shoehorn the Fact That I'm Not a Virgin in Here

When you're nearly thirty, you never expect to have a dummies' guide to sex talk for the rest of your life. I bit back a mix of laughter and rage at his assumption that I did not know how to "have the sex," until I remembered the common theme of all our conversations: the power. I hadn't even had time to think about sex since the powers came. What if I accidentally—

It was a topic that would have made for a really bad plotline on *Smallville*, or at least a very awkward *Spider-Man* read—not a pleasant park-walk conversation. But Nikolas dove into an anecdote, a story about the first man he was with after he got his powers. He mostly cracked jokes about areas where stun guns are not welcome and the similarities between lubricants and nitroglycerin, but between laughs I got the gist of it.

* * *

There was one day, one shitty, shitty day, when he took me to see George Splam. Splam didn't see us. He was lying in a hospital bed in front of the TV in his apartment, where he stayed most of the day. His blinds were open, so we had a clear view of him from the roof of an adjacent building. The lesson that day? Well, that was it.

On the way there, Nikolas had gone on about Lichtenberg layers, the scars lightning left on those lucky enough to survive the storm. I knew about them already from my own research (and my body) but let him drone on about it anyway, because when he was scouring science for a point there wasn't any stopping him. He explained that the marks we had from being touched by a thing that should have destroyed us, should have ripped us to nothing but wind and dust, weren't earned or deserved. They should serve, if nothing else, as a reminder of lessons learned.

Eight. Hours. Nikolas had brought a lawn chair, a few books to read, and the day's paper. Nothing for me, though; I had all I needed to watch right there. Anytime I turned away from the Saga of Splam? *Watch.* Anytime I reminded Nikolas what Splam's part was in our little meeting? *Watch.* And anytime, low enough I thought Nik couldn't hear, I said I was sorry? *Remember that.*

* * *

After two months, Nikolas decided it was time for me to learn more about using my abilities in real-life situations. This roughly translates to: He decided to beat me up. A lot.

Our lessons ramped up to three times a week.

These are the Astonishing Tales of Whoop Ass

I flopped to the mess of broken glass, nails, and other things that promised to tear into me. Nikolas had once again pushed me firmly to the flat of my backside. It was as excelsior a place to be as it ever was.

"You're out of breath already?"

I was, but I made it a point to use control, to not panic, to stay focused on kicking his lily-white ass. I dodged his condescending rhetoric by launching myself forward. Too slow. I knew it when he snatched my hair and swung me into a steel girder.

"You're expending too much energy. You'll run out of electricity if you don't calm down. So calm. Down." He demonstrated controlled breathing. "When you're amped up like this, you're dumping adrenaline into your body. A body that isn't like everyone else's. Adrenaline tells you *oh, it's go time,* and that tells the power inside *he needs more of me.*"

I listened. I calmed. But it was too late—I needed a jump.

"I think we need to stop. I'm spent," I said after crawling up the steel girder that had just cracked something I didn't have the health insurance to get fixed.

"Stop being such a fucking quitter!" Nik was, per usual, too goddamn fast. He pushed his palm towards me and drew out what little spark I'd retained. Then he darted at me; the bony fingers of one hand latched on and the other hand balled into a fist, ready to crash my teeth in. He stopped an inch or so from my face. No flinches, just failures. He released me.

"I'm sorry," I said. "I'm really trying, dude, I just—"

"No, it's okay, man. It's just, well—we *do* have a timeline."

We do? I thought. *First time I'm hearing about it.*

He must have read the question on my face. He scratched the back of his head, offering no words, no comfort, but I shouldn't have expected them. As things connect, they also fall apart. We break and snap, without a spark, oftentimes without sound. I realized that this was how Nikolas planned to leave—that he had a life somewhere outside of Columbus, waiting for him. I couldn't help looking at him as a villain again, if only for a moment.

"Yeah," he said. "I was going to wait until you got a little further along, but I figured that'd be weeks ago."

It's fine, Mr. Tess, I didn't need your help anyway. I don't need anyone's help. I'm a hero—everyone else needs MY help.

"As much as it sucks, I guess I'll just have to take you along as you are."

These are the Astonishing Tales of Oh
the Places We'll Never Go

"I don't understand," I said.

Nikolas pulled me up to my feet. "Yeah, I know, and I'm sorry about that. I haven't lied to you, Donald, but I haven't told you everything, either. I didn't come here just to teach you—that was important, and you've come such a long way, but—what are you here for? Why do you keep coming back?"

I thought of my third-, fourth-, and tenth-grade English teachers. I thought of grief counselors after my Pops died. I thought of the inability of questions to give us their own answers.

"Well, I don't want to screw this up," I said, and it was the truest thing I think I'd ever said to him.

"What is *this*, though? What don't you want to screw up?"

I'm still not sure I have the answer for that one, Nik.

"No, don't try some Yoda shit on me now," I said. "Tell me what you're talking about."

"All right, all right. I'm not an idiot, Donald. I know what you *think* you want—you think you need to become one of *them*. You're itching to rush off to New York or L.A., somewhere with plenty of opportunities to make a fool of yourself in that costume you love so much."

What else was I supposed to do next?

"Do you realize how much you've learned and done of your *own* accord, without the help of those costumed jackasses?" said Nikolas. "I think you know you don't need them, if you're being honest with yourself—if you think of how much you can do to help others already. If that were what you really wanted here, you'd see how much you don't need them.

"I want you to meet some friends of mine. They're like us—Talented—but not in exactly the same way. I know I've been a little evasive so far, but it's about time I make things clear and show you."

* * *

I'd never really left Columbus, save for a few anime conventions. Like many, I'd resigned myself to city arrest in the relatively progressive bubble of Columbus, Ohio. Even though I lacked things the world told me I needed, like my choice of fusion dining experiences or reliable mass transit, it had always seemed like enough.

After my lessons with Nikolas, though, I knew it wouldn't be anymore.

Nikolas didn't let me know what to expect, just where to be. I didn't sleep that night. Instead I wandered around downtown, wafting puffs of smoky cold air at the corner where it all began. After a few hours, I went home and packed some things: my spare costume, my copper rods, and a few outfits. I played counting games as if trying to trick myself into sleeping, but it was more to keep my mind from thoughts of Kat and Paul, of Stereo Hutt and half-paid apartment leases. *What the hell are you doing?* I wondered.

Finally I went out to my car, popped the address Nikolas had given me into my phone's GPS, and drove.

I didn't watch my speed, so I found myself in front of a ramshackle Ohio farmhouse twenty minutes early, having reached Marion in less than forty minutes. I wasn't expecting a lesson that day, so instead of following the rules I'd worn my costume beneath a knee-length jacket, sloshing in my fancy superhero boots over dying snow yellowed with dog piss.

I expected that Nikolas would answer the door, but no one

answered it; when I nudged it open I saw three strangers, all of whom seemed to share Nik's affection for black clothing.

Had I come to the wrong house? Had I typed the wrong address into the GPS?

"Hi, there," I said with a wave.

A big, stocky man snuffled. A wiry Asian dude with an emo haircut played with a switchblade like everyone worth hating played with a vape, flipping it up, up, down, down, left, right, left, right, A, B, start. I thought for a minute that his sole talent was lending the group a 1950s street-gang flair.

The only one who didn't seem indifferent or ill-willed towards me was the youngest, a girl not too far from Natalie's age but with twice the thunder in her eyes. She had a side of her head shaved in that precisely chaotic way I'd never had the balls to go through with on my locs.

"You the one Nik talked about, then?" Biggum McShithewasbig asked, as if I knew what the hell Nik talked to them about. I decided to just nod, while looking around and hoping we weren't all about to be offered mysterious, soul-liberating Solo cups of Kool-Aid. When he started walking towards me, I kicked myself for leaving the copper rods in the suitcase packed away in my trunk.

"He's busy. Told us to be friendly, not to make fun of you if you say something weird," said the big man (which was not very friendly if you ask me). Alvin—his real name, I'd learn; his talent was super-strength—didn't *have* to use his powers to make you feel small. He never unfolded his arms, even as I bit back a dickish retort and extended a hand. The girl with the half-shaved head pushed herself off the wall she'd been leaning against and slapped her hand into mine, shaking it.

"Don't worry, weird is fine here. I'm Maggie, by the way. That's

Alvin—he's the stereotypical big mean guy—and the dude with the knife is Rizal. Donald, right?"

I nodded. "Yeah, Donald—The Spark. So, are you guys registered, then? Like, as a supergroup or something?"

My words seemed to draw the tension that had begun to ebb back in to shore. I stood there, not knowing what exactly I'd done wrong, until that most serene of sounds, that harp of poets, intervened.

These are the Astonishing Tales of *flush*

When Nikolas came out of the bathroom, he met the sight of World War Us. I waited for him to give one of his poignant, nuanced, Jedi-master monologues, anything to prevent me getting punched in the face.

I really don't like getting punched in the face.

"Everyone, calm. The fuck. Down," he said, still shaking water from his freshly washed hands.

"A *suit*, Nik? The hell is the matter with you, bringing him here?" Alvin said.

I hadn't even seen Rizal striding towards me like a Tonberry. His knife was now at my back—while also, in his other body, he met my eyes from across the room. Rizal, you see, could duplicate himself.

"Ah, hell. Okay, so, yes. He is registered, he is technically one of *them*, but—he isn't like them. I brought him here to show him something a little more meaningful. Less barbaric? After everything we've been through, after everything I've done for you, can you give me the benefit of the doubt?" With his hands still wet, he managed to summon enough of a spark to send Rizal's knives soaring across the room, where they clinked on a metal table.

"You should have told us, Nik," Maggie said.

"Yeah, noted. I am the asshole here. So, what are we doing, people?"

Eventually, everyone simmered down. I wanted to apologize, but I also wanted to show them what I could do. Nikolas moved before anything else could go down, putting an arm around my shoulders and steering me into the next room, where he shut the door behind us.

I took in the rickety creak of every floorboard, the warped wood on the walls, the everything that people like Nik and I couldn't connect to. He leaned against the wall, and after I finished pacing around I did the same. We stayed there for a while, and while I wanted to say something to break the palpable silence, I didn't appreciate it when he laughed to himself.

"What's funny?" I said.

He groaned. "You asked them, you dumb—you asked them the one thing I thought you would be smart enough not to ask them. I made it pretty obvious, didn't I?"

My stomach tightened, the fireflies flocking to this spot and that. I knew it had to happen, us talking about his "hobbies," and I also knew I wasn't ready for it.

"You know, right?" Nikolas said.

When I stared blankly he rolled his eyes, pushing off the wall and starting to open a black duffle bag. I did. Know, I mean. The words didn't come, though. I thought of dumb Donald, tripping over myself, doing nothing with nothing and nestling close to myself in the dark. For his trust in me so far, I owed him.

"Yeah," I said. "I know."

"So why did you ask them if they were registered, if we were a supergroup?"

"Guess I was hoping I was wrong."

Another smirk—he had a lot of those stored away, and I had a way of pulling them out. I thought, though—and still do—that they were finite.

He changed his mind about the duffle bag, zipped it back up. "So, what do you want to know first?" he said.

"I'm going to be one of them, you know," I said. "Not just PantheUS but the American Collective for Resolving Overtly Negative Yowled Misconducts. I all but got an invitation from Gunther Gray himself. You had to have known that much—you seem to know an awful lot about me."

He didn't answer.

"You came to *me*," I said. "You told me that you wanted me to be better, but at least some of that was bullshit, wasn't it? You didn't tell me the truth about you all, about you, because you knew if you'd been honest, told me at the outset, I'd have told you to get the hell out. When I realized who you were, I just hoped . . . I don't know, that you had a good reason for doing what you did."

"Was there a question somewhere in all that?"

"Let's start with this: What is it you want, really?"

He stared at the ground. I tried to break the tension threading us to that awkward-as-shit moment with a smoke. I passed one to him first, producing a spark between my pinky and index fingers, and he leaned in to light it.

"There are thousands of Aedans, Donald. Those who have to deal with the consequences of what men in suits in buildings do: in power, in ignorance."

I wanted to hurt him for throwing Aedan at me. When I'd told him that story, I hadn't done so to give him ammunition to make a point.

"The power that we and other Talented individuals have gets

celebrated," he went on, "so much so that we obscure the garbage fire in the distance. Over forty million people live in poverty in this country. Superheroic activity? PantheUS? Lumped in with the national defense budget, which accounts for over half of the US discretionary budget. We're eating ourselves alive. But that problem's not as easy to solve as a supervillain we can punch in the snoot."

I interrrupted with a laugh. "The hell is a snoot?" I asked, and for a moment? Things weren't so damn heavy.

"I dunno, a nose? I read it somewhere." He took another puff of his cigarette. "Look. You can be a superhero, Donald, or you can be something more. You stay the course you're on? You become another one of the PantheUS bullets. You forget what it is to be one of us. You detach from everything that matters, inch by inch. Those dollars, those eyes? They're for clowns who don't even realize who they're putting on a show for."

"Just stop," I said. "So, what? This is the pitch, then? You want me to enlist with the randos downstairs, who looked like they were gonna try to kill me not ten minutes ago, and—what? Hold protest signs in front of the Llama Tower? Organize a march? Aggressively tweet?"

I turned to face him, facing at the same time Paul and his assembly of woke, walnut-headed half-steppers; facing me, five or so years ago, donating an anonymous $5,000 to keep *Kuumba Kollective* afloat instead of investing in something with more boom. Facing all the things my father told me not to concern myself with—until they couldn't see you coming. Until you were more than they could ever hope to handle.

"You're not listening, are you? You're never going to learn anything unless—"

This time I slammed a hand against the wall, near Nikolas's face. He didn't flinch, but that wasn't the point. I was putting a period to his pedantic assertions that I was a student, not of the lightning, but of *this*. This same cynical bullshit that never, ever moved forward. A Ten-Point Program. MOVE. X, after awakenings and asking for bullets in lieu of talking about ballots. A water crisis, pipeline putridly flowing to children in Michigan streets. Take your pick. This was the way of thinking we were damned to repeat over and over until they trampled us.

Every. Single. Time.

These are the Astonishing Tales of Things Never
Ending the Way They Are Supposed To

"I don't need your condescending bullshit, not about this, Nik," I spat. *Anger*: such a small, small word for such a beautifully chaotic thing. Because my father taught me to smile—how to bite anger back but not how to reshape it—it would find life at the oddest of times. Looking back? Nikolas hadn't pissed me off nearly enough for me to react like that, but often as not I'd find myself pointing the pistol at those who loved me the most, who suffered me with laughter. Who would listen.

I pushed myself off the wall and kicked the partially unzipped duffle bag of cash open. I stared at the wealth that allowed him to be whoever he wanted. I'd never had such a luxury.

"I gotta admit, you've given me something I didn't think I would ever have," I said. "I feel . . . safe. I feel like I can make everyone else safe, too—but I'm going to do it the right way. If I'd heard some of this, I don't know, a few months ago? Maybe I could trust you enough to take this for something more than—I don't know. Maybe if you would have given me half of the pieces? But how do I know you're telling me everything, even now? How do I know that whatever you're up to is really worth abandoning all that for?" By now I was talking to the contents of the duffle bag more than to him.

"You *can* trust me. You can show me, right here and now, that you're willing to make a step in the right direction. What do you want, proof? Some sort of promissory note or—or what? A fucking notarized form? I'm sorry, Donald, but I've made mistakes before. I've given too much to the wrong people too soon, and for now—I've given you enough. If you want more I'd have to know you're with us, not them. So: moment of truth, Mr. McDougal. What's it going to be?"

I thought of jokes like *only a Sith deals in absolutes* and other things Nik completely wouldn't get, though I'd enjoy his confusion. Instead I headed for the door.

"I am different," I said. "I hope you know that. I hope you know that nothing you've taught me will go to waste, and that . . . I appreciate everything you've done for me."

He didn't answer.

"I hope I see you again, Nikolas."

He didn't follow me as I headed down the stairs, but he did speak one last time, in a voice weaker than I ever expected to hear from him. "We leave at 10:00 a.m. I hope I'll see you in the morning, Donald."

These are the Astonishing Tales of How He Wouldn't

These are the Astonishing Tales of Sleeping
through Alarms That Were Never Set

These are the Astonishing Tales of My Arch-Nikolas

CHAPTER 10
DEUCES

I'M SORRY, NIKOLAS. If you're reading this, I'm so, so sorry.

These are the Astonishing Tales of We Hate Want You

A couple of days after I overslept and missed my opportunity to dick around with wannabe revolutionaries, I sifted through the three business cards on my kitchen table and found Gunther Grey's phone number scribbled in Wonderful Wanda's handwriting. I was foolhardy enough to think that I'd be able to dial right in and say "Spark here, what's good?"—even though I knew, True Believers, just how exclusive PantheUS could be. I spent an hour on hold, being transferred from extension to extension. I was startled when I finally heard a human voice—and I was pretty sure it was DEATHRAGE. After I'd word-vomited about half of my entire life story until that point, he finally stopped me.

"HOLD ON." I thought he was pissed at me, or maybe constipated, but I'd soon come to learn he had a caps-locked way with words. I heard the clomping of combat boots and racket of gunmetal as he handed off the phone.

"Hello, this is GRAVI-Tina. Who is this?"

"Oh! Hi! This is Donald? Donald McDougal . . . you know."

"No, I don't think I do."

"The, um—The Spark?"

"Oh! The Black Spark, right, right, Gunther said you'd be calling. How are you?"

I thought of correcting her, but only in the way that I thought of correcting everyone and never did. "I'm well, thanks. And you?"

"So Gunther told me he had a chance to speak with you. You're registered?"

"Yeah, I sent in the paperwork a while ago."

"Great, great. Hey, listen, it's great to hear from you, but we've got, well, a *thing* later, so I've got to go. Where are you again? Kansas?"

"Actually, Ohio—"

"Yeah? That's neat. He mentioned he had high hopes for you. How about we get you out here sometime and see what you've got, hmm? I don't know what—hey! DEATHRAGE! Dammit, I told you about leaving your goddamn taco bowls in the microwave, dude."

"Sorry?" I said.

"Huh? Sorry, wasn't talking to you. Anyway, do you have anything going on next week? Let's get you out here and give you a tour of the city, get your people with our people, make a thing of it. Hold on a sec. . . . We can get you a flight out . . . umm . . . Saturday. Saturday good?"

"Saturday is great."

"Great! I'll get you some more info soon. What's your agent's name?"

"Agent?"

"Ha, sorry, forgot you're a newbie. We'll have someone email you the tickets. Listen, I got to go, but we'll chat more when you're here, okay? Later."

Click.

* * *

That conversation with GRAVI-Tina stuck with me all week, through every patrol and every dastardly and diabolical shift at Stereo Hutt. It was easy enough to zone out and daydream at work. I'd expected that when Natalie got back from her vacation I'd get an earful about how she'd found herself, but luckily she didn't seem inclined to drone on that week about how many wokes she'd obtained while away. I should have known her silence meant nothing good, but more on that later, True Believer.

I celebrated the last days of the Donald I'd known. I ate ramen noodles with pugnacity and guzzled Faygo grape soda. I was ready, True Believers—I was ready to be in the house and away from the browning sun. I decided to do some studying during one of my work shifts a few days before my flight. Our usual nonexistent customers allowed me plenty of time to pore over Wikipedia and bone up on my soon-to-be teammates.

GRAVI-Tina was first. I already knew that she was practically a founding member of PantheUS, having been registered for ten years. (The midriff on her costume only had a tenure of one, though.)

She had one of the most astonishing abilities of all: the skill of shifting gravity. Bit of PantheUS trivia for you, True Believer? No one in the American Collective for Resolving Overtly Negative Yowled Misconducts went through half as many wardrobe alterations as GRAVI-Tina over the years. My favorites? Well, version one is up there for no other reason than nostalgia. It was a miniskirt and a long-sleeved purple tunic with arrows stitched on the front. The mask was just a slip of an eye covering, mostly there to contrast with her long, inky hair. When she kept returning from battles with her legs scathed and skinned, though, she requested a change from her stylists. They added skin-tight, flesh-colored protective leggings—but sliced away the shirt around the midsection.

Version three was impressive also. After the Silver Slasher dealt a blow to her abdomen with his Silver Sword that would have been fatal without Patches, they did away with the leggings and skirt entirely. GRAVI-Tina was upgraded to a Kevlar panty guard and combat boots. The idea was, as her stylist put it, to make her more aerodynamic—*maybe less weight will help her get out of those sticky situations.*

I promise we'll move on soon, but the ~~hottest~~ most interesting costume was probably version 4.0. After her waist-length hair was slashed up to her shoulders by The Guillotine in the much-publicized Brooklyn Brawl, a few years prior to my narrow vote into the collective, she requested a mask that would cover her hair. Her stylist then crafted the half-mask with a slit at the top to expose her bun (so as not to insinuate a rebellious shaven head). In addition, her sleeves were removed and electrolysis applied to the hair under her armpits. *Now those dastardly deviants can't snatch at her sleeves*, said her stylist.

Next up: Almighty Asper. What more is there to say about Almighty Asper? After my next espresso, I may be up to going into some of the lesser-known truths, but separating the facts from the fiction can be exhausting. For now, I'll let you stick to the script. From the planet Asspon the Asper was sent, the last son of a planet plagued with holy wars and besieged by a race of monstrous, ferocious beings who with fanatical ideology skipped from planet to planet trying to unify the masses into a "greater society."

The greater society, though, was apparently a myth, and this unification of masses only bred destruction and chaos until the planet collapsed in on itself. The Almighty Asper's father sent his son away to escape this tragedy. When Asper arrived on our planet one summer-kissed July afternoon, he was adopted by Joseph Jack, a humble plumber, and Jill Jack, a steadfast homebody with all the motherly love a village could give rolled up into one woman. Raised on porridge and patriotism, the Almighty Asper would soon discover his true heritage and the myriad of abilities he uses to combat injustice day after day like any good old-fashioned American boy. He would decide that he was sent here to show us that we could succeed—that if we stayed vigilant we could aspire to glory, honor, and expensive tennis shoes.

* * *

The next time I looked up from Wikipedia, there was my manager, fiddling with a battery on the glass counter.

"What's up, boss?" I asked, waiting for a joke or some a comment about how he'd found the search history that proved I spent Monday watching the third season of *Reboot* instead of working.

"Donald. I need you to meet me in the back, man."

"What's wrong?" Part of me seized. Had Allen realized I was The Spark?

"Just meet me in the back room."

I clomped along the mile of black carpet with my head hung low, trying my best to prove to Allen that I was unthreateningly intimidated. The cramped stockroom, also his office, was littered with the dust-speckled boxes of TVs that had never sold, caged cell phones that knew not how to sing, and a tiny computer desk. I smiled at Natalie when I saw her there before noticing that she cradled tissues in one hand while poorly hiding her face with the other. I was about to ask her what was wrong when Allen let me know.

"Here at the Stereo Hutt we maintain a non-hostile work environment, Mr. McDougal. Your coworker has informed me of something. She says you used a word that goes against the peaceful atmosphere we cultivate here. Do you understand?"

I wasn't really listening to Allen. I heard him, but what I was listening to was Natalie: her sobs and sniffles, her misunderstandings and malcontents.

"Um, what did I say?" I asked, because I'd honestly forgotten. Nikolas, PantheUS, and everything else had made me a shitty worker by that point.

"I can't believe you don't *know*!" Natalie said between sniffles.

"There, there," Allen said, mechanically patting her back.

"You said the *N-word*." The last word dripped from her lips and splattered on the floor in front of us. So there we were, Allen's hand on her back, her eyes stabbing into mine.

"Oh, that. Seriously? Um, sorry?"

"You're *sorry*?" She hurled her mucus- and tear-saturated tissues at me. They slapped against my smock before fluffily falling to the ground.

I bit my bottom lip and the pain calmed the laughter I had swelling.

"You know, Donald, I may just be an entitled little white girl from the suburbs, but I don't *like* that word. That word is such a *horrid* thing to say, and you know I can't speak for the Black Spark, but I *can* say he's a hero, and heroes don't deserve to be slandered like that. So—this entitled white girl is going to take a stand, since he can't!"

I felt the bubble swell up through my stomach like a belch, climbing my throat until I couldn't help but let out a chuckle.

"Is this funny to you, Donald?" said Allen. "Because I don't think it's funny at all."

Fucking liar. "No, no, I'm sorry, I really am," I said. "I just don't think the nigga would mind all that much."

These are the Astonishing Tales of the
Pejorative-Passing Spark

"Goddammit, Donald. I've tried to be understanding since you had that—that accident. I've turned a blind eye to a lot of crap from you. All the missed shifts—and don't think I don't know you spend half your time watching TV behind that counter. But this is the last straw, Mr. McDougal. I'm going to have to terminate you."

I let the laughter loose while I took my smock off and tossed it over his office desk.

I'd be lying if I told you it didn't feel bittersweet to get kicked out of the Stereo Hutt. There was a part of me, a strong part, that wanted to show them what they were losing. I wanted to spark in a sudden display of power and show them just how far beneath me they were. I was going to be a superhero, and a high-profile one at that. I was going to be on the television sets we spent all day peddling.

I was kind of an asshole.

These are the Astonishing Tales of Goodbye and Good Luck

"I'm going to New York," I told Kat over the phone. It had only been an hour or so since I'd gotten canned, but I found that standing in downtown Columbus in full costume helped reaffirm that I was headed for more lucrative opportunities. "You know GRAVI-Tina? She's going to show me around. I might join the American Collective for Resolving Overtly Negative Yowled Misconducts! Oh, and I got fired."

"You're going to New York?"

I shrugged as if she was standing there. "Yeah. I mean, it's still early, you know, so nothing set in stone. Can I get some mustard?"

"What?"

"Sorry, talking to someone else," I told her. The hot-dog vendor slid over a few yellow packets.

"New York, *shit*. All the A-listers, right?"

I patted myself down, forgetting my costume had no pockets. Noticing that the hot-dog ninja had taken my lunch back, I set the phone down and flicked my fingers. A few passersby turned to watch the show as wiry streams of electricity pulled in loose change from the sidewalks around me. I scooped the coins up from the ground and dropped them on the vendor's cart. While he gasped I cradled my cell phone between my ear and shoulder again.

"Hello? Donald, are you there?" Kat was saying.

I picked up the foil-wrapped mystery meat and mustard packets. "Yeah, sorry, had to pay the man. Listen, I'll be fine. I'm *made* for this."

"Do you even know anyone in New York?"

"I know Thandie D. Nettle," I said.

Kat groaned with all the might of a collapsing star. "Very funny, Donald."

"I thought you'd like that. No, but GRAVI-Tina and the rest will put me up, I'm sure. It'll be awesome. I thought you'd be happy for me, Kat—I'm going to be a real hero."

"I thought you already were, Donald."

I didn't have an answer for that.

"Hey, look," Kat said. "I've got to go. I'm at work. I'll talk to you later, okay?"

"Yeah, sure," I said. "Whatever."

First Paul, now Kat. Haters gon' hate, I thought before wolfing down the hot dog and continuing my patrol.

Patrol, True Believer, consisted of walking up and down Broad Street and then High Street, not-so-accidentally skipping over anything near Martin Luther King Boulevard. It was one part fear of bullets and two parts aversion to visceral belonging.

* * *

It seemed the Collective was serious about me, because after I'd worked out a few details with GRAVI-Tina over the phone, I had plane tickets and a fat little "travel stipend." I set aside some of it to pay Kat for updates to my costume. She worked fast, adding not only pockets but hooks to hold my collection of rods and disks. Some of the money was spent terminating the contract on my storage unit of solitude, and then I used the last of my savings to buy my way out of my lease. I also shoved a sizeable donation under Splam's door with a note that simply said *Stop doing bad things*.

Sitting in a nearly empty living room, siphoning electricity from the neighbors to illuminate my gutted apartment, I thought I'd wrapped everything up, but as if on cue the slap I knew all too well sounded at my door.

"Hey," Paul said from outside.

I opened the door after waiting a few moments longer than necessary. He was wearing his old Browns coat and holding a to-go cup of coffee. I was still in costume from an earlier patrol; Paul flinched at the sight of it.

"Um, hey man, come on in," I said.

"Sure, but is Donald going to be back soon, Mr. Spark?" he said with a worn-out smile.

"Get in here."

I moved out the way. He walked past me, almost tripping over the long boxes of comic books before plopping down on the carpet where my futon used to be. I sat next to him. He nodded at the open apartment door and I stretched a hand out, connecting with more electricity than needed to the metal knob, slamming the door shut. Paul whistled his *damn, nigga!* noise.

"The Force is strong in you, young Spock."

I laughed. "I think you mean—"

"Yeah, yeah. I was doing a bit."

He pushed the coffee towards me: a peace offering. I looked at him with all the thunder I could muster.

When Paul and I fell out, it could last anywhere from a couple of days to a couple of weeks, but it always ended the same. Spoils of the infamous Prom Date Dilemma of 2003: two cups of coffee and an "I'm sorry, man, I didn't realize she was your date." Spoils of the "So what if there was pork in that, I don't see the big deal" fiasco of 2006: one cup of coffee. Spoils of the cataclysmic "No, man, it goes 'Up jumps the boogie, boogie jumps to UP'" debate of 2004: two cups of coffee and deduction of 73 Black points from Paul James Hughes.

"So, what's up?" I said curtly, staring at the spot where the TV used to be.

"Same ol' shit. We've got some fresh blood in the office. Some big news, too—we're going to get more circulation."

"That sounds good, man. I'm glad your baby is growing up."

"*Our* baby. You were there too, bruh. It's not much, but the folks in New York mentioned they'd really like me to throw someone their way, so pressure is on there. Wish I could find someone I trust to send out there." He gave me a meaningful look.

"So, you talked to Kat, then? About New York?"

"I'm proud of you, Donald. You're really sticking with this thing, aren't you?"

I broke my gaze from the white wall. Paul's eyes were twisted balls of famine and the lies our fathers told us.

"I don't know what to say," I told him. "You know I was always a shit writer."

"Listen, it doesn't have to be permanent. Just to keep you grounded until you get back to Ohio."

"What if I'm done with Ohio?"

"What do you mean?"

"I mean that's the life, broheem. You get powers, you get registered, you get endorsed, you get an agent, and you get paid. The A-listers never stick to the small game. How much can I make as a writer? Fifteen, maybe twenty-five thousand a year? If I want to make this thing worth it I've got to start thinking of the big picture."

"Last time we talked, you told me that wasn't what this was about. You said you were going to be a hero."

"I am. I mean, I *will* be, but heroes don't stay here, man. They go where the fight is."

"Jesus, Donald, I know you don't believe that shit. The fight's everywhere, but not the money. This is about what it's always about with you. *You.*"

"First you don't want me to be a hero, and then you're proud I'm going to be a hero, and then you're jumping down my throat because I'm not joining what, the Urban League? Is it always about race with you, man?" I laughed.

"I'm not talking about *our* community, Don, I'm talking about *the* community. These guys are going to use you. They'll fill your bones with dust and pennies. You'll be adored, you'll be fucking prime time, and you'll be theirs. It's how insta-fame always goes."

It occurred to me that Paul and Nikolas would get along. "Listen, I don't want to get into another thing right now, okay? Can we just sit here and not-watch TV and—and just fucking chill?"

So we sat there and did what old friends do: talk about the past, mostly about the Winnie Coopers and Whitley Gilberts of the past. I was flying out the next day.

These are the Tales of I'm Gonna Make It after All

Thanks to Nikolas, after the flight attendant called for everyone to turn off their cell phones for the seventh time, I remembered to switch off the spark. The rest of the flight went smoothly enough, despite my mind-numbing fear of losing control, sparking up, and crashing the plane. Eventually the little airplane bottles of alcohol brought me sleep, solace, and bittersweet dreams of things I'd rather not remember. Things like my Pops.

Maybe it was because Nikolas was right, and everything connects—things like me to New York, and New York to my Pops, because he'd grown up there before he found himself stuck with a baby in Ohio.

Maybe, though, just maybe, I'm really reaching to segue into a chapter where I can bitch about my daddy issues, under the cheap cover of a dream I never had.

CHAPTER 11
AS YOU'RE SO BEAUTIFUL IN BLACK

"**D**ONALD."

"Kat, this is gonna work, trust me."

"This is easily the worst idea you've ever had."

"You're a chicken."

"You're a doo-doo head."

Kat and I sat cross-legged at the top of the hill that overlooked our apartment complex. We'd strapped mounds of duct tape around the center of the skateboard to ensure the Roman candles wouldn't spurt off everywhere when I eventually sparked them up. I was ten years old; the top of that hill may as well have been the throne of gods. We owned the world.

Kat smoothed back her long, blond hair and tucked it behind her ears, while other loose strands popped out around her head like a ball of twine. She crouched down to inspect the skateboard and groaned, but I knew she was excited as I was.

This was the product of Looney Toons overdoses, of parents erroneously worrying more about their children hearing someone drop the F-bomb than about hours upon hours of a cartoon coyote using explosives on a road runner. Fireworks and other playthings of destruction weren't too hard to come by on the elementary-school black market. It had cost us seventy packs of Gushers, fifteen bucks, and a Star Crunch cookie, but as I strapped the fun-time explosives to the wooden board I was convinced it'd been a steal. Even if only for a moment, we had a chance to do something original, something astonishing. Those are the days they can't take away from me, from us.

These are the Astonishing Tales of Rocket
Skateboards and Gravity Showing No Mercy

I stood up when we were done, and Kat followed. She pulled a lighter from her cropped jean shorts and flicked at it. I stared at the tiny flame, not knowing how well it burned.

"Are you sure you want to do this? It's pretty steep."

I winked. Those were the days when I thought I could win over any girl with my thirty-five-cent smile. I nodded toward the plastic fences at the bottom of the hill around the apartment complex, to remind Kat I planned to turn before crashing. The wind was cold against my nigh-hairless head; I pulled my kufi from my back pocket, stuffing it over my oddly shaped skull.

A helmet would have been a better idea.

I placed the skateboard on the ground. It felt extra heavy, but I reasoned this would give me better momentum on the way down. I balanced myself on the skateboard, nearly sliding away prematurely, but Kat caught at the back of my shirt.

"Remember, as soon as you light it, shove me as hard as you can," I told her.

"I remember." Her voice quivered.

I didn't know then that I should say something to ease her concern. She was always older than her years, while I lived forever in the moment. My stomach bubbled as she bent down to light the fireworks and they began to hiss. She shoved with as much strength as nine-year-old-girl arms could muster.

I blazed down the hill, sparks flaring beneath me. My bare shins felt hot. I still wore a smile, that moronic, galling smile that we all lose on the way down.

The explosions beneath my feet did nothing that the wheels wouldn't have done anyway; the sparks just made things more complicated.

"Zapidy—" I didn't finish. Through the wind billowing past my ears I heard Kat scream my name and realized I was no longer attached to the skateboard. The rocket skateboard, or I guess just a skateboard with a crap-ton of explosives taped to the bottom, had caught on a rock, whistling loudly. The kufi popped off, and for a moment in the sky I was immortal.

Skin tearing over stone: my forearm ripped open, my face ground into the grass. My foot cracking, my teeth crunching.

The first thing I heard came before the first thing I saw. It was Mr. Oldgoer, Kat's father, but he wasn't nearby. The walls of the hospital room muffled his voice. I heard Kat's deep, moaning sobs. Mr. Oldgoer was generally a lukewarm guy who chewed at his thumbnails and stared at people's knees, but that man was gone now. I knew he was gone, because I heard him say one of the most terrifying words in our tiny and recently breakable world. Not *Kat*: *Kathryn*.

Kathryn wasn't the girl who listened to me go on and on about *Wolverine vs. Spiderman* while she made morose gingerbread men in her toy oven. She wasn't the girl who played spy mission with me in our backyard, where we imagined she was the international hired assassin Blood Kurkovia and I was the CIA operative Gerald Vinesnapper, who had a blood vendetta against her for killing my father on one of his many harem-laden expeditions to ensure the Communist threat was never realized.

Kathryn was the girl who got in trouble for skipping a math assignment in order to take part in my Laffy Taffy heist at the corner store. Kathryn was the girl who got grounded for an entire summer when we broke into the closed-down elementary school across the road, because I'd heard from Tommy Jones who heard from Randy Tinkleman who heard from his cousin Fred Decker that it was haunted. She was the girl I didn't know how to save. She was the girl who always failed to save me.

The first thing I felt was a pinching above my left eye, like mosquito bites on sweet and salty skin. I didn't open my eyes; I just imagined that if I did I'd find myself somewhere in the sky, freshly flung from the skateboard and forgetting how to fall. Fingers intertwined with mine over wrinkled hospital sheets. They were thin. The nails would be tinged yellow, from cigarettes not far off from the complexion of the skin. My father's hands were never meant for holding. They were usually content with the business of tying shoelaces and scribbling red pen over ambitious nine-year-olds' essays about the American Revolution.

He was born in Brooklyn, New York, and when he was old enough he'd left to go to college in Columbus, Ohio. His mother, my Nana, told him that the red sun in New York was no good for him and that he could do with fewer distractions. When he reached Ohio, he didn't realize that it'd prove more impossible to escape than any island. He met my mother in exactly the type of place he'd always told me to meet a girl. In a library, in a museum, or during the slow jam of a funk concert. Anywhere their minds were prepped to learn something new. Before they graduated, I was created, due to the unapologetic betrayal of Mr. Trojan and the sounds of the methodical love spell that is Purple Rain. I was born through a willful chaos.

"Donald," said my father's tobacco-shredded voice. His hand tightened over my own, but I still didn't open my eyes. I thought I was under the falling sky of my dreams, but he knew different. He knew I was conscious. "Donald, please, just say something." He was a strong man, True Believer, because he knew when to be weak. "I'm not angry, just wake up, please." He was a strong man, True Believer, because he always believed in the possibility that we can wake up.

"Dad?" I finally managed. "I'm sorry. I'm so sorry."

I let the light of the looming world into my eyes. I turned to him, saw the brown dreadlocks falling across his face, hanging to just above his navel. He got up from the hospital recliner next to my bed and leaned over, kissing my forehead, graciously giving me his tears, the privilege of being present for the third time he'd cried in his entire life, and the last.

I closed my eyes again, fighting my own tears, because the hardest thing to do in this life is give back. He laughed like he'd taught me to do when I was angry: hide behind a smile, and the world won't know it's ever won over you. I knew that he was angry with me, though, because you can't hide anything from someone who's a part of you. Not really, anyway.

I felt the top of my head, happy to find I still had hands, but I frowned when I realized my treasured kufi was gone.

"Where's my hat?" I asked.

My father's cold laughter melted into authenticity. Before I could question him any further, Kat burst through the door, her father hanging behind her, unimpressed with my continued existence. She threw herself over me.

"I hate you," she said, while her weeping and her wobbly arms said the opposite. I started to cry. We shared a moment forged from all the melodramatic scenes of special episodes aimed at our generation.

* * *

Later there'd be a glorious butt whoopin'—and video games after. There was a grounding that included washing each wall of the house with a toothbrush while a Sade tape played on a boom box in the background. There was a fire I'd earned, and a chill I hadn't.

I'd missed an entire week of school. When I returned, I was impressed by the lore everyone had made up in my absence. Apparently I had tried to run away with Kat to Cincinnati. Or I'd blown half my body off and had it replaced with cybernetic enhancements. I let these rumors compound themselves, partially because they were entertaining, but also because I knew the only voices most of them cared to hear were their own.

This wasn't the case with my star bully, Paul Hughes. Paul wasn't always the beacon of Black consciousness that he'd become for the better part of my life. That didn't happen until the teenage years, when he tripped and fell into a box of Dead Prez songs. Before that, he was a plague of such indiscretions as stealing chocolate milk from unsuspecting second graders ("scubs"), gentrifying the east quad of the playground by spitballing the foreign kids, and even inducing the dreaded and torturous "atomic wedgie," the unspoken fear of the entire elementary-school community.

These are the Astonishing Tales of the Serious
Business of Elementary School

I was wearing my kufi—my mother's father's kufi, with its beautiful red-and-blue patterns.

"Kufi? Nigga, that shit's a *goofy*." That barb came during study hall, part of the slow nipping away before the inevitable big bite. The thing is, True Believer, after-school specials, for all the good they did, all the posturing about the world they were preparing us to inherit (or maybe simply to tolerate)—they never told us what to do in the meantime.

These are the Astonishing Tales of
What to Do in the Meantime

My kufi flew off as I lunged at Paul, and the crowd of confused tweens around us hushed. Paul had thirty pounds on me, but I was Donald McDougal; I'd spent the Tuesday prior breaking my first wooden board in karate class, advancing to a yellow belt. I'd ridden rocket skateboards through the sky. I'd once read seventeen *Goosebumps* books in one day. I was not to be fucked with.

Paul wailed while I rained nightmares on his face with fists, nails, spittle, and slaps. Finally I reached back to deliver a dramatic knockout blow, but as I did Paul thrust one of his L.A. Lights into the center of my chest and used those extra thirty pounds to knock me away. It worked, but only for a moment. When he advanced, my fist crashed into his mouth. Blood welled from his lip. Then a giant's hand swept around my torso and I was jerked away from my enemy. It was over.

These are the Astonishing Tales of
Obscenities and Office Chairs

"Mr. McDougal," the principal began.

"Please," said my father. "Malik is fine."

"Of course, Mayleek. Donald is a very special boy—no one is disputing *that*. His teachers are impressed with his scores, and he's a joy to have around . . . for them. That's probably why we've held out on doing anything about this issue until now."

"Issue? I'm sorry, sir, I don't know if I understand what you mean." My father's dreadlocks were tied back, and his horn-rimmed glasses refracted the sunlight. I was surrounded by giants. It's not wise to show weakness in the company of giants, lest they take the opportunity to crush you.

Mr. Graydrake, our principal, wasn't a strict man. He was the kind of principal you could imagine once had dreams of being the cool English teacher who relished calls of O *captain, my captain!* Sadly, he sat instead behind a giant oak desk, playing solitaire or castigating the parents of delinquents-in-training.

"Yes, Merlok, the issue. It's only been five weeks since we last met in here. Jenny Jackson's locker still smells like dead fish."

I laughed, but no one else did. For a moment, I considered reminding Mr. Graydrake that Jenny had called Kat a dyke for wearing boys' polo shirts, but instead I sulked.

"Yes, but—"

"And three weeks before that—"

"I understand. Donald is a rambunctious kid."

"And, lest we forget, the sandpaper-salad incident? Regardless. As exceptional as Donald is, I don't think we can let this last incident slide."

What Mr. Graydrake kept avoiding was the fact that I hadn't *started* any of those things. I never started *anything*. I wasn't a spark yet.

"So what are you saying, Mr. Graydrake?" My father clasped his hands together tighter.

147

"I'm saying that I think we have no choice but to move on to expulsion."

Expulsion. It was the life sentence for children, the word synonymous with a future of loitering on street corners and sipping from paper bags.

My father's expression didn't change. "Mr. Graydrake, I understand how you feel. But this boy, this young man, he hasn't had a lot of opportunities. This school, this expensive school, is one of the only chances a boy like Donald here has to make something of himself. He has friends now, and he's a part of the chess team. I can promise you, Donald will be more disciplined in the future, but to take him out of this excellent school over a childish scuffle when he's finally doing so well seems a bit excessive, don't you think?"

Before Mr. Graydrake could respond my father coughed: a heavy, rattling, hard-luck cough.

"Are you all right?" Mr. Graydrake said, looking alarmed.

My father raised a hand. He was a strong man. "Please, Mr. Graydrake, don't expel my son." He leaned back and adjusted his blazer.

Mr. Graydrake watched my father for a moment and then glanced back at me as if surprised I was still in the room. When he'd stared for too long I smiled awkwardly, and he couldn't help but smile back.

"This is his last chance. Two-week suspension. And I swear, if he causes *any* trouble at all, *anything*, he's out for good. Do you understand?"

"Yes. I promise you, Mr. Graydrake, you won't regret this."

* * *

When we drove home there were no words and no music to fill the silence. My father had set the radio to an empty AM station connected only to static. The white noise was infuriating.

"What did you expect me to do?" I finally burst. "He made fun of my kufi! He's always riding me!"

"Kid, you really don't want to get an attitude with me right now."

"I just meant—you *told* me, Dad, you told me that I should never let anyone walk over me. I didn't start anything! He made fun of my kufi. So I fought back. I always fight back."

"No one's telling you not to stand up for yourself, Donald. You just don't be a dumbass about it in the middle of class. Who did that help? What do you think they see you as now?"

I seethed. I hadn't done anything wrong. It was just another shit day at another shit school. I tightened fists at my side. I had to make him see.

The car jerked so sharply that my head tapped against the passenger side window. He didn't seem to care that I'd just hurled myself from a skateboard a few weeks before, at least not in the moment. The dust kept rising in a cloud even after the car had stopped, even after he'd slammed the door getting out, even after he snatched me out by the forearm.

I was rattled and rage-filled, but only half as much as he was. My father was a strong man.

"You gonna buck at me? Boy, you better get your goddamned mind right." He inched closer to me. He swung backhand, flatly, against my chest.

Thwup thwup.

Two taps were all it took to make me suck my bottom lip tight to my teeth.

"You bad, ain't you? You wanna buck at me? Do something."

Thwup thwup.

"You afraid now? Come on, Donald."

Thwup thwup.

The light backhand hurt no more than if his hand had been a block of Styrofoam. I cried, though, because unlike the lash of belt against bare butt, *this* was personal. There had been an unspoken agreement, somewhere between his old crack pipe and the unsolved case of my missing Super Nintendo. After NA, after rehab, that I could trust him. That he would be astonishing.

"I keep trying to teach you, but you don't want to listen to nobody."

Thwup.

"You think they care if you cry?"

Thwup.

"You think they care if you didn't start it?"

Thwup thwup thwup.

"They care if you *act* like you know better. They care—if they don't kill you first."

* * *

Malik Alexander McDougal knew the dangers of being in the vanguard. When he was a young, tight fade of a boy, he had little choice about finding himself the Junior Ambassador for Black America. Nana threw him into the books, making sure it was always more Du Bois than Woodson, though that's not to say he never had to work. But as he'd explained to me on far more than one occasion, despite the stacks upon stacks of library books, Mathlete missions, and everything else Nana made sure her son was known for, little Malik was always haunted by that incendiary first name.

Nana once told him that had he been born a girl, she'd have

named him Sparrow, or Raven, or anything else that sounded full of sweetness and soared above any need for racial responsibility. As it was, however, Malik was burdened with the name of his grandfather, out of respect for a dude he'd never even met. By extension, he inherited the McDougal mission of surviving proudly in the eye of the storm. Nana kept him primed with first fruits of the tree, with James Baldwin and Assata Shakur, with Haley and Dumas. The warnings, the methods of hiding a hailstorm. Malik McDougal had solid street stone to keep his bones from the hollow. The mirth of maladjusted melanin mood in his mind—and he could have hid it all if it weren't for that goddamned name. *I named you so they'd never see you coming*, he told me once, *because no matter what you do, whatever goodness you can lead them to, it don't mean shit unless they going to listen. Even if you have something? You won't be heard until you have everything.*

After my mother died giving birth to me, no one seemed to listen. HR departments never listened to the resumes he sent, anyway. The pipe listened. It spoke sweet, sticky, and stereotypical seduction in him. It left him hunched, clutching memories of a woman he'd only known long enough to begin loving. It fucked him raw. It told him that if you're lost from everything, you'll never want for anything.

My father was a strong man, because his boy brought him back. I lean more towards the effective rehabilitation services offered freely upon incarceration, but I tended to give him the benefit of the doubt when he told me this.

NA, certification as a drug counselor, and a fuckton of cigarettes later, I'd have him back, at least for a while. I'd also have his mission.

* * *

"Do you understand me?" he asked after the *thwups* turned to tight hands over my shoulders. We turned into the Dynamic Dark Ones once again.

"Yes," I answered between snot bubbles.

"Yes, what?"

"Yes, sir."

That was when Gunther showed up and—nah, I'm just fucking with you. That'd be cool, though, right? If there were a supremely important moment buried here that tied into the great conspiracy of me? If his death, a few years later during a television commercial, a new baby in his veins, blank charcoal eyes staring at me after school, were somehow the source of it all.

If all his compromises and contradictions had gotten him something, I might not have had to pick up those stones and carry that weight.

Don't leave, though, okay? There are some pretty gnarly fights coming up. Oh! And sex, and *boobies*, and someone even blows up! Like, *smaboosh*! Not a metaphor. There's anything and everything you could ever hope for, True Believer, as long as you keep listening. Please?

CHAPTER 12
THE LEAGUE OF EXTRAORDINARY GENTRY MEN

"SO HOW DOES IT FEEL?" Afrolicious Samson asked, arranging his casted arm on the arm of the couch across from me.

I was sitting in the common room, eating a bowl of Fruity Flakes and admiring framed photos of the changing team roster through the years. The only constant was Asper. Year to year, picture to picture, he stood with hands at his sides and a cheese-filled grin, always in the center of the team. I'd been avoiding Afrolicious as much as possible, but stuck in that room with dribbles of cereal milk spilling down my chin, in my PantheUS T-shirt and *Dragon Ball Z* pajama bottoms, I knew escape wasn't an option.

"Sorry?" I said, but we both knew I'd heard him. Sitting here talking with you now, True Believer? I wish I'd just listened to him.

"You heard me. How does it feel to be *in their house*, nigga?" At least he gave me the courtesy of dropping the hard R.

"I don't know what you're—what?"

"Live it up, sellout. It's all downhill from here."

We should take a step back, True Believer.

* * *

After the flight, I didn't collect $200. Instead I caught an Uber to the Llama Tower. I had some homework to read on the way: *The Moral Indignation Cues Code*. It was a hefty tome, 713 pages. Any PantheUS member was expected to have read it from front to back. Not that there was an exam or placement test. If you were *Talented*, you just had to sign a slip of paper saying you agreed to abide by the code. Kind of like those End User Licensing Agreements you click through after your software updates. *Agree, agree, agree—just let me play with my goddamn toy!*

Still, as my daddy only raised a daylight fool, I knew what to be in the darkness. When I was a child, he'd started by feeding me comics, where, although he didn't quite realize I was simultaneously being inducted into a future of wedgies and blerd burdens, my reading speed was augmented thanks to Walter Dean Meyers and Alan Moore, Stan Lee and George Schuyler. The faster I could assimilate the walls of text, the sooner I'd be immersed in my own kind of crack. His kind, the one that ran through his veins, couldn't touch the fiery mayhem of a kid's brain craving swamps and snoot punches. Speed-reading became second nature as I mangled the blocks of text into photographs in my mind.

During the ride from the airport, my driver would every so often glance back at me, immersed in the reading. Like most, he probably assumed I was simply skimming, my Mandingo mind buckling under the letters, skipping through to keep it from exploding. By the time we arrived I'd nearly finished the whole document.

To survive, True Believer, you keep your head low enough to not have it lopped off, until you learn how to make your neck steel. You *zapidy-do* and do nothing that allows you to be seen for anything.

Not in the daylight, at least. More importantly, you learn the rules, insane or inane as they may be, because more than likely you'll need to know how to defend yourself against them at some point.

Some of the more noteworthy entries are seared into my brain, such as:

"In every instance good shall triumph over evil and the criminal [shall be] punished for his misdeeds." *Ain't no rest for the wicked—or for the heroes, either. We can't lose, ever, or goodbye million-dollar contracts.*

"Excessive violence shall be prohibited. Brutal torture, excessive and unnecessary knife and gun play, physical agony, gory and gruesome crime shall be eliminated." *I suppose* excessive *and* unnecessary *are relative. Then again, DEATHRAGE's bullets are only rubber.*

"All lurid, unsavory, gruesome creatures shall be eliminated." *No monsters allowed. Well, that's not so bad. But again, relative.*

"Profanity, obscenity, smut, vulgarity, or words or symbols which have acquired undesirable meanings are forbidden." *Well, shit.*

"Nudity in any form is prohibited, as is indecent or undue exposure." *GRAVI-Tina: the oft-noted exception that eventually became the rule, thanks to the Act for Aerodynamic Superheroine Attire.*

"Females shall operate realistically without exaggeration of any physical qualities." *Unless, you know, they're hot.*

Entering the Llama Tower (named in honor of contributions from a certain tobacco company), I didn't find Hogwarts or the Hall of Justice, just lots of marble tile and gray pillars, the walls bleeding with generic abstract art. It was magnificent in its own way, like a fancy hotel, and while I don't mean to shit on the beautiful landscape—seriously? We were goddamned superheroes. There should have been holographic displays of—well, I don't know exactly, but there should have been stylish entry ports for the flying types, a

155

secret decoder ring that turned you into a rock monster, a mother-fucking tunnel that burrowed underground to a lair of mystifying electronics and the spectacle of the great beyond.

No. There was just the keycard Patches slid me, the nod to security at the desk, and the ever-present mob of office workers just trying to get home for the night. At least Patches spared me the full tour. The Llama Tower scraped the skies and practically paid for itself. The first twenty floors were offices. Above that, there was some residential leasing, where it wasn't uncommon for wealthy New Yorkers to drop my yearly salary for their young scions to live in style. I feel that if I don't use this chance to tell you about the time I got high with Lil' Bruce in his suite down on the twenty-fifth floor, I'll never find a good place to shoehorn it in.

Riding the elevator when you're 168 pounds of pulsating electricity is never calming. When the doors finally opened after 300 or so seconds of horror-movie slow motion, there I was—the newest nigga in the hero suites. And there was the man himself—Gunther Grey.

"Good to finally meet you boy, face to face that is," he said as he shook my hand.

"Yeah, I mean, wow, I'm *here*, I'm with *the* American Collective for Resolving Overtly Negative Yowled Misconducts. Kinda don't know how to digest this, if I'm being honest." I glanced at GRAVI-Tina, who met my eyes with a gaze that was almost a glare. I looked away.

"Well, I'm glad to hear you're so excited," said Gunther. "It's a shame what happened to our man Afrolicious—Jamal—a real god-damned shame. He was one hell of a hero, and I'm sad to see him on his way out. Truth is, though, new blood is always good, shakes things up a bit. Whoever the people go with, you're in for one hell of a ride." He finally released my hand. "Tonight we're having a little get together for the candidates—the *real* candidates. I'm pulling for you, my boy. Can't say I'm playing favorites, of course, but if I were? Well, let's just say I always bet on black." He winked.

I winked back, because, yeah, a little on the nose with that one, but the guy had given me thousands of dollars just to get inside his house, so as far as I could see, he'd earned one ignorant comment, or like a hundred if he wanted.

After the elevator doors closed behind him, I was left with GRAVI-Tina and DEATHRAGE. They were both still stewing in whatever I'd missed happening between them, but since I was a new focal point—oh! since I was a new lightning rod! (heh)—for their lacerating looks, I thought for a moment that this was going the same way as it had with Nikolas's lost boys and girl.

Finally GRAVI-Tina smiled, shaking her head, and extended a hand to me. "I'm sorry, bad timing—that happens a lot around here. We spoke on the phone. I'm GRAVI-Tina, or Maria if you'd prefer."

I shook her hand and turned to DEATHRAGE to do the same, but he only grunted. GRAVI-Tina rolled her eyes.

"Can you be a fucking adult for once, Bobby?"

He left the room without a word. I would have taken it as a slight, but I knew enough to understand that it wasn't about me. DEATHRAGE had to protect his brand as a desperate loner. DEATHRAGE, or Bobby Truthmeadow, was but a boy when he first encountered the grim reality of death. His parents were titans of the cable-TV industry. Paul J. Matthew Truthmeadow and his wife, Miss Iah Martor Truthmeadow, decided to take their young child to a showing of a new Antonio Banderas movie, one that had such a plethora of bad reviews it could only be shown at the Republic Theater on Youwillsurelydie Alley in the wrong part of town. And the rest is history.

"Well, guess I'm showing you around," said GRAVI-Tina—Maria. She started toward the elevator. "You coming?"

While she showed me how to navigate the city-state of a building, I stumbled around my own mind trying not to say anything idiotic. Of course that meant everything I could think of to say was idiotic, so I didn't say much. She seemed okay with that, though, and told me a bit about herself instead. I already knew most of it from my online research, of course, but some things need to be heard more than read. For instance, I knew she'd been a police officer before becoming a superhero, but not about the dinner she and her husband had on top of the Llama Tower to celebrate, or about the time she was out of costume and forgot her key card, and they detained her in the security office and questioned her for hours. Finally I felt comfortable enough to ask one of my idiotic questions: why the name *GRAVI-Tina*? She said that her agent, Christopher Row, had thought it rolled off the tongue better than GRAVI-Maria, which I couldn't disagree with.

She told me that the feeling of being new and not up to snuff never had left her in all her time with the group, so she had a soft spot for the rookies. She was full of helpful tips, such as: housing in the hero suites wasn't free for talented hopefuls. If I wanted to be smart about my pennies, I should get an apartment in one of the outer boroughs. She warned me about teammates' sore spots: never mention knives or parents in front of DEATHRAGE, or religion in front of Patches, and generally don't try to engage in intellectual discussion of any kind with Asper.

* * *

"So you're enjoying yourself, then?" said Kat, interrupting my uncontrollable ranting.

"You have no idea! It's like the world is, I don't know, not crappy? They gave me *more* money, and granted, I won't have as much fun with it as the hospital will, but I'm finally getting out of the hole."

"So have you figured out where you're staying yet? Have you tried reaching out to Paul's friend for something a little more realistic?"

"Well, no, not yet, but did you hear me? Money. Like, lots of the monies."

She only sighed, and I knew exactly what her face looked like on the other end. "Don't get me wrong, that's awesome, dude—just be careful, okay?"

* * *

When the time came to meet my competition, the *other* wannabes, I waited alone, switching on and off like Nikolas had taught me, unsure how much display of talent was necessary for a meet and greet. I'd been the first one to show up—just a thing you do when everyone expects you to be late everywhere, a way to let them know that you're different, that you're not one of *those people*. I'd decided against dry-cleaning my costume. I did, however, tie my hair back and latch-hook it several times more than I needed to.

Gradually the others started arriving. They didn't seem to be anything *that* special: I was one of the few, the proud, the nonthreatening and novel. And I felt about as social as I had during any of the exactly six house parties I'd let Paul drag me to, back when our friendship had first migrated from bully to buddy territory.

"Hey, you're The Black Spark, right? I'm Kendra—or in these circles, you can call me Doll."

I'd jumped when Kendra Kanaway, The China Doll, tapped my shoulder to introduce herself. I'd expected her, like the rest of us, to arrive decked out in her most polished costume. Instead she wore a suit, like she was going to a job interview.

"I'm Donald McDougal, the, um, The Spark," I said. Doll was the only competition I was worried about, and it didn't help that she was so goddamned personable.

She was classified as non-Talented, like DEATHRAGE. I knew not to count her out, though. If anything, she had a leg up in the running. Everyone admired the underdog, the humdrum human who proves that any of us can be exceptional. And *non-Talented* didn't mean talentless. Kendra Kanaway was gifted in the field of robotics, having finished graduate school by the time she was seventeen and then started her own company, Optic Transience. She'd expanded her studies to biology after her son was diagnosed with cancer, which would lead to one of the greatest scientific breakthroughs in history. She built her son a new life: the Jason Doll–1, an exo-suit that integrated with organics to prevent cellular decomposition.

Kendra was hailed as a visionary. She'd found a way to cheat death, or stay it for an indefinite amount of time. The problem, however, was the cost. Her company's stock had plummeted as she poured resources into the development of a single suit for a single person. Undaunted, she went on to create the Doll-2, which she operated herself, achieving astonishing feats of heroism. Publicity stunt? Maybe. But the stock was climbing again.

Fun fact: She also suffers from anosmia, which is an inability to smell.

There were a few other hopefuls present, but honestly, they were probably only as interesting as I am. The Anvil was stuffing his face at the buffet. He was, like, a human anvil, so that's cool. The Depression, almost as mysterious as White Flame, stood in a darkened corner of the room, face hidden behind a thick black mask; being around him for a prolonged period left one feeling profoundly shallow, which was all I cared to know about him. He was rather bleak.

"Black Spark? Is that you?" It was the Almighty Asper. He patted my shoulder and I fell over; China Doll reached down to help me to my feet.

"Sorry about that, friend. It's nice to see you here. GRAVI-Tina told me you were on the potential roster. It's high time we get some fresh moxie and diversity on this team! Are you enjoying New York?"

"Well—"

"Of course you are—it's the best place in the world! Anyone who says different, they're just jiving some silly jive, right, brother? I have to make the rounds, but we'll do something while you're in town. Maybe find ourselves back to back, shoulder to shoulder. You know—hero stuff!" He floated away to the buffet table.

I turned to China Doll after Asper was out of view and smirked. She got it, and we connected.

Our moment was stolen, though. A heavy crash at the other side of the room drew everyone's attention. When I finally got a clear view, I saw Patches, the boy Band-Aid, laughing on the ground beside a not-so-entertained server. He was helping her, or at least thought he was, to pick up the glasses that had shattered when he knocked her over. When he noticed the rest of us staring he took a bow. He'd crossed that line where drunk, high, and dying all look pretty much the same, so no one tried to guess which one it was.

"Meet Patches," Kendra said with a sigh that, to her credit, was a lot less judgmental than I was feeling.

"He's like twelve or something, right? He's like a toddler, and he's fucking drunk at a PantheUS event?" I whispered.

"Eh, I'm pretty sure he's seventeen. Still not exactly legal, but . . . do *you* want to be the one to tell Gunther Grey's grandson—the only person in the world with that kind of healing power—that he can't get shitfaced if he wants to?"

In the meantime Patches had somehow acquired a pair of champagne bottles.

As the night went on and the booze started working its magic I grew less apprehensive about schmoozing. These people were the ones who mattered, who would make me what I deserved to be: a legend amongst mortal men, a hero of Hall H at Comic-Con. They would put me on T-shirts, toys, and taffy paper. Talk long enough with a tequila tongue and someone is sure to start listening, I've realized over the years, and that's how I met Christopher Row. Row was one of the normals floating about. His skin was thick and black and his smiles were twisted and bright between crimson lips. He approached me when I was sipping on my seventh cup of confidence and put a hand to my back, the only time I'd ever feel he really stood behind me during our partnership. When I turned, he adjusted the blond wig atop his head.

"Donald McDougal, The Black Spark, I presume?"

"Um, yes, I'm The Spark," I corrected him, because for the moment he was nothing to me, just another guy trying to hide inside the house. We were two spooks haunting about who'd bumped into each other casually, and we respected the unspoken rule of not calling attention to one another.

"I'm Christopher Row, and I represent heroes. Donny? I've got to be honest, I've been watching you all night, and you know what I see?"

"No, what?"

"I see a dumb kid who doesn't know what the hell he's doing."

And I see you leaning in a little too close to a guy who could electrocute your ass.

"What I also see is a hell of a lot of potential. I see a kid who speaks well, has a charming enough face, and *needs* this. Tell me, Donny, do you think any of these white men here know how to pitch *you*—how to really pitch a Black boy from Ohio—to the masses and get him voted into the American Collective for Resolving Overtly Negative Yowled Misconducts?"

"You're not the subtlest nigga, are you?" I laughed, more than a little drunk.

"Well, I like to shoot straight with my clients, especially the ones vying for a position in this house, of all places. So far, with GRAVI-Tina and Afrolicious—I'm two for two, you understand?"

I did understand. "Is this you buttering me up? Aren't you supposed to be assuring me I'd be your number-one guy or something?" I laughed again, because I had power over him that I was only just learning how to use.

"You watch too many movies. Who do you think you are, hmm? Look at your competition over there. See how they've each got five or six jackasses yucking it up with 'em? You've got just the one. Way I see it, I don't have to prove a thing to you—I'm just trying to help you out." Beads of sweat slid down his face from beneath the blond wig.

"Well, you don't have to be an asshole about it."

"I'm just saying we gotta stick together, my brother," he said. "I can promise you one thing, Mr. McDougal: I won't bullshit you, not now, not ever. If you trust me, I can get your nincompoop ass in front of America, make you the first thing they think of at the polls. No one else is gonna do it, but I will, and I'll make you look good while I'm at it."

I turned back to the rest of the room, watching it spin, realizing how right he was. Much as I hated his approach, I couldn't deny that I *needed* someone like him, and I needed him to let everyone else know just how much they needed me.

So it happened just like that: one bad whiskey, one sour conversation, and I had an agent. Christopher Row had his flaws, but for all the shit advice he'd give me during our prolonged team-up, I never felt he was doing anything that he thought was wrong. I don't know if that makes it any more acceptable, but I do think he tried his best.

* * *

"Today is a day filled with both mirth and marvel. Longtime national hero Afrolicious Samson is relieving himself of duty on the American Collective for Resolving Overtly Negative Yowled Misconducts."

A thunder of cheers and boos. My muscles contracted and released furiously, but—ever in control—Gunther raised a hand and the voices quieted.

"This is a tragic day," he went on. "Afrolicious is one of the finest heroes ever to serve on our roster. But due to his recent injury, and after consulting with his spiritual adviser, Afrolicious has decided it's time to step aside and open the door for a new talent: a new, powerful crusader to take up the mantle of responsibility alongside the other fine members of *your* American Collective for Resolving Overtly Negative Yowled Misconducts!"

Applause.

"We, your watchful warriors: an array of powerful, diverse, intelligent, and empathetic servants of the people. Every day, new heroes rise among us. Ladies and gentlemen, allow me to introduce to you your candidates!"

More applause. Just as rehearsed, Gunther stepped aside as we lined up, one by one, to be weighed and measured at the mic. Christopher had somehow secured the first spot for me. He said it was important to be the first one on their minds, to wow and dazzle and shine.

"My name is The Spark," I said, trying not to look like I was staring at the teleprompter. "I am honored to be amongst you all today. To be standing here, on the same steps where such legendary heroes as the Almighty Asper, GRAVI-Tina, and Afrolicious Samson have stood, is overwhelming. As a patriot wiser than I once said, 'Heroism is endurance for one moment more,' and I believe that. I believe you have struggled, endured, and hoped for so long that we, with our marvelous, astonishing talents, aren't the real heroes here. You are. You, who have braved the fury of White Flame. You, who have longed for the day when, whether you wake beneath blue skies or sleep under white stars, you will be safe.

"I want to be the one you trust to protect you. I want to be *your* Spark. I can't promise I can singlehandedly put an end all those things that haunt and prey upon us, but I will make a start, if you give me the opportunity to serve PantheUS as part of the greatest team of soldiers our nation possesses."

It was probably the best speech Christopher would ever write for me. He was one for big words and empty ideas, but then again, so was everyone in those days, so it worked well enough. Things after that happened faster than I was ready for. My face was symmetrical enough to please the public eye, and my paper-bag pigmentation didn't hurt, either, as Christopher would point out. The key to getting into *the* superhero association, instead of ending up as some no-name street patroller, was elegance, poise, and knowing how to get people talking.

What the key wasn't, however? Continue to page self-sabotage to find out, True Believer.

CHAPTER 13
DANGERS

I **UNLOCKED MY PHONE AND** scrolled down through my texts, past all the unopened ones from Kathryn Oldgoer and Paul Hughes, to make sure I had the right time.

Sunday, 3:15 p.m.

It was only 3:05. But as I stood in front of the abandoned building on North Brother Island and 3:05 turned to 3:30, then 3:30 to 4:00, I remained alone. New Jersey, I'd been told, was to New Yorkers as Groveport is to Columbus types such as myself: a mystery wrapped in an enigma wrapped in get me the fuck out of here. I wondered if I had fucked up the address, but I checked my navigator one more time and found nothing amiss. Finally I decided to take a spin around the building to make sure I hadn't ended up on the wrong end.

These are the Astonishing Tales of You
Probably Know What's Coming Next

When I returned Patches was standing where I'd been waiting. Unlike me, he was dressed lazily, in a pair of slacks and a T-shirt featuring none other than Asper, on the back of an elephant, giving two thumbs up.

"Hey! What's up, man? How was your—"

"You're late, Donald."

"What? No, I've been here since—"

"Listen, man, I know it's a pain, but you really need to try and get here on time."

Patches pulled out an ID and slipped it through a card reader. As he did so Almighty Asper came whooshing past us, and I felt relieved that I wasn't the only asshole dressed in my costume.

I still wasn't used to being around something so almighty. When he crashed into the ground a few feet from us I nearly toppled over, but I found my footing and smiled.

"Yo, man!" I said. Ugh. *Yo, man?* You know what, let's just say that I said *hello.* Yeah, I really need to start utilizing the beauty of retconning. It's probably the only perk of writing in the past tense.

"Yo, yourself, Astonishing Black Spark!"

"Donald is fine, Asper. Or Spark. Whichever."

"Okie dokie, Black. So why haven't we started yet?"

"Donald here was late," said Patches.

"No, I really wasn't! I—"

"It's fine, Black! I mean, you should probably work on that in the future, but we can forgive you, all things considered."

I nodded, feeling like I was falling over myself at Paul's New Year's bash again. Like I was building a fire within, but I could save it for another time. I tried to shrug it off as I followed the two of them inside.

It looked a bit like a fitness center had vomited itself into an oversized Apple store. There was so much white that I was overtaken by a fear of touching anything or even breathing. So clean, so orderly, so expensive. No cool shooty-laser thingies, but the disappointment soon faded. Off in a corner of the room a woman did pushups. Her hair was tied back in a ponytail; everything else about her was a mystery beneath a black hoodie and jeans.

"Maria?" I called. Startled, she stopped her circuit, toppling over onto her side. An expletive from her; a snicker from Patches; and for me, a foreboding dread of what was to come.

"Nice," said Patches.

I suppressed an urge to send a few sparks his way. Seeing GRAVI-Tina without her costume was jarring. I took in her face, sweat-streaked and perfect. My eyes felt confused not having to fight her costume's demand that I stare at the center of her chest. She looked so . . . civilian. I noticed for the first time, as she made her way over to us, that she was shorter than me.

"Something wrong?" she said.

These are the Astonishing Tales of Objects in the Mirror

"No! It's just—are you shorter without your costume?"

Patches chuckled while Maria scratched the back of her head beneath the hanging ponytail.

"Oh. I guess so? It's a gravity thing. So what do you think, Don?" She gestured around the room.

"It's really something. What now? Do we like—fight robots or something?"

"Robots?"

"Yeah, like robots or laser beams or—you know, nonlethal stuffs?"

"None of that sounds nonlethal."

"Um—"

"We're the only challenge we need. We have a physical god, an electricity manipulator, a woman who can change gravity."

"Well, fuck you too, Martinez," Patches huffed.

"Sweetie, maybe when you graduate from juice boxes," Maria said.

The clunking sound of metal brought our attention back to the door, where DEATHRAGE entered with a grunt. You know, he kind of did everything with a grunt, so just keep that in mind. It'll save me some time, which I think is important, as our favorite barista Tad just snapped a pic of me.

These are the Astonishing Tales of Instagram,
Hashtags, and Other Things of Which Less Is More

"So what do we do? Start hitting each other?" I asked.

"It's a little more complex than that, but yeah, we kind of just start hitting each other."

A block of steel collided with my left cheek. Asper's fist.

Luckily, I contracted my muscles in time to lessen the blow, but I still cracked against the wall with a *thunk*. This was insane: I wasn't ready; I didn't know if I would ever be. I rolled over, feeling woozy. So, yeah, thirty seconds into my first training-room montage and I'm already floored. The thing is, it's important to have a wake-up call, and this should have been it. This should have been that moment I could look back on and say, "So then I left, and moved back to Ohio—I ain't about that life."

I was back on my feet soon enough, sparking it up, magnetizing the flat metal weights and shucking them as fast as I could toward Asper, who was distracted by DEATHRAGE now. I didn't expect the weights to do much, but a violet shimmer enveloped them in mid-flight and I realized I'd just set up Maria for a hell of a lay-up. She adjusted gravity enough for them to topple Asper. He slid across the white walls like a caped housefly before hitting the ground.

He floated back to his feet.

His eyes began to glow.

I rushed back to the rest of them. While DEATHRAGE was watching our invincible man, I cheaply clasped my hands together and slammed them against his snoot. He fell, the spoils of his penchant for being the last in and the first out. I knew that if I needed to I could destroy them all—I knew that, if necessary, nothing would survive what I had to give—but seldom, if ever, does life call for such force. Today, I only had to be the best in the room.

I sparked up and dove for Asper. The thing about these almighty types is that they're lazy. Like a band making a sophomore album, they forget what being hungry is. He saw me coming the entire time and kept his arms folded: a floating slab of steel doesn't really have much to fear from a hurtling egg. He extended a fist and my face molded over it like brown jelly.

These are the Tales of Astonishing Let-Downs

I probably set that last part up a little deceivingly, like I was going to do something more than shatter most of my face. I didn't stay conscious for long. I don't know if I count this as a death, exactly, but Patches had to scuttle over to spend his daily Phoenix Down.

"You good?" I heard him say.

I dramatically cracked my eyes open to see the team huddled around me, staring down. I touched my face. Everything was in order, save for the blood of my old face spattered about us. When Asper reached a hand down I flinched, then realized it was to help me up and took it. On the ground nearby lay a few shattered teeth and something white and puffy, like an egg over easy.

"Is that—my eye?"

"No, your eye is in your head. That's not really yours anymore. Or those teeth. Or that skull fragment," Patches explained.

I fought back a tickle of vomit.

"Sorry, Black, sometimes I just get a little excited," said Asper.

Whoopsie daisy!

Asper turned and headed for the door.

"Where the hell are you going?" GRAVI-Tina called.

"Look, you're all severely outclassed here. Adam has used his only heal for the day. If we go on much longer, I'm likely to hurt one of you. I know the contract stipulates that we have to engage in these barbaric rituals. But I've done my part, I've trained." He wasn't being cruel, even though when he said *trained* there were heavy air quotes. He was just being what he considered honest.

GRAVI-Tina's brow wrinkled. "You're staying. You're not above getting an ass whooping from White Flame, are you? No. We're a team, we're partners."

"I will hurt you, and you will gain nothing."

"So, show us you have control. Better yet, if I lose, I'll hop on Hound News tonight and praise the merits of harsher border patrol." While it seemed a random boon to offer, I saw between the two of them the familiar look of an old argument.

Asper's face contorted through a cycle of emotions. "And if I lose?"

GRAVI-Tina shrugged.

My throat tightened, a spark coiling the muscles around my neck. If she was hurt, there'd be no reset button. I'd be responsible. My mind filled with the image of Afrolicious scowling at me. I swam through memories of Aedan. I stepped up beside her.

"Here to save me, masked man?" she said playfully.

Not having the right answer, I let my face melt into heroic calm, doing my best to mimic a Spike Lee–directed Denzel Washington.

Asper was feet away from us. I started to raise a hand, but before I could do anything his was over mine, squeezing. He could have shattered it, crushed it to dust, but he didn't—he only spun me like a carnival ride before tossing me across the room. I'd landed on the flat of my stomach before I knew it, head pressed to the foam floor, hair stretched out like a well-worn mop. I waited for the *thunk* of Maria's body on the ground as well, but there was nothing for a while, and then laughter.

When I looked up she was floating inches from the ground with a shining violet aura surrounding her. Her palm was raised over a struggling Asper. He wriggled under her control.

"She's incredible," I whispered.

Blood rushed into Asper's face as he kept trying to force himself out of whatever hold she had him in. Veins I didn't know existed seemed to be wrenching through the steel skin. It was the most hilarious thing I'd seen in a good long while.

* * *

You know, there were a lot of rumors back then about GRAVI-Tina and me. Hell if I know where they started, but I had a guess. People thought minorities inherently belonged together. Storm always fell head over heels for Forge, or Black Panther, or anyone Marvel could drum up to satisfy the yen for melanin mingling. I could be completely off base. Maybe it's that we both were twenty-somethings. Maybe it's that we had the same agent and ended up at similar events, promotions, etc. Maybe it's because I honestly did like her, which automatically meant the most she could ever be in my life was a romantic interest, even though she's married. All that aside, though, if there's any truth to the pages and pages of GRAVI-Tina/Spark fiction online (shoutout to all those #GravitySparks fans on Twitter), it was in that moment, as I watched her spin our de facto leader up and down with a Cheshire-cat grin.

Without GRAVI-Tina, the American Collective for Resolving Overtly Negative Yowled Misconducts would have probably disbanded before I even got there. When she was still in the closet as an untalented, she explained to me once, she never imagined she'd be able to compare to the rest of the PantheUS, let alone join the most recognized affiliation within it. We had that in common. What she thought, watching all that glitz and glamor, was: who the hell would want to see *her* parading in front of a camera? Well, first, of course, there was her direct superior, who caught Maria in one of those all-too-common having-to-use-your-powers moments.

Seriously: a "secret" identity will get compromised, one way or another, True Believer. It's not worth the hassle.

When Detective Martinez was discovered, her sergeant begged her just to go to PantheUS, make the big bucks, do what she always wanted to do except with a buttload more cash. Help people.

She declined. She loved the police department. The best she could manage in PantheUS would be to join a special-interest superhero group like the Wisps of Wisdom or the Skankyspurs. *Fuck that*, she said.

The second request would come from none other than Gunther "Red, White, and Blue" Grey himself. He implored her to enlist, if not for herself then for her country. Help build his golden age of altruism. This was a little more tempting, but still not enough, and she declined again. She could do the same thing for her country without nearly that much chill between her thighs.

She would be different, she promised herself. PantheUS wasn't really a serious thing. It was a rock of a word. It broke through things, but it just kinda sat around once it made it in.

Still, the rock did a little more than loiter on that second throw.

She began to think of ways in which, if she was silly enough to take that chance, she would make everything different. Just different enough that it would fit her.

These are the Astonishing Fairly Sad Tales

That was all daydreaming, though, because Maria Martinez would never, ever join PantheUS. She wouldn't run around throwing punches, like it was three o'clock in the schoolyard, against people dressed just as ridiculously as she was. She wouldn't give up a badge she'd worked her ass off for. She wouldn't forget who she was.

Spoiler alert.

The final request came from the First Lady. Maria Martinez was something of a local celebrity at that point—North Carolina was as renowned for its superhero activity as Ohio. During her husband's reelection campaign, she stopped by Winston-Salem for a meet-and-greet at a local elementary school (it's always an elementary school) that violently burst into flames, and Maria Martinez saved all the helpless children. This, of course, called for a photo shoot, which led to a phone call.

"So you've heard about this PantheUS project that Gunther Grey has been working on?"

"I've heard of it."

"It's an interesting idea, but a bit of a boys' club right now, no?"

"I guess it is."

"He told me you said you weren't interested. It's a shame. Little girls could use a hero, too."

She called Gunther the next day.

These are the Astonishing Tales of Decisions, Decisions . . .

"Do you give up yet?" she said to Asper.

A few people have speculated about just how fast Asper is—how powerful he *could* be if he were to really try. The best answer to that, I suppose, is that he's as fast as he needs to be. I know, sounds like a cop-out, but you can't quantify a power you've never had and could never hope to understand. Faced with the unrelenting weight of infinite gravity, however, you're always the same speed.

"Okay, okay. Just stop. I give."

Maria floated to the ground and with a wave of her hand Asper became Almighty again, though with his pride a little worn. He glared at Maria as if intent on sending her on a lunar expedition, but it stopped at that. DEATHRAGE moaned as he got to his feet. I jogged up to meet the team at the center of the room. Before I reached them, Asper's body vanished as if cropped from existence.

It was an amazing way to wrap up a day.

CHAPTER 14
WE ~~HATE~~ WANT YOU

"**O**H HEY, HE'S ALIVE," Paul said on the other end of the phone. I was lying on the floor of my recently acquired, sparsely furnished apartment in the Bronx. I laughed. He laughed, too, because he hadn't meant it harshly. It was just a way of saying hello.

Okay, maybe I hadn't called him for a few weeks, even though we'd had that special-episode moment and cleared the air between us before I left town. Since getting to New York I'd been a little pressed for time, between the speaking engagements Chris had lined up for me and the team "training" schedule.

"Yeah, man, sorry, shit's been crazy out here. How are things?" I flicked a spark on and off between the copper-tipped fingers of my gloves.

"Things are thingy, I guess. How about you, man? I see you been making some waves out there. Kind of dope to see you doing your thing."

"Yeah, it's been cool, just kind of crazy, you know? Like, still doesn't feel real. I think it won't until I've actually won." I moved the phone away from my ear for a moment when I felt it buzzing. A reminder had popped up on screen: I had my first major network interview coming up. I needed to get to the station.

"Well, I'm sure it'll work out. Did you hit up my friend Anyla yet? About the job?" Paul asked.

"No, not yet. Hopefully I won't need to."

"Yeah, hopefully. You should try to touch base, though. I'm pulling for you, you know. Guessing you already got that from the article?"

I sat there silent for a while. With everything going on, I hadn't taken the time to keep up with *Kuumba*.

"Yes! The article. Good shit, as always, man. You deserve to be in the *Times*. Like that part when you—ugh, forgot exactly how you put it, but it was, like, so powerful in imagery. Like, yes! Finally, *someone* said it." I'd placed him on speaker so I could Google frantically to find the article.

"Thanks, man. I mean, yeah, I really put some work into it. I thought you'd be pissed, if I'm being honest, me using your real name like that—"

"Nigga, what?"

"Ha—just fuckin with you, man. You always thinking you slick. Anyway, check it out when you get a chance. Sorry to do this, but I got a thing to get to, can we catch up later?"

"Maybe, asshole."

"Aight, talk to you later then. Oh—let me know what you think about the part I put in about Thandie—"

I hung up the phone before he could finish, but only to play along with the bit we'd been doing. I promised myself I'd follow up later, read his article, but after I took care of my own *things to get to*. I found the piece, "A Farewell to Our Midwest Marvel," and bookmarked it. I couldn't help but grin when I saw he'd used a picture of me in my

Spark costume. He always had a thing about the ever-glossy Golden Age of me.

* * *

Back when Afrolicious was running, the only heroes competing against him were The Voice and Navigatrix. The Voice had the spectacular ability of being understood in any two languages at a given time, while Navigatrix was telepathically linked to the MTA routing schedule. Sadly, as these were abilities every New Yorker was gifted with, they didn't get far in the polls, giving Afrolicious Samson the edge he needed to win. This left me to wish I'd gotten struck by lightning just a little sooner, so maybe I wouldn't have had such a tight race there at the end, since the race was never that close between anyone except myself and China Doll.

When you're vying for a closely contested position in the American Collective for Resolving Overtly Negative Yowled Misconducts, you need every publicity opportunity you can garner, even the not-so-savory ones. That's what Row told me, at least, and it's why he'd scheduled me an exclusive interview with Hound News. Even craftier, he set it up to air simultaneously with one of Doll's televised interviews.

It was shady, it was regrettable, but it helped.

I was scared at first, but Chris was judicious in his choice of who would grill me. Keith Kelly Kurskovitch was a known softball player when it came to PantheUS. We dove into the easy stuff early on, discussing the bullshit backstory that Chris had decided sounded better than "I got railed by a lightning bolt." I found it easy, slipping back into things Donald would do: dancing to "Thriller," being everything they needed me to be. This worked until the unfortunate moment when Keith had the brilliant idea to ask me about my association with radical-snowflake publications like *Kuumba Kollective.*

"I'm sorry?"

"We were just curious to hear your thoughts on this article. It seems the editor, Paul Hughes, thinks very highly of you. While I don't doubt for a moment that you're as astonishing as he says you are, what do you think of his other assertions?"

These are the Astonishing Tales of Reading Is Fundamental

Later, when Doll appeared with Keith, do you think she got grilled about her past associations with tiny publications based out of Columbus, Ohio? No? You are correct. When Doll popped on, they went through the same origin story she'd been reciting for years. Afterward, Keith complimented her genetics and facial symmetry a few dozen times, and then they talked rapturously about Doll's libertarian awakening.

While I stared blankly at Keith and then at the camera, I caught a glimpse of a man on fire: Christopher Row, ready to tear out his hair and probably mine too. I gulped like the sitcoms of yore had taught me to. I sizzled, but I didn't spark.

"Well, what did *you* think of the article?" I asked, leaning back into the chair as if I were teaching *him* something.

"If I'm being honest? I was thoroughly impressed by the editor's ability; his writing was solid. What I wasn't so impressed with was the radicalized message that you moving to serve your country is at all a symptom of, and I quote, 'the congested, capitalistic coagulation of resources in the pockets of the rich and powerful.' I mean, that's harsh, if you ask me. Little snowflake may as well have cried." He laughed, swinging a hand at my leg to punctuate his knee-slapper of a comment.

It did sound like Paul. If there was anything he and I had in common more than an exhausted heaviness of being, it was a love of alliteration.

I wanted to laugh. I wanted to shriek into the wind and let the sound soar up, up, up until I couldn't hear it anymore. I wanted to do a lot of things except think of Paul and me, teenaged and tastefully dressed in FUBU Fat Albert. Him pulling it off, me not so much. I wanted to be anywhere else in that moment than on the wrong side of a stop sign.

"Well, maybe," I said. "I mean, distribution *is* key, though. Thinning out the arbitrary concentration of suits in areas that are already saturated with them—suits like Asper. Asper could handle New York with an arm tied behind his back! But we act like the city needs a whole spandex-clad army. If you thin them—if you thin *us* out a bit, cover more bases—don't you think everyone benefits?" I was channeling Paul now, to make up for the fact that I still hadn't read his goddamn article. "There's a lot of work to be done even in smaller cities. Building community, revitalizing neighborhoods."

I reached over to the pitcher filled with water in the center of the table. I really, really wanted that fucking knee slap right about then, but it wasn't forthcoming. The handle of the pitcher was slick to the touch and kissed my palm the wrong way—that awkward, bottle-spin of a kiss that you try to forget as soon as it happens. Keith unfolded his scrunched face.

"Well, now we seem to be getting somewhere. You heard it here first, America: this superhero hopeful, The *Black* Spark, would have us march down to PantheUS with a hammer and sickle and dismantle our defenses, brick by brick!"

Shit.

"I don't think you under—"

"I heard you. *We* heard you: what you just said to me, and to all the viewers of Hound News. Superheroes: no longer the protectors of the American people—they're the new community organizers."

"All I mean is—"

"We'll be back, with more substance and less Spark, on your only news source—Hound News."

These are the Astonishing Tales of Get Up,
Champ, Don't Count Yourself Out Yet

Back in the green room I licked my wounds, using my lessons to quiet the spark. I heard a nine-to-five sigh and turned to see Chris leaning against a wall.

"So how was that?" I asked.

"Well, it wasn't good." He looked around to make sure we were alone before pulling out a smoke. He didn't offer me one.

"Yeah, but—I mean, any publicity, right?"

"That? That wasn't publicity, that was a fucking snuff film. Why are you here, nigga? Why are you—no, you know what? I'm going to smoke this square. Then I'm going to go and get shitfaced, and for a whole eight hours, I'm going to forget that your ass exists." He headed for the door.

"I'm sorry, dude," I called after him.

"Don't be sorry, Black Spark—be smart."

* * *

He was right, there wasn't much time left. Doll was edging past me in the polls, and it didn't help that in the following days everyone had their piece to say about my first major interview. Most of the reaction was lukewarm, from journalists who thought Kurskovitch was out of line but didn't really care, because they were skeptical of the superheroic establishment in the first place and wondered why I'd chosen to appear on Hound News at all. Some of it, from the side of the political spectrum that cheered on superheroes much less critically, was all hot and bothered about my so-called socialist leanings. I hadn't pleased much of anyone, it seemed. Only at *Kuumba* and its parent publication, *Foible*, did I find a truly friendly voice.

ON HEROES
BY ANYLA M. NESSA

There has been massive speculation as to the political alignment of The Spark, a leader among the talented individuals running for the American Collective for Resolving Overtly Negative Yowled Misconducts after the departure of Afrolicious Samson. The Spark brings us something that Afrolicious could no longer provide: a new perspective, an uncompromising view of the responsibility of superheroes to the community at large. In this he follows in the footsteps of GRAVI-Tina, who, let us not forget . . .

Continued on page ohthankgod

I texted Paul to thank him for whatever he'd pulled to get that written. He replied that he had nothing to do with it and maybe I'd better reach out to this Anyla, nice girl that she was. I didn't believe him, but it didn't matter. At least I had something—though it wouldn't be nearly enough to let me overtake Doll in the coming week.

CHAPTER 15
TALES OF THE ASTONISHING
GREEN FREEDOM

FOR A WHILE AFTER THAT, my life as a hero stagnated. I still had training meetups here and there or appearances on late-night shows that Chris arranged to get me more exposure, but mostly I sat on my futon—or, realizing I still had a way to access central air conditioning as well as cable, I'd go hang around the lofts of the American Collective for Resolving Overtly Negative Yowled Misconducts. The common rooms would have seemed wasted otherwise: most of the team had their own lives and never really used them. GRAVI-Tina would pop in with a sandwich and join me for lunch every now and again, but usually my only companion was Patches.

He was quite possibly the worst roommate I'd ever had, even taking into account the fact that I didn't have to sleep there. Kat used to leave bowls of rotting food around the house and fabric storage bins for me to stub my toes on at night. Paul was always hosting parties, and young men clad all in black muttering about Big Brother conspiracies would hang around at odd hours.

Patches—he never stayed in his own room, for one thing. He'd blare the TV while smoking a bowl and laughing hysterically at twenty-four-hour news networks. He seemed to be interested in parties, like Paul, but not ones that revolved around 90s hip-hop and a dozen or so guests engaging in intelligent (if increasingly drunken) conversation. Instead he played music that made me feel old and crotchety, while thirty people I'd never seen before danced and yelled at each other about things I'd never heard of. On one of GRAVI-Tina's lunch breaks I told her how much the kid needed an ass-whooping; her only response was that I should give him a break, since he had the single worst talent of all of us and none of the rest of us could handle it on our best day.

I wanted to laugh in her face. I didn't, partly because I could tell that on a level beyond my understanding she actually cared a lot for the little shit, and partly because she was still a police officer at the end of the day. I bit back my brave notions of raising hell against a teenager and tried to look the other way, but the more I ignored his petulant disturbances, the more impassioned they became.

As I watched him packing a bowl one Tuesday afternoon, I felt the appropriate time had come to let him have it. I hadn't realized my lexicon had so many curse words in it; I'm pretty sure I formed a few new ones while I was at it. Patches only waited patiently for me to tire myself out. When I was through explaining what waited for him if he remained set in his twattish ways, he smiled and I think regarded me for the first time as something more than the asshole who'd taken his mentor's place on the team.

"You done?" he asked, reaching for the pipe that he'd affection-ately named Green Freedom. He packed Green Freedom from a little baggie he had ready and took a long drag of smoke.

I didn't really mind the smell of bud, but that had always seemed like one more reason to stay away from it. It wasn't really about the undeserved punishment of being an NA kid, sitting in the back of a meeting while the grownups would hemorrhage their harrowing tales, though that did pretty much cure any curiosity I had about hitting bottom. It was something else.

I was fifteen years old, riding my bike to Kat's house for the weekly installment of a sad, sad two-person D&D campaign, when I found myself wanted for the first time. I heard the sound of tires slowing behind me: a Jeep was trailing me as I rode through the gated community. No honks telling me to get out of the way, though—only the smiles of two teenage girls, the most tragic form of kryptonite, when they eventually pulled up beside me on the empty road.

I stopped and smirked back at them. In the middle of an Ohio December, I found my body boiling. The nameless beauty in the driver's seat rolled down her window. She moved a strand of her straight auburn hair and tucked it shyly behind her ear, revealing a glinting nose ring.

"Hey," she said.

I considered how I'd frame the humble brag of my first girlfriend for Kat. "Sup," I grunted with a nigga nod. She flushed at this and fell into herself for a moment before sticking her head back out the window.

"Do you know where we could find any trees?" She winked. Her friend in the passenger seat sank her face into her hands, giggling.

I had no earthly idea what the hell she was talking about. I imagined I'd just tripped into some sexually charged banter that I was too young to understand.

"No, but we can find some. Do you climb?" I asked with a coy smile.

She thought about that for a moment. "Yeah? I think?"

"Well, I'm supposed to meet a friend, but Sharon Woods is around the corner," I said with a wink of my own.

My auburn-haired, nose-ringed goddess grew vengeful, glaring at me. "Yeah? Well fuck you." She hit the gas and sped off.

I stared after the car, baffled. It'd be days until I found out (from Paul) what they were really looking for, which very much wasn't me. While I laughed when he chided me about it, there was a dull ache at the pit of my stomach whenever I thought about it, and in some ways, there still is. I filed this experience under the same heading as chicken wings and purple drinks, watermelon and dusty dreads. And that was it: I never wanted to be a Black guy who was into weed.

Watching Patches puff cloud after cloud of skunky smoke, that dull ache swallowed me again. He stayed quiet and stared at the TV for so long that I thought I'd faded into obscurity as fast as Afrolicious Samson. But then he held out the pipe in my direction. He didn't turn away from the TV, being much too occupied with a music video featuring a young woman confused as to why she'd found herself at a party. I took his invitation as what it probably wasn't: a challenge. I snatched the emerald glass pipe and plopped down on the couch beside him, flicking a lighter and sucking deeply.

"Slow, this shit is pretty strong," he said, finally looking at me.

I raised an eyebrow and sucked harder. I didn't think it would be too different from a cig. If Christopher Row's analysis of the age groups I appeal to was right, most of you reading right now probably know how wrong I was. I dropped Green Freedom—Patches caught it in midair—and sank back into the couch, propelled by my coughs. His laughter was intense but without malice. He patted me on the leg as if he were the elder before exchanging Green Freedom for two PS4 controllers. My spark was trembling throughout my body, seizing my muscles; I felt every fiber snapping and twisting. He tossed me a controller.

"So, sorry about the noise."

Those were the first words I heard after the three days I thought we'd spent playing Street Fighter, though it was really more like a half an hour. I shrugged and leaned back.

"Sorry for losing my shit on you," I answered.

He raised a fist and I pounded my own against it, wondering how much of a career Green Freedom would have in protecting the world against domestic disputes.

This isn't the origin story of a pothead, mind you, just a . . . pot enthusiast.

* * *

I was, if nothing else, a creature of assimilation, and I soon learned that the best way to handle Patches when it was just the two of us was with a bowl. Sometimes I just smoked the stories he'd share. Most of them were as shallow as the smoke-hazed, gaming-based relationship we'd developed. *That time GRAVI-Tina dropped a bridge on Asper. The first time I got Afrolicious high. DEATHRAGE was so pissed when I snuck a squirt gun into his belt.*

Since we were the only two dicking around the headquarters most afternoons, we had our fair share of dynamic duo–style adventures. A walking Band-Aid doesn't have much application at a low-risk robbery-type situation, but I would drag him along anyway, if only to get some fresh air every now and again. During one engagement, I took a bullet to the back. Usually I could divert bullets to the chest piece of my costume or magnetize them to some other nearby piece of metal, but I'd been preoccupied with bashing my copper rod heroically into the skull of the gunman's accomplice.

The bad guys escaped, and after healing me Patches stopped speaking to me for a week.

"So, are you just going to stay pissy now?" I said one afternoon.

He was watching a documentary about *ZAPOW!* His eyes had a pinkish tint and he was desperately gripping a hoagie twice the size of his head. I hoped for a moment he'd hand over Green Freedom, but he only rolled his eyes.

"Think I will," he said before filling his mouth with sandwich.

"Are you going to tell me why you're pissed, at least?" I persisted. "Was it me sucking at my job, or the fact that you actually had to do yours?"

These are the Astonishing Tales of Shitty
and Sobering Things to Say

He plopped the sandwich down on the table and stood up dramatically. He was a short guy, but the look in his eyes was six feet tall. I'm not sure what I'd have done if he'd taken a swing at me. I'd like to say I'd have acted like the grownup in the situation, but in all likelihood I wouldn't have. I'd have traded blows with a fifteen-year-old, thrown him into a headlock, and shoved the sandwich into his face.

Thankfully, it didn't come to that.

"Let's go," he said, brushing past me.

I unclenched my fists and jogged to catch up to him.

* * *

Sitting on the D train, I thought of how little I really knew about our pocket-sized protector.

"I'm going to be fucking honest with you, man, I'm fucking blitzed," he announced, sinking back into the train seat after telling me we'd missed our stop.

I can't tell you, True Believer, what you probably want to know: exactly how this kid had become the only person on the planet who could once a day rewind any living being to what it had been twenty-four hours prior.

The first time nine-year-old Adam Robbins played with life and death was in the case of Dotty the dog. It wasn't the most original name, but the black-and-white lab/spaniel mix had a single spot of white on her black front paw, so it just stuck. She had a penchant for chasing squirrels and staring at cars. You could probably imagine how things went after this, but in case not: boy chases dog, dog chases squirrel, squirrel chases the streets for salvation like a clichéd rapper.

Things go *boom*.

The furry carcass of a once-dog flung, tumbling, before finally lying flat against the pavement. The squirrel flattened as well, and the mysterious driver gone.

Adam was beginning, but he couldn't have known it. He rushed to the dog or what was left of it, bones splitting the skin, blood matting the fur. He laid his hands on her.

That was the first.

With shifts and crackles the dog's body knit itself back together like a furry Humpty Dumpty. It was what the layman would refer to as a *miracle*.

After Dotty was restored, Adam, without missing a beat, rushed to what was left of the squirrel and tried to repeat the miracle.

This is the Astonishing Way a Wayward White Mage without
Sufficient MP Ended Up in a Coma for Two Months

It was only the first time he'd have to face that overwhelming, inescapable truth: every talent is limited.

He was forbidden by his parents from using his gifts on anyone outside of their church, from taking into his blessed hands the failures and fuckups and sinners and sadists. He was nine, so he obeyed—for a while. Until Granddaddy Gunther had something to say about it.

When he finally figured out the right stop, he led me to a hospital not too far from my apartment in the Bronx. The scent of cheap healthcare, illusorily universal, took me back to Ohio. As we wandered the halls, the staff mostly ignored us or nodded to Adam in bored recognition. We reached the ICU.

"You got this power, right?" said Patches, who seemed to be sobering up now. "This talent that only a few are 'blessed' with. You got a thing inside you that any-fucking-body would shit themselves to have. Turn left here."

We entered a room with no view apart from the politically correct abstract paintings plastering the walls.

"Are we allowed to be in here?" I whispered.

"Thing is, these gifts? They aren't anything but the residue of being in the wrong place at the right time."

Whoever was lying in the hospital bed moaned. Patches walked right up to the bedside, looking over the burn wrappings that covered whoever it was from head to toe.

"You're a fucking tool if you think anything else, Fuckles. If you think anything is owed to you except when you give back."

This person had had some kind of terrible accident. He was going to die. What I could see of his skin was yellowed and brittle, a brown shell of something that could have been a man once upon a time. I felt very small.

"This guy, I don't know anything about his worldly ass except, well, I can help him," Patches said. "What else are we good for?" He put a hand to the man's sweat-blotted forehead. I watched the shriveled skin reforming, listened to the snap crackle pop of him.

"You want to sit around and complain about your right to what I can do for this schmuck? You want to wag your finger and tell him he's fucking up *your* day?"

"That nurse out there," I said. "The one who nodded. That nurse *knew* you."

He rolled his eyes.

"How many times have you done this?"

"God, you're an entitled—"

"How many times?"

The body below Patches's hands breathed deeply, sleepily.

"I'd say about half the times we're on the field I'm shooting blanks."

These are the Astonishing Tales of *This. Asshole.*

We all have our contracts, our own policies and procedures to comply with. All talents not being created equal, PantheUS tends to adjust the terms depending on what exactly you can do. Adam—Patches, *whatever*—was only permitted to use his abilities in service to PantheUS, and more importantly, any member of the American Collective for Resolving Overtly Negative Yowled Misconducts took priority. He'd be ejected from the Collective if anyone found out what he was doing.

"Why would you show me this?"

"Because you're clumsy as shit, you take too many chances, but mostly? You needed to know what you're really getting your dumb ass into."

These are the Astonishing Tales of a Fourteen-
Year-Old Telling You What's What

These are the Astonishing Tales of Hateful
Half-Pints and Hearts of Gold

These are the Astonishing Tales of Not
Listening Until It Was Too Late

CHAPTER 16
THE ACTUALLY ACTUAL TALES OF
THE ILLUSTRIOUS THANDIE D. NETTLE

I'M ACTUALLY SURPRISED THAT I haven't gotten around to writing about Thandie until now.

In my defense, you wouldn't ask Kyle Rayner to have a casual chat about Alex Dewitt, would you? Or expect to drive around town with Peter Parker and gab about Gwen Stacy? Okay then.

Anyway, she'd finally figured out I was in town and texted my decrepit old phone. I jumped at the chance for some time away from Chris, from the election, from everything. We sat at the bar for a while, watching each other watch each other.

"This is kind of insane, right?" I said. "Twelve bucks for a draft?" I was struggling to even read the drink menu in the dimly lit place, which sacrificed much of its beauty to the dark. I was in full costume, since I'd spilled some wine a week or so prior on the only civilian suit I'd brought with me to NYC. Thandie didn't seem to mind, though.

"Well, actually, it's not so bad for New York," she said. "But I suppose by Ohio standards the pricing here can feel a little high. I miss the old town sometimes." She sipped her red wine through red lips. As usual, she was looking at something in the distance, not at me.

"Hah, yeah, silly little Columbus, right? Anyway, I'm glad you texted. Glad I could find a way to squeeze this in. I was a little surprised to hear from you, though."

She sipped at her glass for at least ten seconds. I studied her, as if I hadn't already failed the final—as if us at that table would be anything other than exactly what she wanted it to be. I felt myself falling, slipping into the history of us. (Granted, not literally, but since I'm obviously setting up a flashback we'll say there was a little time warp going on.)

These are the Astonishing Tales of Thandie D. Nettle

When you're eighteen and trapped in the body of a twenty-five-year-old, it's not so odd to find yourself in a hookah bar on a Tuesday night. So, there I was, doused in the newest Machete body spray that promised an instant harem with one light application and wearing the jacket of thick black fleece that accentuated my speckles of dandruff. It was a quaint little shop with dim lighting and dimmer clientele, in the dead center of the state-college campus scene. I'd been going there for years, since the first time I went with Paul, back before I dropped out. Now, alone with my clean-shaven face and strategically ripped jeans, leaning back in the seat trying to appear as sexily sloppy as I could, I realized that things change, and what we seek is often the furthest thing from what we need.

I kept my eyes on my book, coming up for smoke now and then but otherwise sticking with Vonnegut and his ice-nine. I was the only person there alone. Occasionally I'd see someone of interest, but that was always followed by the murky fear of experiencing a "The thing I like about these high-school girls is I get older, they stay the same age" sort of moment, so I tried to enjoy the privacy of social awkwardness. I was content with this being the way my Tuesday nights went from there until the end of days, but like I said . . . things change. Disruptions occur. This disruption blew into my fortress of smoky solitude much like a leaf soaring through a windless night, full of absurdity and an ethereal kind of arrogance.

She was a myth in action when she removed her glasses and patted the curled hair atop her golden crown. I'd met her before: in letters from my grandmother on the importance of settling down with a strong and conscious black woman, or at the bottom of the fifth and final drink of the night as every woman in the bar stepped into Calvin's transmogrifier box. She wore an assortment of necklaces like bumper stickers that beckoned me to coexist, and across her hallowed skin there were ink stains, constellations in a caramel sky, with pieces that I couldn't see trailing beneath her clothing. True Believer, she was an intricate woman, and though I was never one to understand puzzles or finish lengthy crosswords on Sunday mornings, I was brazen enough to believe this was something I could accomplish: solving her.

I took my jacket off and tossed it to one side, used my foot to slide the seat across from my small table out just a bit, and waited for serendipity to do the rest. I continued to read, glancing up every now and again to see what she was doing. One of those times, I was unlucky enough to catch her looking my way too. *Stupid*, I thought, biting my lip. I believed there was a science to this type of passive seduction—though granted, it had never actually been very effective. My usual plan of attack relied on the target approaching to ask why I'd been staring pins, needles, and daggers at them, to which I would respond, "I couldn't help it—I'm sorry." I know, I know: creepy, right? But there's something mysterious about ~~awkwardness~~ vulnerability, and in that mystery a seed of intrigue is planted, and from that seed of intrigue, well, maybe a phone number sprouts?

This had worked for me exactly twice, and one of those numbers turned out to be a fake, but still.

Thandie D. Nettle, staring at me now, had ruined all that. I had no choice but to take the offensive, the small paperback trembling in my hand, a house of toothpicks crashing down around me.

"Hi," I said.

"Hello. I'm Thandie D. Nettle."

And that's how I met her. In all the years of all the worlds in all the hookah bars I've ever been to, I've never met someone in the way I met Ms. Thandie D. Nettle, and I highly doubt I ever will again. She patted her curls and smiled—teasingly, I thought, although in all honesty I was the sort of guy who might interpret an inquiry for directions as "teasing." Offering me a stick of gum might as well have been second base.

"Are you alone? I don't mean to be too forward, but I thought you might like a seat," I said, my eyes keeping firm, unyielding contact with hers as I succumbed to the kryptonite. Her smile broadened.

"I don't actually think it's 'forward' to ask if I want a seat, but I guess that depends on your intentions." She took a seat at my table, put down her bag, and drew a hit from my pipe. Make of that what you will.

"I'm Donald. Donald McDougal," I said. The way she'd introduced herself forced me to give her anything and everything I could. *My blood type is AB. I have three dollars, twelve cents, and an uncle in the 'joint.' Okay, he's not actually in the joint, he's just a huge dick, so that's what we all say. I once peed the bed at camp when I was eight and nearly killed five other kids in the cabin when I tried to burn the sheets.* And so on and so on.

She listened patiently, taking a puff of hookah every now and again and sipping on her tea, a grand display of moderation. When she finally spoke, after I'd given everything I could, I was consumed with the idea that what she talked about and how she talked about it were extremely important—to me and to the whole universe—but, True Believer, I'm afraid I didn't actually register a single word.

While I have the power to manipulate, control, and absorb electricity, Thandie had the power to hypnotize, to captivate, to control minds. I'd have taken whatever freak accident gave her those powers over mine any day.

"So you study here? At Ohio State?" I said.

"Actually, I graduate in a few months, but yes, I've been studying at *The* Ohio State University."

"What's your major?"

"Ethnic studies."

"Wow, that sounds interesting."

"Actually, it's very interesting."

I nodded in a careful display of understanding the depth of the topic, which was, actually, bullshit. You can pretty much just slide on a black glove and give a complimentary nod whenever you hear *ethnic* or *racial* in the context of overpriced higher education and you're golden. Encouraged, she ended up talking for a few hours, and I listened, for hours, to the tales of Thandie D. Nettle. She didn't laugh at her own jokes or wait for the world to be quiet when she had something to say, and in the beginning those things were enough to ground me. She was from New York originally and had moved to Ohio for school. She loved superheroes—actually, she loved super-heroines—and told me about the ones she'd met and admired. "I saw Lady Lovely stop a car from hitting a little boy with her pinky," or "String Woman was on *Def Poetry Jam* and shared this *beautiful* poem, speaking her power, an unbreakable thread, it's like a metaphor for, for bringing us all together." When she said the word *beautiful*, or anything like it, she would clutch at something, like her shirt or my forearm, and shut her eyes tenderly, absorbing the moment and all its complexity. I remember wishing I did that too. "I *love* the way Almighty Asper volunteers at soup kitchens. Every little thing helps." Clutch. "Beast-Beautician, she's so *passionate* about helping people." Clutch.

I wanted to move her hands with my name, to make them contort and cling in fear of losing hold. She explained to me that superheroes saw the bigger picture, and that lesser people needed them, to bring them up from the depths of apathy and ignorance. She *believed* that this seemingly insignificant percentage of the population could drag the masses, kicking and screaming, into the light.

We ended up closing the hookah bar, which meant it was ten o'clock, and I walked her back to her car. We stood there for a while, me thinking of what to put in the letter to Nana, of giving the skateboard a push—of kryptonite. She pushed onto the tips of her toes to reach my face, wrapped a hand behind my head, interlocked her fingers with my dreadlocks, and then—*flash. Boom.*

* * *

"I'm telling you, man, you're going to *love* her," I said to Paul.

We were at Java Jones, a little coffee shop around the corner from our place where I'd go to listen to him read his poetry every now and then. It wasn't exactly good poetry, though I'd never tell him that to his face (if you're reading this, Paul—sorry, bro); I mostly came to hear everyone else offering pieces of themselves for free at the open mic. I didn't understand how they did it: standing there with nothing, no walls, no masks, just themselves, bare and real. Thandie had promised to swing by after work to meet us. We'd been dating for two and a half months at that point, so we'd made it past the required

199

amount of time I gave any relationship before introducing someone new to my friends. I thought I'd introduce her to Paul first, then Kat, and then whoever else I cared to brag to. I'd spent a good amount of time talking her up to Paul already, but I couldn't help repeating myself.

"She's a genius. She has two majors and she's really political and stuff. She doesn't use the creamy crack, and you know how that natural hair gets me. She's shorter than me and has to get on her tippy toes to reach my face when we kiss. And she's in one of those Black sororities, kind of like the fraternity you're in, isn't that neat? She has so many, like, ideas, you know? She's really conscious."

"Well, I'd hope she's conscious, how else would she get here?"

"Smartass. You know what I mean."

"Yeah, but do you?"

The front door chimed. Thandie stood there for ten seconds or so, giving the men enough time to want her and the women enough time to want to be her. Spotting my table, she walked over.

"Darling!" She kissed me deeply and passionately and any other adverb she could. Paul tapped his finger on the table while we tried our best to be lost in one another.

"I'm sorry, that was rude of me," I said after she broke the kiss. "This is Thandie D. Nettle. Thandie D. Nettle, this is Paul Hughes."

Paul nodded and extended his hand.

"Well, actually, you can just call me Thandie," she said before shaking it.

"So, you two seem to be getting along well," said Paul.

"Actually, we're getting along *very* well." She pecked me on the cheek to demonstrate this fact.

"Yeah, darling *Don* sure is something," Paul said, trying to not laugh.

"So, Thandie, did you know Paul is in a fraternity?" I said, fearing an awkward silence that would give Thandie too much time to size up Paul and find him wanting. She did know that, of course, because I'd already told her, but she acted excited anyway, giving that familiar clutch.

"Oh, really? I'm in blahblahblah, incorporated, what about you?"

"I'm part of bloobloobloo, incorporated—when did you cross?" said Paul.

The question of crossing what exactly came to mind, but I stayed in my assigned position of outsider for the conversation, masking my silence with an empty cup of coffee at my lips.

"Oh, a year ago or so. It's been one of the important milestones in my life, actually. To be a part of something better—this opportunity to be *divine*, to be *elite*. If you look at any important Black figure today you'll find they're in the system too. It's like some private, public, private illuminati."

I listened to her speak, watched the clutch, and tried to ignore the pained expression on Paul's face.

"Well, um—" Paul began.

No, Paul, please, no, I thought pitifully. "Well, um" never boded well when it came to Paul Hughes. It heralded a galactic ego blow. Granted, it was sometimes (if not all times) warranted. For instance:

"Hey, how do you like my Donaghetti? It's like Spaghetti, but more *awesome*, right?"

"Well, um—"

Or:

"You know, say what you will, but *I* think 'Don the Phenomenon' is the perfect stage name. So what do you say, are we gonna blow these guys away with mad style at the talent show next Friday, P Money? Muzak Hughes Child? The Artist Currently Known as Paul?"

"Well, um—"

And, much later:

"So, I was thinking of giving Thandie a call."

"Well, um—"

You understand.

I tried my best to telepathically suggest that he not go down this road with Thandie, but, sadly, telepathy is a power I never achieved.

"I can't say I agree with any of that, *actually*." To his credit, he looked pained to say it, he and I being such good pals and all, and him knowing how long it was since I'd been with someone.

"And why is that?"

"Well, you make it sound like we're better than other people simply because we're organized. When people get swollen heads about wearing a pin, they do more for exclusion than progress. To be elitist, on purpose—that's probably one of the worst reasons for joining the Greek system I've ever heard."

I was sure I'd be buying a body pillow on the way home to cuddle that night, but although Thandie's cheeks reddened, she let it go, picking up again with some harmless small talk. I sighed with relief.

* * *

"I hate to tell you this, man, but I really, really don't love her," Paul told me a couple of weeks later. But I didn't care what he said, or what anyone said: she was special, and by extension I was at least noteworthy.

It was four months before we ended up living together. That was just about convenience at the beginning. Paul had wanted his own place for a while, and her rent was crushing her, even though her mom helped out here and there. It was fun at first, playing house, cooking seven-dollar tilapia and sipping our Walmart white wine.

Having someone's lap to lie on during the nine months of winter that always seem to curse Ohio. It was good, but not nearly everything she wanted, actually. Thandie was accustomed to a higher standard of living. She didn't talk about her family's lifestyle all that much, unless I prodded for a story from her childhood or asked about her mother, and even then, the answers would be quick, jagged little soliloquies. But I guess she missed the finer things more than I realized.

When you break up with someone, you go through phases, True Believer, and the first is undoubtedly the hardest: when you can't help but remember every heartbreakingly wonderful thing about them.

These are the Astonishing Tales of Someone Who Wasn't in That Phase, But Really Liked to Pretend He Was

Sitting at that table in my costume, I watched as Thandie set her perfect glass in the perfect center of her perfect square of a napkin, looking past me to the waiter in the distance, shaking her glass when she caught his attention.

"I'm guessing Kat made you that costume?" she asked.

I nodded, maybe a little too enthusiastically.

"I like it. It has that old, rustic, worn, nostalgic, simple, effortless, safe feel to it, but also—very pretty."

When her next glass of wine came, I made sure to order what I hoped was a very effective twelve-dollar beer. "So, why did you call, Thandie?"

"Actually, I thought you would prefer to talk in person, rather than slinking around my office." She looked me straight in the eyes, taking hold of me with those hazel harbingers of everything I wanted.

So, maybe I didn't mention it, but in that first week in New York, in between doing every single annoying touristy thing there was to do and staring at buildings, I may have ended up on Lafayette somewhere between Jersey and Houston, and maybe, just maybe, this wasn't so much an accident. Maybe I'd looked up, in a state of panic for something I once knew, a familiar face. Maybe, maybe, maybe.

"Yeah, I was thinking of going back to school while I'm out here . . . no, okay, so, I'm a creeper, I just . . . how did you know?"

She laughed with her whole body. "Well, your outfit is kinda hard to miss. And while we academics are busy solving the problems of the world, we do talk." She sipped her wine. "You still know my number, don't you? You could have just called."

I thought of other times I'd made mistakes in the memories of us.

These are the Astonishing Tales of OH MY GOD YOU GUYS I'M SO GOOD AT SUBTLE FLASHBACKS YOU LIKE DON'T EVEN KNOW

During the last summer we spent together, Ohio was ripe with pointless festivals. First on the list was the Juneteenth, which my dad used to cart me to every summer until he passed away when I was fifteen. It was a celebration of the signing of the Emancipation Proclamation, when Abraham Lincoln hopped into his magical sleigh and delivered freedom to all the good little boys and girls of the USA.

"Ugh, oh my God, this is just what we need, to be with the people sometimes," Thandie said, clutching at her bag.

"Yeah, I hear you. Do you want some cotton candy?"

She nodded happily, and I paid the woman five freedom bucks (the currency of the fair, which cost me ten actual bucks). It was nice to see her so ablaze; she couldn't stop gaping at everything and everyone.

"*Thank you* for bringing me here, it's so good to be among, well, *our* people."

I was preoccupied with the ring toss. "Um, yeah, I feel you?"

The vendor patted me on the shoulder after I missed. "Better luck next time, pal."

After we stopped for a bite to eat at one of the taco stands, where Thandie left a generous 10-percent tip, we decided to head home. Four hours of trudging through the heat was weighing on us. I was exhausted, but she was elated; an afternoon of lemonade and merchants displaying the many ways to bastardize an ankh had recharged the down-with-the-people cells that energized her. In the back of the car, paper bags held our loot. For her, that was an ankh necklace with matching earrings and a twelve-dollar car decal of Huey Freeman from *Boondocks* peeing on the White House, with a sinister look on his face. For me, it was a thirty-dollar pair of Tommy Hilfiger jeans that a miasma of irony and bargain-basement pricing had persuaded me into purchasing. I'd have spent more if that was what it took to see her like this. She was, well, glowing. Blech, I apologize; I can't believe I just used *glowing*. I never got that as a compliment for women. Does it mean you look sweaty? But it's the only way I could find to describe it: a brilliant, peaceful glow.

It was one of those preciously rare moments in a relationship when the world goes away and comes into light all at once. Or maybe they're not supposed to be so rare; I'm not sure anymore, True Believer.

Anyway, when we had to stop for gas we were still very much within the *shady part of town*, as Thandie called it. The glow dimmed as beads of sweat sprinkled her forehead.

"Do we have to stop here?"

"Yeah, babe, we're on empty."

"Okay, just, be quick."

I raised an eyebrow but nodded, hoping compliance would bring back the girl I'd been sitting next to a moment ago, but it never did. When I went into the gas station the clerk, hunched over a magazine, took my fifteen to put in the tank and kept reading. Thandie was right to be apprehensive, surrounded by such lowlifes and all.

"Hey, man," said a guy outside. "Do you know where Franklin Park is?"

"Oh, yeah."

After a series of horribly confusing hand gestures he was on his way, but now Thandie was standing outside of her car, waving me to rush back. I jogged over.

"What's wrong?"

"Donald, just, just get in the car, it's so dangerous here."

I took a moment and tried to discern which was more frightening, the broad daylight, the public atmosphere, or the Black faces. She barely gave me time to pump the gas, her body trembling; we retreated as quickly as possible to her fortress.

* * *

"Why did you even agree to meet up?" I asked, hoping against hope that anything about this encounter was in my control. She placed a finger over mine, poking at the copper tab of my costume.

"Well, things have changed a bit since that night I last saw you, haven't they?"

* * *

I supposed they had. The last time I'd seen her, it was the week before Christmas. I'd come over wearing a Speedo and a Santa hat. Mind you, this was during the era of the golden-age beer belly, long before the silver-age electricity-induced washboard abs. You're welcome for the image.

"I think we should call it quits," she said, undressing in front of me before putting on a turtleneck sweater and long black skirt.

"But—I love you, Thandie." The sincerity of my declaration was thwarted by the jingle bells that chimed inside the Speedo when I took a step toward her. She rolled her eyes.

"Donald, you know I care about you, but it's so much pressure. You expect me to be this, this *girl* who's all doe-eyed and sacrifices herself completely—to what? Some impossible ideal of romance?"

About a month prior, Thandie had received word that she was one of ten people selected from a pool of a hundred for a research project in New York. If all went well she'd continue on to get her doctorate. I'd tried to be supportive, but I think we both knew where things were going. She just took the lead, like she always had.

"There's long distance, right? Can't we try that out?" I knew she was meant for more, but I didn't care. I'd happily put in 90 percent of the work. I just needed her to keep me feeling like I was part of her league. I needed the clutch.

"Donald, I wish I was the girl who cared more about being with the boy than about her career, but I'm just not. You're—you're *built* for this life, and I'm envious of you, Donny, but it's just not enough for me. If you went back to school, or—God, I don't know, just showed me you were going to *try* and be better."

"Better than what?"

"If you have to ask, then we really aren't meant to be together. Listen, I just—I'm not good at these things. I'm going to a dinner party. Take your time getting your things together, and—take care of yourself, Donald." After she left, I ~~cried~~ decided to keep my dignity by gathering my things and leaving, resigning myself to a life of never seeing her again. But, as we've covered, that's not the story I get to tell.

* * *

"So what are you saying, we could start things back up?" The words came out so very, very sad. As thin and insubstantial as the seventy-three-dollar tapas I was calling dinner that evening. She took them, my adorable words, and ground them up in her laughter.

"Oh, Don, this isn't Ohio. I would say you're maybe the eleventh most interesting man who wants my affection."

I folded into myself. God, I was a miserable little shit when it came to her. She watched me, sizing up the offering I was, before she rolled her eyes and sighed.

"But I can't say you're not doing anything with your life, not anymore." She leaned in, taking both my hands and reminding me how raggedy they always looked in hers. "If you were to become, say, the tenth? Well, maybe I could be persuaded."

This isn't the part where I snatch my hands away, shove the remaining tapas to the ground, and storm (haha) out of there. Nor, unfortunately, is it the part where I slyly lean back and bounce around the idea before waving it away, before receiving a call from Sanaa Lathan (Sanaa Lathan from *The Best Man*, specifically), who has chosen me over Taye Diggs in a third-act twist.

What do I, actually, do?

"Really?" I said.

These are the Astonishing Tales of *Ughhh*

"Yes, of course. I mean, don't misunderstand, I actually came here thinking that I was going to see the same old Donald and tell him, as graciously as I could, to let it go. But you're not the same, are you? I can tell, sitting there so cute in that little costume, that you're starting to understand what I already have. What really matters. You've grown up." She tightened her hands over my own. Clutch.

She'd conjured, in her own cauldron of bubble bubble toiling tenth, a kind of magic, the almond-eyed trouble all our mommas warned us about. Except mine, of course.

* * *

We parted with that tomorrow on layaway, and with a kiss that left me longing, like a teaser trailer I'd rewatch half a dozen times. I promised myself, as I damn near skipped home, delirious, that this time? I wouldn't lose her. I'd keep her attention, and her everything else.

These are the Astonishing Tales of an Idiot
Who Never Understood You Can't Keep
Something You've Never Really Had

CHAPTER 17
TALES OF THE ASTONISHING PROLETARIAT

IN THE INTEREST OF friendly competition, Doll and I were asked to team up. I wasn't against the idea. Any time I got the chance to shoot the shit with Doll was appreciated, even though I was trying to edge her out of the running.

As much as I'd like to assure you that the showy field operation you watched on TV wasn't staged, I can't. It was pro wrestling on the grand scale, one of those secrets we're all in on but forcefully suspend our disbelief about. Of course, I didn't know it was coming at the time, and that served a purpose. If Doll and I had known about it beforehand, the test wouldn't have been a test. What was silly, though, or at least felt hella silly, was that we were required to proceed as if everyone and their momma didn't know from the thirty or so cameras already on the scene (and the conveniently contained area) that the encounter was not the fruit of serendipity.

When the day came, luckily, I was in full costume already, skulking around NYU for . . . reasons. When my phone lit up, so did I, letting my spark bounce around my emblem while I ran towards the nearest subway station. Since I knew no one in New York and was generally too broke to afford anything like a life, I'd had more than enough time on my hands to prepare myself for that day. I'd treated Navigatrix to a drink, and she'd repaid me with information that would give me a fighting chance against Doll—who could fly.

I ignored the snapping of camera phones as I shoved past a woman with hard eyes and little talent, plinking out my fingers to unlock the turnstile. When I reached the platform the fear kicked in, like it always did and always has every time since then. I'd thought of doing this for a while but I'd been afraid that, like ATM robbery, it might be one of those better-in-theory things. There was no time to second-guess it now, though. I breathed, I sparked, and I gave in to hope.

These are the Astonishing Tales of Third
Rails and the Recklessness of the Rush

I flung myself from the platform edge to the third rail, connecting along the steel flats of my booties. The thing people don't realize is that it's not the third rail that kills you. Really, it's the earth. Electricity wants to connect, but we weren't built to channel it—not you, anyway. It wants to connect so bad that it'll take any path necessary to do so. If you give it the chance, it'll go through you. It's best to never give it that chance.

I unlatched one of my feet from the rail, slowly lowering it to the ground below. The electricity that guided the far-off train rode through me until I tamed it. Sparks flickered from my open mouth, skin tightened without cracking, and I grinned as every part of me became live. I lifted my foot from the earth and latched it to the rail. I sparked it up.

"BBYYYAAAWWWW!" I screamed jubilantly. My body hurtled through the tunnel. It was as close to flying as you wanted to get. I accelerated so fast that I accidentally passed the Canal Street stop by thirty feet or so and had to run back. I bolted up the stairs, and when I arrived on the street I saw Doll in the air, just beginning her descent. It had worked. We'd arrived at the same time; no need to race to catch up. I started thanking God, since I hadn't quite given up smoking yet and my lungs were not so astonishing.

And there was our villain: Dr. Detestable, who, as fate would have it, was Doll's college roommate and had vowed to destroy her for some BS reason or other—you know the type. She'd recently enlisted the help of seventeen-year-old Brick Box, who, encased in granite, had the ability to basically shit out massive bricks to throw at people.

So of course Doll would be extra motivated. Do you know how embarrassing it is to have *your* archnemesis defeated by another suit? Odds are you don't, but it's why I never envied anyone who had one: they become *your* responsibility.

Doll realized this. No matter how little she cared about Dr. Detestable, she knew how detrimental it could prove for her in the polls if I outshone her. Dr. Detestable was monologuing, something about revenge and revolution—hell if I remember. Whatever it was, it probably explained why we'd found ourselves, of all places, in the middle of a tiny hardware store.

News trucks held up traffic and people flooded the streets outside. If you ever find yourself in New York City after being struck by lightning, in spandex, vying for a position in THE premier superhero organization, be sure to mind the potential collateral damage. Make sure no one gets hurt; make sure there's still a baby alive to kiss in front of the cameras, even the ones they think you aren't aware of.

"Spark, we've got to handle this quickly. There are a lot of people," Doll whispered.

"Yeah, aren't there always?"

I wish there'd been two positions available on the team, because I honestly enjoyed working with Doll. She was methodical, and while the charcoal-black and crimson-red color scheme might fool you into thinking she was like the rest of us attention whores, she didn't like doing dances. Working with her, things got to the point. You have no idea how refreshing that can be.

She burst through the air and tackled Dr. Detestable.

When they were students, both ambitious to pioneer the world of tomorrow, both at the top of their class, Dr. Detestable had created a fabric that burrowed beneath the first layer of skin and emitted an indestructible energy field to protect its user. The problem? There wasn't an off switch, and since she'd tested it on herself, she was left permanently unable to feel. Doll tried to help, to find a solution. Her failure resulted only in the beginnings of a lifelong hate. Yeah, it's as stupid as it sounds, but that's the world we live in.

"You're the Black Spark, right?" Box said.

I sighed. "Just Spark is fine, thank you."

"Whatever. You suits think you can walk all over us, don't you?"

"Listen, dude, I'm just doing my job."

"Your job is controlling the masses! How about you control *this* mass!" He clapped his hands. When he spread them out a brick formed between his palms. He readied to pitch it at me but then paused, which I'm guessing had something to do with the fact that I was now laughing my ass off.

"What?"

"I—I'm sorry, dude, it's just . . . wow, man, that's pretty lame. A brick? You throw bricks at people? That's your thing?"

He cackled as he hurled the brick at me. When I skipped to the side he looked surprised. Surprised that I moved faster than a speeding brick. Yeah.

"I guess you're more formidable than I thought, but what about them?" He nodded at the people outside the hardware store.

I wrapped my dreadlocks back, knowing that as cool as they looked, I needed a clear line of sight for whatever was coming next. I grabbed two of the rods hanging from my waist and held one in each hand, waiting for his move. Electricity couldn't do anything against a rock, but then again, it didn't need to. I focused as he started forming another brick, faster this time but not as fast as me. The rods spun furiously, taking more of a surge than I thought, but it didn't matter. If even one dust speckle fell on the onlookers' faces, I could lose everything.

When he hurled the next brick, the copper rod, spinning at such a velocity that it looked more like a disk, sliced through it. But I soon found out that he'd been holding back. Bricks formed and pitched faster and faster, and I felt my connection to the rods loosening. The magnetizing wasn't hard, just . . . consuming. You know, like when you're walking down the street with your cell phone, trying to listen to music while your GPS is yapping at you and you're sending aggravated birds into sickly pigs.

"Wish I would have had these things when I met Maverick," I said aloud, trying to take my mind off my waning charge. I kept it up as long as I could, coated in dust from the exploding bricks crashing against my rods. We were both thrown off guard, though, as Doll crashed down between us from the floor above. Then Dr. Detestable leaped from the hole, landing beside Doll. The dust was hard to see through; I coughed and hacked as it found its way into my lungs.

"Oh, you're the electric one, aren't you? The Black Spark? Whimper in fear of the Detestable!" she spat.

Two on one.

Astonishing.

I sparked it up and aimed my fingers at Detestable, then fired off. Streams of visible electricity coiled around her but only made the force field shimmer.

"Hmm, that tingles a bit. What's wrong, Black Spark? Are you spent? Need a couple of minutes?"

I paused, hoping for a moment that she was one of those honorable fighter types, like Predator, or Vegeta and Nappa in *Dragon Ball Z*.

Doll used the moment to make her move, and I sucked my teeth while watching them trade blows. If Doll took her out, that was it, I thought. The distraction cost me, as Brick Box was back at it. Thankfully he'd taken shooting lessons from movies with stormtroopers, though, and mostly sludged them through the building's front wall. Afterward, the wreckage made the entryway look like a Tetris board.

Brick Box had to use material from his own body to make the projectiles, and now I could see flesh and blood beneath granite. *I can still win this.* I glanced at Doll, who was slowly winning as expected, but there was time. My spark was dwindling, but if I played my cards right, it would be enough.

I'd told Nikolas in our third or fourth session about my foray into the crime world, trying to short-circuit an ATM and coming up with nothing but smoke. He had, as he did with most of my stories, a rather large laugh over that. He also had an idea for a pretty solid lesson plan. You see, electricity is like a language. All you need to do is listen to enough Rosetta Stone tapes and you'll get the hang of it. You may need to narrowly survive a lightning strike also, but if you'd managed that and you were like us, you knew that it all comes down to frequency and wavelength, call and response. You learn to hear, and answer.

Smaller electrical devices that use lithium-ion batteries, like your cell phones and such, sound like the soft buzz of a housefly. No buzz, no charge left. (It's a pretty nifty thing to know when you've lost your phone in the middle of the night.) The bigger the device, the bigger the charge, the louder the buzz. That's how I knew where the cameras were, and how to blind them for as long as I needed to. So I shut them down, bled them of their automated life. I didn't need Gunther or anyone else seeing this next bit.

Brick Box advanced, and I let him, because he'd been slow enough to give me time to figure out exactly how much electricity I'd need to succeed. I feigned a pain at my side and hobbled to one knee, using the talents I had courtesy of the Walnut Grove High School theater company. His exposed hand clenched into a fist, thundering down at me.

I snapped a hand open to catch it, and I'd won.

I guess a little explanation is in order.

These are the Tales of the Astonishing
Absurdities of Mind and Body

It had been a week or so since Nikolas had made me spend a day learning from my mistakes in the broken body of George Splam. The day was ready to give way to night, and I wanted nothing more than to find a six-pack of IPA and then remember I couldn't afford that shit before buying some lager and falling into it. Nikolas was breathing heavy, leaning against a wall. *Yeah, you better take a break*, I thought.

"Good, but think smarter, not harder," he said. "You could have stopped me at least six different ways there. You keep acting with . . . duality. Keep your mind balanced—incorporate the electricity into your actions instead of switching back and forth between fighting with your body and fighting with the electricity."

"But if I use my power while I'm fighting, well, look at George. Look what we're capable of. Shouldn't I use that as, I don't know, a last resort?"

His face lit up before dimming down to a cool smile, as if I'd sparked (haha) understanding. "I see. Listen, Donald, I didn't take you there last week to—I mean, I'm glad you're thinking instead of just leaping straight to it, that's important. But I think you're thinking *too* much now. This spark is a part of you. You can't bottle it up, because that's what gets you out of control, and other people hurt."

"I don't know if I can. I'm just being honest: whenever I use it while I'm in the middle of a fight, or running away, or doing anything but giving it my undivided attention, it just keeps pouring and pouring."

"You're afraid. You're on a tightrope and you're panicking, because you keep looking down and seeing how far you're going to fall. Don't look down. Ride it slow and steady." He raised his hands again, trying to ease us back into the lesson.

"I—okay." I raised my hands, squared up.

Nikolas moved unlike anyone I'd ever come across, and I doubt I'll ever see anything like it again. In my time as a superhero I've seen my fair share of melee marvels, dudes who tried (and mostly failed) to mimic their favorite MMA fighters. When Nikolas advanced, though, it was like a cresting wave. (I apologize for the lost opportunity to make another electricity pun; you were no doubt craving one, but I think you can endure.) What I mean is, there was always something that carried him forward, moved him any way it wanted. If you tried to approach it too aggressively it would snatch at you, in the clutch or the crash. If you approached it too lightly, it would fool you, make you think that you still had the serenity of land beneath your feet, before you found yourself cast as far from shore as you could be.

I'd like to think my EXP bar was filling as I watched him. His breathing was steady, his movements deceptively slow. I felt ignorant and inept as I dodged each of his blows, not realizing that he was leading the dance into a corner. When my back hit the wall, I threw up my arms to guard my face and felt a shudder, a sizzling contraction that started where Nikolas, instead of throwing a punch, had grabbed my arm. I could still breathe, but it was slowed to a dream's crawl. In panic I felt my own spark rattle within, trying to correct, but it only seized things up more.

"You're okay," said Nikolas. "I'm doing this to you on purpose. You see? Once there's a connection, you can gain some control over your opponent's muscles. It takes quite a while to master the technique, though, and if it even works it's reliant on a hell of a lot of variables."

"Such as?" I gasped.

"How much body fat does your opponent have? What's their clothing made of? And, like, a hell of a lot more." He let go of my arm.

I wibbled and wobbled, every muscle tingling as if it had fallen asleep.

It wasn't the first time I'd come across a similarity between him and the Emancipator, but it was the clearest. Even then, though, I told myself that maybe I was reading too much into things. Maybe it was just a coincidence. Maybe, even though his voice sounded an awful lot like the muffled one I'd heard on TV from a guy with an oddly similar penchant for black clothing and banter, it was just my imagination regurgitating what I'd absorbed from watching too many episodes of *SSI: Terse Looks*. Maybe this was something that would just be simple and end the way it was supposed to.

These are the Astonishing Tales of Getting Back to It

I released Brick Box's arm. He stood frozen like a marble statue. I grinned, looking over at Doll to make sure I still had time. I let the cameras see me again, and as soon as I knew they were back on I delivered a Street Fighter–inspired roundhouse kick. It didn't do anything, of course, but his body toppled over from the push.

I knew, or at least hoped, that his paralysis would last long enough for me to finish things with Dr. Detestable. Before Doll could deliver what might have been the final punch, I bit my lip and made a choice.

Using most of what I had left, I flashed the cameras off again, but only for a moment this time. I placed a hand just behind Doll's back, not quite touching, and surged, drawing just enough of her electricity into myself.

"The hell?"

I didn't stand there long enough for her to realize what I'd done. The cameras snapped back on and I was in motion, pinning an exhausted Detestable to the ground, with a rebooting Doll at my back.

I'd won.

Aren't I a darling.

CHAPTER 18
ELECTION DAY

"YOU'RE FUCKING WITH ME, right? Did you see me out there? Wait, okay, just rewind it like twenty seconds. Okay, stop there. See what I did? I was fucking astonishing, Chris."

Chris and I sat on the same side of his desk for once, watching a YouTube video of my team-up with Doll. I'd had him rewind to the moment I took down Brick Box. I looked crisp and elegant, like I knew what the hell I was doing. Chris didn't seem to disagree—he'd smirked at all the right moments. But then he'd told me that my loss was nigh, and that if I could find a way out of my lease in the Bronx shoebox and enough dollars for a flight home, it'd be best to cash out.

"It was good, kid, it was damn good. But I'm doubting it was enough." He closed out of YouTube and opened ten or so more tabs. "Give these a read, and then let's talk about how you're winning."

"Where are you going?" I said.

"Takin' a shit—this'll take you a while."

I flicked the first tab. The site was familiar, a far-right American news, opinion, and commentary website that had gotten some traction lately, regardless of who or what they set in their crosshairs. Insane as they were, people read them—people who had the votes to send my Black ass home.

* * *

SPARKY THE STONER?

Look, in the sky! It's a bird! It's a plane! It's a super-hero who loves to get extremely high!

While subduing the notorious Super Predators Brick Box and Dr. Detestable, the Black Spark decided to proclaim his love of drug abuse. In the heat of the moment, this potential member of America's premiere superhero team cried out, "Let's spark it up!"

Our resident expert on slang terminology, Tyrone Johnson, has confirmed that this is code for "Hello my friend, let us smoke the marijuana." The Black Spark is perhaps best known for apprehending the moderately threatening Maverick Moralist, who has not been proven to be associated with any religious organization or political party.

"His behavior was completely unprofessional. I couldn't really see his eyes from where I was, but I can't say I'd be surprised if they were bloodshot," one witness informed us.

The Black Spark's agent, Christopher Row, was not available for comment.

* * *

"You seem pretty available for comment now, Chris!" I screamed towards the bathroom. Chris, whom I must praise at least for his impeccable timing, volleyed without words and let the thunderous sound of his toot speak for him.

I pressed on.

* * *

A SPARK OF ABUSE: WOMEN SPEAK OUT AGAINST BLACK SPARK

The Spark, until recently a frontrunner for election to the American Collective for Resolving Overtly Negative Yowled Misconducts, is already making headlines. Unfortunately, they're less than heroic.

Sources report that Spark struck the female Super Predator Dr. Detestable with excessive force, revealing a troubling inability to contain his animalistic rage. How long will we let the specter of toxic patriarchy loom over us, under the pretense of "superheroics"?

We here at *Agatha's Woolf Bite* are petitioning for Spark's immediate expulsion from the election . . .

(Also, there were other women there too.)

* * *

"But what the shit was I supposed to do, huh?" I yelled to Chris.

"Oh, I don't know, not punch a white woman square in the jaw on live TV? I mean, that *could* have been one thing, but the hell do I know?" he yelled back.

Eh, at least he was giving me words again.

* * *

A SPARK AND A FURY: DECONSTRUCTING THE RAGE OF BLACK SUPERHEROES

* * *

"Nope."

"Read it, McDougal!"

"Nah, I'm out of here. I'll see you later."

"You better keep your ass in that chair! Donald? Donald, get back—"

I didn't hear the rest of what he'd said because I'd already made it to the elevator. While I rode down I looked at the remaining money I'd gotten from my advance. Sixteen hundred dollars. More money than two months of my salary at Stereo Hutt. More ramen than I could ever imagine. A few round-trip tickets to Ohio and beyond. Absolutely nothing, in the face of the everything I was so, so close to finally having.

I admit that I considered calling Thandie. While I rode the train back to the Bronx I went into my phone's contact list and tapped her photo—well, actually, it was a classic photo of Marvel's Invisible Woman. I usually wasted far too much time scanning Tumblr for the perfect comic-book-character images to go with each of my contacts. (Paul had been cool with my choice of Beta Ray Bill, not that he had any idea who that was. It was just that, as he put it, *dude looks like he could wreck shit.* For Kat, I started with a snazzy early image of Titans' Raven, but after a half hour of listening to the reasons a Western comic could never properly represent her, I switched it to Yamcha in retaliation.) I shifted in the seat, staring at the Invisible Woman, wanting nothing more than to connect. I didn't, though. *Not like this, not yet*, I thought. *It's not over yet.*

It was one of my finer moments.

Instead I decided to go see Patches. As usual, he was the only one in the common room; everyone else was too busy giving more than half a shit about election night. When I slid onto the couch, he already knew what was happening and sparked it up. We chilled, we vibed, we did everything I was supposed to be doing with my constituents and connected for over an hour.

"So, what are you so afraid of, then?" Patches asked, downing malt liquor with a speed and precision that made me wonder if his talent was miscategorized.

"I'm afraid of where I go from here. I never finished school, I can't—No, fuck going back to Columbus. Not after all of this, not after—"

"Getting your eye torn out, getting reamed by Hound News, having a conversation with DEATHRAGE for more than three minutes . . ."

"Among other things, yeah," I said, waving away Patches's offer of a hit on Green Freedom. It was tempting, and since I'd already been boned in the pee test department I didn't see much point in abstaining, but a clear head felt necessary. He groaned, flipping on the TV.

"Could you turn that shit off?" I asked, maybe not so nicely.

He raised a brow without turning my way and, spoiler warning, did not in fact turn that shit off.

"I mean, I could, but you're an ass, so, no." He kept surfing, skipping past the only things I cared to see and along to the many, many channels showing either my own or Doll's face.

"It's election day, all you'll see is this crap," I said.

"Yeah, I know. It's entertaining. It's why these things were made, you know, to be entertaining."

Something in that calmed me enough to make his vegging out a co-op mission. I unlocked my arms, grabbed Green Freedom, and took the tiniest of tiny hits, falling into the chill as much as the storm would allow.

He stopped flipping when we landed on *Hero Station!* They mostly aired such stunningly crafted content as *Is My Girlfriend a Supervillain?* They also had the show we ended up wasting away with that afternoon, *Hero Battle*, in which a not-at-all-annoying host would match up two heroes, analyzing their abilities and social-media presence to determine the answer to a question no one had asked in the first place: Who is better? This episode, like everything else that day, focused on Doll and me. It was informative. For one thing, I hadn't had much time to keep up with how Doll was doing in her own training sessions, or with most of her interviews and coverage, save for what Chris thought was important. Thanks to *Hero Battle* I watched nicely edited footage of her not getting her eye smashed out of her face, instead using Stealth Mode to hide herself from view for the bulk of the session. I'd never had talent envy nearly as much as I did then, that invisibility swallowing her whole, keeping all the things she was to her and her alone. First, she incapacitated GRAVI-Tina. *Shit, that was a good move,* I thought, watching her become visible for a few seconds to let the cameras catch her shooting a tranquilizer dart into GRAVI-Tina's neck. *Optic Transience's very own Sleep Stingers, patent no longer pending,* she said before fading back into Stealth Mode.

She did it fast enough that Asper missed the chance to use his own favorite skill, Ridiculously Strong Punch No Jutsu, and hit nothing but the air. There was silence. I saw in that moment the difference between us, or at least one of the many: Doll was more proactive than reactive, taking the lead in making it them versus her, while I'd flailed around like, well, me.

She made quick work of DEATHRAGE and Patches, blinking back into visibility to shoot, from the center of her chest plate, a flat disk onto the ground between the two of them. She'd waited until they were just close enough to one another; the disk clicked before whipping a dozen thin, metallic cords around the two of them, snapping them against each other. *Wire Whizzers: Simple, safe, and most importantly, cost effective.*

"Oh snap, yeah, those things sucked." Patches laughed.

Asper was the only one left. *How the hell is she going to pull this one off?* I wasn't exactly kite-high while I watched, floating more around paper-airplane levels of lit, but I wondered if I'd miscalculated my intoxication when she blinked back into visibility, removing her helmet to reveal a sweat-drenched, sweetly smiling face.

"The hell are you doing?" Asper said. For once, I was with him.

"Well, we're done, right? I mean, you're the Almighty Asper. *The* hero. You didn't expect me to try and take you on, did you?"

Asper floated down from on high. He eyed her quizzically at first but finally smiled and extended a hand. Shit, was she good.

"You're going to fit in well here, China Doll," Asper said.

While Patches mimed gagging, I felt as if I really needed to puke. The show continued to show my own training, which . . . nope, not touching that shit again. Then they broke down the myriad of reasons why my one impressive display in the team-up with Doll was far from enough to cement a position for me in the American Collective for Resolving Overtly Negative Yowled Misconducts.

These are the Astonishing Tales of Fuck It

I headed for my soon-to-be-too-expensive apartment. That's not exactly right—it was already too expensive, albeit the cheapest option I could find.

The elated escape I'd had courtesy of Patches had worn off. My Black bones were brittle and ready to snap under the weight of a bottle. Before I could stop by the bodega next to my apartment, though, my phone buzzed. I nearly dropped it hoping to see Thandie's name, but it was only Chris reminding me to watch the election coverage. *Like hell*, I thought. In a briefly wonderful moment of frantic sanity, I scrolled down my list of contacts to find the one labeled *Kit-Kat* and used a lifeline.

When she answered I could hear yet another TV in the background, but I heroically fought the urge to hang up.

"Donald? Donald! Holy shit, dude, this is it! Are you watching this? What the hell are you doing on the phone with me? I mean, good to hear from you, but holy—"

"Kat," I said weakly. I'd never heard her so excited in all the twenty years she'd had to put up with me. There was silence for a while; I knew she could hear me choking up.

"Don, what do you need? Are you okay?" Her voice wasn't so much filled with concern as with that thing I really needed at that point. It was firm. Grounding.

"Chris—that's my agent—for fuck's sake, Kat, I have an agent. I don't even know how you *pay* an agent. Anyway, he said I'm going to lose. He said it's over, and I don't think I have enough money to get home. What am I doing here? Why the hell did I think I could do this?"

"It may have had something to do with the whole having superpowers thing," she said dryly.

I managed a chuckle-sob.

"Donald, listen, that shit doesn't matter. There's only so much you can do. Even if you don't . . . holy shit. I hear cars. Are you standing on the street?"

"Yes?"

"GO WATCH THIS, DUMBASS."

I went inside after Kat's call, realizing that whatever happened, I had her, I had Paul, I had people I'd never lose so long as I was brave enough to look. Later, Chris would spin my absence from the public eye that night as an adherence to my potential upcoming duty. Apparently I was too preoccupied with altruism, scanning the streets for thuggish bogeymen to beat into a pulp. Really though, I was sitting on my ass on the sofa the whole time, watching the votes pile up at the bottom of the screen and talking on the phone with Kat.

So, it ended. I lost. I wanted a shitload of shitty beer, but I couldn't afford that. I ended up going home, thanks to Paul and the kind folks who gave him plastic money based on his magical capitalism score. I spent the night at Kat's, dissecting the tale of who we could have been, if only.

I didn't hear from Thandie, but I didn't screw things up with the Ohio girl who believed in me, either. I watched on TV as New York was engulfed in an unforgiving fire, not from atop the buildings, and not one of those bones was my burden.

I eventually realized I could do more out of the costume than I ever did inside of it. I made my way out of my bubble whenever I heard about a storm, or an earthquake, or anything else that brought with it a loss of power and connection. And I offered the spark within.

These are the Astonishing Tales of the Tale I Wish I Had

* * *

"Oh my god, Donald, you won."

"What?"

"You fucking doo-doo head, you fucking won!"

"What? Hooooo, fuck! I won! I have to call you back. Can I call you back?"

"Yeah, that's cool, but—"

I hung up before Kat could finish.

* * *

I'd like to think that other reality, where I lost, exists out there somewhere. Someplace where *The Berenstain Bears* sits on my table while Sinbad's *Kazaam* is spinning in my DVD player. This reality, however, saw the narrow but decisive victory of Spark over China Doll by 210,000 votes. This reality saw my jaw dropping, my legs fire-filled and fumbling to the street.

It was after the call from Chris Row, the congrats from Doll, the calls from Kat and Paul and GRAVI-Tina and Patches and Gunther and anyone else I'd given my number to, that the burner number appeared on my screen. I knew it was Nikolas before I even picked up.

"Hello?"

"Hey," he said.

"How are you?"

"I guess congrats are in order, Spark."

"Nik. Listen, man, I don't know what to say. I'm sorry. But listen, I think I can help you now, after everything you've done for me. I think if you just came in, they'd see—"

"See you at ten, Donald."

Then, click. Then, nothing.

* * *

Wherever you are, Nikolas, good morning.

* * *

These are the Astonishing Tales of My
Power and Your Responsibility

These are the Astonishing Tales of
Houses and Homewreckers

These are the Astonishing Tales of

CHAPTER 19
TO MEND AND DEFEND

❚❚ ❚ *SAID,* **THAT IS SOME** ol' bullshit." Chris and I weren't exactly seeing eye to eye. We stood outside of the headquarters while I had my first cigarette in weeks, thanks to my Cheshire Clarence Thomas.

"That's the game, Donny. You gonna quit now? You came this far, you're gonna go home to sit on your ass and watch some other asshole do what you earned the right to do? Or are you going to suck it up and do some fucking work?"

I looked at the sheet of paper that Chris had spent so much time on, pristine and begging to be booty cleaner.

* * *

A step back, a reboot, True Believers.

The morning after the election, everything had started to explode. It never really stopped.

One thing I learned that day is how powerful a skintight costume can be. After I'd finally finished getting reamed by Chris for not responding to any of his calls the previous night, I went to deal with some more official business: a meeting with Gunther's favorite scientist henchman, Dr. Heller.

Having reached my quota of strangers strangling me with small talk for the day, I'd decided to take to the rooftops. I needed the sky. I wondered how painful the M-Chip would be. Would I be able to feel it in there?

Sorry, you may not know about this. Those times when your favorite members of the American Collective For Resolving Overtly Negative Yowled Misconducts seem to be talking to thin air? Well, that's all thanks to the M-Chip. Put simply:

* * *

THE COLLECTION OF MORAL INDIGNATION CUES CODE, ARTICLE 29

Those sanctioned to work within PantheUS will be required to carry communication devices at *all* times. Those inducted into government-supported task forces, such as the American Collective for Resolving Overtly Negative Yowled Misconducts, are mandated to have a surgically mounted M-Chip.

* * *

When I arrived in the basement laboratories, Heller made sure to get right down to business, rip-the-Band-Aid-off type that he was. The device was a tiny square, no larger than an oyster cracker. It was what was attached to it that made me curdle. Thin, angel-hair strings of translucent plastic hung limply from it, edged at the tips with tiny hooks. I was a good boy, though. I lay in the medical chair, naked, the cold steel stinging a song across my body, as he placed the square beside my ear. There was a *click*, a *whirr*, and then like a less science, more fiction spider it climbed into my ear canal. I started to seize up, my proud flesh wanting to spark everything around me. Heller darted back as the apparatus dug deep. It seemed to melt over my eardrum, the prickly strings burrowing to clutch around my throat. I wasn't sure which parts of it were inside of me and which outside. I wanted to scream, but it took that from me, latching around my vocal cords and tugging upward to find a home within my body.

* * *

I was extremely glad to get out of there. To be completely honest, Heller creeped me the fuck out. I was planning to go up and check in with Gunther next, but when I got to the lobby a buzzed alert told me to get to Kendra Kanaway's press conference, so the old man would have to wait.

I felt mixed emotions about being there, but I hoped for some kind of closure to the rivalry between the two of us. In fact, when she made her way to the podium wearing a suit and a smile, the only thing I could think of was how soon I'd be able to pull her aside to schedule our planned *Arrested Development* marathon.

I was in full costume, which may have not been the best idea, but I felt it was important to show some support as The Spark and not just as Donald.

"Thank you all for coming," she began. "I'm Kendra Kanaway, formerly known as The Doll, or—as some of you, I *hope* affectionately, know me—*that charismatic China Doll*." A bubble of laughter swelled and popped. "I'm happy to concede today that I've lost the election to my friend, *The Spark*, whom I called last night to congratulate on his victory.

"I'm proud of America today. I'm proud of democracy in action, as we've just seen it. What I can't say I'm glad about is that I've been less than fully transparent about my intent to serve."

Murmurs buzzed through the room.

"My company, Optic Transience, strives every day toward building a better tomorrow through scientific advancements that will enhance life for our children and our grandchildren. I don't think it will be news to anyone in this room that the company, over the course of this very interesting election, has experienced a resurgence in investor confidence and research grants. I expected that would be the case. Through the high profile of this campaign, I saw a way to build support for STEM initiatives everywhere. I saw a way to continue fulfilling the responsibilities I had to my employees, their families, my investors, and the public at large.

"I never intended to make it this far. Frankly, I don't know the first thing about being a superhero; I'd thought that would be obvious. No, it was never my intention to funnel my considerable resources—the vast reserve of scientific knowledge developed during my time at the helm of Optic Transience—into punching people in the snoot. This has all been, for me, what you might call a publicity stunt. Not a cheap or disingenuous one, but a chance to show off the power of science in action, building public and private support for research and development.

"America, I think you've chosen well. I think The Spark is the better candidate for this office. This young man's dedication and tenacity have left me with a much more favorable opinion of the superhero program than I had before—even if I remain unconvinced that such an institution is truly a worthy use of taxpayer dollars.

"In fact, you'll find that I've contributed a rather large amount of money to the cause of getting The Spark elected. That's how much I believe in him. I hope you'll give him your full support and confidence, too."

* * *

After Doll was done with the twenty or so minutes of follow-up questions, she met me behind the building. After all her deception, I was glad to see that at least the phone number she'd given me was real and she'd gotten my text asking her to slink out and meet me near the dumpsters.

"Spark! Thanks for waiting. Sorry, they had a million questions."

"What the shit, Kendra?" I was fuming, True Believer. I'd had a good twenty minutes to think about everything I wanted to say to her, but that's what came out of my mouth.

She laughed. "What, you're pissed at me?"

"I mean—all of it was a fucking lie? You rigged it! How is anyone supposed to take me seriously now? They're going to have a fucking field day with this."

"Let them. Listen, I'm sorry. I didn't do anything illegal, the money was all honest. And let me tell you something, kid, *all* elections are bought. You've won, not so fair maybe, but square. I know you wanted this, so—aren't you happy?"

She kind of had a point. "But I didn't want it like this. It doesn't mean anything if it's like this."

She cackled. "You're shitting me, right? Would it have *meant* more if you'd lost, then? Because you would have lost, Spark. Would it have *meant* something if I didn't let you siphon electricity from my suit, if I'd rejected my reboot protocol instead of letting you prance around and beat those jackasses last week?"

My guts melted into the same liquidy pool they used to after the most dastardly benders I took part in. "You knew?"

"I built a suit that runs on electricity, then learned I'd be working closely with some dude I don't know who can *manipulate* electricity, so yeah, I thought it was a good idea to install safety measures. Trust no bitch, Donald."

"I'm sorry I did that. It's just that I—"

"Wanted to win? I *know*. Honestly, I was impressed you didn't try to sabotage me sooner, but water under the bridge, dude. You're the newest member of the American Collective for Resolving Overtly Negative Yowled Misconducts. We both got what we wanted, so why are you sweating it?"

"Because I'm always going to have this hanging over me now."

Kendra smiled, but there wasn't any smugness in it. It was kind and real, meant—along with the hand she'd placed on my shoulder—as a salve.

"Well, make sure you show them what you're really made of," she said. "Listen, I have to go, but you can call me anytime. And congratulations, Spark."

She wasn't wrong. I'd won; I'd gotten everything I ever wanted. Soon I'd have enough money to treat myself to all the ice-cream cones in the world. Was I really still butthurt that I'd had a little help?

* * *

Two cups of coffee were ready and waiting in Gunther's office.

"This is a damn fine day, isn't it?" Gunther said.

I nodded so hard my dreadlocks whipped around, but Chris only shrugged. After all his talk of what was important and what *really* mattered, I thought he could have been a bit more hyped about the moment we'd been enduring each other for. I still planned on keeping him as my manager, but now the work would begin and I'd see him less and less, thank god. No more games. I'd be paid, and

I'd show you, them, everyone, what a nigga could really do. I would finally be Astonishing.

My first check I'd use like a Phoenix Down, paying off my medical bills, upgrading my living situation. After that I'd throw quarters into the slot until I didn't have to anymore, saving up (while of course living it up every now and again). Then, when I'd amassed myself some real capital, when they had no choice but to see what it would look like to pour those dollars back into something that really mattered, I'd make Malik's ashes dance.

"So, we have some materials for you to read, of course, but don't worry, you can take all the time you need. You're with *us* now—PantheUS. Hah! You know, I'll probably use that same pun in a year when you become official."

"Haha," I laughed, sort of.

"So! Fun part, we'll need an account for direct deposit, so when you get a chance, just fill this out for payroll—you'll figure it out. I had legal highlight the important stuff in there, but honestly? That's one of the things you pay this old coon for, right?"

More forced laughter. At least I didn't literally slap my knee like Chris did.

Gunther scooted back and pulled open the center drawer of his desk. He slid an envelope across to me. I'll spare you the details, but I ran through a rehearsed acceptance speech no one had asked to hear. Chris winced. As I opened the envelope and scanned the check I understood why.

A math lesson, True Believer?

Dumbass Donald is on a train, the Compromise-is-really-starting-to-seem-less-worth-it Express. If that train is going X speed, and he must pay a monthly rent of $1,038 with a monthly income of $1,399, how fucked is he?

These are the Astonishing Tales of Please Show Your Work

"You'll notice we threw on a hundred bucks as a bonus. We just wanted to let you know how excited we and the taxpayers are for your upcoming service."

I got instant heartburn. "I—I can't wait to get to—I'm sorry. I thought the supplementary pay was five figures monthly. Is there a mistake?"

Gunther's smile didn't waver. "Well, you're not a tenured member of the Collective yet. You do realize, son, that in the event of an emergency election the newly elected hero isn't given tenure until the next regular election, don't you? I mean, Chris went over that, didn't he?"

I looked over to Chris, who had discovered a sudden fascination with his shoes.

What type of reverse Willy Wonka shit is this? I thought.

* * *

It was true, as I'd find out on my very long, very *loud* elevator ride with Christopher soon after. The thing is, there hadn't *been* an emergency election in the history of PantheUS. I knew of course that my election was different, that a foul ball had put me at the free throw line, but I didn't figure that'd meant my points didn't count for anything at all.

These are the Astonishing Tales of You Are Allowed
on the Council, Anakin, But We Don't Grant
You the Title of Master, or the 401K That Comes
with It, or, Like, Any of the Benefits Really

"You're still a part of the team," Gunther said. "I wish I could offer you more, but the American taxpayer pays us. Unlike those circle-jerkers in the private sector, we have a responsibility to them. The money isn't a problem, is it?"

It sounded like a kind of threat, one I'm not sure he even realized he was making.

"No, not at all, sir. I'm just honored to be serving."

"Good, that's damn good to hear. You know, *this* is why I like you, Donald. This is why you're going to go far, kid. You've got that thing, you know, that—"

"*It*, sir. I think he has *it*," said Chris, patting me on the back.

I tried not to reach across the table and slap him upside the head with all the Odin force I could muster, and succeeded. Because I'd been such a good boy, True Believer, and signed, and smiled, and shucked, and sparked, I was given one gift, at least.

Then Gunther brought in a mannequin—with a fresh new costume on it. A token of appreciation, he said. The only real difference, save for the slightly darker shade of blue, was my emblem. It now illuminated whenever I sparked. Surprisingly enough, the image wasn't an A or something more patriotic but followed the vein of my original. Another Adinkra symbol, this one like two linked chains. I'd be told later, thanks to Gunther's researchers, that it conveyed a more important message while keeping up the whole "African thing." So, that was dope. It also served a purpose: LED lights were installed in the emblem, different colors for different catastrophes.

There was also a cute, not-migraine-inducing-whatsoever sound that happened when the blue LED flashed, to alert me danger was afoot. As a bit of a bonus, I found nigh-invisible pocket slips ... fuck, if I could have that costume back just for the pockets? It just might make all of this retroactively worth it.

Sorry, I'm getting off topic.

I found my first perk in one of the pockets, a pack of menthol cigs that Gunther promised to keep our little secret, explaining that even the most astonishing of us have our vices. I have to admit, True Believer, I was glad to see them. I hadn't had one in a while; later, when I finally got outside, I'd at least have something to do while I imagined the ways I wanted to destroy my amazing agent.

Because as soon as Gunther left the room, Chris handed me a binder.

I flipped it open. "Ha!" There was an image of me from a photo op I'd done during the campaign. But no—my hair had been photoshopped short, and in my hand I held a hacked-off head—*my* head, still trailing my locs. The text? "From Savage to Spark! See the Difference with Naieve!"

"I'm sure they'd work with you, a bald cap or something, but it might be time to think about getting those nigga slugs off your damn head once and for all," Chris said.

I flipped the page and saw a similar mockup for *Pigeon* skincare products. At first, it seemed innocent enough: me in a heroic pose on the left, Asper on the right. But above my head was the word *Before*, and above Asper's, *After*.

I wonder even now how fast my hands could have found Chris's neck in that moment. Would the sound of his squelching voice box trying hard to scream save him? Would it bring Gunther racing back into the room?

"You're out of your goddamn mind."

"Thirty-seven thousand, for the first ad alone. Think about that, and then think about how thick this binder is. *Then?* Before you sing an old Negro spiritual at me, remember how much you're *not* getting paid, and that you'll be risking your life every day when you play dress-up."

He'd known this was how it would play out from the beginning. He'd had a plan.

"No," I said. "I mean, let me think about it for a while at least, all right? And keep an eye out for some less soul-mortgaging shit, aight?" I handed the binder back to him, and that, astonishingly enough, was the end of the conversation. At the time, maybe I underestimated Chris's talent for timing, his patience. The fact that, for him? Things always ended exactly the way he knew they would.

CHAPTER 20
MONSTERS OF THE WEEK

SUNDAY

AFTER A FEW WEEKS with the Collective, I settled into a semblance of normalcy. Most Sundays were low enough on action for me to skid into a church and sit in the back. As crummy as I'd been with church, it surprisingly enough became more appealing when I was risking my life on a daily basis.

Then I'd give Kat a call, if I wasn't trying to conserve my prepaid minutes, and sometimes Paul too. I'd wash and wind my locs through a latch hook, or I'd waste away in front of a book and wonder what it'd be like to live in New York with an actual income.

Fink foop!

I was halfway through a fantasy book Kat had recommended one Sunday afternoon when I heard the sound coming from my costume. I loved that sound at one point, True Believer.

After calling up the HQ response line, I was told I'd be paired with DEATHRAGE in apprehending a couple of bank robbers. Intercepting such mundane criminals was, I'd learn, far more common than any other type of assignment. Unfortunately, this also meant I worked with DEATHRAGE more often than I would have liked. If you're the only member of America's premier superhero association without a glint of a talent, you'll probably be useless for most situations beyond garden-variety robbery, True Believer. Joining him on those calls was something of a dues I had to pay, being the new guy.

I never knew anyone with more of a gun-boner than this guy. Some days GRAVI-Tina and DEATHRAGE had competitive shootouts in the HQ range while Patches stayed locked in his room, using the circumstantial sobriety to dredge his way through stacks of past-due schoolwork from his online classes. You'd think the guy whose power was having a pistol would win, but most times GRAVI-Tina, after her years of training with firearms, would outclass him. He tried to get me to fire one once, but I declined. When he pressed I did the same thing I always do to get an angry white dude to chill the fuck out, which was flatter him. *How could I ever hope to be good as you?* Or: *Aww, man, I can't let you embarrass me like that. I ain't no good at that stuff!* He would accept this and go on about his bullet-time business. GRAVI-Tina was a harder sell. She tried everything short of dragging my ass into the range to teach me about respecting and understanding the weapons that were fired at us on a semi-daily basis.

That Sunday was pretty standard. I met DEATHRAGE, but I didn't hope to milk any conversation from him while we raced to the scene. I'd tried once to find some common ground with the dude, but somehow it always circled back to his dead parents. Like, don't get me wrong, tragic and all, but as a fellow orphan? Shit gets played out, fast.

"So, I see you got a new gun there. What do you call that one?"

"I CALL IT THE DEATHPISTOL NUMBER 34, SO I ALWAYS REMEMBER MY PARENTS ARE DEAD."

Or,

"Do you really believe that shit you said in your Hero News interview the other day? About Talented immigrants not being trustworthy enough to enroll in PantheUS?"

"THE MAN WHO MURDERED MY PARENTS WAS PROBABLY ONE, THEY ARE DEAD BY THE WAY."

I did admire his tenacity, though. Hell, given all the times he's been rendered unconscious in engagements with Talented individuals without suffering critical brain damage, he must have *some* kind of talent.

When we arrived I let him take the lead—not that I wanted to, but Gunther had suggested (ordered) that since I was the new guy I should only work as backup. I did get some practice in that way: I don't think I'd be nearly as good at using my powers to magnetize objects if not for having to constantly save his ass from speeding bullets. He'd give me a knowing, *good-job-kid* smirk whenever I did that. Afterward, he would of course receive all the press, but every now and again they'd come ask me what it was like working with the tragic and talented DEATHRAGE. I probably should have made more of a stink about how much *I'd* done in those encounters, but rule number 732 of showing gratitude for what you've been "given," True Believer? Take your bullets, take your kicks, take your everything if it means they let you hang in the house for one more night.

These are the Astonishing Tales of
Taking a Bullet for the Ballot

* * *

MONDAY

Fuck Monday. Fuck that saying *fuck Monday* is a fucking cliché. Even though it's completely fucking true, at this point it's like saying, oh, hey, it's a fucking dark and stormy fuck of a night.

Last Monday I stubbed my toe when I ran from a group of newbie Talented hacks looking to make a name for themselves.

Nine Mondays ago my phone got jacked when I fell asleep on the bus.

A billion Mondays ago I held a remote control, turning off the TV that my father's corpse seemed to be staring at. Rakeisha Harrison had taken the $6.99 box of chocolates that I offered her, but not my love, earlier that day at school. So that one was a twofer.

I woke up this Monday with a thin, steely string of pain radiating through my forehead. Thankfully, since I hadn't gotten my insurance info yet, I didn't need a doctor to tell me the all-too-common side effects of my friend with the black label. I rolled off my sunken inflatable bed and sprang not-so-spryly to my feet.

These are the Astonishing Tales of Taking Back Monday

When I arrived in the Situation Room, the monitor showed nothing, not even some frizzling static. It was just black, in an eerily empty room that did nothing but make me regret all the horror movies I'd pretended to be okay with watching in Kat's basement.

The expectedly unexpected jump scare I had thrown at me moments later came from none other than Patches, who nearly got his ass electrocuted when slapping my shoulder from behind and making me implode.

"Haha, shit, you're easy," he said. When he reached into his pocket and clicked at something, the *fink*ing and *foop*ing stopped.

"You?" I said, half pissed off and half still terrified.

"Oh, yeah. I wanted to hang, and your phone went straight to voicemail. Like, can we talk about that? How are you a walking charger with a dead battery? Anyway, GRAVI-Tina is upstairs. We never celebrated your induction, so I thought we could go kick it, you game?"

"You used an emergency alert system for America's greatest collective of talented individuals to see if I wanted to chill? How is that even possible?" I asked. Scolding a teenager who gave at best half a fuck might have been the most like an adult I'd ever felt up to that point.

"Oh, yeah. Gramps gave me a communicator like his, so I can get any of you fuckles on the line anytime I need to. Neat, right? So, you trying to hang or are you just going to stay all pissy?"

I rolled my eyes. My wallet, however, did not, and as mentioned, there are worse ways to spend a Monday.

* * *

TUESDAY

"I didn't say they were animals, Black. I said, you can't deny there's a problem with their presence *here*. Sorry if I happen to *trigger* you, but we'd be far better off not having to deal with them at all."

I was rarely in the same vicinity as Asper without the presence of cameras or some catastrophe brewing. That day, though, was one of those rare, precious moments that I cherished oh so much. The powers that be had seen that we were *fink*ed and *foop*ed together at a Zuccotti Park that had been empty of troublemaking anarchists for years. It was a low enough priority alert that Maria could keep her plans with her family. Patches was off doing that thing he wasn't supposed to at the hospital, and DEATHRAGE was no doubt busy shooting his dick off somewhere. So that left the two of us: the outsider from a doomed planet, and Asper.

We sat on a building overlooking the park where, in 2012, people from around the country, including Paul, had flocked to occupy the ground until something didn't even so much get fixed as maybe noticed. Like a dude with a missing limb or hemorrhaging wound sitting in the emergency room, waiting to hear his name called.

I'd seen Paul afterward. He seemed physically, mentally, and spiritually (as much as his atheism allowed) exhausted. Through his depleted everything, though, a euphoric glow seemed to envelop him.

"At least we did something," he said.

I'm proud that he did. I'm not so proud that the only response I had for him at the time was, "But did it matter?"

Sitting there with Asper, I couldn't say it had. The park was empty, abandoned.

"How long do we have to sit here?" I asked.

"Until they come back, and we have to remind them again why America will always—*always*—put a stop to terrorist activities."

I thought about correcting him on the difference between protests and terrorism, but I didn't have tenure yet, and pissing and moaning wouldn't help my staying power.

So we waited, and I let his mouth ramble at me. I listened to all the reasons why sloth was the true cause of disenfranchisement, not some sinister 1 percent. I zoned out, watching the wanderers of the world tick and tap across the park.

It was a bit of a relief when we finally saw something. One man, with one sign and one very bad idea. Great: this Tuesday drudgery would end soon, and I'd be able to go home and lie around and forget that Asper and his ilk would never be deterred, not this day or any other.

Asper soared into the park, cracking the sidewalk (the repairs would be of course billed to the not-so-super predator with the sign). His blue eyes burned, but to his credit they didn't zap. The man, the sign, and the seed were sent packing with a ticket and a reminder of what to do with freedom.

I got a bratwurst. I went home. I drank, heavily.

* * *

WEDNESDAY

When I met Paul at the train he smiled, crooked in tooth but honest in form, dropping his leather I'm-a-professional-writer satchel from his shoulder before enveloping me in a tight hug. It was always with a kind of apprehension that I let him that close. Silly as it was, there was still a holdover from the days when being within a few feet of him might provoke an attack of opportunity in the form of a wedgie, a wisecrack, or some other schoolyard classic.

"You have an okay trip, man?" I asked as he picked up his satchel.

"Yeah, it was cool. Missed this city, forgot how many costumes pop up as soon as you get off the plane. Speaking of, thought you'd be all decked out in your getup."

"Nah, honestly, Wednesdays are pretty chill. We're meeting up with your friend for lunch still, right? Didn't want to unintentionally block you with my superhero getup in case you were trying to holla at her," I said heroically.

"My nigga on his Adonis shit now? Damn, I knew it. I knew that all those times, those corny-ass jokes and that time you were really trying to make hats *happen* was all a front. You was just tryin to teach me something all along."

"Well, *you know*," I said.

He hated it when I used those two words of his against him—as if by not being a part of his secret dick-fiddling band of fraternal brothers I wasn't allowed to string them together in a sentence.

"Anyway, she's just a friend," he said. "She cute though, so don't be weird."

I nodded. Tucked away in my phone was the promise of Thandie, but he didn't exactly need to know that.

We spent some time catching up before lunch. I was glad to hear he'd been doing so well—not that he was ever in a place of actual struggle, but it was still nice to be reminded of the contrary. He told me Kat would have tagged along, but her pops had slipped into bad health. I made a mental note to check up on her.

We spotted Paul's friend as we walked down Sixth Avenue in Greenwich Village. The freckles on her face were scattershot like a night sky in Ohio. They were plentiful, chaotic, but there was a method to the magic. That crafted chaos continued to her 4-C crop of hair, which frizzed around her face and down to the bottom of her earlobes; the brightness of her natural reddish tinge made each swirl impossibly visible. I began to deconstruct each one in my imagination.

Shit, Paul was right, I thought. *She is cute tho.*

"Anyla? That name is pretty familiar. You're—you wrote that piece about—*The Spark*," I said, with italics.

I couldn't understand the confusion on her face at first, or why she traded looks with Paul, who shrugged in response. I finally took her hand to shake it.

"Yeah!" she said. "What did you think about it? I'm sorry, is that weird? I don't really meet many of the people I write about, and can't say when I do it's usually in a positive light." She laughed.

I, however, did not laugh. I didn't continue shaking her hand. I didn't release it, either. I didn't do much of anything before the rage set in and I spun to Paul.

"Nigga," I said, letting all my sense of betrayal and some palpable malice sink into the tofu-like word.

He rolled his eyes. Hell of an underreaction to the person who's just learned you've been passing out his secret identity like [insert metaphor I'm too angry to come up with since I'm currently reliving it].

"You. Have. White. Dread. Locks. My. Nig. Ga," Paul said. "You don't even wear a fucking *mask*."

Thankfully, as Anyla asked for her hand back, I let it slide.

We took our time getting to the restaurant for a bite. It was odd hearing about that missing bit of time when Paul didn't live in Ohio but instead was kicking it with Anyla at Columbia, although it was nice to talk about something other than PantheUS crap for a while.

"So how long are you in town?" Anyla asked.

Paul, who was smashing on his burger, took a moment to remember where the universe began and the plump patty ended. He'd told me more than once that of the few things he desperately missed about the city, his monthly splurge at Minetta Tavern was one. As I didn't have the means to dump nearly forty bucks on a slab of cow carcass, though, I mostly watched while snacking on some fries and a water.

"Well, I had to check on my boy here. I have a meeting with Chester, then I'm pretty much bouncing back."

"Sorry to hear that. I hoped you'd stick around and get an actual look at the people you slam so much in your pieces," said Anyla.

"Ha, ha," said Paul. "You write, what? One positive piece on a superhero from your hometown and suddenly you're PantheUS's poet laureate or some shit? Get the fuck outta here."

We all laughed.

"So what about you?" said Paul, turning to me. "You gettin' back to Ohio anytime soon?"

I split a French fry in half, trying valiantly to fool my body into thinking it was being fed more than it actually was. "Not likely. Too much going on. They're re-evaluating the budget for PantheUS and there's a vote in two months, so getting time off isn't really an option right now. A few months after that I have the final vote."

"I heard about that—the budget, I mean. How are you feeling about it?" Anyla asked, shifting seamlessly into her journalist cap.

I ate the other half of my fry. "I mean, we provide a service. It costs money to keep that service organized, keep the heroes compensated. There are a lot of wheels to grease and all that."

Paul eyed me with his arms crossed.

"Yeah, I get that," said Anyla, "but the current budgetary allotment for PantheUS is in the billions. Do you think it's worth that much? Of taxpayer money?" She shoved her credit card into the leather fold the waiter had left.

"Well, it's just—" I started. I didn't have the balls to keep going.

"I think if we were to really look at it, the structure of the superhero complex as a whole? It's a bit counterproductive. Funding, compensation, insurance—all of that's important, don't get me wrong, but the budget is absurd. If we took a quarter of the income for PantheUS members in the most well-known affiliations and invested that back into the areas most highly impacted by villain activity, invested in education or, you know, housing development, we could eliminate the need for superheroics, at least in its current form, altogether."

"That's all well and good, but I don't see either of you jumping to promote a cut in your paychecks," I said.

"Yeah but, I mean, you spend more time and resources on defending yourselves than anyone else," Anyla said. "Don't you?"

"Uh, I mean, yeah, maybe you have a point. You know, I read your article about PantheUS's shitty approach to assisting those impacted by the first appearance of Asper," I said.

Anyla's eyes widened. "Stalking my work, McDougal?"

"Well, you *did* write something nice about me, so I guess it was mostly narcissism, wanting to confirm you knew what you were talking about. But I knew one of those people you wrote about. And you're right. He was more than a number. Forget human decency, it would have been in PantheUS's best interest to do something for his family."

"Can I quote you on that?" she asked, seeming impressed for a moment (or at least that's how I let myself remember it).

I played the ponderer, rubbing my chin and staring at the ceiling. "Hell no."

"This nigga," Paul said with a sigh.

Fink foop!

The sound of my masters' call made me shrivel a bit; the two of them stared in confusion.

"I gotta go," I said. "It was nice meeting you, Anyla. Hit me up later, Paul."

"Yeah, you too," said Anyla.

Unfortunately, I didn't catch up with Paul later. I didn't even have time to answer the text he sent about meeting up before he left town.

The Carnivorous Crane, some winged wonder, had thought it a wonderful idea to attack a charity event in Tribeca. He had help from the Great Gavin, a teleporter of all things. GRAVI-Tina and I made quick enough work of them, but not so quick that I had a chance to see Paul off.

* * *

THURSDAY

Fink!

Mother.

Foop!

Fucker.

That Thursday at least had an upside: I'd be teaming up with GRAVI-Tina instead of DEATHRAGE. We'd been sent to take down the Great Gavin, who'd escaped us the night before. Fuck, do I hate teleporters. Gavin, whose real name was Alberto Acosta, had started out as a vigilante. He'd explained, to anyone who would listen, that while he had indeed teleported back and forth across the US–Mexico border a number of times, and while, yes, maybe the US had a few new migrant workers as a result, it was only in the hopes of furthering the cause: ending Onyx-level threats like White Flame.

PantheUS was not amused.

> These are the Astonishing Tales of Bring Us Your Tired,
> Your Poor, Your Huddled Masses, Although We'll Turn
> Them Away If They Are Kind of a Little Brown Even

"A minute," I whimpered.

What I needed a minute to recover from, True Believer, was the shattered, splintered thing I'd become when Gavin tried to teleport the two of us during our battle on a rooftop. GRAVI-Tina had placed a field around us, stiffening the gravity so that if Gavin tried to piece himself away he'd fall flat as he crossed it. That left nowhere to go but up.

It did feel a little odd that what we were trying to stop his getting away from wasn't exactly a crime scene. He'd been using his ability to teleport people out of a burning apartment building, but his altruism had taken too long, giving us, the heroes, a chance to bring him to justice.

A note on teleportation, True Believers.

There isn't some vomit-inducing cloud of smoke or dimensional sliding door you step into. It's death and rebirth. It's being everything in one moment and nothing in the next. It's one of the most excruciating horrors our universe has to offer.

When Gavin touched me I was torn from the inside out. Starting from my navel I peeled apart but didn't spill an ounce of anything, as if every molecule was Saran-wrapped. I was separated from time and it went on forever and a second. I felt every splice, every imperfection of mine being perfectly pulled apart, until the world went black.

When I had eyes to see again, I was a few hundred feet in the air, tumbling down through cutting wind and wild laughter.

We were too far up for GRAVI-Tina to intervene, and Gavin, apparently not wanting to add "murdering a PantheUS official" to the list of crimes he was wanted for, tore us apart yet again between the sky and the ground. When I reformed I had only a few feet to fall—but the thud was still crushing, True Believer. GRAVI-Tina had no time to react when he appeared behind her. I couldn't speak, couldn't warn her. He touched her, taking her who knows where—far away from the fight.

He reappeared from wherever he'd taken her off to. My body shuddered and sparked on the ground. He just left it there and went to check on those he'd saved. The dastardly villain.

* * *

However his power worked, it wasn't supposed to work with *me*, because I couldn't stop shivering. The light of my spark radiated furiously around my body. I groaned.

He heard me and sucked at his teeth, hesitating but ultimately making his way over to check on me too.

It was more than a mistake, True Believer, because when he approached, he got caught in my untethered pulse of energy. Pain took ownership of his body like the country couldn't. It became all he knew, and like me, he lost control.

His left arm began wilting away like a milkweed. He tried to call the rest of his body to teleport with him, but it disobeyed, and bit by bit I watched it reform. Bones from his elbow protruded where his shoulder should be. His limp hand dangled from them, the skin grafted over it tight but incomplete.

I'm sorry, I thought. *God, I'm so sorry.* I closed my eyes and remembered Nikolas's lessons the best I could. I undid the pulse, but that was all. Gavin flailed madly, unable to form words but emitting violent shrieks.

"Holy fuck," said GRAVI-Tina, who'd found her way back to us. In the distance there were sirens as police cruisers sped towards the scene. The victims of Gavin's vigilantism kept their distance as they watched the altruism their taxes had paid for.

* * *

FRIDAY

"No, no way, man," I said.

We were sitting at Dilly's pub. In the world of up-and-coming heroes, Dilly's had become something of a refuge for those who hadn't "made it" yet and therefore wanted to imbibe at a relatively low price. She'd invited me out for a lunch date—probably to check in on that favor I owed her for the help back during my campaign.

"I know, fucking crazy," she said. "I tell you man, some shit? Even when you run around in spandex all day? Can *still* surprise you."

We'd been talking about roommates. Most PantheUS members who hoped to make it onto an A-list squad had to live where the heroic heartbeat hemorrhaged the most, a.k.a. very expensive cities. One had to get creative to survive, and that's where Ronin Rooming came in. It was an app where hero wannabes could find cheap, sublet housing and link up with other randos who needed to do the same. Navigatrix and I had both used it.

My roommate (didn't know I had one, did you, True Believer?) was the all-too-common nonhero who had, thanks to a friend's invite to the exclusive app, found affordable housing with an actual superhero. I didn't so much care that he wasn't a hero. In fact, he was so invisible that the only way I knew he was a dude was a bit of deductive toilet-seat-related reasoning.

He kept his door locked, which I only knew because I'd tried to use his fire escape once. The only clues that led me to knowing of his nonhero status were in the crap he'd leave in the living room. No hero had so much hero-related trash. HeroCon weekend pass; copies of *Hero Scope Weekly*, whose mission was to snap candid photos of PantheUS members eating burritos or picking out wedgies.

Having moved in with someone who wasn't actually a hero and didn't have the decency to say so up front was a bit of an annoyance, but it was nothing compared to Navigatrix's drama. Her roommate was a bit of a ghost as well. She worked nights, which wasn't all that uncommon, so at first Navigatrix attributed it to her aspiration to be a brooding, *I am the night* type of hero. The truth, though—as she'd found out due to a laundry-bag switch that was a sitcom level of serendipitous—was that this roommate was in fact the D-list supervillain Victorious Steel.

"How do you know she wasn't just a cosplayer?" I asked.

"I stayed up one night and watched her Netflix bingeing on the couch after she got home. She was covered in welts and bruises. Cosplayers don't get that banged up on the regular—or pay in so many loose bills, or choose some no-name like Victorious Steel to dress up as. Know many cosplayers who can transmute their appendages into steel at will? No? Me neither."

"Shit, that's rough. So, the great hunt is on for a new roomie, then?"

"Well . . ."

"What?"

"It's just that she's the best fucking roommate I've ever had."

"You're shitting me."

"She barely uses electricity, there are no weird dudes, or, like, baggage floating around, and she doesn't just pay on time, she pays *early*, like clockwork. She's also a neat freak. I completely hit the jackpot."

"Save for the whole supervillain thing."

"Yeah, but I read up on her PantheUS file. It's a one-pager. She isn't even *classed*. She's nonviolent, even though her talent is physical. She loves animals. Her biggest crime was releasing penguins from a zoo or some soft shit like that. Okay, maybe she doesn't get the money through the most legal of means, but she's out there busting her ass all night to get it. She pays her bills *early*, man, I mean, who *does* that?"

"A supervillain with lots of disposable dirty money? I'm a card-carrying member of the American Collective for Resolving Overtly Negative Yowled Misconducts, Nav. I can't know this."

She played shyly with her fingers. Fuck—*this* is where the favor lived.

"So, listen, I would really appreciate if you did me a solid."

"What's that?"

"I know that she mostly picks up odd night jobs here or there, and pretty much does her villain thing on Friday nights. So, here's the thing, you *owe* me. Not being an asshole here, it's just the truth. So I can give you her usual starting route, and I thought you could maybe, you know, keep tabs on her for a little while? Make sure she really isn't hurting anyone? Cause if she's not . . ."

"You want me to do this *tonight*?"

"What else are you doing?"

Shit. She wasn't wrong. The A-listers, True Believer, mostly fought their ferocious foes between Sunday and Thursday. Only the lesser-known among heroes and villains alike—the ones with something to prove—spent their weekends working. Me—well, with an A-list-type gig that gave me quiet weekends but not the pay to enjoy them, I spent my Saturdays training, reading, or doing anything else I could to distract myself from the reality that I was too broke to live it up in any way at all.

"Besides, there's something in it for you," wheedled Navigatrix. "I'm basically giving you the potential for a free collar, you know? If anything goes down. So—you're welcome."

That kind of pissed me off. "Are you serious? Do you want to get electrocuted? Because this is how niggas get electrocuted."

"Sorry, it's just that—I don't want to lose a good situation, and I don't want anyone to get hurt, either. Can you just help me out?"

I don't want anyone to get hurt. Crap. Those seven words bore into my ears, past the M-Chip and down to everything that mattered. I wanted to burn every Spider-Man comic I'd ever owned that even slightly referenced power and responsibility, but it was too late. I knew I had an obligation to fulfill my debts. And I didn't want anyone to get hurt, either. I groaned and shook Navigatrix's hand.

"*Fink foop,*" I muttered.

"What?"

"I said we're even."

* * *

SATURDAY

Like I said, I usually had Saturdays to myself. I thought about wandering around at the Strand or doing a rooftop run to clear my head, and definitely not about spying on Thandie. I went out to do a little of each. It was during those blessed non-*fink*ed, un-*foop*ed moments that I stumbled across the Cheetacker.

Once a brilliant scientist, Stanley Spade—who had tragically lost the ability to use his automobile—developed a serum incorporating the genetic code of the cheetah, which would increase the running speed of an average human being to somewhere in the ballpark of sixty miles per hour. It worked—all too well. He achieved the inhuman speeds, but at an inhuman cost. His body morphed into a cheetah-humanoid hybrid. It was initially thought that he was not to blame for his wicked wrongs, until a brain scan during his last incarceration revealed that, neurologically, nothing had changed in him whatsoever.

He liked to spend his days terrorizing those who made the tragic choice of driving in the city. He was something of a white whale for the lower-echelon PantheUS members. He didn't so much hurt people as jack up their rides and then hurl an insult while darting away.

So, True Believer, there I was practicing on a rooftop when I heard someone screaming obscenities in the street below. Usually that wouldn't have drawn my attention, but I caught the flash of spotted fur out of the corner of my eye. I hopped and sparked from rooftop to rooftop, chasing him as he cut through alleyways.

He eventually stopped, unaware that I'd been watching, and laughed to himself. How fortunate that he'd decided to do his dastardly deeds in the Bronx that night. I could wrap this up, call for a pickup, and still get to bed at a decent hour for church the next morning, yay for me. Also, it was something of a bonus to know I could now hope to secure the votes of most urban automobile owners. Two birds, one cheetah-man hybrid.

I leapt from the building above him, using a flashy display of electricity to both intimidate him and slow myself down via magnetization to nearby metal. When I landed, he wasn't very quick to run away, which was a little wounding to the pride but worked out for me.

"Cheetacker! You nefarious foe! I am The Spark! I have come to put an end to your—"

"You won't stop me, you suited scallywag!"

"I wasn't done, man. Like, that's just fucking rude."

He readied himself to leap. I'd learned enough about fisticuffs from Nikolas, but most times? I didn't need them all that much. Even as Cheetacker twisted his way through the darkened alley towards me, I knew that electricity? Well, it kind of works the same on one person as it does on another.

These are the Astonishing Tales of What Happens
to a Toad When It's Struck By Lightning

I began to spark it up with a smile. I should have kept my eyes on the prize, but I was giddy to speed this along and catch the season finale of *Supernatural*. Before we could engage, however, Cheetacker stopped short, his feline eyes riveted on something behind me. When I turned, I realized why so much fear filled them.

The creature, which had no name, was like the melted husk of a human, dream-muddled, malformed. Its mouth didn't so much open as snap triangularly. It shrieked.

I think I've made it clear that I had quite a lot of time on my hands back in those days. I'd scanned thousands of PantheUS files, trying to shovel information into the messy room that was my noggin, creating space among the memorized scripts of *X-Files* episodes past and John Cusack movies for the rogues gallery of PantheUS. This creature was nowhere to be found.

Its nigh-invisibility sank into me, its paper-white whirlpool eyes the only thing I could make out clearly until it flopped down on all fours with the malevolence of a Lovecraftian haunt. Worse, I felt something as it arched its back to leap: a tingle. A connection. The same as when I'd first met Nikolas.

These are the Astonishing Tales of It's
Electric, Boogie Woogie Woogie

A flash. A spark. A lightning-licked limb cracking through space into Cheetacker's arm. Whatever the shit it was, it latched a talon into him. When the appendage whipped back, Cheetacker's arm hemorrhaged.

Nightmare, the solar-plexus-deep, garish kind that makes you force *garish* into a sentence, filled me. The creature leapt through the air while I cradled a fallen Cheetacker, who'd gone in the span of a few seconds from villain to shivering, scared-shitless victim.

I barely had the chance to yank Cheetacker to the side. The creature slammed into a fire escape. I got up, leaving Cheetacker in a pile of garbage bags, and summoned a bolt of energy, focusing it behind the emblem of my costume. When the creature's mouth snapped open, a swirl of light formed within it. A connection latched in my belly as the ball of lightning swelled in its jowls.

The lightning popped and fizzed and bled from intense white to brilliant violet before it shot towards us. I opened my palms instinctively. When it crashed into me, I felt like the black-haired noob I had been on that New Year's Eve when lightning first struck. The heat of it was like nothing I'd ever known. It coursed throughout me, bringing me to my knees. The creature scuttled in our direction.

"Run, fucking dammit!" I cried to Cheetacker, but there was little left of him to respond.

The thing whipped its tendril across my body, and I fell flat.

When I got to my feet the creature was hulking over Cheetacker, the darkness of its form shadowing the intense spark spilling between their bodies. When it moved off, the smell of seared flesh filled the alley.

I needed help. I needed anyone who could fucking save me.

I screamed.

The creature screamed in return, a scream that electrified every hair on my body. I wasn't brave, but I knew I wasn't willing to die running. I poured everything I had out at it, moron that I was, sending a spark into it that shone brilliant white and then violet.

It regarded my outburst as little more than a breath of wind on a cold Columbus night. The creature crawled toward me, chaotic and slow, emitting a low growl—but even that growl latched onto a part of me, in the pit of me.

"Aaaa," it moaned.

I froze as it crawled up my body, its limblike appendages clasping my own. Those eyes, spiral pools of white, met mine. This was death. This was the end.

(Of course, it wasn't. Frame narrative, duh.)

It seemed to survey me, weighing what I was—the greatest horror of that night, True Believer: being weighed in the scales, and no doubt found wanting. But whatever it decided I was, apparently I didn't merit the same fate as Cheetacker. It lurched off, it kept those pools on me, and finally it scuttled off up a brick wall and to the roofs.

A real hero might have tried to follow the creature, to make sure no one else would fall victim, but—staring at the body of a now-exsanguinated Cheetacker—I went a bit catatonic for a while.

I'd eventually report to HQ that night. I was told they'd use the information I gave them to create a new record for a John Doe Super Predator, since I only had a story and a body and a knowing that it all sounded insane. No name; no description. *Eldritch horror* didn't quite convey what the sketch artist had in mind.

I wouldn't see Gunther for a few weeks afterward. He'd been busy with a conference on the expansion of Super Predator Patrol within allied countries. But he'd read my report, and—of all the things to say—congratulated me on the successful apprehension of a Super Predator who'd evaded capture for months.

I reminded him that it was really more of a fatality than an apprehension.

"That's an apprehension of sorts, though, right? That speedy bastard has been slipping through PantheUS fingers for too long. Sounds like he got what he had coming."

"What about the thing I saw? The creature?"

The elevator stopped. I stepped out but kept a hand against the door until he answered.

"Right, the creature. Well, we'll look into it, and if we dig anything up we'll be sure to get the full weight of PantheUS behind tracking it down," he said pleasantly.

I nodded and took my hand out of the elevator door, not wanting to force an issue with the dude cutting my check.

He put a hand out and blocked the door himself. "Spark? Now, this has nothing to do with nothing, but you really should make some time to study your regulations. You know that PantheUS members have authorization to use lethal force when a Super Predator endangers their life, right? That, say, if a PantheUS member feared repercussions for exercising said force, he should really know he's got nothing to worry about. Here, more than anywhere, honesty is the best policy."

I added up the words. "Are you saying you think I made a false report?"

"No, of course not, my boy. Just thought I'd make sure you're taking the time to study up. You have a good day now, Spark."

Weeks went by, *finks* went *foop*, but I wouldn't see my monster again, not for some time, anyway. The space between that time and the next seemed so far then. Each week I spent wondering if I'd see it again. In every alley or alcove—was it waiting?

I could only do my job and hope, for the sake of any life I'd promised to protect, that it would stay away, tucked in its own little space of the world. As if a space existed where our own machinations don't come home to roost.

CHAPTER 21
BOTTLE EPISODE

"**H**EY MAN, I DON'T WANT to be that guy, I just asked for it black." I'm overhearing a customer talking to our favorite supporting barista, Tad. Tad is full of apologies, filtering all the masculinity from his voice. It's amazing how fast the switch happens. I don't know much about the barista wonder outside of this place, outside of that ill-fitting smock, his mask. He's smart enough to make himself look weak when necessary, and I feel that I can relate.

When Tad finishes helping the Gratuitously Grumpy Bear, he turns and his hip smashes into my table, spilling my coffee down my body. I've never been much for heat, but since I'm currently down to a total of two shirts, coffee stains are my most dire Super Predator. Tad apologizes profusely, to which I smile and ask where the restroom is.

It's serendipitous. I'm rather stank-filled. I shuffle off my clothes to take a sink shower and get the best news I've had all day: three dollar bills falling to the ground. I have money! It's like being in the final dungeon of *A Link to the Past*, ready to throw the controller across the room after yet again getting face-fucked by Ganondorf, but then, when all seems lost, a fairy floats over—one you forgot you had in that overstuffed inventory. And you've got a chance to fight again.

A three-dollar coffee is enough to keep the thoughts flowing.

Shit, maybe I should have saved those three bucks for the laundromat I saw three blocks away. Eh, hindsight, True Believer.

So I'm sitting back at my table, dreadlocks draping the sides of my face as they've done for months now—my very own invisibility cloak. What am I going to do with the next blank page in this whatever-it-is? Where should I go next? What will just keep you fucking *listening*?

I mean, I do have quite a few options.

There could be a chapter about the Carnivorous Crane. GRAVI-Tina and I spent a week hunting him down after he robotically cloned DEATHRAGE's parents to torment him. DEATHRAGE dissolved into a pool of useless sobbing, leaving us the only teammates who could pursue the villain.

There was that stint I had with the Power Pride. It was a sadly one-shot type of thing that went by way too fast, three weeks I think, but I got to fly out to San Francisco. They were awesome and even gave me an honorary membership that afforded me the right to chill whenever I wanted to at their base, The Rainbow Room, and that was pretty rad. I'd have probably stuck around longer, but if I didn't have New York money, I sure as shit didn't have California dough. Well, that and anytime I'd hang in Boys Town, outside of their HQ, I was asked so consistently if I was *supposed to be there* that I got the message: I wasn't.

Oh! *Noodle Man*. I could probably write a whole book about the Noodle Man debacle. Ugh, with the amulets of absolution and the multiple earths and that poor, *poor* unicorn. That story, though, has been told to death, and while I'd love to elaborate on how two basketballs, a game of Horse, and the very lackluster knowledge I'd gleaned from three years of high-school French ended up saving our entire galaxy, I'll be merciful enough to spare you yet another rehash of that week.

* * *

And then these thoughts evaporate, because someone is standing over my table. Probably has been for longer than I realize, because, you know, world's most perceptive superhero, ladies and gentlemen. He, Vivan, is pleasantly alive—thanks to anything but me and the places we're getting to, True Believer.

This would be more of a moment, I guess, if that meant something to you yet, but, well, just trust and believe, and know that the Indian fellow with an iced coffee in his hand is the undeniable proof that every New Yorker who exists in this city alongside 8.5 million others is cursed to have awkward run-ins with people they know.

"Holy fucking—you're *alive*." My body shivers, it tightens and twists everywhere he's trying to find me at.

"Spark—" he starts to say.

"Cliff Fern," I interrupt, spinning my coffee cup around so he can see the name *Cliff* scrawled on it. I give him a glare that I hope says *Read the room, motherfucker.*

He does, thank God. "All right, um—Cliff? How did you—no, sorry, that's not important. Are you okay?"

"You need to leave, V, *please.*" I lower my eyes to the blank page and all the things I hope people will believe someday.

"Oh—are they, you know, *watching*?" he whispers, leaning in.

I can't help chuckling. "No, V, no one's watching. That's the problem, though, isn't it?" I jot that bit down because I am the type of asshole who thinks everything he says is unbearably profound. "I don't know how you found me, but—"

"I didn't. I live a block down, sir."

After a moment, we laugh like there isn't a world of dried blood between us.

We talk for a while, longer than I feel comfortable with. We touch on—well, spoilers, True Believers. We do spit takes every now and again at the absurdity of our dreamy past of altruism and asshats.

"They're calling them *nigghts*. With two g's." He doesn't look me in the eyes when telling me this.

I lose my sanity for a moment, hacking up hyena laughs. The eyes of the other coffee-shop sulkers find time for us, if only for a few seconds. "Sorry, that is just—*fuck*, dude. You can't make this shit up, can you?"

Maybe I could better use this time to blab about the great escape of The Maverick Moralist, and how Gunther sent me all on my lonesome to take him down as he attempted a heist at Fort Knox. Gunther seemed annoyed that I didn't crap butterflies at the "offer" of the collar. I mean, in the end I did go take that asshole down (again), but I'd be lying if I told you I was happy about the job.

These are the Astonishing Tales of Nah, That Shit Is Boring

V, I can tell, is getting tired of catching up. He doesn't even seem to care much about the present. He wants something more than that. Real talk? I owe him. And if this piece of espresso-stained shit ever gets read by anyone, I want it to be *you*, V. If only so I can tell you two things. First of all, I don't think you ever needed the feather to fly. Second, I'm so, *so* sorry that you had the misfortune of meeting your misanthrope hero in real life.

The first time I met him—met *you*, V—we were too preoccupied with the business of saving lives to talk about anything that mattered. We'd get our chance for that a few weeks later. Me, sitting behind a desk; you, timid but talented. You spoke about why you wanted to work with my partner and me.

I've never told you this, V, but I almost told my partner no when we discussed you coming to work with us. You seemed too young. Not in years, of course—what are you, three younger than me? No, something more telling. You rambled on and on about my so-called "feats." The time I saved a child from a burning building, not realizing that a two-by-four had crashed over my back. I'd have been burned alive if not for tiny hands tugging at my dreadlocks. The time my team intervened when The Uncanny Cadaver, a talented Super Predator with the ability to manipulate the nervous systems of corpses, attacked a church in Tribeca. You praised me for letting a camera follow me when I "returned" to Africa to thank the tribe that had "given me my powers." You didn't know then, at that desk, that things didn't go down like that, but you also didn't question how I could have made that video and then appeared on SNL the next night without a trace of jet lag.

I feared—wrongly, I know now—that I was seeing another version of that Ohio kid who couldn't see the truths that were obscured by misdirection but obscenely visible if you looked under even the first layer.

These are the Astonishing Tales of It
Wasn't You, It Was the Me in You

"You don't have to protect me, sir. You don't have to do whatever it is you're doing here, whatever it is you're *planning* here, alone. I can help you."

By now you've probably realized that you were once more falling victim to my bile and bullshit.

"What?" I ask.

"There's a reason you're back. I know you wouldn't come here, you wouldn't risk being seen, unless you *had* to, unless you were planning something. You're going to need help, sir."

You're a wonderful moron, V. No, this isn't some White Fang–inspired insult to make you run, though it's not entirely a diss, either. Everyone who has ever done anything of substance has had to be a wonderful moron on some level. The thing is, all the wonderful morons who wanted to help me, V? I've learned by now that they only end up dead.

Oh!

Okay, what about that time I took down The Cranky Counterclock? He'd turned most of the American Collective for Resolving Overtly Negative Yowled Misconducts into prepubescent versions of themselves, without control of their powers. Thankfully, Patches and I were late to the scene due to an impromptu smoke session, surprising Counterclock before he could do the same to us. (That bit may have been left out of the report.) I beat him, but his ability had a run time of about a week and led to some very stress-filled days of crusty socks and teen angst.

These are the Astonishing Tales of OMG
Everything Is the Worrrrst

These are the Astonishing Tales of Nah, I Only
Want to Live through That Week Once

"You're going to botch the operation, V," I say, clasping my hands in front of my face. If he'd seen even one episode of *Neon Genesis*

Evangelion, he'd probably have seen right through my very poor Gendo Ikari impression, but the way he wilted at my glare let me know he hadn't.

"Operation, sir?"

"There's a reason I've come back, you're not wrong about that. It's not over. Not by a long shot. Did you think I just happened upon this coffee shop? Where you'd happen to be at this exact time? Maybe I've been observing you the last few days, maybe I wanted to make sure I could still rely on you. Maybe I thought you'd be smart enough to not engage in a public conversation with me, to simply await instruction."

"Sir, I—"

"It's *fine*, V. Not much we can do about it now, is there? This is what you'll do. You'll leave, and tell no one you've seen me. You'll be at Grand Central Station three days from now at 10:00 a.m. That's when you'll get your answers, and we'll have our justice," I say—taking inspiration from Nikolas, I suppose. I can tell, V, that a question rests on your lips before you bite it back and get your happy ass out of here.

These are the Astonishing Tales of Take Care of Yourself, Gon, You're Free, Gon, Get Out of Here, Go Go Go!

If this reaches you, V, I imagine you will already have waited until 12:14 p.m. and found nothing. That's one thing I could apologize for, but believe me, it was better than the alternative.

Know that, I think at least, I meant to do better. Know that—eh, just be good, V.

These are the Astonishing Tales of Not Meaning Well

Well, True Believer. I guess this leaves us in a bit of a pickle, now, don't it?

So. Three days.

Paul told me once that any writer works better beneath the cascading ball of shitfire that is a deadline. Now I really have only three days to finish this thing if I want to avoid V and his thunderous *What the hell, sir?!* assaulting poor Tad's ears. Or I guess I could, you know, change coffee shops.

I've decided that we will, sadly, be skimming by Noodle Man. There also won't be any discussion of the time GRAVI-Tina and I swapped bodies. Freaky that it happened on a Friday, but that probably deserves a book on its own.

Yeah, if I hope to get this done in three days, we're going to have to skip a few beats.

CHAPTER 22
THE NIGHT EVERYTHING CHANGED

IF YOU'VE COME HERE by reading through my whole whiny but whimsical memoir: I thank you for reading so far, True Believers, and I'm sorry that there's nothing to find in this chapter. But hey, now's the perfect time to take a pause and grab a nice peanut-butter sandwich for our friend Chris before moving forward. Continue to chapter 23.

If you skipped here from the beginning: You sadist jerk. Shame on you, because *you know the rules, and so do I*. Don't you value yourself enough to take the time for an enjoyable reading experience? Seriously, all this coffee Tad's loading me up with shouldn't be in vain, and goddamn you if you think I'll *give* you anything without knowing who Barkley is.

But I'm not mad, or even upset, really. In fact, I want you to know that I'm never gonna give you up, I'm never gonna let you down, and I'm certainly not going to run around and desert you. I probably won't make you cry, while this chapter is a lie and I hurt you.

Spark it up from chapter 2.

CHAPTER 23
HEISENBERG

THERE ARE SO MANY WAYS, True Believer, that they'll try to keep you safe, keep it away, keep you from being a fucking moron. Don't take the elevator, because it's always better to run run run, down down down.

Watch out for doors, or more specifically handles that are too hot to the touch, that plunder from you all avenues of escape. Raise the alarm, sans Beyoncé but in apt observance of the astrobleme, cosmic and uncontrolled. The heat.

These are the Astonishing Tales of White Flame

After Aedan's family were through the worst of the mourning, it was high time to get mad. Back then, though? The fact that these were the first Talented individuals operating in public unfortunately meant that no one knew what the hell to do about them or the lives they'd torn apart as collateral damage. Who *should* be held accountable when a space alien imbued with godlike powers tussles with the personification of all things chaotic and combustible? There wasn't exactly insurance for that shit.

The family fought, though—not with snoot punches but with litigation. Kayla, Aedan's widow, was well practiced in the subtle art of getting shit done. I know that because as badly as Aedan turned out to have bungled managing the shop's assets, the East Columbus nerd collective still had a shop to escape to after he was gone, a refuge far removed from the bastard boys who played with balls and their predilection for face farts and gratuitous yo-momma jokes.

These are the Astonishing Tales of I Do Stand
Behind Aedan's Purchase of 9.9 CG *Secret Wars*
Number 8, Though, Because That Shit Is Metal

At the time Gunther wanted to roll out his baby, PantheUS, with all the appropriate fanfare, so little green hush papers were doled out as needed. After that came ways to protect their pockets, in case of further casualties in the pursuit of something we called justice. Super-Predator Insurance did become a thing, in case man-made malevolence should find its way to your area. There was also research done in the interest of protecting the country from another White Flame attack. No one really knew what he'd been aiming for when he first appeared—a bright, terrorizing flame that tore through downtown Detroit for hours until Asper descended from the skies like an angelic asshat. He'd been watching the entire conflagration under the guise of his American alter ego and had not so much decided but was forced by the brilliant patriotism within his heart to knock the almighty fuck out of this foreign threat. When they met, it meant war. It meant a battle that would ravage the entire country. After Michigan they'd battled all the way from Ohio to Pennsylvania to Wisconsin and Virginia and New Hampshire and Florida and Iowa and Nevada and Colorado and beyond. It wasn't until they reached North Carolina that we had time to collectively blink as a country and consider what this all meant. Even after that, though, they continued to rage, finishing in Iowa with burning bushes and barley—and Asper distracted, finally, by the burden of the feeble proletariat. The whole deal was something of a swing and a miss on Asper's part, but he'd tried. He'd done as much as he could and that would have to be enough.

There were other Aedans, but honestly, as shitty as it sounds, I couldn't be bothered to find out more about them then, because they were not in fact Aedan. And we all mourned our losses.

We realized soon enough that Asper had been chasing White Flame away from multiple government establishments in these states, and could call the attack what it was: terror. At least we found a strategy to defend against the terror more quickly, an immediate means of raising the alert. What did we do to protect the proletariat? Yeah, it was a fucking phone number. When they first announced the 9-1-6-1 emergency number they got a ton of prank calls, but that changed after the institution of Monopoly-worthy fines for false reports. And to my surprise, the phone line paid off when it alerted everyone to the third sighting of White Flame and Asper met him face to face in DC, right above the White House. He proved to be fire in every sense of the word. He came, he erupted, he vanished.

I hope all this backdrop gives you some idea of where I'm going with this.

A superhero's first death—that's got to be a hell of a tale, right? And it kind of was. I mean, it was mostly pain, but since that's the stuff of all the best tales anyway I guess it doesn't tell you all that much.

Let's start where it starts: Thandie's smiley face popping up on my cell phone, an exhilarating—and crushing—way to start my day. Exhilarating, because seeing her name flit onto the display swelled something inside of me, stirring the spark enough to make me illuminate every light bulb within ten feet of my body.

Crushing because it was soon followed by a *sry! Wrng persn!*

So yeah, I guess this is all to say that the day I died started off standard.

These Are the Astonishing Tales of
Getting There, Getting There . . .

After I responded to Thandie's apology with one of my own, apparently for existing as a contact within her phone, I tapped and scrolled through the texts to discover what fresh hell awaited the Astonishing Black Spark.

Kit-Kat:
Hey, sorry if you're busy but can you call me?

Paul:
Sup man! Have you read that shit about . . . ?

Dickhole:
You tryna to team up with Green Freedom today?

Chris:
Jsyk, they're ready to pay you. Fifty
THOUSAND dollars. Today.

Chris:
CALL ME.

Chris:
You really want to see me beg, don't you?

I let them stay unread and slid the phone into my pocket.

I promised myself I'd read whatever doesn't-the-world-suck link Paul had sent me later.

Kat and I would touch bases eventually.

With everything going on, and the time for my final confirmation only a few months away, I thought it best to politely ignore any request from Patches for a Green Freedom break. Chris, well, we've been over it so many times. He kept up his one-person campaign to coon and cash in on my ass. I'd taken to ignoring his calls.

The months I'd been with the American Collective for Resolving Overtly Negative Yowled Misconducts had been filled with fantasy, tales of suspended disbelief and comical action. They weren't filled, however, with much momentum in my popularity. The election was around the corner, and I felt it every day. I was thankful to Chris for at least getting me some extra screen time during those months. It was a compromise that helped us both, an opportunity to play up an angle that they all say shouldn't matter, in fact they don't even see it—but it totally gets you on a panel.

"So that's why I'm interested in your opinion on all of this. It's an egregious oversight, sure, but when does personal responsibility come into play? When do we stop placing the blame on the enigmatic *man* and start doing something to fix *our own* problems? What do you think, Black Spark?"

I stared into the camera, ready to respond in kind as the talking head that I was.

I was sharing the panel with several official, card-carrying (they showed them to me after) Black intellects. It was moderated by Adam Apple, a CNN correspondent, and the topic was "the state of Black America." We spoke candidly and without colloquialisms about people who shared a similar skin tone but not much else.

The talks had spun off into a surreal discussion about a recent news story. I didn't watch the news as often as I should have, which means I watched it about as much as everyone else. I'd been mostly silent during the panel, giving head nods and cosigns for the better part of thirty minutes, until Apple addressed me directly. Luckily, I wasn't completely lost. I knew that Dark and Disappeared was a nonprofit that festered with angry rhetoric and conspiracy theory, and that it had built a bit of press for itself with its outspoken rage at law enforcement's supposedly callous handling of missing Blacks.

Adam Apple had covered a story about one of these alleged kidnappings, and he'd taken some heat for lambasting the errors that minority youth found themselves making on a day-to-day basis. My opinion on this subject was the reason, I realized, that I was there. The slowly rising approval of my work within the American Collective for Resolving Overtly Negative Yowled Misconducts had improved my brand enough to let Chris finagle this interview, which was supposed to help me out of a jam caused by the cameras having caught me out late one night in a not-so-professional state.

"I think you're kind of right, Mr. Apple. If we work on these key things, things we have complete control of, we have the potential to bring a resolution to all of this. The violence and aggression against us and among us," I said.

One of the other pundits—was it Dr. East? Dr. North?—scoffed at my agreement with Apple's remarks.

"I think, humbly echoing the words of the prophetic Lauryn Hill, that 'everything you drop is so tired,' my brother. I love you, my brothers, but you do *not* seem to love yourselves," he said.

"Oh, there's *some* legitimacy to this five-point plan," interjected someone else. "Perhaps if I, a Black intellectual, had followed it, I might not have been accosted by the police whilst attempting to enter my own home." That, I was fairly sure, was sarcastic.

"Thank you so much for your input, ladies and gentlemen. I really think we've made some progress in the last half hour, but unfortunately we're out of time. I'd like to thank all of you, especially The Astonishing Black Spark, for joining us today. For CNN, I'm Adam Apple."

I was supposed to return next week, and the week after, to sit in front of the camera and occasionally throw in a not-too-substantive remark. We were shooting on a Friday, which meant I had to decline going out for drinks with Apple afterward and instead take to the streets. I was still monitoring Navigatrix's roommate. Miranda was, as far as steel-limbed Super Predators went, predictable. She'd get off work, run some errands, then have dinner with her aunt and cousin in Queens. After that came the costumed shuffle around town.

I'd found some benefit in the patrol, which was why I'd stuck with it. Following her meant the rooftops for the most part, and if there's one skill every Talented PantheUS member should keep in tip-top shape, it's that. Back in Ohio, when Nikolas was training me, grooming me, whatever, he'd made sure my clumsy ass knew how to use the spark to skip across the sky.

These are the Astonishing Tales of Sparking and Swinging

"Just watch," Nikolas told me.

In Ohio there weren't many skyscrapers available. We mostly worked at our dramatically abandoned little practice site. I was wearing my Kat Oldgoer–variant costume then, the hanging threads blowing this way and that while we stood at the window.

He spun the foot-long copper rod in the air before snatching it. Always had to be so fucking cool. He took a few steps back, then darted toward the window. When he hurled the rod, I felt him starting to spark it up. He spun around and winked before diving, back first, out of the window. My chest fluttered. Granted, he didn't seem the type to say *just watch* before offing himself, but I couldn't be completely sure.

He didn't go splat. With a buttload of class he swam through the sky. A bolt erupted from the palm of his hand and he rode the silver lining. The magnetized rod had buried itself in the concrete ledge of the adjacent building. He caught it and swung, then pulled himself up onto the ledge.

"Get up here!" he called.

I'd seen *The Matrix*, so I knew how this would play out. I'd jump, I'd fall, I'd die. Something told me, as Nikolas glared disapprovingly in the distance while I shook my head, that he really, really needed to see *The Matrix*.

"Stop dicking around and get up here, spunk," he shouted.

It helped, in a way. I got out of my own head, which was mostly filled with pop-culture quotes and internet memes. I ran, I sparked, I leapt. For a moment I fell back inward, fumbling with the abstract image of what would be left of me on the streets, but I didn't let it take over. Something else did: my desire to raise a middle finger to Mr. Tess as I cut through the derelict wind. So, I did. I sparked, focusing on the ledge where Nikolas stood.

I spun haphazardly upward, dreadlocks whipping me in the face the entire time. I wish I could paint you a suspenseful picture of my body nearly hitting the pavement first, of me finding the resolve in the last second to pull myself up. I can't. Somehow, I just *got* it. I'm not saying it's easy, finding a groove—most times we just end up stripping bolts—but that moment when you just *have* it? Astonishing.

I grabbed the rod when I reached the top of the building and swung myself up. He didn't lend me a hand, which was pretty much status quo for us, and I panted as I hauled my body up over the edge. I almost fell on my ass, apparently too preoccupied with the whole defying gravity thing to realize how much it had taken out of me.

"How was that, asshole?" I said.

He rolled his eyes. "It was okay—even though you cheated."

"How do you *cheat* at something like that?"

"You connected to my rod. You were supposed to break through the brick and mortar."

"Brick doesn't conduct. I can't do anything about that."

"I did."

"I'm not you."

"Yes, which, while tragic, doesn't matter. How did I do it? How did I connect?"

I'd hated the seventh grade. More importantly, I'd hated my teacher, Mr. Maxwell, who liked giving obtuse answers to obvious questions. *I don't really know why I should use a semicolon here instead of a comma, Mr. Maxwell. Why does anyone ever need a semicolon?* To which he'd answer, *Why do you think you need a semicolon, Mr. McDougal?* I didn't know; that's why I'd asked the goddamned question.

In the case of Nikolas Tess, I had no principal's office to be sent off to for snarky commentary, so I swallowed the unusually acidic lump of banter rising in my throat and thought. He waited, grinning like an apple had just been placed on his desk, when my face lit up and so did the literal light bulb above my head.

"You didn't connect to the brick."

"Nope."

"You found something else, something that was past it or inside it, and *broke through* the brick."

He nodded. "Shoot for the stars, Mr. McDougal."

* * *

Following Miranda was, to Navigatrix's credit, a pretty low-risk gig. You usually expect someone with a talent like that to have a more violent rap sheet. Her most common dastardly deed? Breaking into pet shops after closing and smashing the locks to allow the creatures to roam free in the night. This created more than a little bit of hell for the owners in the morning, but when there was so much actual crime happening, this Padfoot-and-Prongs, mischief-managed type of shit didn't seem too pressing.

She was smart enough not to get all PETA on the lions, tigers, or bears down at the Bronx Zoo, so I never saw any point in stopping her. Letting some fellow mammals act out their own rendition of *House Party* seemed pretty harmless. Besides, my TV was busted, and it was kind of entertaining to watch. I couldn't bring much in the way of snacks for the show due to the tragedy of spandex, but an Airhead was flat enough to slide in my pocket.

That night, however, the show had an unexpected but very welcome interruption: the name of a certain Thandie D. Nettle flashing on my screen.

"Hello?"

"Hey Don, what are you doing? Are you free?"

Shit. She'd said my name, which meant she was talking to me on purpose this time, but was I free? This was it, I realized: the shining "What If?" issue of *Don the Phenomenon* where he ended up with the Talented Thandie D Nettle. One issue only.

"I'm, uh, kinda working," I said, watching a pile of pit-bull puppies tumble viscously into Miranda's lap.

"Oh, it's just so good to actually hear that, you know? To actually hear of a Black man making a point of displaying work ethic in these times," Thandie said.

I kept my laugh inaudible while watching Miranda try to shove off a pup that was trying to hump her.

"Uh, thanks, Thandie. I have to say, I am, like, definitely happy to hear from you, but it's a bit unexpected. You've been a little MIA lately," I said, trying not to sound so very, very pathetic.

"Yes, well, I'm sure you understand, being of a better brand now and all, that life isn't all booze and old cartoons."

"Yeah." *More than a little fucking personal, fam, but yeah.* "So, are you okay? Did you need something?" I asked, muscles tightening throughout me as I did. I could feel her smiling on the other end of the line.

"Well, number seven is out. He tweeted—you won't believe this— he *actually* tweeted a heinous tweet about Kanye West that was just so actually racist I can't—ugh. Anyway, I was hoping to share the good news of your new status with you over a drink? I *have* been thinking of you, Don, and now I think I'm ready to discuss things, actually, more deeply."

By the time she finished I was already halfway through figuring out the best route to each one of the four drinking establishments she could be referring to.

We made plans: those things that everyone's almighty gets a good lol at.

I watched as Miranda finished up, finally getting that rage against cages that creatures don't really understand they're in out of her system for the night. I paused in my vigilance to enjoy a stick, forgetting about dark nighttime antics for a moment to answer the all-consuming call of nicotine. (I'd given them up by then, for the most part—when you're darting from roof to roof, the lure of lung hara-kiri dwindles. Well—I'd cut back, anyway.)

It was at that moment, in the glow of the lighter and the call from Thandie, that I felt the rumble and the heat. Far away, a brilliant burst of white fire swirled in the sky, raining down in a spiral that set a building ablaze.

I couldn't see him, but I knew, like we all do when the first flash of white fire booms, that it was White Flame. From the looks of it, he was somewhere uptown, and before I could even unlock my phone the *fink foop* blinked white through the LEDs.

I forgot that Miranda existed. I nearly forgot my phone while crawling on all fours across the rooftop, trying to find my rods in the dark, finally calling them to my hand with a quick spark before making my way to HQ. I nearly crashed to the world below more than once, not paying enough attention to the fact that I was hundreds of feet in the air. A tsunami of spandex was pouring through the streets and the sky around me.

When White Flame reared his head, we all had jobs to do, True Believer. The civilians had their asses to cover. The Super Predators? The real ones? Well, what better time is there to be a criminal than when everyone is focused on Flame? This caused a problem. Usually, when White Flame had reared his head, the larger cost to the country was an accumulation of more minor aggravations.

The American Collective for Resolving Overtly Negative Yowled Misconducts was the only group authorized to initiate engagement with White Flame, leaving those of lesser talents to deal with making sure others wouldn't also bring the fire. I wish I could tell you that the spark shuddering through my body was all born of fire-forged fear and not the lure of a chance to garner much-needed public support by taking down the world's most infamous supervillain. It carried me, that potential, from rooftop to rooftop until I finally arrived.

I caught Patches in the main hall. He was playing on his phone and couldn't be bothered to look up.

"You're not coming?" I asked.

He took on the unbearable task of rolling his eyes up to meet mine. "This *is* me coming. When it's White Flame, I'm placed a sizable distance away." He slid his phone into his back pocket as I pressed for the elevator.

"How far away?"

"Can't tell you."

"Well, screw you, too."

"Nah, I mean I legally can't. White Flame protocol. Only Gramps, Asper, and a security detail have my exact whereabouts. A safety measure to keep me from healing the first of you to come hobbling over to me."

"That's kinda cynical, isn't it? I mean, we're superheroes. We're friggin' paid paragons."

"All right, *paragon*, let's see how cynical it is when you're flailing around with your body covered in pick-any-degree of burn. When your skin's all melted, though if you're lucky your eyelids will have seared shut and you won't have to see it. Shit, man, the last time I saw him he didn't even need to burn anyone, he lopped off Afrolicious's legs in one swing. The blood almost doesn't seem real, you know? Like, I think there's a point at which it just seems like a Tarantino movie and somehow cycles back to bearable. Anyway, see you out there, hero." He waved as the elevator doors closed.

When I arrived in the situation room, the sight of all of us there at the same time on the same day felt torn from a comic-book page. As much as I appreciated the strength of numbers, it was a little inconvenient. Stuck behind the towering personification of patriotism, I couldn't see the screen.

"As I'm sure you're all aware, we are receiving multiple communications regarding White Flame sightings. We have evacuated all high-risk government facilities and thrown a few up-and-comers a bone, lending Talented patrol to hospitals throughout the city."

I raised a hand. "Shouldn't we be more concerned with evacuating them? The hospitals and schools, I mean."

My teammates chuckled, snickered, and made some other condescending AF sounds.

"Give the boy a break, he's still pretty green. Donald, White Flame is insane, but we've been here before. He hits hard and goes on a crawl. He'll blow over the Bronx, make his way down to Midtown, put on a show for the kiddies, and end up in Federal Plaza," Gunther explained.

My hand flew up again. "If we know where he's going to be and what he's going to do—um, I really don't mean anything by this, I'm just asking—why does he keep getting away?"

This time, the room didn't swell with condescension so much as indignation.

"White Flame isn't a person, Donald. He is a force of nature who's proven, time and time again, that he can't be contained. We can't all be so lucky as you and have a *monster* do our dirty work for us."

Lucky. Oh, the luck I'd been blessed with, True Believer.

"So, why the exposition then?" said GRAVI-Tina. "The hell are we doing in here and not out there?"

I still wasn't fully hearing her through the field of feels. I was steaming so high with words I couldn't let loose that I nearly missed, up there on the screen, the face of the guy who spouted shit about blind trust while wearing a mask: The Emancipator.

"Well, this is some fucked-up timing, isn't it? Not only White Flame, but we have this clever dickhole to deal with," said GRAVI-Tina.

I nearly knocked DEATHRAGE over closing in on the screen.

It was a live feed. Every PantheUS Prime Bank had one. He wasn't alone; there were others with him, dressed in their usual greaser-sleek black from head to toe. They seemed to have skimped on whatever astonishing tailor had made The Emancipator's slick plastic mask, though, because the rest of them only had bandanas covering the lower halves of their faces.

The weird part was that the money was again sitting in plain view, in those heaps of cartoonish bags that might as well have had dollar signs stamped on them. Also that The Emancipator—by now I knew it was Nikolas, which probably doesn't surprise you either, True Believer—didn't seem at all bothered about the cameras recording his every move. In fact he'd occasionally bow to one of them, knowing, of course, where each was located, the same way I did. There was a spray-painted message at his feet that simply read, *Connect.*

Shit.

"Sorry, this was a little before you joined. Have you heard of him?" GRAVI-Tina asked.

I swallowed hard. What was I supposed to say? *Yes, I watched it all on the television screen and have had no other interaction with the Super Predator of whom you speak.*

I nodded, offering my best display of indecipherable chill. I couldn't let them know how I really felt, equal parts cloud and iron and all the while utterly breakable.

"Well, Black, you have a chance to meet him in person tonight," Asper said, nudging me.

Gunther sighed. "We can't deal with the both of them, and Flame is the bigger priority. It's not ideal, but we may have to let The Emancipator go."

I felt sandpaper and nails settle in my belly. GRAVI-Tina got up in Gunther's face. I admit, I was a little impressed.

"That isn't going to work, sir," she said.

"Giving me lip isn't going to get you any closer to handling both Flame and The Emancipator," Gunther shot back.

I'm sure there were terse looks aplenty, but I was too busy watching the screen. Nikolas's black mask completely obscured his face and *still* he was managing to give me a smarmy smirk through the camera.

"White Flame is predictable and trackable, *and* he can be stalled, leaving enough time for the rest of us to take The Emancipator down and then come in as backup. All we have to do is keep whatever shiny toy he wants dangling. He'll throw a tantrum, which Asper can contain. This other guy? I don't know if you remember, but he kicked our asses—and said some shit about ending us. This isn't just some hero posturing, Gunther. We can't *afford* letting that one get away," GRAVI-Tina finished.

"He did kick your asses. And now he has four other individuals accompanying him, most likely Talented as well. And he isn't the White Flame. He won't cause a shitstorm if we let him have some shitty credit union and don't fall for whatever it is he's looking to start with us. He won't inspire a think piece on our misjudgments or one of those tweet things they spend hours replaying on the news."

"You're honestly saying we let him go because it won't *look* good?"

"Oh, you *are* an Onyx class, aren't you? I ain't saying I'm happy about it, but we know how to handle White Flame. We can't risk looking like we don't know how to do our jobs."

"This is fucked."

"This is you doing what you're expected to do. You, *all* of you, are responsible for White Flame. We were founded *because* of White Flame. There isn't anything to debate here, Maria. We go for Flame."

Seeing that this could go on for a while, I did that whole go-ahead-and-screw-yourself thing I should have a badge for.

"I can do it," I said. "Get him. The Emancipator dude, I mean."

Gunther sighed. So did GRAVI-Tina, finding some common ground with Gunther once again. That's what matters at the end of the day, right? I'm nothing if not a catalyst for bringing people closer together.

"Son, you want to take on a guy who has taken out *all* of the American Collective for Resolving Overtly Negative Yowled Misconducts—this time, with a team at his back? How exactly do you propose to do that?"

"I'm not a member of this team. Not fully, not yet. White Flame is the only thing that really matters, but let's be real, I have electricity powers. The hell is that going to do to a guy that controls fire? This Emancipator guy, I don't think I can take him down, but *him* I can probably stall, or I can keep my distance and follow his crew. I can do that, and you all can get White Flame." I watched the live video feed and listened to him screaming what the rest of them could only ascribe to insanity. *It's 10:00 a.m., suits, time to wake up and get your asses down here.*

I could have said something different. I could have told them that he wasn't so much calling *them* out, but me. I could have told them that everything in me wanted to be seen, finally, taking on someone who demanded visibility. I could have told them that, this dude on the screen? He was really, really deserving of an ass whooping that no one else in that room would be able to give.

"The kid has a point, sir," said Asper, of all people, and patted me on the shoulder.

"You don't have to do this, Spark," said GRAVI-Tina.

"I'll rendezvous with you all once I take care of him," I said, just as astonished to be casually using words like *rendezvous* as I had been on my first day with the team.

Gunther considered it for a moment before cracking his toothiest grin and nodding. "You got moxie, boy, and a point. You're getting what you want, Maria, and honestly, no one is gonna think twice about him being absent. No offense. We'll keep a close eye on you, but get the hell out of there if things get hot, all right, Black Spark?"

More than a few parts of me marveled at how quickly that decision was made, but it was just like the city, the job, the life . . . things happen fast. Once they explode they never really stop. I nodded and started collecting details from Gunther.

* * *

When I arrived, the scene was eerily calm: another bank, another late night under black skies and New York's approximately six visible white stars. There were no cameras, not yet, and no quaking pens poised to present prolific truths. You see, True Believers, big daddy Gunther had his hands over your eyes, but only to keep you innocent, to protect you from the things that would otherwise break you. Because heroes are only heroic in the full light of day. In the dark, where all things are beautiful and unkind, the gray lot of us are bare.

Subtlety? Yeah, that would have been a swell idea, but being in the midst of a feels explosion I might not have been thinking much beyond the need to show those assholes what's what. You know, me, the guy who came alone to meet four Talented, well-trained Super Predators, one of whom was imbued with the same talents as me, though with an extra helping of wisdom.

So I just walked right up to the bank and knocked on the glass door. With the stankiest of stares, one of The Emancipator's men— we'll call him the Duplicating Douchebag—let me in. He looked me up and down.

"You okay? You seem scared, suit. Like you know that coming here alone, while ballsy, was perhaps ill advised."

He didn't try to stop me, though, just walked alongside me while I went to meet the man with a plan.

"I'm not scared—not of you, anyway. I'm not sure if you realize this, but whatever bullshit you're trying to pull? It's right in the middle of a White Flame appearance."

He stopped. "The White Flame? Shit, okay, you go, I'll tell him that you—never mind, I'll just come up with something. What are you waiting for? Get the hell out of here!"

It's a little more telling than showing to say we didn't like each other much, True Believer, but yeah, when I turned around I met a stiff arm belonging to his doppelganger, into which I crashed and fell on my ass.

They both laughed, right up until the double sank back into DD's body. So fucking creepy, that dude. While I patted at my nose, trying to find the nonexistent blood, he crouched and pulled the bandana down.

"Yes, we know about White Flame, of *course* we know about White Flame. Shit, you're as dumb as they say you are, aren't you?

You don't deserve this; you haven't *earned* this. I could kill you right now. I'm—"

"Wanted in twelve systems?" I chuckled with a hand still holding my nose.

"What?"

"Nothing, just—listen. You don't want me here, I get that. You don't need to Charlie Brown me in the nose for me to get that. You don't like me, and I sure as shit don't like you. Can we just, I don't know, not like each other in silence, and you take me to your leader and shit?"

I'd decrypted some kind of code. He watched me for a moment, then shrugged his shoulders and helped me up.

I glanced around the bank. *Two floors. Stay away from that vault; a closed space means your ass. Don't let the dickbag here go all* multiple *man without you seeing it. Oh, okay, Nik has a flyer, and a fuck-you-upper too. Standard enough talents; you're ready this time. You got this. Wait, are you serious? You really, really shouldn't be thinking of Thandie right now, you moron. Hello? Are you even listening?*

I wished I was at a bar or on a rooftop or in the fight with White Flame or really anywhere else than here, in whatever this ongoing arc was between Nikolas and me. I froze when I finally saw him. From the way he turned to look at his team and a few of them rolled their eyes, I knew I'd just earned someone twenty bucks by showing up.

There we were, me and my arch-Nikolas. The rest of them were eyeballing me hard, but this time I wasn't so keen to impress them. This time, they stood between me and what would ensure me an actual income. They stood between me and an opportunity to take off that mask he'd oh-so-quickly decided to hide behind. They stood between me and the ghost of Aedan.

"You're pretty quiet, after all that ranting on the screen," I said.

"I didn't do all of this to get whatever it is *you* are to come here. I called for the PantheUS team supreme. I want the American Collective for Resolving Overtly Negative Yowled Misconducts."

"He's their newest member. I think his name's Spark, Emancipator," Maggie chimed in. It was a pretty crummy performance, mostly because after glaring at me she turned directly to one of the cameras, then back to me.

I decided to play along. "I'm here on behalf of the team. Your heinous crime shall not be tolerated!"

"Yes, I do remember the name now. Spark. You weren't officially inducted, though. Do you get to live in their fancy schmancy mansion? Do you have a room, a 401k? Do you even have one of those communicator thingies? An M-Chip?" said Nikolas.

I would have written it off as just another typical Super Predator rant, but when he said the word *M-Chip*, the lot of them seemed to rustle or tighten, or forget lessons their bodies had learned at birth about how to get oxygen. I realized that amid all the filler, that was the only word that had connected to anything.

"Of course I do, fiend. I may not be official yet, but it's required when working with the American Collective for Resolving Overtly Negative Yowled Misconducts," I said. I must have chosen the wrong adventure—that much was evident by the sullen swipe-to-the-left looks, the nigh-orgasmic glee dancing on Double Dickhead's face, and the nothing, per usual, that Nikolas gave me.

"Ah, well, you really are one of them, I guess. Shit," Nikolas said. Again, only one word seemed to connect.

"He's theirs, Emancipator. I mean, I *told* you that before the van, and before the fucking gas-station meat paste, but, not going to be that guy about it. He was theirs then and he's theirs now. Can we go?" Rizal said.

Nikolas didn't say anything—not in the way I expected, anyway. He ducked out of view of the cameras, scribbled something on a memo pad, and showed it to me.

No time. Here to save you. You're going to die. Serious.

I stared at it for a while. "The hell is all of this? Seriously. No more school notes bullshit. Why. Are. You. Here. That's it, that's all I want to hear from you."

"Spark, was it? There are two ways this can happen, and one involves a lot less pain on your part."

I looked around. They couldn't have known, save for Nikolas, that I was pouring electricity into my limbs, ready for fight and flight all at the same time. "I think you're underestimating what I can do."

Please, Nik, just run, just run, just run.

"That's the whole problem, Spark, I don't think I am," he said. "Formation Zeta Epsilon."

"What?"

Rizal was first, dropping low and splitting in two. Thing One sucker-punched me in the jaw while Thing Two delivered a swift and steel-toed kick to my groin. As I fell, I thanked whatever deities of padding and pelvic armor may exist that the kick had only knocked the wind out of me, but that was enough. The big guy had me in a bear hug before I could recover. I slammed my heel into his toes. I was released and, more importantly, educated as to the fact that Nikolas's bruiser wasn't so durable. There wasn't much time before the next attack was on me, and I saw that that was how Nikolas wanted it. Unlike Gunther, Christopher, or anyone I'd worked with, he had the benefit of knowing what I was actually capable of. Hell, he was mostly responsible for it.

This time it was Rizal One and Rizal Two—and, astonishingly enough, Rizal Three and Rizal Four. Apparently, like me, Rizal hadn't been so quick to overshare just what he was capable of, and I'd been an idiot for underestimating him. They tackled me. Since I'd spent most of my life in basements and bookstores, the intricacies of a dogpile weren't my forte. At least I did know about proximity, and power, and just what the dickbag had coming to him.

I sent a spark shuddering throughout his bodies, seizing their muscles. Nikolas sauntered over, as he tended to do, and crouched down beside me and the pile of Rizals. This, I realized, was what he'd been counting on. Gravity became my trap when six hundred pounds plus of hater, perfectly immobilized, became a living cage that I couldn't break free of.

"I could kill him right now," I gasped.

"Sure, but *will* you? I know you could probably get out of this right now if you wanted to, but then you definitely *would* kill him. You could also generate enough electricity to pull your body away from his if you latched on to the vault, but you have no time to figure out just how much more electricity you'd spill into him doing that, and whether it would be fatal. You could do a lot of things—hell, we could all do a lot of things—but *will* you? No, I don't think so. I wouldn't be here now if you would. At least, not all mild-mannered like this, anyway."

"So, what? Because I don't want to murder a dude I'm suddenly just shit under your sneakers? Listen, man, just listen to me. You've got to let me go. You've got to let me do my job, *please*." While I spoke, I wriggled one of my hands down to a copper rod at my waist.

"This isn't going to hold for long, Emancipator," said Maggie.

"Right, well, up to eleven, then. Have to make it faster than he can reverse it." Nikolas opened a palm. I felt the start of a connection. He'd latched on to me, to my spark, like I'd done so many times before with outlets or batteries. It seemed he was aiming more for a manifest destiny than an emancipation.

I saw the vault in the distance, all that wonderfully conductive metal, and I connected, but not with my fingers. I'd finally gotten the rod into my hand and scooted my arm out the side of the pile of bodies. I magnetized the metal with enough force that it hurtled at full speed, slamming against the vault. Nikolas's crew watched it, which was of course the intent. Like a bumbling, barfing boy-man on New Year's Eve, I had them listening to the *zapidy-do*, the thought that I'd stumbled spectacularly as the rod clung there on the vault, doing nothing.

Then it rattled, but more importantly, the bags filled with coins also began to rattle.

These are the Astonishing Tales of
Fuck Yo Prep Time, Nikolas

The coins burst through the bags and sprayed through the room in chaos. Between the rod and my fingertips I'd created a line for protons to play against, and I'd shot for the stars.

These are the Astonishing Tales of
$$\oint B \cdot d\ell = \mu_0 \left(I + \varepsilon_0 \frac{d\phi_E}{dt} \right)$$
and Other Shit I Won't Waste Time Diving Into

I'd only really thought that far ahead, though. If I could distract them, then maybe, with a prayer and a powerup, I'd suddenly be able to shovel six hundred pounds away.

What I didn't expect, but will completely take credit for if you let me, was Maggie, or rather the result of her whipping her head around to look at the coins. As soon as she shifted her attention, Rizal's Thing Three and Thing Four foamed with shadows and melted into nothing.

I grunted, shoving the remaining two bodies to the side. They stirred, recovering slowly from the effects of my spark. Nikolas was right: there wasn't time to make a decent judgment about how much more electricity I could pour into them without lasting effect, so I had to find a way to end it before I'd need to worry about Stabby McGee.

I called the rod back to me. While it snapped to my hand, I leapt at Nikolas. When the rod hit my palm I brought it down across his mask.

The mask cracked. Our bodies spun, his hand catching hold of my costume as he fell. We tumbled and slammed into the floor. Then I groaned as Nikolas, The Emancipator, That Dude I Used to Know, plugged his shoulder into my diaphragm. I gasped for air, blinking back tears.

He took the moment while I winced and writhed to breathe. "You stubborn fuck," he said.

I kicked upward, but he caught it. He was better. He was always better. At fighting, at teaching, at empathy, at altruism. So what to do, exactly?

"Nik—Emancipator, your dastardly deeds won't bring you anything but a pair of handcuffs . . . when I spark it up!"

Nikolas's crew surrounded me. Nik's face was halfway visible through the cracked mask, and what I could see of it was sullen. I ducked out of view of the cameras for a moment and motioned for the notepad. Nikolas jumped after me as though to hit me again before I could spark, but once we were both hidden, he handed me the pad and pen.

My chicken scratch is hard enough for me to read, even when I'm not writing under duress, and now I was scribbling, but I had to try anything I could to connect. If only he could see that this was ridiculous. All of it. The entire story of us, from beginning to end. I just needed him to see the truth of it, of his halfhearted attempts at being better than the rest of us and of how his hubris would end.

It's White Flame, Nik. It's the end of everything if you don't let me go right now.

At about this point I considered an emancipation joke. I'm proud to say I was above it.

Whatever this is, it can wait. It has to wait.

Nikolas read the note, and of all the fucked reactions to give, he sighed. He was yet again lording this bullshit Morpheus Obi-Wan Kendouchedick superiority over me. He had the knowledge, he had the way, and he also by the way wore a mask. Granted, my lack of mask was intentional, but I digress.

He passed the notepad back to me.

There's no time. I can't say everything. Take a fucking leap. Please, just trust me—

"This is ridiculous, Emancipator," said Rizal, interrupting my reading (there was more scribbled on the back of the page). "He made his choice—how many chances are you going to give him? We're in New York, the one place we shouldn't be. You didn't just give them a gun, you strapped a goddamned nuke on it. Live with it."

So, listen, True Believers, the unfortunate-misunderstanding-of-cosmic-importance trope isn't one I want you to dwell on too much here. Oh! What if Romeo had known the whole plan?

Oh! What if Buffy had realized Willow knew a way to save Angel's soul when she went to kill him?

What if Dumbfuck Donald had taken a sec to finish reading the note to come to the grand realization that he was really in a computer program or in purgatory or some shit?

I've spent enough time sitting in front of a TV screen, in the deep, destructive maelstrom of a binge, watching superheroes do their thing, to know what a difference one sentence can make. I stuffed the note in my costume, beneath the cuff of my wrist. But when I got a chance to read it later, I'd merely be disappointed at the clever but rambling plea Nikolas had written. There were no revelations. I hadn't missed anything, not really.

After Rizal spoke, though, I didn't need to know anything else anyway. My choice had been made thanks to that final grain of truth: I was a living weapon. Nikolas had taught me how to control and more importantly how to capitalize on that power, and that made me dangerous. He wanted trust, from something he ultimately couldn't trust.

These are the Astonishing Tales of Iron
Fist Ain't Got Shit on Me

"I'm not just going to murder—"

"He's right, *Emancipator*," I said. "The fuck kinda name is that, anyway?"

I knew I was outmanned, outeverythinged. I didn't really care anymore. If I'm being honest? I also wasn't afraid. Nikolas had a few different ways to stop me at that point, if he really wanted to. All the Talented individuals at his back were equipped with devastating abilities. But I was at worst a little bruised, slightly winded. Also, I knew now that they feared me.

The fear of those who think you a beast is all you'll ever need to play one.

I knew that, as far as he'd go to get shit done, Nikolas wasn't a murderer. I don't think he was so sure about me. My life, True Believer, had been lived just like my father taught me. Never let them see you coming.

"Fuck, Donald, don't make me do this," Nikolas said, taking off the half-broken mask to look me in the eye as if sending love to his Old Yeller before putting it down.

Rizal had already started to separate into double the dickhole, double the fun. I had only the one unknown variable in Maggie, but whatever she had up her only-kinda-postpubescent sleeve was either minuscule or OP as fuck.

To play it right, I'd use that terror and be the thing that was coming right at them.

I moved back into view of the cameras with my arms raised, as if surrendering. But at the same time, I charged my fingertips with violet lightning. All lighting is fire, True Believer—stay away from it if you can—but the color tells you something about the heat. To keep it as simple as I can, since I need to get back to the shelter soon and would like to wrap things up here, and since I'm hungry: Yellow lightning is a low-level saag. Blue? That's a nice and spicy tikka masala. Violet?

Violet is a New York vindaloo in a shop that never took the time to implement a one-through-five spice-level scale.

I shot the lightning at Maggie, who barely realized what was happening. Lightning, to use technical terminology, is hella fast. To slow it down, however, I made it take the scenic route. There were enough conductive points in between us to filter the flow, make it zigzag as it bolted to its destination.

For the plan to work, I also had to play up the other character. The one that fell over himself while yelling *Zapidy-do!* and couldn't possibly understand why the color of lightning shifted, let alone control it. The one who thought of power as some mystical thing he could never hold. When Nikolas moved to protect Maggie I felt like every episode of *Death Note* I'd ever watched was finally paying off.

These are the Astonishing Tales of Just as Planned

While everyone was concerned with this nonexistent threat of violet death, I had a rod unclipped and in hand. I sparked it up. I used caution, internally kicking up my mental processing with electricity as Nikolas had taught me, since I needed the world to slow to nothing. My sights were set on the bruiser first. I threw the rod his way.

There is a difference, thin as it can seem, between super-strength and super-durability. The super-durable types are essentially encased in armor. Super-strength operated differently. I'd learned that best when I saw Nikolas break through Afrolicious Samson's skin months earlier. Super-strength is a product of muscle, triple-woven or hypercharged. Unlike with the super-durable types, though, the joints, ligaments, and organs remain mostly vulnerable.

I aimed my rod at Greg's elbow, connecting to a metal shelf behind him to boost the force as much as I could. The way he cradled his arm after it hit let me know I'd bought at least ten seconds from his respawn. Double Douchebag was next. I needed to take a hit, but sometimes there isn't any other choice.

My one interaction with him had taught me that subterfuge was his bread and butter. Not cowardice, just pragmatism. My mind was racing faster than he could move, though. I fell with the expected blow, exaggerating its actual impact by dropping to my knee. As I did, I cracked my arm backwards into the double's shin, seizing his muscles with a jolt. The B-side bastard tried to yank him away from me. Fucking idiot. They both toppled over when I ramped up the voltage.

Then? The hard part. The last double (triple?) was already standing over me—faster than I'd anticipated, but not by much. I had to be quick, because (a) Maggie could get hurt, even if I was pretty sure I'd distributed the flow of my bolt so as to not threaten her life, or (b) I could supercharge Nikolas and essentially fuck myself anyway.

I connected with the rod again, as I'd need it momentarily. It flew through the air and into my open palm. Between finger tabs, rod, and emblem I had enough conductive tools to redirect the lightning back to myself, denying Nikolas the boost. The violet bolt curved in answer to my silent call, veering off inches from Maggie as a few splintered offshoots frizzed her hair. At my command and through my control, the bolt split on the way to my conductors. When it reached me, I clenched my fists and let the electricity constrict my muscles tight as stone before swinging both fists upward to Rizal's jaw. He went down. I released the spark in my mind, switching off my mental modifier. Time sped up again.

Ignoring the migraine that ensued, I tackled Nikolas, pinning him down with the rod at his throat.

"That was pretty fucking awesome," he said after we'd glared at one another for a moment.

"I'm going to go," I said. "The motherfucking White Flame is back. You have officially extended beyond being a pain in *my* ass and are now one for the entire country, wasting tax dollars with this useless shit fit of a movement. You're no better than he is, for all your bullshit about 'what really matters.' I. Am. Leaving. You can't stop me, so don't try."

"Don't!" he commanded. It made me chuckle, True Believer. There he was, completely defeated, and he had the sheer testicular fortitude to command things. Astonishing.

"I'm through playing at whatever this is. You need me to be clearer? Fine. I, The Spark, in the name of the United States government, hereby order you to stand down."

"Donald, please."

"Nikolas."

"Oh, for fuck's sake."

"*Tess.*"

These are the Astonishing Tales of Say His Name

He only sighed, True Believer. He didn't poof into a cloud of dust; he sighed, and glared. He continued to glare even as the screech in my ear announced an incoming message from Gunther Grey.

These are the Astonishing Tales of
Computer Programs in Purgatory

"Spark! Spark, report. I've received notice from your audio channel—mention of Nikolas Tess. Are you near someone with that name currently? The man referenced would have white hair and abilities like your own. Is he working with The Emancipator? Report."

Nikolas mouthed, as slowly and obviously as he could: *Say no.*

"Nikolas Tess *is* The Emancipator, Gunther. I overheard one of them calling him that. Who is he? You know him?"

"Listen, Spark, are you in range to execute Nikolas Tess? If so, you are fully sanctioned to use lethal force."

"Sir, I—"

"Did he tell you to kill me?" asked Nikolas. I knew damn well that he had the same power I had to overhear every word. He was putting on a show. "Spunk, was it? Hey, Greyhound, you can hear me, can't you? You think this little knockoff can do what your other science projects couldn't? You think anything will stand between me and you? You think Ralph, Alberto, won't be the last names you hear before—"

"Kill the fucking terrorist, Spark. Kill him now."

These are the Astonishing Tales of What the Shit

I let go of Nikolas, and no, I didn't follow that up with a daring escape set to any song from Rage Against the Machine's 1992 self-titled album. I sure as shit didn't trust him any more than I had before, but I wasn't going to kill him, either. Instead I killed the cameras and helped him to his feet. The others were startled enough not to make a move.

"Sir! He—he—*ah*! He *has* me, I can't—" I must have performed too well, because next thing I knew, the familiar *fink foop* sounded as the LEDs shimmered purple. The color to let me know my GPS tracker had been activated. More importantly, the color of incoming heat.

"Asper en route," said Gunther.

"Asper?" I echoed.

Shit.

Those times when you're weighed down by the knowledge of your own fuck-ups, try to keep perspective, True Believer. For example, as I, during a throbbing migraine, wondered how I could be such an astonishing moron, perhaps the more pertinent question should have been: Why was Gunther so quick to take our biggest, maddest gun and turn it away from the most powerful villain in the world?

"Hurry," I gasped.

"Hold on, Spark," said Gunther. "Backup is on the way."

Nikolas signaled for his group to make their escape. I expected a trademark stab of snark, at least, but he only turned and ran, the others following. I felt a strange disappointment at the thought that it was probably the last I'd see of him.

I wasted no time in collapsing to the floor. Three, maybe four minutes later, the *boom*, the *croom*, the Almighty Asper and his aversion to using a door. He burst through the wall behind me. By the grace of a few dreadlocks, Asper found me through the cloud of drywall dust and dragged me to my feet, slapping my face as gently as I could hope for.

"What happened?" I groaned, starting to peel my eyes open. They quickly shot wide when I realized Asper's own eyes were burning bright.

"*Whoa*, holy dicks, man, it's me!"

He dropped me. I landed on my feet.

"Where is Tess?" he demanded.

"That, uh, Emancipator guy? I don't know." I looked around. "I think he got away."

Asper considered this for a moment before finally seeming to calm, his eyes dimming back to normal. "Sorry, Black. It's not your fault. He's incredibly dangerous, cunning. You slipped up when you said my name. If he hadn't known I was coming, I might have gotten here in time."

I tried to look astonished, drawing inspiration from Kat and the way she'd look when men were under the impression they had some celestial level of knowledge about topics too intricate for her small female mind to understand. I wasn't so much trying to castrate him with a glance, though, as to hide my affiliation with the dude I'd been ordered to kill not fifteen minutes prior.

"Oh, shit. Of course, I shouldn't have done that," I said, summoning my best stunned, slipped-and-cussed-in-front-of-Nana face. And the Oscar goes to . . .

"Are you injured? If not, we should get back to the team. White Flame isn't letting up anytime soon."

"No, I think I'm okay. Just got knocked out there for a minute. Let's spark it up!"

Before I could protest, Asper touched my hair again, this time firmly grasping with both hands. We soared through the gaping hole he'd made, in one of the most excruciating flights I've ever experienced.

CHAPTER 24
FLAME AND SPARK

WHEN WE REACHED THE site of the battle, Asper came in low and slowed down just enough before releasing my hair. I landed in a sprint and didn't stop running. Thankfully, I'd never had an issue with recharging my spark anywhere in New York City. I borrowed bolts of electricity from the air around me, calling to them like a lame Aquaman (before DC Comics made one of the few notably awesome moves of the 90s and turned him into a total badass). I don't know what, exactly, in a power set revolving around fire gave White Flame the ability to fly, but there he was, high in the sky, the blacker-than-black cape billowing in the wind.

I still had a massive headache from boosting my brain earlier—Nik had tried to warn me about that once, though I couldn't remember exactly what he'd said—but that was the worst of my physical pains. As for the other kind of pain—the implications of everything that had transpired between Gunther and Nikolas? Yeah, that shit was super effective. I sparked, though, and tried to keep my head in the game, straining to focus on Gunther's words streaming through the M-chip.

"White Flame is insane, but he ain't stupid. He's gonna try and separate the lot of you, push you each into a corner, but don't let him. You get separated, you're toast."

"Do we have any more support on the way?" I asked, connecting with a nearby fire escape and flinging myself to the roof above.

"White Flame is too dangerous. The B-listers would just be liabilities. You and this team are it, kid." Though *kid* was leagues above *boy*, which he usually preferred, I didn't exactly crap lightning bolts at hearing it. Still, I ignored it like a professional and pressed on.

Just as I'd been confused with Nikolas at first, I didn't understand why, of all the places to make an appearance, White Flame would ever choose New York. What was here that he couldn't find elsewhere? Nikolas could have found a bank to rob anywhere, but *I* was *here*, and that was what he'd been after. The news reports would write off an Onyx-level threat like White Flame as doing, with ultimate power, ultimately whatever the hell he wanted. He seemed a bit too focused, though, to behave like a thirteen-year-old kid in a basement going ham in *Grand Theft Auto* for stress release. For one, the thirteen-year-old usually gets bored after twenty minutes or so and runs into the bathroom for a quick "shower" instead. I got the sense that White Flame wasn't going for that option anytime soon.

It was ridiculous to hope for an answer, quite literally, because unlike the first time I'd met him, sans spark, this White Flame had a slab of metal drilled over his mouth. The gashed and thickly puffed skin around the metal made it obvious he'd chosen to go DIY with that project.

Its steel shone in the shades of a brushfire. He was always on fire. His power was raw and danced with a pale, hellish rage, as if knowing the truth of what it should be. The team had been battling him for a while, and the only thing they'd accomplished was to slow him down a bit while igniting him even more. He'd cut a blazing path all the way up Centre Street to Federal Plaza.

If I were a supervillain, hellbent on anarchy and on taking out my frustrations against my fellow white dudes with power (the paper-pushing, make-life-or-death-decisions-without-ever-having-to-see-a-single-one-of-the-people-affected kind of power, as opposed to the hotty-hot kind), I'd probably know that the superheroes would be sent in to stop me. I'd know that I needed to bust ass and do the damn thing. But by some silver-aged stroke of luck, no one had been killed by the time I arrived. The federal buildings had been miraculously emptied prior to our arrival there, as the battle that bustled through the streets had allowed time for high-risk buildings to be evacuated. I wondered, briefly, if there was a comic-book shop anywhere amid the mayhem.

GRAVI-Tina had kept most of the fire on the ground contained, while DEATHRAGE fed White Flame bullets. (These he easily melted, but they kept him sufficiently annoyed to focus on trying to shoot streams of, yup, white flame at DEATHRAGE through the clacky clunk of guns and piss.) White Flame stayed out of GRAVI-Tina's direct range. He never lost sight of her and sent heat whenever she tried to climb or do anything that would close the distance between them.

Patches, as expected, was nowhere visible, hidden away off some break-glass-in-case-of-emergency avenue.

Asper engaged. It was like I was a kid again: two unstoppable forces and me, watching instead of finding the will to move. I blinked and nearly missed Asper wrapping his arms around Flame, smoke rising from his body as he did so. They dive-bombed towards the ground. Then the crash, the boom, the two staggering bodies struggling to their feet.

I watched them from my rooftop. Standing in the street, White Flame looked less like a monster and more like a confused homeless man of a certain age. GRAVI-Tina acted quickly, increasing the gravity immediately around Flame to keep him grounded, but she was struggling to fight on a lot of fronts, smothering flames with pockets of zero gravity wherever she could. She wouldn't have to hold on for long, though. Asper was with us, and his super-strength could end it. Once and for all, we'd have a world without that light.

What happened next? Well, I'm sure you remember, but there's an important director's-cut bit that, *I* think, needs mention. Asper was moving as fast as he could within the weight of GRAVI-Tina's field. I could tell the field was relatively high, so dense that DEATHRAGE, caught on the edge of it, smashed against the ground, the snap so sudden that his head seemed to crack on the pavement. Luckily, though, he was only—say it with me now—rendered unconscious.

Then? I fucking saw it. I saw it, I saw it, I. Saw. It. I don't care what they say or how many think pieces slam me for—as one Pulitzer hopeful put it—ride-or-dying with my blatant lie. I saw Asper throw a haymaker with enough destructive force to crush a semitruck—at the empty space next to White Flame's face.

No, I didn't say that he missed. Asper doesn't *miss*. And no, things weren't moving so fast that I didn't understand what I saw. And no, I wasn't fighting the shattered delusion that just because Asper was better than me, he was infallible. I knew he wasn't infallible, True Believer. Did I ever.

Which is not to say that I was entirely up to speed. My first thought—you might have figured out by now that I didn't exactly *like* Asper—was that the overpowered alien was a traitor. That he was in league with White Flame, only pretending to fight. Where did that leave the rest of us?

My head was still throbbing, but I had no choice: I sparked up my brain again. I needed, for an instant, to be a genius, because I had a hell of a problem to solve: how to escape the jet of supercharged flame that shot my way as soon as GRAVI-Tina's control wavered, blotting out all other thoughts.

The human brain, your brain, transmits electricity via dipole stimulation—at least, I think it does; I was always more of the *please buy my zine* guy in college. Anyway, electricity in the human body is just the way we transmit information from one bit to the other, like a really, *really* fast expressway. I'd show Nikolas that I could *spark*. I could grab hold of the me inside and become everything I wasn't meant to be. Someone who could see. Someone terrific and foolhardy enough to give himself the equivalent of fourteen PhDs without the wait. If I took what Nik had taught me and pushed it to the limit, farther than he'd ever let me take it? I could be one of the smartest men alive.

I clocked the trajectory and speed of the jet of flame, hell if I remember how, and knew exactly which way to jump, and how high, in order to evade it. Then, suddenly understanding electromagnetism in the minutest detail, I created a field of lasers—lasers, True Believer! all different colors and shiny and everything—that caged White Flame where he stood. That wasn't a trick Nikolas had taught me. I'm pretty sure it wasn't even one he'd discovered.

"Spark! Get out of there!" shouted GRAVI-Tina.

"Shhh, I'm doing stuff here!" I said with a laugh that, if I'm being honest, was probably fairly maniacal. "Hehehehe, I'm doing stuff here and there and everywhere with science! I'm doing things that thought provides power for! Silly Cheshire cat, you can't fool Alice!"

Yeah, sometimes screwing with your own mind comes with mixed results.

If I could have sent a jolt of lightning into White Flame right then and there, that would have been the end, but GRAVI-Tina had needed years of experience to enact zero gravity for a few moments. Me? It took all my supercharged brainpower to hold him for three seconds, True Believer. But it only took me three seconds to get to what I was after all along. When the laser light show released him, I was standing with a sadistic smile atop a manhole cover.

I soared, cackling with laughter that I couldn't control and didn't want to. I knew that Flame was following me, but I couldn't have given any less of a shit. I was flying. I was above it all. I was Astonishing.

Also, I was out of my fucking gourd, but that's beside the point.

These are the Astonishing Tales of Man, It's Like
I Came Straight Out of a Comic Book

"Head spinning, head splitting, can you spare a cup of spark, neighbor?" I shouted to White Flame. "Haha, need to stop these furies, speed up the tick-tock-tick-tock ticker! I get to save the day! Donald delivers final blow! It'll be all in the papers, oh, won't matter in a few seconds, man, shoulda wrote a will, Will Smith is funny. Daddy loves you, aha!"

I slowed down. He sped up as if I'd done it by accident. Adorable. His fingertips grazed the manhole cover when we were a few thousand feet in the air, and as soon as they did, I leapt off of it. I leaned back in freefall—*Oh noooooooo! White Flame, don't let me die like this!*—and then I connected with the metal disc through my emblem, smashing it right into White Flame's face. He cried out, or at least I think he did behind the metal slab.

Calmly, I rested my hands behind my head and cackled all the way down, down, down.

"Aha, one jump ahead of the lawmen, and that's no jo-ho-ho-hoke!" I sang, while the manhole cover, feeling the call of my electricity, connected with my boots just ten or so feet before impact.

I bumped from manhole to magnetic manhole across the pavement as if surfing over squishy ocean waves, skidding to a stop a few feet in front of GRAVI-Tina.

"Spark?" She sounded worried.

"*Aladdin* was such a dope moooooovie! Dopey dope, ropey rope, gravity on this make Flame go boom in the face?" I said, raising the manhole cover and pointing at a very fast, very incoming Flame. GRAVI-Tina nodded, and I let it go. It floated in midair, sinking slowly, before both of us focused our Talent and shoved it towards the incoming predator.

His robes enveloped the manhole cover like a blot of ink, the impact so strong his body felt the need to try and wrap its way around it. He fell, limp on his back, just as Patches finally made his way to us.

I stepped over to White Flame, plinked my copper-tipped fingers, and pointed them at his face.

"Aedan," I growled, finally the beast I was supposed to be. Staring into those worn, glass-shielded eyes of his, I sparked it up, magnetizing the copper to the metal over his mouth, peeling it off forcefully. He cried out, but this time with a breath of fire that would have swallowed me, GRAVI-Tina, and everything else whole if he hadn't raised his head up to the sky and let the stream swirl upward.

The whiteness filled everything above us. I thought it wouldn't stop, and I also thought, *good*.

It did stop, though, when he clenched his teeth tight. Smoke spilled between them. I began to spark, my body surrounded by a field of violet, of amber, of all the colors I'd never called upon.

"Please," he said through his gritted teeth.

This, I suppose, is where the end began, because I stopped. I let my own Talent dissipate to listen to the dying pleas of a madman.

"Please," he choked.

I stood there, frozen and fascinated, as he raised his hands to let out the white and bring nothing but the black.

* * *

I know what happened after that. There wasn't a TV over the next three weeks that didn't show my charred, life-plundered body lying there in the street. We'll touch on that, but in the interest of linear storytelling that doesn't hop back and forth, which I'm totes known for at this point, I'll just skip to the life I knew next.

CHAPTER 25
WHATEVER HAPPENED TO THE GRAVITATIONAL GODDESS?

"YOU KNOW, WHEN I got here, I thought I'd be, I don't know, *not* working? Like, crazy, I know, but kneeling with your fat ass in my face wasn't how I imagined using my *very* limited vacation time." Kat was kneeling behind me in my Bronx apartment, her measuring tape wrapped around my waist.

"Come on, you're loving this. I could turn around, if you prefer. We could finally cross that threshold every 90s movie told us we would and have a go at it."

"Oh, wow, haven't heard this bit before, hitting on your lesbian friend. Holy shit, that was so funny, OMG, ILU." She groaned as she got up, snatching the notepad she'd had me use to jot down my measurements.

"I mean, isn't it *possible* for a personality to transcend your myopic standard of attraction?"

"If that personality is attached to a vagina, sure. Put your arms out."

I huffed before stretching my arms out. Then my body seized. A tremor of lightning played around me and rebelled against me from within. Kat leapt a few steps back; I think she called out to me. She tried her best to hide it, but I knew terror when I saw it, even if she was better than most at covering it up.

"No no no, nooooo . . . haha! Ahaha . . . keep me from . . . keep, Kat? Kat?" I swayed back and forth before finally collapsing. Tears spilled from one of my eyes; the other just couldn't close. It took another thirty seconds before I stopped shaking and fell into myself, still sobbing at the man I'd made myself into.

Kat scooted over, cautiously, as I lay there balled up in a fetal position. She found me, like she always did. Eventually my head was in her lap and my locs were being stroked. The comforting smell of clove cigarettes and Mountain Dew. Bony legs. Trying to make sure you're loved, and nothing else matters even if everything matters and you—

"I can't do this," I sobbed.

"Shhh. Hey. Fuck you, doo-doo head. You've made it through worse, just take it slow. Breathe, Donny."

A sssstep back, True Believer?

* * *

He'll be fine.

Those words probably never met with as much resistance as when they were uttered to Kat and Paul, who were powering through a ten-hour drive to New York to see what was left of their darling, dumbass Donald. They'd started their trip, they told me, when—along with the rest of the TV-watching country—they saw me burn.

I, of course, only kind-of-sort-of remember this, because when I was revived, I came back wrong.

The red tape it takes to get a reverse of fatality by Patches is, well, murder. That's not even considering that on this occasion there were other, higher-profile heroes to consider. First—well, let's just get to it. What happened to the Gravitational Goddess? She was right behind me. After I fell, there was GRAVI-Tina, and there was White Flame.

"Patches, get out of here," she said to Adam, who for the first time, staring at a wobbly but waking White Flame, looked his age. He trembled, looking back and forth from my corpse to Asper's wounded face and then to DEATHRAGE, not yet knowing he was only unconscious.

"But—Spark and Asper, and—"

"And what? What are you going to do right now? Revive them so they can die again? What we need right now is for you to *leave*. Spark is the only one who's fatally wounded, and I can keep his body safe. Asper will be fine, but it'll be pointless if you aren't around to—shit, he's getting up. Fucking go, now!"

"What are *you* going to do?" He was resigned to leaving, but he needed to know that she, the best of us all, was going to be fine too.

"Only thing I can. Really going to regret this when TMZ gets a hold of it in the morning." She chuckled, and Patches, good kid that he was, forced a laugh before darting off.

When I say she is, or was, the best of us, it's not just sentimental bullshit. Like Asper and Flame, she was one of only six (seven now, I suppose) individuals in history to receive PantheUS designation as Onyx-level talents. The thing that links most of them (Asper being the only exception) is the elemental nature of their power. GRAVI-Tina, Rinse and RePETE, SkyScraper, and White Flame: all could control one of the most basic forces of nature. They bent the laws of physics by their very existence.

Anytime GRAVI-Tina's status came up in debate on the PantheUS nerd forums (where I'd never, ever spent time trying to find out what *you* think of me, True Believer), her Onyx designation got dismissed as mere political correctness (the liberals wouldn't shut up about the patriarchy, so PantheUS threw them a bone and upgraded her status). Without the heroically hypermasculine magnificence of her colleagues, according to the nerds? We'd see that the closest thing the Dominican Danger really had to Onyx was her skin tone.

While I find this a little tragic? At least, in the end, she shut those asshats up.

These are the Astonishing Tales of My
First Friend in PantheUS

She stepped forward, putting my smoke-wreathed corpse behind her. White Flame's eyes bore past her to my body.

The first thing she did was release the constant gravitational field that made her the woman of Wednesday crushes. Her hair fell limp; her corset strained, unsure how to contain that body, so different from the one it had held a moment before. She kicked off her heels.

White Flame's eyes darted. "PLEASE, DIE FROM THEY THAT ARE BEAUTIFUL MAKING HAPPY ME DO A BEAUTIFUL DEED THIS DAY." He coughed between bursts of white fire from his mouth.

"Uh, okay." A violet aura pulsed around her, much as it had the day I'd sparred with her months before. White Flame unleashed fire and GRAVI-Tina met it with her own Talent. She screamed, cursed, and was generally, in the words of Adele Givens, a fucking *lady*. The deathly void she created swallowed the flames whole.

Amid the heat of it all, GRAVI-Tina slapped a hand to the pavement beneath her and a focused tremor shook the ground, making White Flame's body shudder and rise into the air. Darting at him, she grasped his dangling legs, shifting the gravity with pinpoint precision to slam him into the ground in a display of super-strength we hadn't known she had. Fire roared from his cloak on impact, but not a lick of it touched her skin—it danced around her body as if frightened of something that really burned. It began to spread, though. White Flame, however his powers worked, seemed to disregard or at least bend the rules about what was combustible, because the concrete jungle we called the city might as well have been one giant pile of tinder.

"Motherfucker." She watched the buildings, the ground, the everything catching fire. Having let go of her personal gravitational field, she seemed not to struggle at keeping up the protective shields, but as more and more of the city melted she seemed more and more absorbed by the vistas of destruction.

My question, and Paul's too when he wrote about it later, wasn't so much what we do when faced with such an unbridled force as why the shit did he take so *long* to go nuclear? I guess it sounds a bit hypocritical as I type it. After all, I had more power than I'd ever displayed prior to my death, so why didn't *I* use it? Even GRAVI-Tina could have done more, as evidenced by my ashen remains. But then again, we were the good guys. GRAVI-Tina hadn't used her every-thing until she absolutely had to. None of us really ever wanted to be seen using much of anything if we could help it. But White Flame? What fire ever holds back its rage just because?

I digress. When GRAVI-Tina saw that White Flame had lost whatever modicum of self-control he'd had, she didn't flinch. She met his eyes. He stared back, like a sleepy-eyed child looking at the mess he'd made of his sheets, and flew off. GRAVI-Tina worked fast, floating into the sky to get a better view of the damage. At least ten blocks were engulfed in thick smoke. There was screaming, there were sirens, there were other PantheUS members doing what they could, but most importantly there was her, saving our asses.

319

Her expression betrayed, as the news reports would highlight, a peculiarly feminine terror in the face of the fire, but she persisted. She extended everything she had, invoking powers that nudged every brick and pebble, defying all the known laws of physics to corral the fire into burning orbs that ascended slowly into the sky.

As Asper awoke to a day that had already been saved, watching the violet aura around GRAVI-Tina dissipate, he rejoiced that at least he'd be able to rescue a damsel and be again the hero of AM, FM, all-M radio that he'd always been. He caught her just as she passed out from the overexertion of her talent and tumbled down into his arms. The orbs of fire ascended into the sky, dwindling until nothing remained but the night.

What came after?

Well, I can tell you that the rumors of my death weren't exaggerated at all. I was, like, completely fucking dead, and I would have stayed that way.

Gunther had a hell of a mess on his hands, but his extraordinary talent for cleaning shit up was as astonishing as it ever had been. And he had his secret weapon, Patches, who'd gotten out of the line of fire and back to his hidey-hole in time to stay useful. (His ability is constantly misunderstood, by the way. He was more time machine than healer. With a touch he'd rewind a part or the whole of you back to what you were precisely twenty-four hours ago. So I'm glad I wasn't around to know that at hour fifteen, I still lingered in the void.)

To Gunther's credit, I was at least third on the list of problems to be fixed, so, that was pretty dope. First, there was Asper's face. America's sweetest stubble-free mug had had its glow of innocence burned away in the fight. But the public face of PantheUS couldn't be scarred, couldn't show a blemish or share the wounds of the world. Asper had to be made whole. Then there was GRAVI-Tina.

She wasn't mortally wounded—in fact, she'd woken up an hour or so after saving all our asses—but she'd woken up without the one thing that made her matter. The overexertion of her power had left her talentless. She couldn't alter gravity enough to move a nickel. Only then, coming in third just like at his fourth-grade science fair, was The Astonishing Spark.

The way I imagine it, they had the three of us on gurneys somewhere: my lifeless body flanked by GRAVI-Tina and Asper. It was somewhere appropriately brooding and dramatic, I'm sure. They wouldn't let the press in; they sure as shit wouldn't let Paul or Kat in, no matter if they were my emergency contacts. The mad-scientist henchman Dr. Heller, who'd installed my M-Chip, was allowed in, of course. He was immensely saddened by the loss of me, they told me later, and in honor of my legacy sought to begin harvesting my everything immediately in the interest of continuing my service to the nation. Gunther, stickler for the rules that he was, forbade such action until I was fully and irrevocably gone.

GRAVI-Tina didn't have trouble making up her mind. She refused her chance at healing. She didn't hesitate, just stared at Gunther. *How are we even discussing this?* But discuss they did, for fifteen hours, while Heller salivated over my remains. Asper? Well, being the hero, he found himself at a tragic crossroads. He had nothing but kind words for the departed, but he was forced to point out the obvious truth. I wasn't yet a member of the American Collective for Resolving Overtly Negative Yowled Misconducts. I was just another registered PantheUS member, and therefore, regardless of the relative severity of our injuries, I had to wait my turn. The PantheUS brand depended on it.

Patches was ordered to heal Asper.

"No," he said.

These are the Astonishing Tales of This Asshole,
This Wonderful Moron of an Asshole

Sometimes, True Believer, it only takes one *no* to tear through every last strip of red tape. Sometimes, even more surprising, that *no* can come from a teenage asshole who spends most of his time higher than the Almighty Asper in flight. When Patches disobeyed a direct order to heal Asper, he did so with a careless word and a loose shrug, as he did most things. This was just how it was going to be, and good ol' Grandpappy Gunther would have to fall in line.

This, from what I heard, didn't go over too well. Gunther placed his grandson under arrest and locked him up inside headquarters— that is, until Asper's time was up, but mine still wasn't—just barely. Gunther reasoned that there was still something to be saved in all this mess; it had just so happened to work out that it was my Black ass.

I don't remember much about coming back—not about the beginning of it, anyway. When, to Heller's dismay, Patches revived me, I was in the same unfortunate state I'd been in exactly twenty-four hours before: a muttering, misanthropic miscreant, body healed but mind a shattered mess.

Kat told me later that I didn't seem to have completely forgotten who she was—that while they kept me sedated for the most part, there were moments when I sprang to life and looked at her the way I used to when we were kids. I spent a few weeks in a PantheUS-funded facility for those who'd fallen victim to a very particular sort of circumstance. My mind, though they dosed it with anything they could pump into it, had forgotten how to shut down, how to *slow* down. They called it a miracle when eventually, one morning, I woke with the same sad brown eyes any Black baby has at first. I had a vague memory that something had happened the night before—a gentle hand in the darkness, placed over my own. I remembered feeling found. I remembered the mad circling spark in my brain quieting until only Absolute Resistance remained.

I was sidelined. Gunther was kind enough to send some appearances my way: charitable stuff, mostly, where I didn't have to do much except be a body in a costume in a room in a house. This, I knew, couldn't possibly be enough to get me permanently elected to the team. Chris knew it, too. Oh, did Chris know it too. (To his credit, he didn't lose his shit about it right away. Even he seemed to understand that a modicum of tact should be applied when your client is only recently resurrected.)

During my unofficial leave, Kat decided to stay in town while I stumbled into whatever life it was I had before me. She was a nurse, an adviser, a stopper of doo-doo-head tendencies, and a piece of something I would always want and never get back. She was there when I got the call from Chris, asking me to come to his office. I knew that his patience had thinned, and it was time to tackle the business of tomorrow. I wore my costume beneath a trench coat: I wasn't looking for attention, but I was looking for the safety I felt in Kat's upgrade to my suit. She was sitting on the couch, reading the next book in the obscure-fantasy-that-believably-writes-women series she was into. I tried to think how best to bug the shit out of her without bugging the shit out of her.

"Hey, so are you gonna just chill out all day?" I asked.

She took a mental note of her spot in the book and then closed it to look at me. "Yup, this place is expensive and I'm poor, soooo . . ."

"Well, if you're bored or, you know, want to get some air . . ."

"Do you want me to come with you, D?"

"I mean, if you want to, I guess I'll drag you along. You're welcome," I said with a smirk.

She rolled her eyes, grabbed her hoodie, and followed me out the door.

* * *

When we walked into Chris's office, I nearly ran into a woman walking out. It was her: not GRAVI-Tina, but Maria. I knew she'd been a cop before, but it had never quite computed. Dark skin and death-warrant badges always formed a frazzled kind of juxtaposition in my brain. But there she was, in civilian garb, the badge glinting from the interior of her coat. For some reason that I couldn't understand, she smiled at me.

I froze. Kat, seeing my static, rubbed my back gently to bring me back to life.

"Donald, you're late," Chris said.

I wasn't, but I didn't care to correct him. He motioned me inside. Maria looked as if she wanted to say something, but Chris rushed her out and closed the door behind her.

"You have to start thinking, seriously, about what your chances are," Chris said after we got through the pleasantries.

I looked away. "I'm getting better. It's slow, but—"

"You know that shit doesn't matter, Donald. If you ain't no good in the right now, then you ain't no good at all."

I'd been feeling hollow for weeks, but his words whirled in deep to show me there were still a few pieces left to excavate.

"So . . . what do we do, then? You want me to just give up, after everything I've done to get here? I died for this, Chris. Like, I literally rotted, for nearly a whole day."

"So why the shit would you want more of it?" Kat interrupted.

Neither Chris nor I knew what to say for a second.

"Got a mouth on her," Chris said finally, with a laugh. (He'd probably have seen what else she had on her if I hadn't squeezed her hand *very* tightly at that moment, one of those times when words weren't needed for us to understand one another.) "She has a point, though. This is your swan song, Donny boy. You can claw and bite and all those other niggardly things you want, but nine times outta ten it ain't gonna do you no good. We can however, capitalize on your ripe ass for something that will still get you something out of this deal." Chris had now used the word *niggardly* in the wrong context twice since I'd known him, which made me think that either he hadn't quite grasped its meaning or he just liked how it rolled off his tongue, the way liquor rolls down the back of my throat.

These are the Astonishing Tales of You Can't Be
Niggardly When You Got Nothin to Nig

I knew what he was reaching for when he opened one of the lower drawers in his desk. When the black binder flopped in front of Kat and me, she eyed it quizzically. I, again, looked away.

I thought of my apartment. I thought of how I'd accrued a rolling ball of interest in the form of payday loans in order to eat and sleep within it. I thought of promises of pie slices, or a bite of an apple, or anything else that stained your teeth but never kept you full. I thought of Paul, and shackles, and coffee, and everything, and me. I thought of *thwup-thwups* on my chest, too. The weight of my father's hand, even then.

These are the Astonishing Tales of Black

CHAPTER 26
ALL THIS AND RABBIT STEW

I'**M SORRY, SIR, YOUR** card was declined," says Tad, my barista. He's standing behind me. He must be reading what I'm typing, because I can see his face reflected in my computer screen.

Isn't there a rule against that? Doesn't it say somewhere in the ethical code of conduct for baristas that a proprietor of bean juice shall not pry into the rough drafts of budding Nobel Prize winners?

I reach into my satchel and hand Tad a five, my thanks, and the curt nod of a night crawler.

So anyway, back to the Adventures of the Advertising Spark.

After we left Christopher's, my milky-white life companion tried to keep me contained with words about nothing. It was approximately our thirty-seventh debate as to which Kevin Smith movie reigned supreme, and we were just getting into it when GRAVI-Tina—Maria—stepped out of the shadows in the middle of the day. I stared at her for a moment. While I immediately knew her, I didn't. The long trench and the rest of her bust-yo-ass getup made me wonder if she had an audition for *SSI: Terse Looks*, but the badge looked a little too real for that. I stood there, not knowing what to say: long enough for Kat to introduce herself, long enough for them to break the ice with some lightweight crack about me that I can't remember, long enough for the chill to creep back over.

"It's good to see you, Spark," said Maria.

My eyes watered, which really didn't do a fucking thing to help anyone feel less awkward in that moment. "Maria, I . . . I'm glad to see you're good." I couldn't keep my eyes on her for more than a second or two before they'd wander off.

"Are you sure? You don't seem like it. Are you okay? I mean, not trying to give any credence to the rumors about us, but a girl feels a way when you don't return her calls." She said it with a laugh, but I'd brought her world to fire and I couldn't see the joke.

"I just . . . I, like, never meant for any of this to end up so shitty, and I'm sorry. I'm so fucking sorry. I thought—I saw Asper go down. If I'd have just stayed on that roof, you—and you saved me. Well, I mean, kinda, I was already dead, but semantics, I guess. And I wouldn't be here without you, and what was it for? Now, like, *two* heroes are down for my dumbass mistake, and—I just, like, never meant for any of this to end up so—"

"You're looping," Kat chimed in from behind me, and there was this moment when the two of them laughed and I felt less like the nothing I'd changed into, but it passed.

"Damn, man, I mean that is a lot of words," said Maria. "You really just need to get better at picking up your goddamned phone, my dude."

"Preach," said Kat. I flashed her a look that did absolutely nothing but entertain the two of them.

"Look: I'm sorry if you think I'm carrying some, I don't know, resentment toward you for doing what you were paid to do," said Maria. "What you *promised* people you'd do when you accepted your position, temporary or not. You tried to use your gift to save people. I ain't ever gonna shit on you for that. So don't let it swallow you. I'm working. I wasn't injured, not really. I picked up where I left off, and yeah, sure, it sucks sometimes, but I had a hell of a going-away party. I didn't wait for you outside here because I wanted an apology. I waited because I was pissed I'd let Chris get one more over on me before I dropped his ass. Do you know he rescheduled me so we'd be here at the same time, because he thought we were lovers? I should have known something was up. This is what he does, man. Manipulate. You think he didn't know we'd pass each other going into his office? You think that crabby-ass dickhole didn't hear your, um, really ill-advised radio spot about me, didn't get the idea of using me, like they all wanted to use me one more time, as a tool to yank at your guilt strings?" She stopped, looking worried that I'd gotten lost in her maze of words.

"Shit," Kat said.

Yeah, shit, True Believer.

"I . . . thanks," I said, which may be the lamest thing I've ever said in a very long history of unquotable quotes.

"It's cool, man. Just stay good, and don't fall for Chris's shit, okay?"

"Yeah. I promise," I said.

With that we parted. Kat and I flew back to Ohio, and—ah, hell, I already did that bit, didn't I? Right, sorry, True Believer. Limited time, all that.

These are the Astonishing Tales of
Falling for Christopher's Shit

I gave Chris's binder of advertising campaigns another look. He'd done his homework. Each of the many, many offers we'd received was thoroughly researched, with numbers showing the maximum return we could expect for taking it. I'd never imagined that the payout for a commercial could be so impressive. While I'd mooched off of Paul's cable subscription even more often than Kat, she and I being economic twins, I preferred the same method of idiot-boxing as she did: streaming. No commercials; limited content but enough stuff there to melt the mind just as well as Paul's 837 advertisement-laden channels could, and for way less money. And if that isn't the precise dichotomy of mankind, I don't know what is. Streamers and Subscribers. Those who want enough for enough and those who'll pay for all of it to get some of it, if you call it premium. All of which is to say, it'd been a long time since I'd even *seen* a commercial, except through the haze of Green Freedom.

Flipping through, I stopped at a page that read, "Black Spark vs. Hunger: Ad proposal for Colonel's Chitlin Fried Chicken and Gumbo." I fought back a laugh, trying not to wake Kat up. I wanted to laugh and laugh and laugh until my skin slid off my naked bones, but I couldn't, because Christopher Row wasn't laughing. He wanted me to be his hero.

I hated chitlins.

No, I *fucking* hated chitlins.

I hated that they felt like hot rubber between my teeth. I hated that my grandmother had made sure to wait until *after* I'd eaten them to let me know what the hell they were. I hated that I'd spent my ninth Thanksgiving huddled over a toilet after they'd wrought maximum carnage in my digestive tract. I. Hate. Shitlins.

This wasn't for me. It wasn't for anyone—but maybe, just maybe, the trail of zeros following the number eight made it worth considering.

We've all heard one version or another of the same astonishing tale, True Believers. Be twice as strong, twice as fast, three times as

329

lucky, and maybe you'll get half as far. My father had learned it from his mother and taken it as a paint-by-numbers way to fast-track a child past years of obscurity.

That tale, like many, wasn't entirely true. You don't have to be faster than a speeding bullet train to make it to work thirty minutes before everyone else. You don't have to leap tall grade-point averages at the HBCU you attend. You don't have to *be* the best, True Believer. You just have to reflect what they see in NBC sitcoms.

Your mother, God rest her soul, wanted to name you differently, my father once told me. We were sitting on a bench at the edge of a park, right where the city streets started to bleed through the greenery. *I named you Donald because they won't hire Devonte, they won't listen to Darshawn, and they're scared shitless of Tyrone.* His voice was always gravelly, but when he swore it dug even lower as if to tell me: these are the words of men. *I named you Donald so they'd never see you coming.*

This lesson was carved in my bones, and through the years it had blossomed throughout my consciousness. And so, I thought, if I broke away for just a moment from everything I wanted to believe, sliced just a pound of me and sold it for a share of what had been kept from us, that wouldn't be so bad, would it? I could gag on chitlins for that. I could be their *Oh, Donald,* their beloved clown, for just a little while longer.

I apologize for the fire in my fingers. Thankfully, it's a cold day.

At any rate, I didn't have much of a choice. Chris had already been brokering deals, printing up contracts, and doing basically everything except forge my signature on the documents. However much my thoughts might have soured on the man by that point, I had to give him this: he knew his shit. I needed as much visibility as I could get, as quickly as I could get it.

To get my face in front of Middle America, I'd be a regular on the *Superpower Hour* on Hound News with Keith Kelly Kurskovitch. The show was billed as a chance for ordinary voters to get to know the heroes they were paying for. First, I had an origin-story interview. Not my real origin story, of course, but I think we've covered that. After that I was given a weekly spot, *The Spark Spot*, where I just had to show up in costume every Wednesday and do three things:

Smile and nod in agreement with Keith's in-depth understanding of the politics that surrounded being a minority hero.

Cringe and condemn public overreactions to perceived unfairness against people with not-so-fair skin.

Wave a forgiving hand and laugh off the most recent misstep of a prominent (white) hero, usually Asper.

The spots I did with Keith were just supplemental to the other half of the job: crafting the most lucrative public image I could. My first ad was for the Flying Forty, a supercharged forty-ounce malt-liquor *experience* that would *shock the spirit*. The theme for that campaign revolved around me accidentally letting a supervillain escape while distracted by the shockingly sharp appeal of a Flying Forty bottle.

While that message might have been, um, questionable, I barely had time to think about it, because my inner fanboy was racing straight on to the next thing: doing motion capture for a video game. That's right, True Believer, I was going to be featured as an unlockable character in the wildly popular *PantheUS Brawl*! It was strange being in that motion-capture suit, waving my arms around like I was using my powers without firing off a single spark. The developers were jazzed to include my newest costume enhancement, the Spark Bracelet, as a power-up available only to my character. They also included a

Clubbin' Spark alternate costume, where I'd be dressed in a baggy, zebra-print pair of jeans and white wife-beater. Unfortunately, these bells and whistles did little to boost sales of downloadable content relating to my character, and while they tried to correct this with bonus coupons redeemable at Congregation Chicken, among other vendors, the numbers remained disappointing overall.

Despite the rapid leveling up of my public profile, of course, I was still just a twentysomething manchild from Ohio. Kat tried her best to keep that in mind while she stood by my side as stylist when roomfuls of executives critiqued my hair and while she sat through all the late nights of me training my mouth to hold hot rubber bands of meat for more than three seconds.

Although, when I got to that shoot, no amount of leveling up could defend against the sight of chitlin chunks circulating around the set. Adding to the bubbling in my stomach was finding out on the day I arrived that the script had been switched up. I'd be working on the Colonel's Chitlin Fried Chicken ad with a rapper: none other than Lil' Bruce, a.k.a. Young Breezy, my buddy from the twenty-fifth floor.

The now-infamous thirty-second spectacle began with a super-villain viciously attacking a schoolyard amid the suburban bliss of Somewhereville, along with two henchwomen who sported practical, battle-ready bikinis. They would be stopped by none other than yours truly, The Black Spark, and my sidekick, Lil' Bruce.

I wasn't really hip on new music. My search for new sounds had rested in peace since 2003, the final nail tacked in the coffin by lyrics lauding lip gloss and how it pops. Lil' Bruce wore leopard-print pants and diamonds in his teeth. Between takes I tried to spark conversation. His answers were sharp and to the point, though not really rude, which is how I realized we were playing the same game.

We both knew better; our Black asses cherried at the thought of being caught, but there we were.

We didn't owe each other anything. It was all about business, and I respected that. I eventually stopped trying to pry conversation from his glittery mouth and instead spent my downtime rehearsing lines of which we'd only use about 10 percent in the end. Kat spun on a chair beside me, reading a book and probably praying that the words would make the world her doo-doo-head homie had fallen into disappear. She slipped out for a smoke, and I was sure she was busy regretting even this brief return to the world of us. Because, well, I never stop doing the wrong thing, True Believer.

I've never felt like anyone important. I know how emo that sounds, and I apologize, but real talk: even when I was still part of the American Collective for Resolving Overtly Negative Yowled Misconducts, the cameras didn't instantly cure my self-loathing. I didn't feel like I'd be the one to show up on TMZ, mouthing off to the cop with a *Who the hell do you think I am?* Maybe the only thing that ever did make me feel truly visible was Thandie D. Nettle—or rather, the sight of her seeing me. There's something to be studied in the relationship between dopamine receptors and the most phenomenal woman in the world. And just then, that woman was walking onto my set.

Thandie gave me a tight hug and a kiss on the cheek. "It's tiny, isn't it? But I think this is where it really matters. The visibility of our people has to start everywhere if we hope to get anywhere."

When Jaquan, one of the grips, wandered a bit too close for comfort, she latched onto my arm. I smiled, the origin story of how she'd gotten there not mattering much, just the fact of her getting there. The knowing that there was still a chance for me to be astonishing enough for her to stand beside.

When Kat came back inside she stood there for a minute, looking from me to Thandie and back again. "Hey," she said to Thandie, flashing me a look that telepathically told me we'd be having a conversation later.

The charisma that my old friend Maverick Moralist had at the pulpit might have been his real talent the entire time. Like, no dispute here that he was totes insane, but the power of commanding an audience is no joke. I saw that in how Thandie watched me, watch her, watching me. How her eyes, both electric and earthy, clutched and held and did everything else that Kat's didn't. When we shot the last scene, I only needed one take to get it right.

For the most part, Kat kept her mouth shut until the filming was done. She scrolled obsessively through 4Chan, Reddit, and anything else filled with better garbage than what I was forcing her to sit through. She didn't bother looking up when I peeled a chitlin-greased costume from my body. She sighed when I regaled Thandie with the topic of my next HNN interview and the unstoppable force of finger-waving. She even stayed relatively silent on the way back to my apartment, as if asphyxiated by the smell of pig intestines that clung to us.

"So?" I said finally. I could see that her phone was running low on battery.

"Donald, you're going through a lot, and I don't want to criticize. But do you really think it's a good idea to—"

I dropped some dishes into the sink, purposefully making a loud crash against the basin. I flashed a smile when I turned back to her, but it wasn't mine: it was the tight-lipped one I'd picked up from my Pops.

She didn't flinch, because Kathryn Westermarck Oldgoer didn't flinch. She hadn't flinched the day she'd stepped in front of Tarika

Larso, ready to be my hero against the new bully who'd taken Paul's place after he became a piece of my everything. She hadn't flinched when her dad told her that if she really wanted to go to hell, she could go ahead and do what she wanted. She hadn't flinched when I spilled all the tears I had in me over the corpse of my father.

"I fucking jusss—fucking jus-jus-just—fuck!" I closed my eyes, trying to recover the stillness. When I thought I could get words out again, I said, "Just say it, Kat. Be real with me."

"D, what the shit is all this? Like, fuck, man, you are so—is this what you are, this life? Thandie fucking Nettle? Christopher Whatshisface? That asshole is what, your Jiminy Cricket? You know this shit is wrong. You have superpowers, you're an official PantheUS member, and that's enough. You can come home. I love you, Paul loves you. Come home."

There was no such thing as home for me anymore. Why couldn't she see that? "I fucking *died*, Kat. Who gives a shit about a commercial? Who gives a shit if I do some shit that a million people see but only like five people remember? You don't understand what it's like to—"

"Shut up, Donny. You act like I haven't been here before. Like I wasn't there all along, like I didn't see your Pops's body and everything else. I've watched you crawl down this same shithole a million times. Usually I don't say much, because I get it more than you think, these spirals of yours. I let it go, and Paul does too, because on some level you're trying *your* best in *his* way. You mess up, though, because unlike him, you're afraid. This time you're just getting *paid* to be a chickenshit and lie to yourself."

Paul's name was the only thing that hit home, skidding and skating through me, dragging it all down, down, down. "Don't be a cunt," I said, regretting it almost as soon as the words flew out of my mouth.

"Don't be a coward, and don't use words that'll get your ass beat."

"You don't get it. I don't even think Paul ever got it. I know what I look like, what they'll see. I know this shit is ridiculous, but I also know that people like Chris, or Thandie? They've built something for themselves that can ultimately be used. Power isn't all chaotic evil or lawful good, it's a fucking MacGuffin. It's something you accumulate and steal while never letting the ones that want you bleeding in the street know about it, not until the time comes to use it. I have this chance to get enough blocks together to build something so much bigger than a fucking blog. I think I can finally, I don't know, not be fucking useless. Help make someone who looks like me not so afraid to look like me."

"Yeah, not gonna listen to your race shit right now, not after you just did a fucking chitlin ad," she said.

That was a shank in the kidney. I sucked in my bottom lip as the air became hot and stale between us. Kat gave a low, growling sigh: I think I was somewhere on it, riding my way out of her life. She laughed like my father had before the *thwups*.

"I need your Metrocard," she said.

Shit, Kat, I'm sorry, I wanted to say.

"Why?" I said.

"Because I'm cheap, I'm fucking done with you, and I can probably catch the Megabus back to Columbus if I leave right now."

Hey *asshole*, you're going to need her, don't do this. Hey, asshole, she's going to need you, don't do this. Remember how you waxed poetic about rocket skateboards and childhood bonds? Yeah, that was her. She's walking out. You're stubborn but you're not even that stubborn, so don't let it go to your head, you're not an immovable boulder, you're at best stubborn like a thumbtack that falls out of the wall and gets buried in the carpet where no one can see it but they damn sure always end up stepping on it. Unrelated, but FYI, you're making this moment, this post-moment, about you, aren't you? Oh look, she stopped! She stopped for a minute! Are you—no? No, you're just going to watch her watch you and take it as what, some kind of challenge? That's not a challenge in her eye, not that it matters to you a fizzle-fuck, but—and, that's the door.

When you eventually end up in a coffee shop staring at a blank page, you'll desperately (and quite insanely) hope that writing about the past will mean that maybe just this once you can rewrite it, re-get-her-to-call-you-a-doo-doo-head, but you'll know that you can't, and that everything is still pretty much just as on fire as you left it.

So, good job with consistency, I guess?

CHAPTER 27
RED BONES AND BASTARDS

THE PROBLEM WITH WAKING up at the apartment of someone who should be a stranger is that neither your self-respect nor the cereal bowls are anywhere to be found.

After Kat left, I'd started composing a text message full of apologetic lies and avowals of regret, until I realized something: I was *done* with that. I was *better* than that. I was the Astonishing one, after all; she was the supporting character. After the third or fourth draft, I decided to call Thandie instead. One thing led to another, led to another, and anything in this world sounds better than self-deception on repeat, so let's do body flaps!

She seemed to remember all the things about me that I'd shown, not told, so we bungled along well enough. As shitty as I've made her sound, take with a grain of salt the ravings and the oh-so-reliable narrative angle of a cis-toxic ex. I can't say she didn't care about things that mattered. I can't say I didn't watch how she sobbed at an article about penguins and fishing nets. Then there was that night when she sat curled up against me, a laptop nestled on her thigh.

She'd created a ten-page PowerPoint showing what schools I could best afford, which frats I might join, what networking events I could attend. She tried to save me. She must have realized that every ten seconds I didn't move meant she'd take a hundred strides, and that I couldn't be bothered to catch up, but she tried anyway.

Anyway, while we stared at the ceiling waiting for the spinning to stop, she said it was fine if I crashed, and that brought us back around to cereal bowls and their enigmatic placement.

* * *

As the advertising dollars rolled in, I started making some adjustments to my lifestyle. I started buying monthly passes for the subway, for instance. While I could have shot through the tunnels on my feet at twice the speed, now I didn't have to. I didn't have to spark up my powers much at all, in fact: the only powers I needed were a smile and a jig, and I'd go home with checks to cash. Best of all: I'd stayed in the Bronx—but now I had a big, sun-drenched one-bedroom that I wouldn't hate bringing Thandie to.

This was our spark, our new beginning that would—

What the hell am I doing.

You know what, True Believer? I think maybe I should just tell you now that it ends. I think maybe I should try on a bit of realism for once.

Not that I haven't done it before. Hell, giving me some perspective on the real was Green Freedom's greatest talent, but since I don't think the bathroom here has windows, and I'm not eager to get myself arrested and stripped of the last few worldly possessions I treasure, I'll have to make do with whatever blessings a fourth cup of coffee can grant me.

I did some writing experiments earlier, trying to see if I could make Thandie's and my second separation sound even more wrenching than the first. The tragedy of her wanting to be with me, but also wanting me to be something more than I felt, was the destiny stamped on my giant forehead. The way she so suddenly decided to cut out the rot—a rot that hadn't so much filled up with maggots as opted for street meats and gaseous apathy. Not to mention that a hundred or so pages ago I activated 90s-teen-movie, socially-acceptable-because-charming nerd-stalker mode on her.

Shit, Donny boy, did you ever think that maybe the reason everyone who cares about you has an issue with her *might* have something to do with the whole two of them standing on the other side of the "save him or hope he saves himself" spectrum? Like, fam, did you even ponder on the meek-geek manipulation that somehow you haven't gotten around to confessing anywhere in these pages, abridged or otherwise?

> These are the Astonishing Tales of You Thought You
> Were the Hopelessly Romantic Paragon Who Must
> Endure the Tragedies of Infallibility, But It Was I, Dio!

I guess I can tell you something, True Believer.

I can tell you that it ended, but beyond that I have a mouth filled with wanting, and it's not fair to tell a tale from one side. Her absence would go on to propel the important mission of the guy who, sane and sour in his spandex, leapt from rooftop to rooftop to *hmm, it's four hundred feet to the ground, I wonder if it would really have been that hard to walk to the bodega?*

How about we say that the White Flame dropped her off a bridge.

How about we say that she was, *actually*, a shapeshifting alien the entire time, and the real Thandie is trapped in some stasis cube of clandestine convenience.

How about I just say that the last time I saw her, it was on a train. How about neither of us was right or wrong; we were just two very different people looking for the ship that those who came before us said we needed to find. How about we finally just got out of each other's way.

Also: If I've learned anything from muscle-bound heroic types about relaying a compelling story over the years, it's that there's not really anywhere for her arc to go in this one beyond the successful romantic conquest that crowns the classic dick-centric narrative. Maybe, in the end, what she really deserves is a book all her own.

These are the Astonishing Tales of Sue Storms

So, I guess, back to me?

After R. Kelly pissed across a teenage girl's forehead, he released the remix to "Ignition." After Chris Brown beat the holy hell out of a woman, he fried his head and piggybacked on any track that would have him. I've never had much of a singing voice, but I was finally making sound all the same. That sweet, shoe-shined fantasy of Blackness. I'd be only the second African-American superhero ever inducted into the American Collective for Resolving Overtly Negative Yowled Misconducts. I was their champion. I could talk right and walk white. I needed people to remember this.

Other people, not *you*, True Believer. If I tried to pull that shit with you, well, it'd never fly. It was for them: the ones who write the checks, the ones who have the power to bestow on us what we've earned. They're the ones who mattered. I needed to get my message out, craft my public image into something I could stand looking at. It was in this very vulnerable, very stupid moment that I decided to reach out to my old friend, Paul Hughes.

These are the Astonishing Tales of HeroCon

Six weeks.

That's how much time hung between me and the still-precarious prospect of permanent tenure on the nation's flashiest superhero team. I'd been invited to speak at the tenth annual HeroCon thanks to my recent surge in popularity. Supposedly, the convention was purely for the benefit of fans who wanted to revel in the glory of superheroics, as well as being a chance for taxpayers to get up close and personal with the Talented individuals they helped to elect. When a small group of freelance Talented individuals first founded HeroCon, they described its purpose as "celebrating the institutions aimed at dismantling the scourge of superpowered crime." Since then, though? It's become a finely tuned advertising machine. I can't tell you what flying out to San Diego to discuss my upcoming biopic had to do with connecting to the fans, since I mostly got rushed on and off the stage without talking to a single one of them, but at least I got to meet Pauly Shore wandering around the convention floor. That was kinda rad.

I'm being a little rough on the convention, perhaps. There was always a panel here or an interview there where no cameras waited around to pounce on the cute kids dressed up as their favorite heroes and squeeze them for packageable sound bites. Little moments when we just got to thank the fans and they got to thank us, with no agendas and no bullshit. And that was pretty astonishing.

When I got the HeroCon invite, I was still trying my best to connect with Paul. As a kind of olive branch, I even had Chris send him a free press pass for the convention. When Chris got back to me and let me know the pass was registered for an Anyla Mannes Nessa instead, I almost had it cancelled out of some inherent need for phallic measurement. Thankfully, I was heroic enough to think that move through.

My recent advertising opportunities were working. My name wasn't synonymous with one of the greatest failures in PantheUS history anymore. I was becoming the laughable darling whose name was on everyone's lips. I was zapidy-doing my way to victory. What I thought I really needed, though, to hammer things home for the upcoming vote, was for some reputable news source to capture the support of the staunchly snooty.

Paul and I had never been out of touch for such a long time. I'd reached out after the first TV spot aired for Colonel's Chitlin Fried Chicken. After my texts made their way to him, the subtle reply of *WTF* clued me in on his opinion. (Little did I know that this would be a drop in the blackened bucket compared to what came after.) When I got over being pissed off that he'd dumped the press pass off on Anyla, I tried giving him a call.

"Hey! Paul?"

When he answered it was from, of all the shocking places, a coffee shop. I could tell from the background noise of clanging spoons and subtle chatter. When he didn't respond right away, I almost hung up.

Just in time, he said, "Don? Hey, man."

I expected him to follow that with a sarcastic remark about something I'd done in front of a camera recently. When he said nothing more, I blundered on. "How are things in Columbus?"

He sighed. He'd been a constant, exploding cyclone of sighing since I moved to New York. "What do you want, D?"

343

So I told him. I told him about the opportunity I could grant the *Kuumba Kollective*: the chance to sit down and hear the true-life story of The Black Spark, hero of his people.

Paul laughed for nearly four hundred years before finally telling me that he wasn't interested, but he appreciated the offer.

I didn't take offense. I hadn't really expected him to agree in the first place; I just wanted to massage his ego with the thought that I'd consider his blog for such an exclusive story.

What I did need, though, were his connections. What I needed was for anyone from the independent Black press to shine up my sold-out image. Chris and I had agreed to offer the exclusive behind-the-scenes interview to one of these little publications, figuring it'd be easier to get a paper that needed the exposure to play by our rules. These rules would be simple enough: no questions about my relationship with GRAVI-Tina; nothing regarding my political affiliation; and, above all, no mention of my godawful spot on the Superpower Hour.

What would that leave us to discuss? Blackness. That, I'd decided, was my wheelhouse, the one topic I could excel at speaking about.

And so it was that I found myself facing Anyla Mannes Nessa at HeroCon.

She fit all of Chris's criteria. A Midwestern girl living in New York City who knew how to appeal to both regions. Black, but not *too* Black, at least by appearance. She spoke *right*, as Chris put it, which was to say, she spoke like the America you see on TV.

These are the Astonishing Tales of Her

The interview room was bright and vacant, spotlights flooding a stage that held only two stools and the two of us.

"Thank you for agreeing to this interview, Black Spark. We really appreciate your time."

"Hi, Anyla! It's nice to see you again. How've you been?" I said, as if we'd been acquainted for years. I mean, not entirely untrue, but—yeah.

"It's nice to see you, too. I've been following the developments since White Flame attacked. I hope you're in better health?"

I nodded. "I am, thanks—and just 'Spark' is fine, by the way, my sistah," I said, hoping the colloquialism would score me a few points with the group whose votes I most needed to recapture if I was going to get into the Collective for real. I expected maybe a fist raised in solidarity or something, but she only smiled. I opened my hand and let some sparks dance about, hoping that was at least a bit impressive.

"Very well, Mr. Spark, shall we begin?"

"Yes, let's do, Ms. Nessa."

"Perfect. So, aside from your advertisements, we don't get to hear much about The Spark. How has the superhero life been treating you since your induction?"

"It's been great, Anyla. Just *so* tight! And being the only African-American superhero in the Collective feels like a pretty big deal. I feel like I can finally give something back, you know? I feel like real change is happening." A wink, a spark.

"How do you mean?"

"I mean, I think it's a sign that finally we're moving into a postracial age. I couldn't be more honored and privileged to be at the forefront of that."

I saw then how fake Anyla M. Nessa's smile had been, because it was falling apart as she fought the real one bubbling through, and that was the carnivorous grin of a wolf about to pounce. Like the professional she was, though, she forced a cough to get rid of it and reached for her water mug.

"So, you're saying that your induction into PantheUS is a win for the African-American community at large?"

"Well, yes. I mean, I think it's a milestone. I respect and appreciate the task I've been given."

"I'm sure that being the *second* A-list African-American hero, following in the footsteps of Afrolicious Samson, seems like a pretty big deal. But if postracialism is your thing, why is it that you've chosen to play up race in your recent endorsement deals?"

"Wait, what are you doing?" I tried to whisper, nearly forgetting about the cameras.

Anyla leaned in. "I'm interviewing you, *my brotha*."

I crusted a smile over my terrified face and leaned back, edging myself into the game. "I just try to take the high road whenever I can," I said. "I don't want to get caught up in the nastier side of identity politics."

"And this high road includes the recent ads you've done for Colonel's Chitlin Fried Chicken? Which, blatant pandering to racial stereotypes aside, is a company currently under investigation for pumping their products full of harmful chemicals."

"Well, they're a fast-food chain that specializes in fried chicken. They have to make sure they don't give anyone salmonella. Right?"

"I think that every company needs to be held to certain standards of quality. How much do you think about the ethics of the companies you have advertising contracts with? Many of the ads lean on humor, as if it's all a big, harmless joke—saying for instance that you go 'toe to toe with da munchies,' all but confirming suspicions raised about the double entendre behind your motto 'spark it up.' But you must have some thoughts on the subject. You once wrote for *Kuumba Kollective* yourself, I believe."

"There's no double meaning," I grumbled. "Sparks. Electricity. I'm the guy with electric superpowers."

"Okay, or what about your interview on the Black Station after controversy broke out over the new album *Shockin Dem Bitches*? You asserted that, and I quote, 'Well, sometimes snitches need to get got, am I right? We live in an age where most of these bitches out here need to be shocked. We need to take personal responsibility and stop bitchin about how everyone else is holding us back, you know, my brotha?' End quote. I personally look forward to picking up the album myself, but I've got to say that for someone who is so postracial, you clearly direct a lot of criticism against one particular group, don't you?"

I imagined that somewhere, at that moment, Christopher Row was having a bowel movement in his pants. I thought of Paul, who must have been going apeshit when he set this up, laughing his talentless ass off knowing that I'd fall apart in front of America, feasting his imagination on the grandest display of Black on Black violence since Ali and Foreman.

I wouldn't fall apart.

"I suppose I can understand how you'd think that," I said. "But listen. For us to forge a way out of the darkness we've found ourselves in, we first have to understand how we got there, then drag our asses to the light. And that means owning up to the ways we've failed ourselves. Taking responsibility. Right?"

These are the Astonishing Tales of the Droids
Anyla M. Nessa Wasn't Looking For

"How we got there. You mean, by enduring centuries of slavery and systemic oppression?"

These are the Tales of No, Wait, Actually Those
Were the Droids I Was Looking For I Will Take
Them Fuck You and Have a Nice Day

"I'm afraid I don't understand your hostility, Ms. Nessa. Everything I've done, I've done to move us *past* the anger and hate and misery that weighs us down."

"Your assertion, then, is what? That, genetically or culturally, we are predisposed as Blacks to have a controlling share of ignorance and fallibility? That it's on us to take all of the blame and none of the credit?"

"Uh, no, of course not."

"Even if you're right, and a postracial America would be a paradise of equality: How is it possible to be an advocate for equality while practically plastering on blackface and doing a somber jig across the country?"

Super combo breaker.

"Well—this is exactly what I'm talking about, though! Getting hit with all this rage and judgment, when I'm out there every day risking my life—dying, even—to save people. "

"Mr. Spark, I'm simply making an honest attempt to understand what you're trying to accomplish in this community. I'm simply relaying to you the thoughts and concerns of Black America. How do you respond?"

"I just wann—jusss—" My mind sparked, overloaded, and then—nothing. As blank and empty as it had been the night I died.

"Mr. Spark?"

I stared dumbly at Anyla while the remains of my career circled the drain. To her credit, she waited until I started blinking again to ask her next question.

"Mr. Spark, is it true that you were clinically dead for almost twenty-four hours after your confrontation with White Flame?" All of a sudden her voice had gone low and husky, like this was a super-intimate chat instead of an ambush. She'd scented blood. She was coming at me where it hurt.

I nodded.

"What was that like?"

"It was, um—it was pretty much the worst thing you could imagine. It was—" *Don't cry in front of all these people, don't do it . . .*

"Do you feel it was fair for PantheUS to send costumed civilians into that kind of heat, instead of a properly equipped military unit?"

"I'm not a civilian! I'm a member of the American Collective for Resolving Overtly ~~Negative Yowled~~ Misconducts!"

"So what kind of training did they give you?"

"I mean, I had training, just not—not official. You know."

"Mm-hmm."

"He was going to burn the city. You think we should have just let him?"

"Your predecessor, Afrolicious Samson, sustained an injury that ended his career after the same kind of fight. And so, if the reports are accurate, did your colleague GRAVI-Tina."

You weren't supposed to mention Maria. You promised. "They were just doing their jobs."

"And that's you, too? Just doing your job?"

I gave a classic Patches-style shrug, not really caring anymore if I was coming off as an asshat middle-schooler.

"Mr. Spark, if there's one thing you wanted to tell our audience about yourself, what would that be?"

I gulped. "I guess it's, um, zapidy-do!" I said with a goofy grin.

True Believer, do you know how loud a glug careers make when they get slurped down drains?

Anyla M. Nessa might have set out to rip me to shreds in front of millions, but she only succeeded in making me realize that I'd been ripping myself to shreds for years. And that the masks we wear mold us maliciously, mangling what we hide behind into what we are.

As the camera light faded from green to red, so did I. She paused for a moment, looking at me, seeing me, but I could only see the ground between my legs and how crashing into it felt like the thing to do in that moment. Before I could, though, Anyla put a hand over mine, and while faint, it clutched, it felt like Ohio and basements and things you're not ready to see.

"You know, I wasn't trying to railroad you here today. I want you to know that. I came here hoping that Paul was full of shit about—anyway. I'm sorry if that felt harsh. It's my job to ask the hard questions." Her soft voice told me I still had some shred of dignity hanging around somewhere. Hell if I could find it, though.

"Then why did you do it?" I snapped. I expected—shit, if I'm being honest, *hoped*—to see some sign of fear when I met her eyes.

There wasn't any. There was something, but it wasn't what I felt I was owed. Instead? There was a little of Paul, and a lot of Kat, and, mostly, there was Aedan. A catalog of connections built in a constant state of Absolute Resistance.

"Because I think you can still make this shit right," she said.

* * *

Is it obvious here that I preferred our first encounter? The one where we'd met charmingly under the tacit assumption of mutual esteem? That woman, where the hell did *she* go?

This woman, well, she wouldn't be so eager to shoot the shit over a burger with me.

This fucking fire that my nanna would slap the shit out of me for calling out of her name.

This bit of an itch.

This memory of all the things, like my father's mother, who picked up this blerd-ass baton of me after he was gone, like the heaviest breath born from the heaviest hurts that I neglect to speak on because of something I'll try to convince you isn't a preoccupied eye.

These are the Astonishing Tales of This Astonishing—

Do you want to know a secret we all have to learn, True Believer? It's in here somewhere, beneath the shoulder blades of the body of us, in places you can't scratch or see.

Spoiler warning: You're going to find it, but not before they find you, and by that time you'll want to grab hold of it and scream, you'll want to bite at your cheeks. You'll also hate that I'm not giving it to you here, you'll think me one cruel coon, but you must find it for yourself, because Dumbo ears and Michael's Secret Stuff and ballot boxes and the short end of sticks you can break into jagged, piercing edges.

* * *

Chris thought it pragmatic to delay any further advertising opportunities until the election. I think it's safe to say we'd never been so calculating as when we decided I should stay cloaked sans dagger in my apartment until the fateful day came. For the first few days, phone calls poured in. Some names I hadn't expected blipped across my screen.

Missed Call: Kit-Kat

Missed Call: GRAVI-Tina

Missed Call: Asshole

Missed Call: Kendra Kanaway

Missed Call: Kit-Kat

Missed Call: Thandie D. Nettle

Missed Call: Anyone but Paul

While I didn't expect to hear anything like an apology from Paul, I still missed his voice, but I sure as shit wasn't starting that conversation. I checked my mail, half-hoping he'd send me a bag of coffee beans and that that would be one more peace treaty in the annals of our friendship, but of course it was just bills and reminders from nearby stores about what a beloved and valued customer I was.

That might have been the end of it all, I guess. Wilting away, too proud to sob my way back to Ohio, probably becoming the Super Predator you know and loathe so much sooner.

I worried for what ultimately amounted to Yamcha. I declined a few interviews. I wasn't up for anything but taking my time, rooftop shenanigans, and street meat.

I wasn't up for Paul, I'll tell you that much.

I for damn sure wasn't going to send out fourteen phone calls with no response.

I definitely didn't spend an afternoon finding this really dope coffee shop, scuttling through the Cave of Wonders that is SoHo for a bag to express ship with a note reading, *This one's on me, all of them are on me.* I'd be offended, in fact, at any accusation that I would feel the need to buy a weekend plane ticket to Ohio, and then wuss out at the last moment before boarding.

Only if I were a weaker man would I dare consider taking time out of my dwindling life points for such things. I'm just not the one, while sipping an (at best) hour-old brew, to tell ankh-wearing assholes that I take back every word I said about Common or to concede that spelling *Kollective* with a 'K' is deep.

Yeah, anyway, let's get back to the shit I did do.

* * *

I forgot what day the election even was, True Believer.

I woke up thinking it was a Monday when really it was a Tuesday.

I was blissfully ignorant, until the midnight banging at the door.

Until, on the other side, Chris Row stood with a champagne bottle.

Until he told me I really needed to get a damn TV.

Until I found out that, by a landslide, I was still your hero.

CHAPTER 28
EARTH'S MIGHTIEST MANEUVERER

I **HAVEN'T SEEN** *GLORY*.

Ugh, it feels so good to type that out.

(I'm kind of doing a thing with this, don't worry, mostly still A-OK up here.)

It was strictly prohibited in the McDougal household.

Aghast! The morbidly melanized Malik McDougal had a beef with the one movie that nearly completed his Black film trinity of Freeman-Washing-Jackson?

Yup. Not to mention the tragedy of his banning a movie that starred his 80s-movie man crush, Matthew Broderick.

Why would he reject something so intrinsically redeeming as the idea of glory? It was, he explained, the same reason he rejected *To Kill a Mockingbird* and *Dangerous Minds*: tales in which to have melanin was to have a malicious, malevolent mind—redeemable or not. Of course, he also rejected *Blankman*, but that was only because he didn't vibe with the high-caliber comedy of perhaps the most fire movie Damon Wayans has ever made. Anyway, digression being bae and all that, we'll move on. I have a point here, I swear.

When Milestone comics first appeared, he made another rule. For every *Iron Man* issue I bought, Aedan had to tuck a *Hardware* into my bag. For every *Action Comics*, an *Icon*. For every *Spidey*? A *Static*. It wasn't so much that this would ever make up for the inescapable tale of the decay of our communal body, built for booms and for autopsy. He believed, though, that it would at least keep that health bar holding strong at half-full.

All I'm trying to say is that really, there are no heroes. There are at best people who know things are fucked. At best, there are people who ask themselves: Am I going to do something to *unfuck* them, to make the fucked-up-ness known, or am I simply going to turn down the lights?

I wasn't the first Black superhero, not by a long shot, just the first that didn't make a big fuss about banging my knee on the end table every night while searching for shit that only sorta kinda belonged to me.

Ever heard of Ninety-Four? Nah, didn't think so. Hailing from Milwaukee, Ninety-Four was an early PantheUS hero who had the ability to multiply himself a total of—can you guess?—ninety-four times. Unfortunately, unlike my favorite sadistic body-splitter Rizal, Ninety-Four could only split for two minutes at a time, with a cooldown of about three hours.

He was likable, though. Who knows, he might even have made it to where I am, if it hadn't been for Florida and Fayth Wright.

After an all-too-common mishandling of powers blue and break yo'self, which resulted in justice-laced lacerations laid across Fayth after a traffic violation, there'd been a spark of momentary outrage. While the content of her character was in question for some, others decided to protest at the precinct that held her. Conley, or Ninety-Four, didn't feel he had much of a choice in joining with them. He

355

didn't know Fayth, but he knew every time he saw her on the news that it could just as easily have happened to some; not so easily to others.

He knew that this seemed rather fucked.

So what happened? For two minutes, Ninety-Four doubled the size of the small protest. His copies filled out the crowd. After he'd attended two or three more protests to do the same, bad branding won the day.

Now, if he could have stayed split for longer than two minutes, he might easily have been an A-lister regardless of his mistake, but as it was, criticisms abounded. One interview snippet that I caught on YouTube questioned the integrity of artificially padding a protest's numbers.

"It's just about doing what's right," Ninety-Four responded. "I'm not fudging the numbers, I'm just a proxy. You don't see or hear from dozens of people who *want* to be here, but who have to go to work or else starve their kids. I can represent them with my Talent, and I intend to keep doing so."

But did it befit a man working under the benevolent banners of PantheUS to wield that brand politically?

The answer eventually came in the form of radio silence. Disobedience, civil or otherwise, for two minutes or twenty, was deemed, as one article put it, a thing too divisive for a public servant to engage in.

There were also the Soul Sirens. Don't worry, I didn't know about them either—probably still wouldn't if it weren't for Anyla. But their power set was solid and paired with a sleek Afrofuturist design that might have worked—anywhere else but in Alabama.

They only managed two encounters with Super Predators. The first fight almost dissuaded them from trying it again, as reports came in of the "she-thugs" who wouldn't set aside their ridiculous attempt at work meant for more tenured hands. The second encounter, though, was the one that would ultimately consign them to obscurity.

They'd uncovered, during an election year that had thus far been monotonous, that a major contender for office was a Super Predator. Randy Montgomery's ability revolved around manipulating shadow. Instead of using this ability for something as mundane as padding his income, he decided to wear the mantle of Predator as maliciously as he could. He was responsible for the disappearance of at least five women by the time the Soul Sirens came calling.

The Soul Sirens engaged in a lengthy battle with Randy just days before the election, attacking him publicly while he delivered a speech. Unlike in the case of Ninety-Four, the public reaction here was unanimously positive. The internet was full of memes and gifs praising their actions. Not much happened after that, though. If they wanted to keep patrolling, they'd have to do it with the same old bottom-tier PantheUS payments. They couldn't make a living that way, so they hung up their suits, and eventually they were forgotten.

So what do you do when everything is fucked? You punch in your weight class, True Believer. You choose your battles wisely, and if the big one, the one that really means something, never comes, then at least you can say you tried, and that's enough, right?

These are the Astonishing Tales of Talent

Gunther called me into the office without any *finks* or *foops* the morning after the election. I went in my costume, not sure if I'd need it. Maybe they'd want to have an impromptu televised sparring session with the whole team? But when I reached his office, the only thing I found there was the man himself, pointing an angry finger at his grandson Patches.

The healing hash-lover was apparently getting his suspension lifted. He was cringing before the finger, but if you ask me he didn't seem all that worried. He knew he had the power. Gunther was never going to kick him off the team, no matter what he did. He was the only one with the healing touch.

Gunther finished yelling at Adam and spritzed a bit of love on the scene by half-embracing him. Then he looked up to see me, standing there with my hand halfway to knocking on the door, as if I hadn't been there the whole time.

Patches gave me a droopy grin; the one I returned was probably just as wilted. I couldn't remember the last time I'd seen him, and I'm being literal there. The way *he* told it, I'd been pretty out of it the whole time I was in the hospital. During one visit, I'd flipped over in my bed and slapped a hand over his on the safety rail. The skin around my eyes seemed thin, eroded at the edges. I stared, or something like me stared, cracked open to transmit a truth of the world that even Green Freedom hadn't taught us.

"Save Point," I rosebudded.

Patches looked around. The ever-present Kat was asleep in a corner. No nurse to be found. "Uh, what?"

"What's a Patch? What's a patty pat patch? You don't—haha—you don't patch, you save, you spiral through time and and and and your name is stupid, Save Point is better, bah zip bahadoooo hoo hooo, save a point."

"Yeah, man, I'll think about it," Patches said. He then listened to me map out the location of every save point in *Final Fantasy 7* before peeling my hand from his and beating my pillows back to maximum fluff.

Afterward, Chris had thought it best for me to distance myself from him, for both our sakes. It wouldn't look too good for the suspended treason tyke to be seen hanging with the Talented individual who'd led him to break protocol. Just as importantly, it wouldn't reflect my boundless appreciation for being saved by the powers that bleed. I gave him a nod as he passed me on his way out of Gunther's office. He hummed the theme song we'd made up for Green Freedom back in issue 420 of our ongoing team-up. It was enough to tell me we were cool. Time was never a real threat for Adam; he was full of raucous, sickeningly hopeful adolescence, devoid of worry. I wanted him to stay, but as the heroes say, this was something I had to do alone. Besides, I hadn't had a moment with Gunther since waking into my new life. A life I wasn't sure he was all that on board for me to have, but there we were. I'd made it, I was in the house, and we both knew that, like everything I'd been building, it was made from his blocks.

The malingering mess of me, Scotch-taped and zip-tied together, wasn't built to start whatever it was I needed to do now.

"I have to be honest, my boy, when I first met you—hell, when I first learned about you—I wasn't sure we'd end up here. I was hopeful, but—anyway. How are you feeling? The hard part is through, isn't it? I mean, what haven't you been through at this point, am I right?" He laughed and poured himself a drink from his fancy-schmancy decanter of scotch.

"Yeah, I wanted to just say thanks for everything, for all of this. I can't begin to—"

Gunther raised a hand. I stopped weaving my standard, silk-spun sincerities.

"We're past that now, aren't we, Donald?" he said.

"I'm sorry, sir?"

Gunther got up and went to stare dramatically out his window. I should have been more anxious, I suppose, but instead I found myself tumbling through the wasted space in my mind, counting all the comics, TV shows, manga, and anime that had promised this moment. I found myself wondering what white dudes with bewildering power did when they wanted to create a moment of palpable tension, if they didn't have any fancy scotch or high-rise windows around.

"You sacrificed your life, son. Now, I know you may be feeling some sort of way, given how things went down." He went quiet long enough for me to realize I had the talking stick in my hand.

"Oh. I mean, protocol is protocol, and rules are made for a reason, right? Like, honestly, sir, after everything you've done for me so far, I don't feel any sort of way but euphoric at this opportunity. I promise not to let you down," I said.

"Well, that's good to know. We need more people like you, you know that, Donald? Who understand that the past is the past. If more people got that, maybe we wouldn't need any of this business. It's why I don't regret my choice, and I don't think I will, as long as you keep your nose clean and everything else alive." He laughed and raised his glass. I don't know if he'd forgotten to offer me a drink or just chose not to. I cupped my hand like it had something in it to return the toast.

"I'm sorry—your choice, sir?" I asked, placing my nonexistent cup back into pretend land.

Gunther reached into his desk and pulled out an envelope. It felt the same in my hands as the last one, but there was a cling in Gunther's hand that told me it was different.

I opened it. Booms and sparks and the end of ramen noodles filled me. I was finally Astonishing.

"So, how's it feel to be a millionaire, Donny boy?"

I'm sure that if I'd been able to look up from the check in my hands, I'd have seen Gunther wearing that Nikolas type of smile, full of knowing that the other party doesn't have.

A million dollars.

The fuck.

I'd find out that the standard signing bonus was much, much less. Though they're well paid, even the ACRONYM wasn't on that *Friends*-cast-member level. I figured that the successful passing of a budget increase for PantheUS might have had something to do with Gunther's sudden generosity.

"I can't—this is mine?"

"Yeah, *thought* you'd be pretty happy. Don't go getting used to that, now. But didn't I tell you? I take care of my soldiers, and you've more than proved that you're one of the good ones." He leaned back in his chair and waited for me to stop bawling.

I tried to will the tears away. "I'm sorry, I'm just . . . What did you mean by choice?"

Gunther laughed. "What I mean is, I make good on my promises, Mr. McDougal. I take care of the ones who not only take care of me but know what hard choices need to be made to take care of this country. From Sally Thomas out in Little Rock to Mandy Ross in Florida."

It helped calm my tears to have the challenge of not laughing. It was a sweet sentiment, especially coming from Gunther, but I'd heard some of that stuff before—word for word—in a speech Asper made.

"Thank you."

"Of course. Not another word on it. I want you to *realize*, though, that it's a cross to bear, son. It's a responsibility to defend against threats our forefathers couldn't have fathomed. Flying assholes and superpowered thugs, I *swear*—every day I'm getting news of some new threat, *some* thing that belongs in some shithole country somewhere, not in mine. Some of these threats, you know, they're smart. They aren't so quick to come into the light. Enemies like those? They're the ones that keep us up at night. They're also the ones, though, who impose on us the duty of silence."

He stared at me. If not for the recent raging boner he'd displayed for silence, I would have thought he expected me to contribute.

"I mean that I was the one who put you in that chair," he said. "I mean that if you think for a moment the Senate has any real power over my PantheUS, well, you may not be as smart as I thought you were. You've done astonishing things, Donald. Not just against Flame. You were ready, instinctively and without any need for direct command, to protect the country from something even worse."

These are the Astonishing Tales of Damn It,
Nikolas, Why Do You Ruin Everything

"The order you gave me—" I started. I was smart enough to stop when I saw how serrated was the cut of Gunther's eyes over me.

"What order, son?" he asked, so innocently I thought I'd found myself in a retcon.

"Nothing, sir. I was just—ha, I don't know, I just get so silly up here sometimes, you know?" I said, without so much as a fucking flinch. "What with the dying, and all."

"No worries, son—from what I've heard you're still on the mend, right? Well, we have resources for that too, now that you're official. We'll make sure you're well taken care of." He stood up in a you-can-go-now kind of way.

So I did.

I ran and ran until I stood in front of a bank teller with sweat dripping from my dreads, holding a check for slightly over a million dollars. Of course, if I'd known more about Gunther's penchant for theatricality, I would have known that the check itself was just for show. The actual money was in a direct deposit that had already been transferred into my account by the time I left his office.

I'd walked into that office with a thousand questions running through my head. About Nikolas, about how I'd be able to perform considering my recent injuries, about pale moonlight and promenades and horns that poked me as we shuffled, about how to move with two left feet.

He'd given me a million answers, so I considered us square.

* * *

Another unpopular opinion? *The Never-Ending Story II* is the superior tale of a kid riding around on a cotton dragon-dog.

The switch of actors for Sebastian was a good move, the budget was better, and the threat wasn't so damn vague. I didn't have to sob my eyes out for a week over a drowning horse, and the villain was the most pragmatic mastermind I ever saw during my rocket-skateboard years. Imagine filling your head with world conquerors and mustache-twiddling tricksters before landing on a baddy who decided in the first act that, nah, I'm not going to beat that kid with a book who defeated literal nothingness. She knew, too, that the right carrot could be a rod.

If you've failed at life and haven't taken the eighty-nine minutes to sit through the movie: Xayide, a sorceress, isn't so messy as to throw down in a throne room. She listens to our heroes' demands and lets them go free. Well, she doesn't just let them go—she sweetens the pot by giving our protagonist a way of making wishes.

I won't spoil the ending of a thirty-or-so-year-old movie, but the gist is that she was smart enough to let the hero corrupt himself. See, the wishes? Each one that Sebastian used meant another memory was gone. You want a fresh bike, my dude? Fine, you didn't need those multiplication tables anyway.

I respect her hustle. Wishing didn't give him some mangled appearance; it wasn't fueled by sacrificing a family dog. It was something invisible, something insidious.

Not that you need this unimportant and highly arbitrary opinion of a children's movie that has no relation whatsoever to the issues at hand.

* * *

When the day came for me to move into headquarters, I didn't let go of my apartment. I didn't need it, didn't really even have plans for it, but it was like that faulty-doored storage unit back in Ohio: I thought a day might come when I'd want the solitude.

There were more speeches, more pledges, and another big endorsement from Gunther and the team while the cameras zoomed around us, which gave me a chance to introduce myself to the public all over again.

"I'd like to take this opportunity to reassure the American people that I've grown over the last year, both as a hero and as a human being. I understand the power entrusted to me more than ever. Ladies and gentlemen, I am The *Black* Spark, and as long as I serve you, I will never let you down."

CHAPTER 29
ASIDE

I **HADN'T NOTICED UNTIL NOW,** but once again, I'm nearly the last one here. Tad isn't being very subtle about his desire to get the hell out of work and to the unbearable lightness of Natty Ice. I want to get out of here too, buddy. I want to get as far from *here* as I can. (I'm not saying these things out loud of course, just to you, True Believers.)

Maybe I should talk to Tad. I should answer the questions he has at the tip of his twentysomething tongue. Yes, I am The Spark. Yes, I did become the greatest of all time. Yes, I did kill *him*.

Maybe, maybe, maybe.

I'm reaching that point of caffeination that curdles the intestines and bleeds out the chill. It's a hell of a thing to be dying in the past and present tenses all at once. Then again, Daddy McDougal would just muse that this is the melancholy of melanin. This is the stuff of nigga bones bred for basket caskets and endless retellings of slave narratives.

In the end, after I have a chance to edit things down, I don't think I'll keep this bit. This whining that everyone asks for but no one wants to listen to without interruption.

Why can't anyone take a second to just listen? Tad would listen. He'd keep the store open for five more hours if I confirmed for him that I was one of the Talented.

Tomorrow, I might make it to the end of the story. If I were smarter, as smart as Nikolas always wanted me to be about shit like this, I'd switch coffee shops. Gunther is going to find me one of these days, so that's kind of whatever, but what if *they* do? The Nigghts? I've been shut down, powered off, rebooting for so long that I don't know if I could face them like this.

Since things have changed, since *I've* changed, it's not so easy to conceal-don't-feel, True Believer. Standing in front of the bathroom mirror a moment ago, I was reminded of this. As I stared into the bronze-brown of my eyes, I remembered when this color didn't just mean I'd made a simple cosmetic shift from the silver. It used to mean I was one of you.

V must have worked me up more than I realized. I'm halfway to my old maximum charge, which is way too much energy for me to safely contain now, even just sitting here doing nothing with my shoddy little dinkputer.

I bleed out the spark, dumping it back into the wall where it belongs. Oops, might have overshot that: the fluorescents are flickering.

"The fuck," Tad mutters, squinting at them.

"Zapidy-do," I say under my breath.

I've got no more writing in me today, but I don't want to leave the coffee shop. What if, when I leave here and crawl back to the undisclosed corner I've been kinda-sorta sleeping in, I get clipped? Guess it's been fun, True Believer. The end. To be concluded never.

Or maybe I just don't want to stop writing because when I do, that's when the shadows find me.

Maybe, maybe, maybe.

* * *

Writing about tomorrow, well, that's not as fun as this other stuff. Not for the obvious reason of not knowing what will happen next— that would make it more bearable. It's the fact that I know *exactly* what will happen next. Every plot point and palpitating heart. Every sidekick and drop-kick. And there isn't a damned thing I can do to change it.

Tomorrow, I'll be here again. I'll tell you about more astonishing moments. I'll explain why it is we heroes focus so much on redheads, and I'll even squeeze in a bit more about daddy issues if I can, between bites of a very, very expensive croissant.

What I won't do tomorrow is tell you anything you haven't heard before. I mean, maybe a bit, but that's just semantics, silly putty. Keep reading, though. If not for the boom, then for the spark, the substance, and the everything they told you is in between.

Shit, I sound like a fucking nutcase right now. Maybe Flame was right. Maybe we're all meant for ashes, insane membranes and all.

Anyway, for me it'll be a lifetime, for you it'll be a page turn. Good night, True Believers, and sleep well.

ACKNOWLEDGMENTS

IT'S DANGEROUS TO GO IT ALONE.

First of all, this book is dedicated to the memory of my mom, Vicky J. Smith. She gave everything.

Without the love and support of my family, I don't think I'd ever have known that some things, the things that matter, will keep you going. My maybe-wife-at-this-point-since-the-publication-date-is-so-close-to-the-wedding, Morgan: I'll "things" you forever and a day. Harsh times never felt so good. For Gage and Christian: You two are basically my heart, and Mom would be proud of how strong and how fucking brilliant you are becoming.

To Mike, my big bro. If I hadn't had you to chase, I'd still be dicking around with sparks.

Pops, thank you for giving me the pen and the talk from page 309 of *The Official Black Dad Manual* about twice as much and half as far. Thanks for being, now and forever, on your Green Lantern ish and trying to get into my head the importance of overcoming great fear.

To Lanternfish Press. HOLY SHIT, Y'ALL, WE DID THIS SHIT. Amanda Thomas, Feliza Casano, and Christine Editor-of-the-Fucking-Millennium-aka-Word-Whisperer-aka-Don't-Be-Afraid-Just-Do-the-Damn-Thing-aka-Fuck-Nazis Neulieb. Thanks for your care, your partnership, and pretty much everything that made this book a book. Thanks for basically fulfilling my life's dream, but, no big.

To my teacher, Jedi-Jōnin-Master, and friend, Dr. Phyllis Burns. You put me on the path to get here and gave me the tools I needed to keep going. Thank you, Teach.

To my beta readers. Bill, you have no idea what this meant. Thank you so much for your time and willingness to contribute. Izetta Thomas, Beth Gilleon, Kevin Williams, Bryan Harsh, Josh Howard, Lillie Teeters, and Jacob Life, thank you. And all the others who gave me phenomenal feedback, such as Ella Chappell, David Moore, and Elizabeth Earley.

To my writers' group, the Columbus House of Scribes, for constant motivation and dedication.

To all my friends and family: uncles, aunts, Wasabi Samurais and Nanas, Bruhsins and Browns fans. The ones I miss. Abaddon and other allies. Blurple Aliens and Garrett Rabens of Old. All of you who were part of this in so many ways. I hope you know who you are, and how much just having you in my life helped.

To every comic-book-shop owner who created a space for flights of fancy, especially Rob Moore. You, sir, are fucking excelsior.

To so many authors and artists. To the legacy and life of Dwayne McDuffie, who believed in the importance of expanding the range of experiences captured in comics.

I know I'm missing so many people; that becomes clear in the writing of this bit. I thank you all.

Oh, snap, so there was this time my favorite Mediterranean spot lost power, and I didn't have cash. After an awesome conversation, you paid for my meal. I had nothing to offer you at the time, so you jokingly asked me to throw you a mention in the acknowledgments if I ever got published. So, wherever you are, thank you, Donna Culley.

To True Believers.

CPSIA information can be obtained
at www.ICGtesting.com
Printed in the USA
LVHW080606121218
600076LV00018BA/649/P

9 781941 360163